Ryder locked himself on the tail of the Red fighter. He was still in the high energy dive, roaring along at Mach 1.7. But he had to close the gap. In one motion he kicked in the F-14's afterburner. The Tomcat exploded forward. The airspeed indicator blurred as it passed Mach 2. Ryder felt himself pinned against the 'Cat's flight seat. And suddenly he was on the jet's tail, twisting and turning just below the fighter's smoky wake.

"Jesus Christ . . . *burn* him, Ghost!" Woody yelled, his words gurgling in the high g-environment.

Ryder squeezed the gun trigger hard. "Come on, you bastard," he whispered. *"Blow!"*

THUNDER ALLEY
MACK MALONEY

ZEBRA BOOKS
KENSINGTON PUBLISHING CORP.

ZEBRA BOOKS

are published by

Kensington Publishing Corp.
475 Park Avenue South
New York, NY 10016

First printing: July, 1988

Printed in the United States of America

PART 1

Fightertown

1

Two US Navy F-14 Tomcat jet fighters roared down the runway, both kicking in their afterburners as they lifted off. In a flash of flame and jet exhaust, the Tomcats twisted to the north and climbed, nearly straight up, disappearing into the high clouds in a matter of seconds.

The small Scramble House at the edge of the runway shook from the sound waves left behind by the powerful jets. Inside the cement block structure, D.J. Woods, Captain, United States Air Force, was stretched out on a battered couch, trying to get some sleep.

"How the hell can I get any shut-eye with all this noise?" he yelled out.

Ryder Long, also a captain in the USAF, was flopped in the dilapidated chair next to the couch, reading an old copy of *Sports Illustrated*, trying his best to relax. He and Woods were fighter pilots. Each was wearing a flight suit and a pair of nylon "speed jeans." Their helmets were hanging off the edge of the splintered coffee table in front of them; the one marked "Ghost" belonged to Ryder; the one marked "Wood Man" belonged to Woods.

Two more jets—Ryder knew they were F/A-18s—took off. Once again the inside of the Scramble House began to shake. The fluorescent lights blinked. The lone wire-meshed window rattled. An ashtray vibrated its way off the coffee table, falling to the floor, spilling two dozen cigarette butts.

"This is getting ridiculous," Woody said, opening his eyes just in time to see the small cloud of cigarette ash rising in front of him.

The Scramble Room was a dreary place. It looked like a high

7

school detention center. The three couches and half dozen chairs were pre-World War II. There wasn't a magazine in the place that was under three years old and the wastebasket hadn't been emptied in at least that long. The room's only luxury—a black-and-white plastic TV set—was silently flickering in a far corner, its volume control long ago broken.

On the wall next to the TV, a crooked clock was ticking off the last few minutes until noontime.

Ryder gave up on the ancient *Sports Illustrated*, rolled it into a ball and sent it flying across the room. It landed perfectly into the overflowing wastebasket next to the Scramble House's only door.

"God, this place is a dump . . ." he said, taking in the surroundings for the hundredth time.

Who would have thought the Scramble Room at the famous NAS Miramar-San Diego would look so unglamorous?

But then again, who would have thought that the Navy would be playing host to two *Air Force* pilots here?

Woody was thinking the same thing. "I was awake all last night," he said, staring up at the ceiling as he spoke. "Wondering *what* the hell we are doing here. We have to be the first Air Force guys ever even allowed inside this place . . ."

It was a question Ryder had been asking himself for the past three months. And still he didn't have a satisfactory answer . . .

He and Woods were part of a highly classified project codenamed "Distant Thunder." And, at this point, that was just about all they knew. The project was so secret, they not only didn't know why they were selected, or by whom, they had no idea where they would eventually be deployed or what kind of mission they were even training for.

Not too long ago, both of them had been flying unglamorous Air Force C-130 cargo planes; Ryder peddling a yawn-filled Utah-to-Michigan route, Woody plowing the skies between Texas and Alabama. Then one day, Ryder and Woody received orders to get to Miramar, immediately.

That was nearly three months ago. The first six weeks were taken up by attending classes, lectures, seminars, more classes, homework, and simulator time. And plenty of flying, in Navy trainers mostly. Many times, Ryder told himself that if it wasn't for the flying, it would have been *very* boring.

Then, once they got out of this initial training phase, to their great surprise, they were assigned to the US Navy's Fighter Weapons School—better known to movie fans as Top Gun.

Ryder shook his head slowly every time he thought about it. One moment he was flying Air Force C-130 "Humper" cargo planes; next thing he knows, he's flying F-14 Tomcats, the Navy's *preemo* "Tits Machine." It was like being traded from the worst team in baseball to a World Series contender.

But their training had been twice as extensive as the usual Top Gun jocks assigned to the Navy's Fightertown.

Woody continued. "They got us flying round the clock, Phase One alert for the past four days. Even the regular Top Gun guys don't do that."

Ryder and Woody had already flown three missions that day and it wasn't quite noon. And these weren't ordinary training missions. These were "scramble-intercept" missions, complete with a flashing red light and an ear-splitting klaxon horn above the Scramble House door. They knew it could go off at any second. When it did, they had to be up and out on the flight line in a matter of seconds.

And perhaps that was the strangest part of all: Their "enemy" were the pilots of the Navy's Adversary Force— American pilots flying airplanes that were painted like Soviet MiGs. But it didn't take long for Ryder and Woody to learn that the pilots of the Adversary Group—known as the Aggressors— were the strangest bunch of fighter jocks in the world. They spoke Russian. They wore Russian clothes. Their headquarters flew Soviet flags. They even ate Russian cooking. All designed to know what it was like in the mind—if not the pants—of a typical Soviet pilot. The only force better to train Navy flyers against would be the Soviets themselves.

The name of the game was ACM—Air Combat Maneuvering, better known as Dogfighting. For weapons, both sides used computers. So-called sensor pods were carried on all Top Gun and Adversary fighters, usually slung under the jet's wings right where the real weapons would go. The sensors registered "kills" during the simulated aerial combat between the Top Gun pilots and the Aggressors.

The rules were simple: Hit someone with your computer beam, you put another notch on your belt. Get hit by someone else's computer beam and you were "dead." Bounced. Scrambled. ACM was an exhilarating, sometimes frightening, high-speed video game. And it was as close to the real thing as a pilot could get.

Incredibly, Ryder and Woody were doing well. In fact, in their handful of weeks at Top Gun, they had yet to lose a single aerial engagement against the Aggressors. No other pilot teams in their Top Gun class could make that claim. And because Ryder and Woody were Air Force, the Navy guys were really burning ass over the situation.

That morning, in three engagements, they had iced two Aggressor A-4 Skyhawks and a F-5 Tiger II. The last battle—the one with the F-5—had been a particularly hard-fought, hard-won affair.

Woody whistled. "That F-5 was tough. But we made it. Clutch flying, Ghost, my boy."

They exchanged a ritualistic high-five. In the past three months they had grown as a team. They had been up dozens of times together and they had won the simulated dogfights each time. Their secret: Stay pumped up. Keep it cool. Keep it tight. Keep the edge. It was necessary.

Finally, the room was quiet for a few moments.

Woody stretched and tried to reorient himself on the overstuffed couch. "That's more like it," he said, closing his eyes and enjoying the silence. "Maybe they'll leave us alone for a while . . ."

No sooner had he spoken the words when the red scramble light started to blink. A second later the damnable klaxon was blaring. Ryder clicked a stopwatch he was holding.

"*Damn!*" Woody said, rolling off the couch. "Here we go again . . ."

Both Ryder and Woody were up and running in two seconds. Out the door, down the path and out on to the flight line

10

toward their F-14 Tomcat. It was hard running in the "speed jeans," the nylon G-suits that would help prevent them from blacking out due to high *g*-forces during heavy dogfighting. Plus, their "ready fighter"—an F-14 known as VF-333—was about two hundred yards from the Scramble House. They were both out of breath by the time they reached the airplane.

The Tomcat was ready to go—as usual. A swarm of Navy ground mechanics were always babying the airplane. As the two pilots hoofed it to the F-14, they saw the twin blast of jet exhausts already spewing out of the rear of the plane. Its navigation lights were flashing, its twenty thousand pound-thrust engines were screaming. It *looked* ready.

Ryder met the ground crew chief at the foot of the airplane.

"You're all set, Ghost," the chief told him. Ryder would be piloting the two-seat fighter. Woody would be in the rear seat of the Tomcat, serving as the backseat Weapons Systems Officer, better known in Air Force parlance as "The Wizzo," or simply "Wiz." That was another unusual thing about their training: At Top Gun, there were pilots and there were Radar Intercept Officers, the Navy's term for its backseaters. But both Ryder *and* Woody were pilots. However, since arriving at the Navy's Fighter Weapons School, Ryder had done most of the flying. And, strangely enough, they had discovered they worked better as a team that way.

The Air Force pilots climbed into their seats and were strapped in in a matter of seconds. Ryder was keeping a close eye on the stopwatch. Early on, he and Woody had figured out that the quicker they got off the ground, the better prepared they would be for the dogfight ahead. They had worked hard at being the fastest airplane off the flight line and in most cases, they were. But now, for this flight, they were the only ones going up.

"This looks like another solo for us," Ryder said to Woody over the cockpit intercom once they had their face-mask microphones connected. Normally, the Navy sent its Top Gunners up in two-ship pairs: a flight leader and a wingman whose sole job was to keep an eye on the leader's tail. But this hadn't been the case for the Air Force interlopers; they hadn't

11

had a wingman since their second week in Top Gun training.

"Damn," Woody replied disgustedly. "No back-up. No one watching our six. It's getting very lonely up there, Ghost."

Ryder did a quick check of the F-14's control panel and made sure everything important was "lights on." He was especially concerned about his computer sensor pod, better known in school as the Airborne Instrumentation Subsystem or AIS. About the size of a AIM-9 Sidewinder missile, the AIS pod was locked onto the side of the Tomcat's weapons pylon. Its specific function was to transmit a constant stream of data on the aircraft's performance, position, acceleration, and altitude, back to the Miramar/Top Gun central computer. Using this information, the computer knew every move the F-14 and the similarly equipped Aggressors made during an aerial duel. When either aircraft "launched" one of the unarmed Sidewinders they carried, the AIS would determine if the launch resulted in a "kill" or not. This was how The Game was played.

Without a properly functioning AIS, Ryder knew it would be like going into battle without bullets. He was glad to see the AIS confirmation light was burning deep green, telling him the unit was functioning.

He called back to Woody and read a quick checklist. Woody yelled out an even quicker "Check!" to each item, sometimes even before Ryder had finished saying it. Ryder didn't mind. They were in a hurry. Time counted in The Game. Their fuel tanks were full and the AIS was working—that's all he gave a damn about. They couldn't be bothered if some of the incidentals were slow in lighting up.

Ryder reached out of the cockpit and gave the flight crew chief a quick thumbs-out. This was the signal for the chief to get all his guys off the airplane, pronto. The F-14 was already moving when the chief gave his reply wave-off. The chief understood; they'd been playing The Game, too, for these past weeks. As the Tomcat rolled by him, Ryder gave him a quick thumbs-up, followed by a friendly salute.

"Go get 'em, Ghost!" the chief yelled over the scream of the Tomcat's jets.

They rolled right past the mechanic crew waiting at the entrance to the runways. These EOR (for End of Runway) mechanics were assigned to check the airplane for any last second problems that might have sprung up during the rollout, especially in the fighter's landing gear. But Ryder was in a rush. In his several years of flying, he had never had a flat tire. The chances were he wouldn't get one this time, either.

Woody gave the EOR crew a casual wave as Ryder applied power to the 'Cat's engines. Quickly, they rolled out onto the short arterial taxiway and headed toward the runways.

Ryder was already arguing with the base's control tower.

"Tower, what's holding up our take-off clearance?" he asked with the right touch of exasperation added to his voice.

"F-14 Flight 17, wait on East Runway-Right," the controller came back to him. "Comfirm an E-2C take-off before you. Wind is at fourteen knots."

"I don't care about the wind, Tower," Ryder said, checking the stopwatch. "We're on a priority launch. We can't wait."

There was a short silence, then Ryder's radio crackled. "Confirm an E-2C take-off ahead of you Flight 17," the controller said firmly.

Ryder immediately shot back: "Tower, I repeat. We are on a priority launch. Request that you insert us before the E-2C . . ."

Again, there was another silence. All the while, Ryder had been gunning the Tomcat's engines a little at a time, increasing his roll speed along the taxiway.

Then another voice, this one deeper, more authoritative, came over Ryder's intercom.

"Flight 17. Negative on insertion. Confirm take-off before you of E-2C."

Ryder wasn't paying any attention. He was already out on the main runway and taxiing in parallel to the squat, propeller-driven E-2C Hawkeye radar airplane. He gave the pilot a wave as he passed the slower airplane. The pilot of the E-2C, who couldn't care less as to when he took off, waved back.

That's when Ryder booted the Cat into afterburner . . .

Both he and Woody were slammed against their seats. One

13

moment they were going 45 mph; five seconds later, they were up to 180. They could physically *feel* the engines greedily sucking in the JP-5 jet fuel, spitting most of it into their combustion chambers, saving the rest to dump raw into the last stage of the jet engine, giving the ship an extra powerful "after-burning" kick in the ass.

They lifted off in a rush of adrenaline and pure sonic power. Ryder immediately put the F-14 into a totally vertical climb. In seconds they were roaring straight up into the heavens and closing in on .75 Mach.

"*Fly it,* Ghost!" Woody screamed with sheer excitement. "Fly this *motherfucker!*"

"Consider the pedal applied to the metal," Ryder called back, clicking his stopwatch as they passed ten thousand feet. Four minutes, five seconds. Their fastest time yet.

The base control tried to call him and rip his ass about the unauthorized take-off but Ryder had already switched his radio.

Channel 10, 255.3 frequency. That was the band where he got his dogfight instructions. No one but those involved in the aerial combat exercise could use the frequency.

Ryder leveled off at 12,500 feet and called into his microphone, "Control, control. This is F-14, Flight 17. Awaiting intercept information and vector."

They were about eighty miles from their aerial play-ground—the skies over the Navy's China Lake Weapons Proving Ground—a "strictly military personnel only" patch of desert northeast of Los Angeles. Somewhere, out over the range, Ryder knew two, maybe three Aggressor aircraft were waiting for the Tomcat.

The radio crackled once, then a faraway voice came on. "Flight 17, three bogies at southwest, bearing one-three-zero. Flying at 17,500."

Ryder reached down and snapped on the F-14's "do-it-all" radar computer brain, the Hughes AWG-9. Instantly a small TV screen, one of three on the control panel before him, flickered to life. A similar screen blinked on back in Woody's compartment.

14

"I've got cross-section acquisition," Ryder called out. "Ditto," Woody reported.

Right away they both saw three simulated aircraft moving from top to bottom on their TV screen.

"Better than Saturday morning cartoons," Woody said, making minor adjustments to the TV screen.

The AWG-9 was more than a super-sophisticated radar set. The device could locate an enemy and gave his position, display a miniature simulated profile of the type of enemy aircraft—in this case, three Aggressor F-5s. But there was more: The AWG-9 also gave accurate readings on the target's speed, altitude, probably total weapons load, and probable attack profile. The device also controlled and guided the jet fighter's arsenal of high-tech weapons.

"OK, Woody," Ryder called back to the rear seat. "What's happening?"

"They're thirty-seven nautical miles from us," Woody reported. "Bearing Two-Three-Niner. I read armed with Sidewinders and cannon. They haven't picked us up yet."

"Roger," Ryder replied, looking at the exact same readout. "Let's keep it that way."

Ryder put the F-14 into a steep dive, booting up the throttle at the same time. He could feel his speed jeans fill up with compressed air and start squeezing him. This action helped keep him conscious by keeping the blood in his head where it belonged. Still he could feel the tremendous g-force build up as the airplane continued its dive. They were closing in on Mach 1—the invisible barrier that opened at about 750 mph into the almost ethereal world of supersonic flight—when he finally pulled back on the control stick.

They were only two hundred feet off the ground when he leveled off, a maneuver only an F-14 could pull off. The amazing thing is that the airplane did it without missing a breath. Soon the low hills and desert of China Lake came into focus.

Ryder knew the approaching F-5 Aggressor pilots were

among the best in the States. But they were also very, *very* strange cats. Their role in life was to play Russian. The best adversary the Top Gun pilots could practice against were the ones who flew and fought like the Soviets. That was the reason that Top Gun flight training was enacted. The US military didn't have to kid itself about who'd they be up against in the next war; it was a short list: 1. The Soviets or, 2. Soviet-trained pilots. After a less than honorable kill ratio over North Vietnam, the military thinkers realized that having US jet pilots practice-fight against each other was great, if you were intent on shooting down F-4s Phantoms. The problem was, the US pilots wanted to shoot down MiGs.

So the Adversary groups were born and ordered to mimic MiGs to help Top Gun pilots train. The Navy filled up three squadrons with their best pilots and made them the Designated Russians. In the twenty or so years since, service in the Adversary squadrons was the most requested duty in the Naval air service.

Nevertheless, Ryder knew that no matter how good the Adversary pilots were, in the initial stages of the dogfight, he would be better. Partly because he had a lot of confidence in himself and in Woody, partly because he was better equipped. The reason was simple: the Aggressors didn't have the AWG-9 nor a "look-down" radar. The F-14 did. So Ryder knew he could fly low and the Aggressors couldn't. That would be his advantage in the upcoming engagement.

The F-5s were still at 17,500 feet when he passed right underneath them. He was flying so low he thought the F-14's arrestor hook might snag a tree. Once he was sure he was beyond them, he called back to Woody to strap down. Then he put the F-14 into yet another, screaming climb.

Up they roared. Five thousand, six, seven thousand feet. Incredibly they were gaining speed as they climbed. Eight thousand, ten thousand feet. The sky was crystal clear and the visibility went on for hundreds of miles. Good dogfighting weather. Twelve thousand, fourteen thousand, sixteen thousand feet. Ryder knew that Woody was checking off the Tomcat's electronic weapons systems. He called him for a readout.

"We got four Sidewinders showing ready," Woody radioed back, his vocal chords straining against the high *g*-force of the climb. "Cannon is armed."

"Roger, Woody," Ryder replied. "Now just sit back and enjoy . . ."

They passed seventeen thousand feet and still they climbed. Sometimes in these Top Gun mock engagements, the controllers put a twenty thousand-foot ceiling on the flight. This day they had no such restriction.

Only at twenty-eight thousand feet did Ryder level off. He throttled back and was soon cruising at four hundred mph.

"High noon, Ghost," Woody reported from the backseat.

Hunter checked his watch. Sure enough, it was straight up twelve o'clock. He took that as a good omen.

"OK, Wood Man," Ryder said. "Start taking notes . . ."

He was going to play the oldest trick in the book. Come out of the sun. Get on your first opponent's six o'clock position, dead behind him. Then *pounce* . . .

Ryder punched three buttons on the AWG-9 and in a flash relocated the three-ship Adversary flight. They were now about eleven miles west of him, a full eleven thousand feet below. And still, they had yet to spot him.

Ryder pushed his microphone button. "Woody, old boy, everything still working?"

"Roger, Ghost" came the reply.

"Got your shades on?" Ryder asked, as he began to nose the Tomcat down. Both pilots had fallen into the ritual of wearing their sunglasses on the first pass. It had worked on their first few missions and both were highly superstitious.

"Wait a minute," Woody said. "Lemme get them on . . . OK, all set . . ."

Ryder pushed the 'Cat into another dive. He watched as the jet's speed indicator started to whirl around the clocklike dial. Mach 1 was signified by the numbers 1.0 on the dial; increments of one-tenths were added as necessary. Ryder gradually opened the throttle, gained speed from both the powerful engines and the momentum induced from gravity. In the jet fighter biz it was called a "high energy dive."

He quickly passed Mach 1 and effectively broke through the

17

sound barrier. But still he added power to the throttles. The engines screamed in response. Only when he saw the speed indicator hit 1.8 was he satisfied.

"Still lit, Ghost!" Woody called from the back, making his periodic weapons status check.

"OK," Ryder replied. "HUD screen up . . ."

Ryder pushed two buttons and was immediately staring at a miracle of technology called a HUD. The *Heads-Up Display* was a transparent TV show flashed up on a see-through screen mounted on the F-14's dashboard. What he saw was a video projection of all the important flight instruments and weapons system data. With the HUD in operation, he could fight without ever having to look down at his cockpit panel instruments. This was important. Top Gun was smeared with signs that said: *"Lose Sight, Lose The Fight."* It translated another cardinal rule of dogfighting: Keep your enemy within eyesight.

Ryder took a deep gulp of oxygen. He'd been in many engagements in the past four days, yet when it came to an aerial knife fight, he knew the best way to do it was by the book.

He counted off an imaginary checklist in his head. He had secured all the best advantages. He had good position, he'd be attacking from behind. He had the height, the speed. Best of all and most important: Surprise. He would bounce these guys right out of the bright sun.

Now his targets were just four miles in front of him and about two miles below. He knew they still hadn't spotted him; they were flying along like a trio of Sunday drivers. He was so close now he could pick out their individual colors. One of the F-5s was sporting a reddish camouflage scheme that was right out of the Kremlin's crayon box. The other two were wearing blue camouflage for the occasion.

"Which one we going for, Ghost?" Woody called ahead. As in all the engagements, the pilot actually fires the weapons, the back-seater took care of them as soon as they left the wing.

"The red one . . ." Ryder answered, ". . . *and* the outside blue one."

"Yeah, two at once!" Woody yelled, pounding his dash-

18

board in the excitement. "Balls, Ghost. *Balls.* Let's do it, man. Grease these guys."

They were on the F-5s in the next instant. Ryder yelled "Fire!" at about a mile out as he hit the appropriate button.

"Sidewinder away!" Ryder heard Woody yell. At the same second, Ryder saw the Red F-5 break. He knew a warning buzzer—known as the "low-warning tone"—was rattling in the Adversary's cockpit indicating a missile lock had been achieved on his aircraft. But the Blue fighter had reacted too late. Suddenly its pilot heard another sound: the shrill "high-warning tone" meaning a missile had been launched at him. But just an instant later, a third sound blasted through the cockpits of both the Aggressor airplane and the F-14. This was the "Confirmed Kill" tone. The pilot of the Blue Aggressor fighter knew what it meant: The computer in the AIS sensor pod was saying he was dead. The F-14 had shot him down.

Normally a fighter pilot would pull up at this point after the kill and try to line up another target. Not Ryder. He believed in the conserving of energy and surprise. When the Blue fighter was hit, his two Red companions broke to the right. Ryder instantly locked himself on to the tail of one of the Red fighters.

"Pump him! *Pump* him!" Woody yelled from the backseat.

Ryder squeezed the Tomcat's cannon trigger and heard the confirmation sound of the gun's imaginary firing.

"Come on baby, blow!" he yelled out, beseeching the Con Kill to blare from the cockpit speaker. No sound came. Meanwhile the Red fighter started gyrating in a superb effort to shake the Tomcat.

"Stay on him, Ghost!" Woody urged him. "Stay on his ass. He's running!"

Ryder never let up. He continued to pour the invisible shells into the F-5. Still no sound came.

"Christ! Check the batteries on that Con-Kill horn!" Woody yelled. "We're all *over* him!"

It only meant one thing, Ryder knew. He had to get closer to his prey. He was still in the high energy dive, roaring along near Mach 1.7. But he had to close the gap. On one motion, he

19

kicked in the F-14's afterburner. The Tomcat exploded forward. The airspeed indicator needle blurred as it reached and passed Mach 2. Ryder felt himself pinned against the 'Cat's flight seat. He immediately started breathing in short, quick gulps.

Now he was right on the F-5's tail, twisting and turning just below the Red fighter's smoky wake.

"Jesus Christ . . . *burn* him, Ghost!" Woody tried to yell, his words gurgling in the high *g*-environment. "Burn *his ass!*"

Ryder squeezed the gun trigger harder. "Come on, you bastard," Ryder whispered. "Blow!"

An instant later the kill tone sounded . . .

"Yeah! Ghostman!" Woody yelled, once again banging his control board. "It's another two-fer. *Two*-fer!"

Ryder saw the F-5 pilot grudgingly wag his wings in acknowledgment of his electronic demise. He immediately yanked back on the 'Cat's control stick and pulled up out of the dive. Woody was still smacking his dashboard in victory. Ryder on the other hand was looking for the third and last F-5.

"Where the hell is the third bandit, Wiz?" Ryder called out to Woody.

Woody twisted and turned in his seat, trying to get a visual on the last Aggressor. "I don't know . . ." Woody yelled back. "The bastard just disappeared!"

Suddenly the low warning tone went off in their cockpit. It was the "death warning," indicating that an enemy's missiles had acquired a radar reading on them and were about to fire.

"Jeesuz, he's got a lock on us!" Woody yelled, turning to see the F-5 bearing down on them from their six o'clock. "They suckered us, Ghost. Gave up his two buddies just to bounce us . . ."

"Hang on, partner," Ryder said coolly as he put the Tomcat into a deep dive. Immediately, both pilots were once again slammed against their seats, the *g*-forces rippling their skin. Their speed jeans were furiously pumping air around their legs and torso, in an all-out effort to keep the blood in their heads and to keep them from passing out.

The buzzing got louder. "He's gonna fire on us!" Woody

managed to yell.

"Stay cool, Wood Man," Ryder called back, increasing the angle of the already torturous dive. "And give me a cannon status . . ."

"Cannon?" Woody gulped as he watched the earth come shooting up to meet them. "How the hell you gonna knock him with the cannon . . ."

Ryder didn't answer. He was too busy adding figures in his head. Rate of drop. Speed of his airplane. Speed of the F-5. Fire rate for the cannon. All the while the Tomcat was plummeting to the tune of Mach 1.7.

The warning buzzing got even louder. They were at 7,500 feet.

"Ghost! He's about to launch!" Woody yelled. "Get us out of it, buddy!"

At that moment Ryder yanked back on the Tomcat's throttles, while simultaneously engaging the Tomcat's speed brakes and yanking up all the 'Cat's flaps.

The result was like a big ole' semiscreeching on its brakes. The 'Cat's speed dropped from twelve hundred mph to just three hundred mph in a matter of seconds, giving the occupants first a strange floating sensation, then slamming them against their seat.

The F-5, its pilot bewildered that anyone would pull such a gut-wrenching maneuver, predictably shot right past them.

Ryder flicked the F-14's control stick a little to the right and found what fighter pilots call "the ultimate angle"; the F-5's tailpipe was dead zero smack center in his HUD sights. Without hesitation he pulled the cannon trigger. It took less than two seconds. The Aggressor was dead.

"*Jeesuz Christ*, Ghost!" Woody yelled, laughing. "He's gone, gone, *gone!*"

"Another day at the beach," Ryder said, turning the 'Cat toward home.

2

It was an hour later. Having landed and gone through a routinely boring debriefing on the simulated dogfight, Ryder and Woody were now trudging back to the Scramble House. Both men were exhausted and still drenched in sweat—both the unpleasant but natural side effects from the intensity of the dogfight.

"That's *got* to be it for the day," Ryder said, flexing his fingers. They were almost numb from squeezing the F-14's control stick so hard.

Reaching the Scramble House door, they found that Commander John Slade was waiting for them.

Slade was a Navy Instructor pilot, a balls-out, high-powered job around Miramar. As such, he was more experienced than the Top Gun students; tougher than the Aggressor pilots. But ever since Ryder and Woody arrived at the base, Slade had become their twenty-four-hour-a-day babysitter, a duty he clearly didn't relish.

"Stand down, guys," the Navy officer said, in his typically dour voice. "That was your last exercise of the day."

"Hallelujah!" Woody said, slapping Ryder with a trademark high five. *Stay cool. Stay tight.*

"How long a stand-down?" Ryder asked the rugged, compact man.

"Can't say," Slade answered with a shrug. "I don't really know."

Ryder knew that was Slade's trademark ass-covering answer. Slade was all-Navy, he didn't much like the idea of two Air Force guys cutting up the skies above Top Gun.

"Long enough to have a drink?" Ryder asked him.

Slade thought for a moment then nodded. "Yeah, you can have a drink."

"How many?" Ryder asked quickly. He knew the more they were allowed to drink, the longer they could stay on the ground and relax.

Again the Navy officer shrugged but said nothing.

"Four? Five?" Ryder asked, knowing he was pushing it. "Are we clear to tomorrow morning?"

"Look, Captain," Slade fired back, "just go have your goddamn drink. But do it quietly. And that's an order."

Ryder smiled. He and Woody were Air Force; Slade was Navy. In a military sense, Slade couldn't order them to do anything.

"Where do we drink?" Woody asked him.

Again, Slade immediately shot back, "Drink in your goddamn quarters!"

"How about the Officer's Club?" Ryder said.

"*No way*," the Navy officer said, shaking his head.

"But why?" Woody protested.

"Because you tore the goddamn place up last time you were there, that's why!"

"But that *wasn't* us," Ryder said. "It was your Top Gun guys that did all the damage."

"That's *bullshit*," Slade said. "We have sworn statements that you two guys started that fight. That mirror you broke cost *ten thousand dollars*. You know, the admiral had it flown over from Naples? Just to put behind the bar at the Top Gun's officer's club? It was like a family heirloom to him. And you Air Force guys trashed it. I can't believe it."

"Look, Slade," Ryder said, "we've been up four times already. We're beat and we need to cool out. We couldn't get in a fight now if we tried. We just want a couple of drinks. Maybe grab some chow. See some girls. Then get some rest."

Slade was relenting. He knew that if he allowed Ryder and Woods to go to the Miramar Officer's Club, there was a high potential for trouble. There was no love lost between the Air Force pilots and the Top Gun jocks who frequented the bar. This was especially true since it looked like Ryder and Woody would capture the Top Gun Class trophy with their so-far-perfect kill rate. To lose the coveted trophy to the Air Force would be an enormous embarrassment for the Navy, to say the least. And the Top Gun jocks never missed a chance to try and psych out the Air Force pilots. Alcohol would only inflame the situation.

23

Still, Slade realized that Ryder and Woody were due for some stand-down. As a pilot himself, he knew fighter jocks of all services needed to blow off steam every once and a while or their performance in the air would be affected.

"OK," he finally said. "Go to the OC. Get shit-faced for all I care. But do it *quietly*. And if anyone over there gives you any grief, just walk away from them."

Ryder and Woody were already out of their flight gear and throwing it all inside the door of the Scramble House. Then they sat out to hoof the full mile across the huge Naval Air Station to the Officer's Club.

Slade shook his head as he watched the pair walk away across the tarmac. "What the hell *are* Air Force guys doing here at Top Gun?" he asked himself.

It was barely 1:30 in the afternoon but the Officer's Club was already crawling with white-uniformed Top Gun pilots enjoying their day off. Some were already drunk. The usual complement of good-looking girls was also on hand. Off-duty base civilian personnel and town girls mostly, the girls—all Eights, Nines, and Tens—never missed a chance to dress up and head for the Miramar OC in hopes of meeting an airborne Mr. Perfect.

"Look at these guys," Woody said as they entered the club. "White dress uniforms in the middle of the day?"

"These Navy guys will do anything to get laid," Ryder said, heading toward a table in a dark corner, far away from the high gloss, glass-and-neon bar area.

Wanting nothing more than to be able to sit and drink the afternoon away, the Air Force pilots had agreed to take Slade's advice and avoid trouble.

But, as usual, trouble found them . . .

They had just sat down and ordered two Scotches when a pair of Navy pilots passed their table on the way to the men's room. They were wearing the mandatory lily-whites, sunglasses, and overgrown *moussed* crewcuts.

At first, Ryder thought they were going to pass on by

24

peacefully. But then one of them stopped right beside them.

"Hey, look," one said, pointing to Ryder and Woody. "It's the Boy Scouts . . ."

"You mean the shit-movers," said the other, mumbling the Navy's universal dumpname for Air Force pilots.

Ryder and Woody took deep breaths and stared straight ahead. *Stay cool.*

"Hey listen, Air Force," the first Navy guy said in mock seriousness, but still drunkenly slurring every other word. "I think it's time we talked . . ."

Ryder and Woody glanced at each other and shook their heads. *Stay cool . . .*

"C'mon," the man continued. "Let's find out why you Air Force guys are *really* here."

"Weren't you girls on your way to the ladies' room?" Woody asked.

The bigmouth Navy pilot leaned right over the table, his face now only about two feet from them. Ryder felt his right fist tighten. The man was just a punch away.

"Just what is all this crap about, guys?" the man said, spitting out the words.

"Take a walk, pal," Ryder said sternly.

The tone of his voice made the other Navy pilot stop and think. Ryder was a strapping six-feet-one; Woody was a little taller, a little thinner. Both were lean. Both pumped iron. Both were veterans of barroom brawls. And both looked it.

"C'mon, Panther," the second Navy guy said, starting to walk away.

"Panther?" Woody said, derisively mimicking the Navy jock's nickname. "Excuse me, you got the wrong kind of cat. You mean, *pussy*, don't you?"

"Fuck you, back-seater," the Navy man said, turning to Woody in anger. "Learn how to fly."

Both Ryder and Woody laughed in the man's face. Unlike most of the Navy backseat Radr Intercept Officers, Woody *did* know how to fly.

"I can fly rings around you, Kittycat," Woody said calmly.

The Navy man's face went red. "You want to see just how

25

well I can fly, shit-mover? C'mon, let's take our birds up. Right now. Let's mix it up."

Once again, they laughed in his face. "You've been watching too many movies, boy," Ryder told him.

The Navy guy was at a momentary loss for words, finally slobbering out, "Yeah, well I've seen your old lady in the movies . . ."

At that moment the drinks arrived—just in time for Woody to throw one in the Navy guy's face.

Ryder was on his feet as the man lunged forward. He managed to step aside at the last instant, popping the guy with his right fist as he went by. Propelled by the punch, the Navy pilot flew right past him, taking out two chairs and knocking over another table in the process. His head hit the floor with a particularly nasty crack.

Meanwhile, Woody had grabbed the man's reluctant partner, blocked his first punch and was presently administering a bone-crunching headlock on him. They flipped backward, taking out yet another table and set of chairs. Turning back to the pilot called Panther, Ryder calmly ducked as a chair flew by his left ear. Springing up, he hit the guy square on the chin, knocking him back to the floor. A girl at the bar screamed. Panther landed hard on his ass.

Now, out of the corner of his eye Ryder saw a gang of Navy pilots were moving toward him. They were soon going to be outnumbered. He had a feeling that cooler heads would *not* prevail.

Ryder turned to meet the onslaught, but was surprised to see that two enormous Marine guards had suddenly appeared. Behind the Marines stood Slade, arms crossed, face crimson. Their "scoutmaster" had taken the precaution of rounding up a couple jarheads and heading for the OC to keep peace between the rival pilots.

"Take these guys out of here," Slade barked at the Marines.

The guards quickly got the Navy pilots to their feet. Their ruffled appearance and the smears of lip blood on their white Top Gun uniforms told the tale of who won the fight.

"Remember my name, glory boy," Panther hissed at Ryder.

26

"I'll catch up with you. Over the range. We'll see who gets the last punch in . . ."

Slade cut him short. "Panther—my office, one hour," he said curtly, giving the Marine the sign to get rid of the two.

The Navy Pilots were quickly hustled out. The bar was very quiet. But within seconds, the incident was forgotten and the others in the club went back to its chatter and drinking.

Slade was steaming, though, a large vein bulging on the tough-as-nails instructor's forehead.

"Look, Slade, that wasn't us . . ." Ryder began to say.

Slade cut him off. "Save it," he said with barely controlled anger. "You Air Force guys are walking and talking trouble. I can't wait until the day you are out of here. That's the day *I'm* going out and get 'faced."

With that, he stalked out of the bar.

"Why does he get so pissed off at these things?" Woody asked.

Ryder straightened out the table and readjusted his chair. "I'm not going to lose sleep over it," he said. He motioned for the waitress and she quickly brought them two more drinks.

"That last round was four dollars even, honey," the attractive middle-aged waitress purred.

Ryder frisked himself and realized he had no money. Woody was drinking his Scotch at lightning speed, so this meant he didn't have any money either. Finally, Ryder looked up at the waitress and said, "Please put these on Commander Slade's tab . . ."

Eight hours later, Ryder and Woody stumbled back to their quarters, a concrete structure located in the most remote section of the sprawling base. They had succeeded in drinking Slade's tab over $120. That didn't include several rounds of free drinks the waitress had seen fit to bring them. "My third husband was Air Force," she had told them.

They entered the small dormitory-style housing—a main living room-dining area surrounded by a half dozen separate rooms—which they alone occupied. Woody immediately

27

staggered into his room and collapsed on the bed, passing out before his head hit the pillow. Ryder closed his partner's door, turned out the main lights, and moved on to his own room.

He was exhausted and drunk. He lay down on his bunk and found himself thinking about his father. Captain Ryder Long, Sr., had also been a fighter pilot. He had been shot down over North Vietnam more than twenty years before. And now Ryder was following in his footsteps, flying fighters.

As he drifted off to sleep, Ryder wondered what his old man would have thought of all this . . .

3

The knock at the door was so forceful that Ryder nearly fell out of bed.

"Captain Long!" the voice on the other side called out. "Important message, sir!"

Ryder glanced at his military-style digital alarm clock as he rolled out of bed. It was 0610 hours.

He opened the door to find a young Marine lieutenant waiting for him. Ryder noticed several fresh welts on the plywood door where the Marine had done the knocking. The lieutenant handed him an envelope, saluted, and walked away.

"Thanks for the wake-up call," Ryder said.

Ryder ripped open the envelope and found a one-line, typed message: REPORT TO MAJOR NORTON, AJAX RIGHT, IMMEDIATELY.

Now what? Ryder thought as he quickly dressed. He was certain it wasn't a scramble call. When they first arrived at Top Gun, they had told all the Power Projection students to expect a survival exercise sometime during their training. Ryder had a strong suspicion that he was about to go for a walk in the desert.

28

He was out the door in less than five minutes, unfed, barely showered and unshaven. As he sprinted through the barracks he noticed that Woody was still sleeping, snoring the rafters off the building.

"Ajax Right" was a landing strip about a half mile from the barracks. It was an auxiliary runway used mostly to service the base's supply and transport aircraft. As he jogged to the strip he could see a large Marine Corps Sea Stallion helicopter waiting on the taxiway, its rotors whirling. Two of the chopper's crew were walking around the huge helicopter, checking various critical points. Ryder knew the Sea Stallion was preparing to take off.

The rest of the strip was deserted so Ryder ran up to the helicopter and approached the nearest crew member.

"Is Major Norton here, Sergeant?" he yelled to the Marine who was checking over the chopper's nose. The noise of the helicopter's engines was deafening.

The Marine pointed straight up and yelled back, "That way, sir."

Ryder followed the man's finger up to see the chopper's pilot sticking his head out the cockpit window. The pilot was motioning Ryder to come aboard. This is all I need, Ryder thought as he ran around to the chopper's open door, to go for a helicopter ride with a bunch of jarheads.

He climbed inside the big chopper and walked forward to the flight deck. The noise was only slightly less deafening inside. The man he assumed was Major Norton was sitting in the left pilot's seat, fiddling with the copter's controls; a co-pilot was doing the same in the right seat.

"Major Norton?" Ryder asked, tapping the pilot on the shoulder.

The man turned and nodded. "You're Captain Long?" he asked, giving Ryder a quick handshake. "Please strap down in one of the seats in back, Captain. We're about to take off."

"Where are we going, Major?" Ryder asked.

"Survival exercise, Captain," the Marine pilot said, returning to his flight instruments.

The words didn't do much for Ryder's empty stomach. The last survival exercise he went through was back in Air Force Officers' Training. Three days and nights in the slimy, bug-infested Florida Everglades.

"What's the destination, Major?" Ryder asked.

"I really can't tell you that, Captain," Norton said, briefly looking up from his instruments.

Ryder knew it was useless to further question the Marine pilot, so he stepped back down from the flight deck, folded down a seat near one of the copter's port windows and strapped in.

The Sea Stallion's engines gunned up and the noise grew even louder. The two flight check crewmen jumped in, closing the large sliding door behind them. Both men then strapped into their flight harnesses and braced themselves. Ryder braced himself too—he'd been in Sea Stallions before and he knew that take-offs in the big chopper were a jolting, sometimes violent, experience.

A moment later the helicopter's engines roared and the aircraft lifted off. It was a furious take-off, one that for a few moments made Ryder glad he *hadn't* eaten any breakfast. He didn't know how these helo guys did it, the shaking alone must scramble the intestines over a period of time. Maybe that's why most chopper jocks were so thin.

Just seconds after take-off, one of the crewmen unstrapped himself and dashed through the copter's cabin, shuttering one of the aircraft's windows including the one Ryder had sat next to. The compartment was completely blacked out for several seconds. Then a dim orange bulb clicked on over the emergency exit, giving everything in the cabin an eerie glow.

Typical, Ryder thought, hanging on to his flight brace and staring into the orange-tinged darkness. Not only do I not know where I'm going, I can't even see how we are getting there.

The flight lasted more than two hours and he had no idea which direction they were flying. The pilot had performed several jarring 360 turns early on, screwing up any sense of direction he might have had.

Just then the two compartment crewmen suddenly sprang to life. At the same time, Ryder felt the chopper go into a steep, winding decline. He knew wherever he was going, he'd be there soon.

The co-pilot came back and stood next to him.

"Get ready to go, Captain!" he yelled to Ryder over the din of the chopper's engines. "We're coming up on your drop-off point," the man explained, cupping his hand and just about screaming in Ryder's left ear. He handed him a standard flight helmet. "Put this on. Every once in a while we have a rough landing."

Then he gave him a small cloth bag with the Marine Corps emblem on it.

"Here's some essentials," the co-pilot said. "Not much, just a jackknife, a first aid kit, a can of water, and a transponder. It's a standard location beeper and it's being monitored back at the base. Now, if you get in real trouble—and I mean, catastrophic trouble—hold your finger down on the beeper button and we'll come out to get you. But I have to tell you that in three years of doing this we have yet to go out looking for someone at night because we ain't equipped. And neither is any chopper on the base, so be careful. There's also a map and instructions inside the sack, but don't read them until we land. OK?"

Ryder nodded.

"Good luck, Captain . . ." the co-pilot said, shaking his hand and returning to the flight deck.

Suddenly a large red light began flashing in the cabin. Seconds later the big chopper hit the ground so hard, it actually bounced up once then came down even harder. Ryder had caught the "every once and a while" rough landing.

One of the crewmen helped Ryder unstrap his flight harness and led him to the chopper's cargo door.

The man then turned to him and said, "Would you please strip, sir?"

"*Strip?*"

"Yes, sir. Sorry, sir," the man, a sergeant, said. "But those

31

are the orders. You have to leave everything here. Except your shorts and boots, sir."

"Where the hell you dropping me?" he yelled at the co-pilot, as he climbed out of his flight suit. "At the beach?"

"I can't tell you, sir," the Marine yelled back, pushing hard on the chopper's large sliding door.

Ryder was down to his shorts and his boots. The door of the chopper now fully open, he could see that he was indeed somewhere in the desert.

"Ready, sir?" the sergeant asked.

Ryder nodded. "Just one question," he said. "Is it true you guys don't come out to get anyone at night?"

"That's right, sir," the man said. "The Corps don't want us flying at night . . ."

"How come?" Ryder asked.

"Beats me, sir," the man replied. "They sometimes do black ops out here and I guess they don't want us jarheads seeing what they're doing."

With that comforting thought, Ryder stepped off the helicopter and out onto the hard, scorched desert ground.

He walked a short distance away and the sergeant gave him one final wave. Then the big Sea Stallion took off, its blades kicking up a mini-dust storm. The hot flying particles of sand felt like BBs hitting his unprotected skin all over. With a great roar, the Stallion lifted straight up, then turned south.

Ryder huddled himself between the two boulders and waited. Suddenly everything was quiet.

What a fucking show . . . he thought as he watched the helicopter disappear over the southern horizon.

He ripped open the sealed envelope containing his instructions. Inside there was a typed message and a map that strictly indicated terrain. It gave no information as to where he actually was located. A penciled-in star indicated his pick-up point to the southwest.

Just from this information alone, he figured he was somewhere at the northernmost corner of China Lake. Following the dotted line on the map, he had to walk about 25 miles to the southwest, where he would eventually come to a large body of water and some kind of large waterway construction. He was somewhat familiar with the China Lake area from flying over it so many times. The body of water was most likely the Haiwee Reservoir and the large waterway construction, probably the Los Angeles aqueduct. If this was the case, then he knew his pick-up point would be near a town called Coso Junction, California.

He quickly took a position fix on the sun and determined which way was southwest. Then he studied the terrain around him. He was on the side of a slight rise, the flattened-out portion of which was just big enough for the Sea Stallion to set down on. To his left was a wide natural path which spilled off the rise and out onto the desert floor. He could see a mountain range off in the far eastern distance—he figured it to be the Panamint Range, the mountains that formed the western edge of the Death Valley. There was an unnamed set of low hills to his north. A road intersected the desert north to south about six miles from his position.

All told, he was a good three-day walk from the pick-up point. No food, water, or protection from the sun.

And he never even got to eat any breakfast . . .

"What happens if I don't survive the survival test?" he wondered as he set out down the path to flatter ground.

He wasn't completely unprepared for the survival test. He and the other NWS pilots had been given two classes since arriving on how to endure the desert, what and what not to eat, and so on. Apparently raw lizards were the most nutritious, though Ryder had no intention of eating one. He had learned a long time ago how to control his metabolism. He had gotten by on little more than roots and water during his Everglades excursion, there was no reason he couldn't do the same thing this time.

He knew the whole idea was to get himself in the right frame of mind. He had a desert to conquer. The daytime temperature could reach a hundred and ten degrees; at night it went down to thirty-five or so. So he decided to move slowly during the heat

33

of the days and then try to make serious time during the cool nights. Instead of looking for meals he would constantly munch the moist desert roots that he knew could be found in many places. Eat a salt tablet every few hours, don't do anything stupid, and he knew he'd reach the pick-up point with no problems. Just another three-day walk in the desert.

But this was no ordinary desert. He knew these hills and flatlands were covered with highly sophisticated sensing devices, computers that monitored the aerial dogfights via each plane's AIS and sent the data back to the base. Plus there were radars, video cameras and radio transmitters and even simulated surface-to-air missiles.

He also knew that all of these devices were on automatic control, thereby requiring no humans to be out on the range. But that didn't matter. Rule Number One in survival exercises was to avoid any human contact whatsoever. Doing so would negate the test, meaning he would have to do it all over again.

The remainder of the first day passed uneventfully. He took frequent breaks from walking, munching on the bitter yet semimoist desert roots as he went. To prevent sun poisoning, he fashioned a crude hat of sticks and leaves which he supposed gave him a proper Robinson Crusoe look. He had also found a good-sized walking stick as a traveling companion. Using a piece of shoelace from his boot, he tied the open jackknife on to the tip of the stick, giving him a crude but reassuring weapon.

He walked toward the direct southwest whenever it was possible. Besides the sun, his main navigation aid would be the road six miles off his left and in the belly of the desert valley. While most of the roads in the desert ran either true north-south or east-west, according to his map, this one ran in a rough southwesterly direction. So, if he kept the two-lane highway in sight and tried to keep roughly parallel to it, he'd stay on a course.

The road also served another purpose: it provided him with a mind-link to civilization, a weapon to ward off the demons the desert could implant in one's mind. If something catastrophic *did* happen—like a snakebite, a broken bone coupled with the loss of his beeper—he told himself he could always crawl to the road and wait for someone to come along.

But he also found other links to civilization. As he walked along he would occasionally come upon a sensing device or a clump of wires sticking out of the desert floor. They were reminders that while he was miles from nowhere, he was still walking the floor in the midst of a billion-dollar technical video game.

Only in America, he thought.

Night fell quickly, offering him a magnificent sunset, but bringing on the brutal desert night chill. The road was getting harder to see, so once he spotted the North Star he started navigating in its opposite direction. He also quickened his pace, hoping to make another seven or eight miles before sunup. For once he was thankful that he'd kept his thirty-year-old body in shape—he knew that only someone in good condition could survive a three-day trek in the desert. All the jogging and time pumping in the weight room was finally paying off.

Bats. There were thousands of them flying everywhere, sometimes diving at him to get a better look—or more accurately, sonar reading—on him. He was also aware of many little creatures scurrying about the desert floor, dispersing as he passed through. He learned that upon coming to a gully or dry stream bed it was best to heave a rock in first to scatter all the furry and squiggly things that tended to congregate in the depressions. It wasn't that he was so much afraid of the little critters, he was just averse to stepping on something unknown in the middle of the night.

It was around midnight while he was taking his second

nighttime break when he first heard them.

Jets. Off to the south. Coming closer.

He waited and soon could clearly see their red-and-white navigation lights heading right for him. He waited for them. There were three of them, probably at four thousand feet, heading due north, flying single file with about a half mile between them. They went right over him. In the inky blackness he could see no more than their navigation lights and the flare of their exhaust tube. But, that was enough for him to determine the blue-gray camouflage scheme on the aircraft's tails.

"*Aggressors!*" he said out loud, hearing his voice for the first time in almost a day. "What the hell are they doing, flying over the range at this hour?" They passed over him and roared off to the north. He waited until they passed over the horizon and he could hear the engines no more.

"That was very strange," he said aloud, realizing that he was talking to himself. As he understood it, very rarely did any of the fliers from the Miramar—students, instructors, and Aggressors alike—fly at night. In his six weeks at Top Gun, neither he nor any of the Thunder pilots had been given a night flight assignment.

Then it came back to him what the helicopter sergeant had told him about black ops in the desert at night. Ryder wondered if that was the connection.

The airplanes were gone a full five minutes before he finally shrugged it off and started out again.

The sun emerged from a spectacular sunrise and instantly started warming up the bone-cold desert.

He had made good time—possibly as much as nine miles. His strength was holding out well, as was his supply of the moist desert roots that he kept in the plastic map case and stuffed into the crotch of his shorts. His bug bites were at a minimum, and nothing major had tried to take a larger bite out of him during the night. He checked his map to the surrounding terrain and judged that he was roughly on course. The road on his left looked farther away than before, but he still had it in sight.

"Two more nights like that and I'm home free," he thought.

Now he had to find a good place to sleep off the heat of day before starting out again.

He diverted off the desert floor into the low foothills off to his right. He found a group of boulders, two of which formed almost a perfect shape of a woman's bosom. The vision both excited and depressed him. The last time he'd been with a woman was nearly two months before. It was in Seattle, the point of his last stopover before proceeding to Utah where he received his Distant Thunder/Get Your Ass To Top Gun orders. She was a pretty blond barmaid—he had an acknowledged weakness for waitresses and barmaids—and she spent the entire day and two nights of his layover with him.

It seemed like a million years ago . . .

He crawled into the cleavage between the two boulders and found a suitably shady place where he could stretch out. He meticulously checked for any evidence of snakes or rats. Satisfied there were none, he took the precaution of taking a leak at the entrance of the place to keep any curious animals away. Then he lay down and closed his eyes.

Almost immediately his thoughts went back to the barmaid in Seattle. "What was her name?" he wondered as he drifted off to sleep.

4

The sun was starting to dip down in the west when he suddenly woke up. It took him a few moments to get his wits about him. Then it all came back to him: The chopper ride. The desert. The survival exercise. The strange world of

Distant Thunder.

He had been having the most curious dream. He was walking in the desert with a woman. He didn't know who she was, but he felt like he had known her all his life. And she was absolutely gorgeous . . .

But now he was wide awake and something was wrong. He was filled with an uneasy feeling. It was his fighter pilot's instinct, telling him something was amiss. He took a deep breath and listened.

It was a noise, coming from the entrance to the cleavage. It wasn't a snake rattling, thank God. It was more a combination of sounds—rustling or snapping of branches, combined with an occasional clump.

What the hell can this be? he thought, planning his next course of action. He lay completely still and continued to listen, trying to dissect the noise.

The rustling was definitely being made by bushes being brushed together. Could be an animal, he thought. Maybe even a big cat? There were a lot of cats out in this part of California. He fought down an anxious feeling. The infrequent clumping noise almost sounded like small boulders being hit together. That would be some trick for a cat.

He stayed frozen in position, although the mid-afternoon sun was still beating down on him unmercifully. He didn't have many options. There was only one way to get out of the cleavage and that was the direction the noise was coming from. He could get up and see what the hell the story was or he could lay there and cook and hope it went away.

It was too damned hot for Option Two . . .

He slowly reached for his walking stick/spear, hoping the pocketknife on the end would hold up as a weapon should he need it. He quietly removed his improvised hat and toed his way into his flight boots. Then he sat up.

The noise continued. Rustle. Snap. Clump, clump. More rustling. More clumps. More snaps. It sounded vaguely familiar . . .

Then he had it.

The rustling-cracking was the noise of sticks being broken,

the clumping was rocks being hit together. To make a spark. Like someone out there was trying to start a fire . . .

Now he faced a whole new dilemma.

If it was a human out there and if he came in contact with whoever it was, technically the survival exercise could be negated. And, after one long day into it, he didn't feel like starting over and spending another three days wandering around in the desert.

But he knew he had no choice.

He slowly got to his feet and moved to the front of the cleavage. He gradually moved so he could see the small clearing in front of the two boulders. The noise continued, with some foot shuffling added to it.

Ryder stuck his head out far enough to catch a quick glimpse of the clearing.

He saw a pile of sticks and desert scrapings first, with a ring of boulders surrounding it. A wisp of smoke was rising up from it and a small but growing flame crackled in the center. A makeshift spit was built to one side and some kind of small animal—skinned and limp—was skewed on it.

But whoever made the campfire was nowhere in sight. Perhaps they'd gone to get more wood, Ryder reasoned. He edged himself out of the cleavage, staying close to the big rocks . . .

Suddenly he whirled around and had the walking stick up in a flash. He moved so fast he surprised himself. The man had somehow come up in back of him. But Ryder had instantly placed the pocketknife point of the stick up and under the man's jaw.

That's when he noticed the man was holding a nasty-looking knife right at his belly.

"Hold it!" they both said simultaneously.

Both of them stayed frozen for a few, very long seconds.

The man was a soldier—or at least he was dressed like one. He was wearing a desert camouflage uniform, authentic Army-issue boots, a wide-brimmed desert hat, and a military service belt. He also had a sweaty blue scarf tied around his neck.

But there were two things unusual about him: One, his hair

was way beyond allowable service length. Second, his right leg was heavily bandaged.

"Who the *hell* are you?" Ryder demanded.

"I ask you the same question," the man said quickly, his voice slightly forced.

Both men eased off a little.

"All right, this ain't the movies," Ryder said. "You sheath the knife, I take the spear away. OK?"

"OK," the man agreed.

On the count of three, they lowered their weapons. Both breathed a sigh of relief. Then they took a quick account of each other. The man was younger than Ryder, possibly only twenty-two or twenty-four tops. And he had addressed Ryder as "Sir," leading him to believe the man was a GI of some kind.

"Well?" Ryder said first.

The man hesitated, looking at Ryder's somewhat scanty attire. "Are you from Miramar? A pilot on survival training?" he asked.

"Maybe," Ryder said. "And you?"

Again the man hesitated. He was obviously trying to find the correct words to say. "I'm also on a survival exercise," he finally said, adding, "But I'm really not supposed to have contact with anyone, sir."

"Neither am I," Ryder told him. He looked at the man's banged-up leg. "By the looks of that bad wheel, you're lucky we ran into each other."

The man grimaced. "I guess you're right," he said. "My name is Simons. Lieutenant Bo Simons."

Why did that name sound familiar to Ryder?

"I'm Captain Ryder Long," he said, shaking the man's hand. It was obvious the guy was having a hard time standing. He helped him slump down and lean against the side of the boulder.

"What happened to the leg?" Ryder asked.

"Had a run-in with a mountain cat," Simons said, trying to adjust the ragged bandage. "Someone had already shot him. Wounded him. Left him for dead. Probably some jerk hunter in a chopper. I was up on the hill a little further, getting a bearing. Goddamn thing came out at me from nowhere! He was crazy. Foaming at the mouth. He got the leg before I got my knife into him."

"*Jeesuz!*" Ryder exclaimed. "You're lucky he didn't carve you up . . ."

The man was obviously in a lot of pain.

"You were right," Ryder said. "I *am* from NAS Miramar, on survival training. Where's your base, Simons?"

Simons shook his head. "Can't say, Captain," he replied.

The fire crackled a little, drawing their attention to it. "I caught a rat just before I got cut up," Simons said through clenched teeth. "I've got to get something in my stomach before I pass out. Do you want some, sir?"

Ryder looked at the small skewered rodent, its skin now black and smoking. It was disgusting.

"No. Thanks," he said.

Ryder lifted the man up and helped him hobble over to the fire. Simons painfully knelt down and pulled the cooked animal from its skew. Without hesitation, he started pulling off parts of the rodent and eating them.

Ryder felt his stomach do a 360-degree flip. "How many days you've been out, Lieutenant?" he asked the man, sitting down out away from the smoke.

"This is my seventh day, sir," Simons replied.

"Seven days?" Ryder said, surprised. "How long is your exercise supposed to be?"

"It's a two-weeker," Simons answered. "My second one in three months."

Ryder shook his head in admiration. "That's some training, Bo. What are you? Marine Recon? Or SEALS?"

Simons had already finished off the critter and was picking his teeth. "Actually, I'm Army. Airborne."

"Army Airborne?" Ryder said. "I thought this was all Navy property."

Simons shrugged. "I guess it is," he said. "But I sure wish they had taken the time to clear out all the cats . . ."

Just then, the man slumped back, barely catching himself with his elbow.

"Where's your pick-up point, soldier?" Ryder asked him.

"I can't tell you anything, Captain," the young man repeated. "As it is, my whole exercise will be scrubbed because I've made contact with you."

"Look," Ryder said to him forcefully, "*both* of our exercises are scrubbed. Can you understand that? If your pick-up point is any distance from here, you ain't going to make it on that leg. So for now forget all the flag waving and tell me where the hell they are meeting you. And when."

Simons grimaced again. "Sir, you don't understand," he said with some effort. "I'm attached to a special unit that's out in the field. There *is* no pick-up point."

"Out in the field?" Ryder said, looking around the vast desert wasteland. "Your unit is in the field—*out here?*"

Simons nodded.

"And they just send you out and you walk back?"

Again, the soldier nodded.

Ryder knew that the guy wasn't going anywhere. "Well, I'm sorry," he told him. "If you don't get to sick bay, those rodents—or something bigger—will be eating you."

Just then, an enormous roar came up. It was so loud it seemed like the boulders themselves were shaking.

Ryder instantly knew what the noise was. He looked up and saw the telltale contrails of a flight of A-4 Skyhawks passing over high above them. The airplanes, like the F-5s he saw the night before, were attached to an Aggressor Squadron.

They both shielded their eyes and watched the flight of A-4s go over, heading west. There were eight of them in all, flying in pairs. Ryder knew they would eventually make contact with Top Gun pilots somewhere farther out on the range and the electronic, shoot-me, shoot-you computer battles would commence once again.

"*Those bastards!*" Simons said sharply.

Ryder looked at the man. He had cursed the jets so forcefully it surprised him. What would the Aggressors have to do with an Airborne trooper on a survival exercise? He let it pass and concentrated on the immediate problem of saving the young officer's life.

"OK, so you don't have a pick-up point," Ryder said. "So how far away are you from your unit?"

The man shook his head. "I can't tell you, sir."

Ryder was getting fed up. "Look, soldier, you are being very valiant and all that crap, but start forgetting about all your Top Secret stuff right now. You got to level with me so I can get you the hell out of here."

The trooper continued to shake his head. "I can't tell you, Captain!" he said, tears of pain coming to his eyes. "It's beyond Top Secret. My unit . . . is *different*. I mean . . . look at me. Do I look like regular Airborne?"

At that point, Ryder didn't care.

He crouched down and looked the soldier in the eye. "OK, Simons, I ain't got many options," he began. "My pick-up point is twenty miles from here. I could leave you here and hoof it, if that cat had any friends or relatives, they'll get you tonight for sure.

"I suppose I could drag you to that roadway over there and hope a vehicle comes by. But we probably can't make that either. So, I'm going to beep my locator and get a chopper in here."

"*No!*" Simons said with all the force he could muster.

"You'd rather stay out here and die?" Ryder put it to him bluntly.

The trooper winced once again in pain. His bandage—it looked like it had been made from an undershirt—was soaked through with blood. The sun was beating down without mercy. They had very little water—Ryder had about two-thirds of a canteen, the trooper just a quarter.

"All right," Simons finally managed to say. "Fuck it. Beep them. But not now."

"Not now?" Ryder asked. "When the hell do you want me to do it?"

"Tomorrow . . ." Simons just barely whispered. "They'd never find us now anyway . . ."

The man was close to passing out from the pain, but Ryder knew he was right. It was getting dark—and quickly. He could beep his locator and maybe a chopper would be dispatched—

43

maybe not. But if one did come out, it would be a long and maybe dangerous search for the chopper crew to try to figure out the coordinates in the dark. By nature, very few helos were night creatures.

"OK," Ryder said, looking around. "I'll start beeping at sunrise. Think you can last that long?"

Simons nodded and even managed a slight smile. "Sure I can . . ." he said.

5

They moved out of the boxed-in terrain of the cleavage to the very top of the hill. Ryder carried Simons as carefully as possible, but he knew it was a very painful trip for the wounded soldier. Luckily the hill's summit was flattened out, giving them more space to stretch out. Plus the high, flat terrain allowed Ryder to keep watch on all sides for any hungry animal that might be out prowling around.

"Light three fires," Simons told him upon reaching the top of the hill. "That's what the Indians do. It keeps the animals away."

At that point, Ryder wasn't about to argue with the soldier. Despite his condition, Simons obviously knew something about the ways of the desert. Ryder gathered some brush and sticks and built three separate fires, arranging them in a triangle, per Simons' instructions. Then he made Simons as comfortable as possible, building a makeshift bed out of brush and leaves.

It was completely dark by the time he finished and now he had time to think about how hungry he was. His neat little scenario of conserving strength and positive thinking had been thrown completely out of whack by meeting Simons. And while the desert roots would provide the bare essential of

44

sustenance and moisture to his body, the bitter weeds did nothing to eliminate the feeling of his very empty stomach or his perpetually dry mouth.

He offered a few roots to Simons to munch on, but the man was having a hard time swallowing, plus his pain was increasing.

"I can't eat those goddamn weeds," Simons said, reaching down to his utility belt. "They make me sick." He produced a plastic bag filled with plant buds of some kind. With great effort, he took out three and handed them to Ryder.

"Take these and boil them in a little bit of water . . ." he said with obvious struggle.

Ryder looked at the plant buds. They resembled miniature green acorns.

"What are they?" he asked the wounded trooper.

"*Penticus sausilitcus,*" Simons answered, rolling off the Latin name for the plants. "It's an old Indian remedy. They'll relieve the hunger and thirst and help knock out this pain. My unit uses them all the time."

Ryder carefully doled out about a quarter of their water supply into Simons' canteen cap and rested it over one of the fires. Once the hot water started to bubble, he threw in the three seeds and stirred them around. Several minutes later, he had a boiling mixture of green tea.

He helped Simons take a few long sips from the cup then he drank the rest himself. Amazingly, the pangs of hunger and thirst disappeared almost immediately.

Simons managed another smile. "Works good, doesn't it?" he said, leaning back on the bed of brush and leaves. Five minutes later, he was asleep.

Ryder added some more brush to the fires, then leaned against his own mat of brush and leaves which he'd propped up against good-sized rock. He had his walking stick/spear on one side of him, Simons' survival knife on the other. He had also took the precaution of making two brush-and-stick torches, tied with shoelaces. These would be lit only if he had to scare some animal away.

*   *   *

Time passed and the night grew colder. But he was amazed how well the sausilitcus plants worked. Despite everything that had happened, and the fact that the next day was going to be uncertain, he was beginning to feel extremely relaxed and confident. Gradually all his wants—food, water, a beer, a soft place to sleep, warm clothes—seemed to disappear.

"Those Indians knew what they were doing," he thought.

The moon rose, large and white, giving everything in the desert a sharp, almost ethereal shadow. He looked up at the brilliantly star-filled sky. The thick, wavy band of the Milky Way was directly overhead. Everywhere he looked he saw constellations: Hercules. Cygnus. Leo Minor. Pegasus. The Triangulum. Corona Borealis. Ursa Major. They were blazing so brilliantly he imagined he could feel their heat. He felt an overwhelming sense of euphoric magnificence well up inside him. All that seemed to matter in his life at that moment were the stars.

Billions of galaxies, each one filled with billions of stars, he thought. What's really going on out there?

Although he had intended to stay up all night, he soon found himself pleasantly drifting off to sleep. He immediately started dreaming about hundreds of individual stars moving across the sky—moving like airplanes, or spaceships, high up, darting here and there as if outer space were some gigantic intergalactic highway system.

His dreams moved slowly from spaceships to visions of women. First, many women. Lovely. Soft faces in the sky, passing before him. Then, just one woman. She looked vaguely but gorgeously familiar. Was it the woman he had met in his dream walking through the desert? He wanted to find out. He wanted to reach out and touch her face. Feel it. Kiss it.

Then her face disappeared and that's when he heard the rumbling . . .

It was tremendous. The ground underneath him started to shake violently. He opened his eyes. I'm awake, he thought, aren't I? He tried to move, but couldn't. He was paralyzed—

frozen in place, looking up at the stars. What was going on? Why couldn't he move?

Then he saw the lights. Off to the south. Red-and-white navigation lights. Getting closer. First one set, then two, then three. Despite his frozen-in-place condition, his mind flashed back to the trio of F-5 Aggressors he saw the night before. Maybe these lights belonged to the same flight of jets. With great effort, he managed to barely lift his head. Then he saw a fourth and a fifth set of lights. Then more. More than he could count. The southern sky seemed suddenly dotted with the navigation lights, about twenty-five miles away and heading north.

Jeesuz! he thought, trying but failing to move anymore. "There must be three squadrons of them . . ."

The noise became more intense. It was a deep, thunderous roar almost too loud to be caused only by the still far-off three dozen jets.

He stiffly turned his head and strained to look to the north. More lights! These were different in color and arrangement. Amber lights mixed with green and strobe-white. What kind of airplane carried those kinds of colors? As he looked, more amber lights appeared, as if they were materializing out of the thin air. He quickly counted as many as twenty of them. These aircraft were heading directly south almost on a collision course with the others.

He tried to identify this second group of aircraft. By the light of the moon he could see they were larger aircraft, flying very low. Almost too low. They were about eighteen miles from his position. Then, as he watched, they changed direction almost as one. He was astounded. Such a maneuver was hard to accomplish in the day—at night, almost impossible. Unless . . .

He slowly turned back to the force approaching from the south. They were now about twenty miles from him, but coming on very fast. As he watched, some of these airplanes began changing positions too. But not as one. Instead they were splitting off into pairs. Some climbed, others dove. Some streaked off to the east, others to the west. Still others continued on the same heading.

His head was swimming. He made a strong effort to move, but couldn't. He felt like he was floating—floating in place. What was the matter with him? Suddenly the fragile quiet of the desert was reverberating with the roar of more than fifty jets.

"What the hell is going down here?" he asked out loud.

He turned to the north once again. That group of aircraft were now only a few miles from him.

They look like B-1s . . . he thought, straining his neck to identify the mystery airplanes. That would explain the group's intricate low-level maneuvering. The B-1 had a top-notch terrain guidance system which allowed it to just about hug the ground. This way the multi-million-dollar bomber could make its bombing approach while flying under the enemy's radar.

He turned again to the south to see the many pairs of smaller jets scattered across the sky were now converging from all directions. They weren't yet close enough for him to pick out individual designs. Were they A-4s? Or F-5s? Whatever—he had no doubt they were Aggressor fighters.

And they're going for the bombers . . . he thought.

Never had he seen such large groups of airplanes in one mock engagement. Nor had he seen or heard about the Aggressors going after bombers like the B-1. But to do it all at night was really insane!

The crazy bastards must all be flying on instruments, he thought.

No wonder they didn't let nosy choppers fly out here at night . . .

He felt a chill run through him. The two groups were approaching each other in such a way that he knew they would meet almost exactly over his position.

He heard a separate roar coming out of the west. He turned slowly to see a pair of the fighters heading right for him. That's when he got his first good look at the smaller jets. The two jet fighters flew right over his head, so close he was enveloped in their jet exhaust.

They were F-5s painted exactly like Soviet MiGs.

The two groups met head-on no more than a half mile and overhead from his position. Suddenly it seemed as if the whole night sky suddenly caught on fire . . .

Streaks of lights were flashing out in all directions. The fighters were firing on the bombers and the bombers were firing back. He could see missiles, trailing smoke, leaving the fighters. Long thin beams of light were emitting from the bombers. There were explosions in the air. Smoke. Flames. The screams of whining jet engines.

"This is crazy . . ." he said, his jaw agape. He closed his eyes. *Was this really happening?* He opened them again to see another F-5 pass right over his head, no more than 150 feet above him. Instantly he was once again covered in the jet's hot exhaust as he watched it dive and head for a B-1 skirting the valley. Suddenly a line of tracer shells shot out from the F-5's nose.

"This is nuts," he whispered. "These guys are really shooting at each other . . ."

Suddenly a B-1 flashed close by, its engines shrieking. It was so close, he could see the pilots working the controls by the greenish light in the cockpit.

Two more F-5s roared over; he could distinctly see realistic-looking missiles under their wings. A B-1 swung low around his hill position trying to shake a pair of attacking fighters. Another B-1 screamed through the valley so low, he expected it to impact on the desert floor at any second.

The melee continued unabated. The whole time he could only lie there—frozen in his spot, unable to move, watching the action, his mouth wide open. It had such a dreamlike quality to it, he closed his eyes on many occasions and commanded himself to wake up. But every time he opened his eyes, the incredible dogfight had become more intense.

Then, as suddenly as it began, it was over . . .

It was as if every jet involved got a single command. The aircraft dispersed—the B-1s turned 180 and disappeared to the north. The F-5s did likewise and vanished to the south. They were all gone in less than a minute. Suddenly the desert was quiet again. A strange, deathly quiet. The stars had once again taken over the sky.

He fell back into a deep sleep.

It was impossible to determine how long he slept for—maybe hours, maybe just a few minutes . . .

But he suddenly reawakened to find two people were leaning over him. An extremely bright light was being shined in his face—too bright for him to clearly see who the people were. He tried to move, but found he couldn't. The light in his eyes was so intense, his pupils began to sting. Still he strained to get a glimpse of the figures hovering over him. His eyes finally focused and he saw the men were wearing helmets and Army uniforms and camouflaged face masks. Then he saw the distinctive blue scarves.

Instantly he knew that men from Simons' unit had arrived . . .

Ryder started to say something to them when he suddenly felt the hand of one of the men covering his mouth. Then the other man put a fountain-pen-looking device under Ryder's nose and pushed a button.

It all happened very quickly. He was aware of a greenish mist shooting out of the device. Then he felt unconsciousness come crashing in on him, like being knocked out at the dentist.

"You bastard . . ." was all he managed to say before going under.

6

He woke up hours later, his head pounding and the taste of blood in his mouth.

At first he still couldn't move. Then gradually he was able to roll to one side and lift himself up on his elbow. It was almost midday; the sun was directly over head. His skin was sunburned to a deep red and a colony of desert ants had spent the past few hours devouring his lower extremities.

He tried to get his bearings, but he was dizzy and his eyes were going in and out of focus. Finally, he squinted and strained them into working. He looked around, but he couldn't recognize any of the surroundings. The mountains, hills, and desert valley he expected to see were gone. Instead all he could see for miles in every direction was flat, open, barren desert.

He smelled smoke and he realized that he was lying near a small campfire. Beyond the campfire was a road. With great effort, he managed to sit up, his head feeling like it was suffering the worst hangover possible. That's when he saw his locator-beeper was stuck upright in the sand a short distance away. Someone had taped down the send button. He could hear it softly beeping, meaning an emergency message was being sent back to the base.

His canteen also lay nearby, as was his walking stick/spear. But Simons was gone . . .

Suddenly a wave of dizziness came over him. He painfully laid back down and closed his eyes, trying his best to stay conscious. But it was a losing battle.

Just as the darkness closed in once again, he thought he could hear the far-off sounds of an approaching helicopter.

7

"How you feeling, Ghost?"

Ryder opened his eyes to see Woody looking down at him.

"Howdy, Wood Man," Ryder managed to say. "What's shaking?"

"The whole base is shaking, my man," Woody said with a smile. "Everyone's wondering what the hell happened to you . . ."

Four days had passed. Ryder was in a private room at the Miramar base hospital. A search and rescue helo from Miramar had found him, attracted to the place by his locator. He barely remembered being lifted back to Miramar or his first two days in the hospital. It was only by the third day that he realized he was suffering from a handful of ailments, heat prostration being the most serious.

He was presently covered in salves and oilments and had an IV unit stuck into his arm, replenishing his body's fluids. The doctors were also injecting him regularly with sedatives, giving him an all-too-familiar dreamlike feeling.

Nevertheless, it was good to see Woody.

"Been up lately?" Ryder asked him.

"No way, Ghost," Woody said, slipping into the chair next to the hospital bed. "They got me on indefinite standdown. I told them 'I don't fly unless the Ghost is with me.' So they got me booked overtime into the flight simulators. That's where you're going, too, once you get out of here."

Ryder managed a laugh. "I'd probably crash one of them, the way I feel now."

Woody was quiet for a moment, then asked, "Hey, Ghost, what the hell really *did* happen out there? I mean, the stories going around the base are just wild."

Ryder shook his head. "I gave them the whole story yesterday. The best I can remember it anyway."

"Well, you're the talk of the town," Woody told him. "I've heard everything. One story says you got heat fever and spent three days hallucinating. Another story's got you claiming you was carried off by a UFO!"

Ryder shook his head. "Frigging Navy scuttlebutt," he said bitterly. "These swabbies are like old ladies when it comes to this kind of stuff . . ."

"So, what *did* happen, Ghost?" Woody asked again. "Do you realize they picked you up more than 120 miles from where you were supposed to be . . ."

It was true. One of the Navy doctors—Ryder had him pegged for a psychiatrist—had filled him in the day before. The chopper had found him not in the Panamint Valley where he'd been dropped off but on the other side of Death Valley, right on the border of Nevada. It was 127 miles from his drop-off point.

Everyone—including himself—was baffled as to how he got there . . .

Ryder took a deep breath and told Woody everything. Finding Simons. The incredible midnight dogfight. The black F-5s. Getting gassed by Simons' rescuers. His partner sat on the edge of the bed and listened to it all, his mouth wide open in amazement.

"Christ, Ghost," he said when the tale was complete. "You actually *told* them you saw a *real* dogfight between B-1s and three squadrons of F-5s. Real bullets?"

"I *did* see it," Ryder said. "Real bullets. Real bombs, missiles, you name it."

"OK, let's take this a piece at a time," Woody said. "Where could these three squadrons of black F-5s come from. Certainly not here . . ."

Ryder closed his eyes and nodded. "I know it *sounds* crazy," he said. "But, maybe Nellis. They were F-5s. But they weren't painted like the usual Aggressor squads. And they weren't just using AIS pods, either."

"What's the brass say about this live ammo stuff?" Woody asked.

"They laughed," Ryder said. "Told me that no way were there any large scale aerial maneuvers in that area that night. Or any other night. They had the nuts to tell me that I was actually looking at commercial airliners going over."

Woody let out a whoop. "What the hell you tell them after that?"

Ryder gritted his teeth. "I told them that I've been playing their fucking dogfight games here for six weeks with F-5s painted every which way but pink. I *know* what a goddamn F-5 Aggressor looks like. And I know what a B-1 looks like and I know what real ammunition looks like . . ."

Woody was quiet for a moment, then asked, "What about

53

this drug angle? Where did they dig that up?"

"What drug angle?" Ryder asked, somewhat defiantly.

"Well, one of the main stories on the buzz line is that you . . . ah, ingested something out there," Woody said, selecting his words carefully. "Made you high, Ghost. Tipsy. Stoned. One guy said he heard you were picked up by some hippy-dippy people—Manson Family people—and that you partied with them for three days before they dumped you."

Ryder was livid. "What a bunch of Navy scuttlebutt bullshit!" he said, the frustration showing in his voice. "This guy. Simons. He had these little plants. It was like an old Indian remedy, he said."

"Like . . . peyote?" Woody asked, trying to be diplomatic. "Pretty powerful stuff, Ghost. Makes you see very funny things. I'm telling you, back in school . . ."

Ryder cut him off. Suddenly it was coming together. "So they're saying I was tripped out on peyote and made all this up?"

Woody started to say something, but couldn't.

"Give me a fucking break here, Woody pal," Ryder told him. "Is that what they're saying?"

Woody shrugged and said, "What they are saying is you were found 120 miles from where you were supposed to be. Lying in the middle of the desert. Cut up. Burned to a crisp. Claiming you met some Airborne guy who is not around and that you saw a bunch of mysterious black F-5s shooting it out with a bunch of B-1s in the middle of the night. With live ammo."

Ryder actually laughed a little. He had to agree with his partner. "Well, when you put it that way, I guess it does sound kind of crazy . . ." he said.

Suddenly Woody was shaking his hand. "I believe you, Ghost," he said. "You got a straight head and you got the nuts. You say all this happened, then *I* say it happened."

Ryder felt a bad vibe run through him. "Jeesuz, they won't let me anywhere near a cropduster, never mind an F-14 after this," he said.

"Screw 'em," Woody said, getting up to go. "You're the best

stick jockey in this whole fucking place. You make those Navy jocks look like clerks. They take you out of your speed jeans, they're making the biggest mistake since selling guns to the Iran towelheads."

Ryder thought for a moment, then said, "If I could find out who this Simons guy is. What his unit is. I'll drag his ass in front of them and let him tell them the straight jack."

Woody nodded. "Now there's a good idea," he said with genuine enthusiasm. "What was the guy like? You said he was Airborne. Did he mention any unit number or nickname or anything?"

Ryder shook his head. "No, he was out of it most of the time." He paused for a moment, then said, "But, come to think of it, he *was* wearing a blue scarf around his neck . . ."

"Blue scarf?" Woody asked. "So what?"

"So, the guys who knocked me out were also wearing blue scarves," Ryder said. A light had just clicked on in his head.

Woody rubbed his chin in thought. "Could be some kind of unit identification thing," he said. "I mean, look at the Top Gun jocks. Ever since the movie, they've been running around wearing ascots, checkerboard scarves, you name it."

"Yeah, I know what you mean," Ryder said, pulling himself up on the bed. "The other thing is, the guy's name, 'Bo Simons' sounded familiar, too."

"OK, Ghost, I'm gonna do you a favor," Woody said, getting up to go. "Let me see if I can track down any units where blue scarves are in vogue."

Ryder smiled for the first time in a week. *Stay cool. Stay tight.* "Thanks, pal," he said. "I owe you . . ."

"I know you do," Woody replied, giving him a thumbs-up. "If you ain't out of here in two more days, I'll *break* you out . . ."

The Wiz disappeared out the door, leaving it open just long enough for Ryder to see that two Marine guards were posted outside.

As Woody would later tell it, the librarian had a body that

55

could stop a Sidewinder a mile away.

"I think I can definitely help you out," she was saying to him.

He had used a few hours off-time to borrow a car, head down the Cabrillo Freeway to the University of San Diego. He guessed correctly that they would have a fairly large library at the school. He had some research to do.

But from the moment he wandered up to the Information Reference desk, he couldn't take his eyes off her. He didn't know whether she was a blonde or brunette. Somewhere in the middle. Blue summer minidress. Deep plunge front, practically no back, held up by a pair of very thin straps. Sun-tanned to perfection. Face courtesy of *Cosmopolitan*. Body from *Sports Illustrated* swimsuit issue. Legs from a silk stockings ad.

The library at the University of San Diego was filled with California girls—doing God only knows what. Woody couldn't imagine any library in California actually *filled* with people, never mind one near the beautiful San Diego beaches on a warm July day. But crowded it was. However, all of the academic beach bunnies paled in comparison with the card catalog lady.

"Here's one that might be helpful: 'Department of Defense Guide to US Army Unit Identification,'" the librarian said, bending over a catalog drawer just enough for Woody to catch a glimpse of her powder-blue bra. It was his favorite color. The librarian looked up and caught him staring at her bosom. "Is that what you are looking for?" she asked him, smiling.

Woody could only nod weakly.

"Well, good. But if that doesn't . . . well, satisfy you," she perked seductively, bending over a little further, "there are similar volumes for the Navy and Marines . . ."

"I'd . . . I'd like to look at both of them," Woody managed to babble.

She stood up and straightened her skirt. "You're from NAS Miramar, aren't you?" she asked him. "A pilot?"

"Yes, ma'am," Woody answered.

"That's funny," she said with a smile, fixing one of her shoulder straps that had slipped down. "We *never* see you Navy guys in here."

"That's because those Navy guys can't read," he said quickly. "I'm in the Air Force, ma'am. I'm assigned to Miramar as part of a . . . well, I mean, it's classified. A secret mission. Top Secret."

"*Really?*" she said, her eyes going wide as she adjusted her profession's mandatory tortoise-shell glasses. "I *am* impressed."

She handed him a slip of paper with several card catalog numbers on it. "These are all reference books," she told him, tapping him lightly on the hand as she spoke. "You'll have to read them here."

"Where?" he asked, fingers crossed.

"At that desk," she said, pointing. "The one right next to mine."

Ten minutes later Woody was plowing through the first of the ten huge volumes. The book contained page after page of hundreds of Army unit badges, patches, medals, citations, flags, banners, mottos, and insignia. Each item was accompanied by an exhaustive history of the emblem, its origins, its service record, and its present status. Woody was amazed at the detail of the book. He could just picture an office full of Army desk commanders putting in hours upon hours of research into such military minutia.

It took him more than an hour to go through the Army book. And although he'd seen instances of units that wore everything from odd hats to funny boots, he didn't find what he was looking for: a regular Army outfit—Airborne or otherwise—that wore the blue scarf.

"How are you doing?" he heard a sweet voice say.

She was standing right beside him, leaning over his shoulder, turning a few pages of the Army book herself. She was standing *so* close to him, he could *feel* her aura, that's what the Californians called those things.

"No luck here," he said, glad he had showered before leaving the base.

57

She leaned in even closer, innocently brushing up against him. "Well, I know there are those two other books—on the Navy and Marines," she said, her lovely powder-blue supported breasts now mere inches from his face. "But they are quite . . . large."

Sticks' next breath got caught in his throat. "Just how *big* are they?" he heard himself saying.

She laughed a little. "Well, I guess I should have said: *thick*. About as thick as the one you have."

He swallowed hard. Was she kidding?

"I'd like to look at them," he finally said. "Both of them . . ."

"It will be my pleasure . . ." she said.

The Navy and Marine book yielded nothing. Yet the trip wasn't a complete loss.

"Well, I couldn't find anything," he told her, as he got up to leave. "But thanks for your help."

"It was my pleasure," she said, beaming. "I'm glad I finally got to meet one of you fighter pilots. It must be a very exciting job."

Woody nodded. "That it is, ma'am," he said.

"I just *love* airplanes," she said, fingering a long blond strand. "I even know a little bit about them."

"Really?" Woody asked, seeing his best opportunity. "Well, it's noontime. If you want, I'll buy you lunch and we can talk about it."

She thought it over for a couple seconds, then smiled and said his favorite two letters: "OK . . ."

She quickly got her things, then called over to a fellow-worker sitting at a desk nearby, "Helen, I'm going to lunch now, and I may be back a little late."

Woody closed his eyes. Maybe all this was a dream, he thought.

8

The E2-C Hawkeye early-warning aircraft circled high and lazy above the China Lake range, its topside saucerlike radone slowly revolving.

On board were the two pilots, three generals, an admiral, and a civilian. The civilian and the general officers were riding in the mid-section compartment, seated next to a battery of radar and communications consoles. None of the equipment was turned on, however. Instead the five men sat huddled around a fold-down table usually used by the aircraft's crew for chow during long flights.

The stubby, twin-turboprop Hawkeye was being used as an airborne "secure room"—a place that was completely impervious to any kind of eavesdropping, even by spy satellites. A solid, soundproof door separated them from the two pilots. Nevertheless, the five men were somewhat nervous, and therefore when they spoke, it was in hushed tones. So sensitive was the matter they were to discuss, each man knew that by right, nothing short of the cabin of Air Force One could provide them the absolute security they needed.

But they were at the mercy of time and logistics. So the E2-C would have to do.

Each man sat quietly reading a lengthy document marked only: "Program Evaluation."

The topic was Project Distant Thunder. No one was smiling . . .

The civilian, an assistant secretary of defense, had read the document several times before and only skimmed it quickly for this occasion. Still, its message chilled him. He thought of his family—at home just outside of Washington, D.C. He closed his eyes and realized that he wanted to be with them more than anything. While they still had time.

The officers finished reading the report at roughly the same time. Each seemed to take a moment of private reflection before closing the document and returning it to the special "burn bag" on the table in front of them.

"My God, this is grim, *grim* stuff," the Marine general said.

"It's all been confirmed—several times over, by the DIA and the Company," the assistant secretary told them. He had brought the reports out from the Pentagon earlier that day. "I saw the reconfirms myself."

"How about all these photos that are mentioned in here?" the Navy admiral, the top officer at NAS Miramar, asked. "Do we know if that KH-12 has been working OK?"

"The NSA guys say it is," the assistant secretary replied. "I was there when the transmission came down. Clearest goddamn satellite photos I've ever seen."

The E-2C hit a patch of turbulence, rattling the inside of the aircraft momentarily.

"Well, it's clear that time is running out," the Marine officer said. "And according to this latest evaluation, we'll be lucky if the Navy's Air Training Program is completed on time."

"There are always problems instituting even the slightest new training procedures," the admiral said in his own defense. As NAS Miramar commander, he was in charge of all the project's air crew training. "Never mind the . . . shall we say, *unorthodox* procedures connected to Distant Thunder. Add to that the security that's been layered on top of this, the delays were inevitable. And the timetable given to us was close to impossible in the first place."

The assistant secretary held up his hand and signaled he wanted quiet. "The secretary and the President are well aware of the timetable, General," he said. The man from Defense knew the admiral was not happy about the Navy's major role in the project—that was to usher the Air Force crew through the Navy's very provincial Top Gun.

"Can your air crew training timetable be accelerated, Admiral?" the assistant secretary asked.

The admiral was getting annoyed. What did they want of

him? "The truth be known, it's the Air Force pilots themselves that have caused the slowdown," the admiral fired back.

"How so, Admiral?" the Air Force colonel asked.

"Well, one of your Air Force pilots had a rather . . . unfortunate experience on his survival exercise," the Navy officer answered. "They tell me he got a hold of some kind of poisonous root out in the desert. He's still in sick bay."

The Air Force officer reached into his briefcase and came up with a file. He leafed through it momentarily, then said, "Which officer was it: Woods or Long?"

"Long was the one, Captain Ryder Long," the admiral told him, then added with a sarcastic smile, "Maybe our survival course was too much for him."

"I doubt that," the Air Force officer shot back. He was just as unhappy that *his* pilots were going through Top Gun for the crucial mission training. By rights, they should be going through the Air Force's version of Fightertown, better known as Red Flag out of Nellis Air Force Base in Nevada. But the intense security of the entire Distant Thunder project dictated that the Air Force pilots had to be "submerged" at Top Gun. "In fact, from the numbers I've seen, I'd say the Air Force pilots were doing quite well."

Touché, the admiral thought. As much as he hated to admit it, the Air Force guys were performing better than any of the Navy pilots in their group. In fact, the Air Force pilots—Long and Woods—were the top scoring pilots for all of Top Gun. But he sure as hell wasn't going to mention it.

"Gentlemen," the assistant secretary interrupted. "I would like to reiterate at this point how much of this very critical mission depends on the cooperation between your respective services . . ."

Each of the officers shook his head. They had heard it over and over.

The assistant secretary was trying to keep his temper under control. It was not the first time he had warned them about inter-service sniping and bickering.

"We cannot have another Iran Rescue Operation here, gentlemen," he said, his voice filled with a sternness that gave

61

the normally unruffled military men a momentary pause. "And to quote the President directly: 'Any inter-service bull*shit* will not be tolerated.'"

There was a long, uneasy quiet around the table, the only noise being the whine from the E-2C's props and the whirring sound from the aircraft's revolving radome.

The admiral finally broke the silence. "Your pilot Long will only be out for a week. He is scheduled to put some time in on the simulator in the next couple days, then he'll be back flying '14s again. He'll be ready for the exercise against Red Flag."

The Air Force general smiled. Within the next two weeks his Red Flag pilots would be pitted against the Top Gun jocks. It was the normal ending for any Top Gun or Red Flag class. A chance for his Air Force guys to do battle against heavily disliked Navy pilots. Those aboard also knew that after the exercise, the two Air Force pilots would be moving on from Top Gun and into their next training phase for Distant Thunder. But the secret Thunder project aside, the Air Force officer was confident his crews would whip the Top Gun cover boys.

"If I could ask a question," the admiral said deliberately. "What is the status of the other nations' pilots? I haven't heard a thing about them in three weeks. How is their training proceeding?"

"They are just completing their First Phase training, too," the assistant secretary replied. "They are scheduled to arrive right after the exercise with Red Flag."

"How many can we expect?" the Air Force officer asked.

"Just four in all," the assistant secretary said, consulting a memo he retrieved from his briefcase. "One each from the RAF, the French Armée de l'Air, the Luftwaffe, and the Royal Indian Air Force."

The Air Force officer spoke up. "So counting our two Air Force guys, there'll only be six Distant Thunder pilots in all? Is that enough?"

The assistant secretary shook his head slowly then said, "Probably not. But they put their pilots through the same profiles as we did ours. Only one guy from each fit."

"Well, so much for international cooperation," the Army general said, a taste of bitterness in his words.

"The allies *are* cooperating . . ." the assistant secretary said firmly. "But please remember the sensitivity of what we are dealing with here. Plus, some of our allies' security apparatuses leak like sieves. We don't have to be reminded of the consequences should this get out. To the press. Or to anyone who doesn't have a need to know.

"Now, I realize that mission calls for a squadron, but seven pilots is all we have. We don't have the time to train anymore—assuming that any more 'suitables' could be found. Plus you all know that the security undertaking for these seven was awesome. We simply can't go through all that a second time without compromising the entire project."

"But we should at least have one more pilot, a back-up," the Air Force officer said. "Is there anyone close to the program who could jump in easy? One of the Aggressor guys or an instructor, maybe?"

"I'll work on that," the admiral said, jotting down a message in his notebook.

Once again, a stone-dead silence filled the compartment.

"Getting back to the allies for a moment," the Marine general said. "Have they firmed up cover stories for their pilots yet? If so, I think we should get copies or something, just so we're all talking the same gameplan should anything get out."

The assistant secretary quickly nodded and said, "They are in the process of doing that right now." It was this particular program—inventing the cover stories—that bothered him the most about Distant Thunder. He tried not to let it show. "Being assisted by the US Information Agency," he added. "I'll make sure they get a copy of our cover stories, when it's appropriate."

The E-2C's engines whined as the pilots began yet another long, lazy circle.

"All right, gentlemen," the assistant secretary finally continued. "I trust that all the other training schedules are firm?"

"Army is ahead of schedule," the Army general said quickly.

63

"All three of our units have been in Deep Training for four months now."

"So have ours," the Air Force officer reported. "I have only good reports from the commander of the Adversary Tactics."

"How about the Corps?" the assistant secretary asked.

"On schedule, sir," the Marine officer said. "All armored units have been Deep for two weeks."

"Good," the assistant secretary said. "Then I think I have enough for my report to the secretary and the President. Thank you, gentlemen."

With that, the admiral got up and opened the specially sealed door that led to the E-2C's cockpit.

"That's it, guys," he told the two Hawkeye pilots. "Let's go home."

9

It was three days later when Ryder got some surprisingly good news.

"You're going back up," Slade told him. "Report to the briefing room at 0900, tomorrow. You, too, Woods."

Ryder had been out of the hospital for a full day. Although he was told that his medical evaluation as well as the whole file on his incident were now "classified," the Navy doctors sent him off with no more than a prescription to "rest up and take it easy."

He had spent the whole day doing just that, sitting with Woody at their regular corner table at the OC. That's where Slade finally caught up with him.

Ryder was ecstatic when he heard the news. He had imagined the bizarre desert incident would lead to everything from court-martial to being bounced back to C-130s. Sure,

Woody's recon mission to the San Diego library had gone bust—that was secondary at the moment. Ryder was just glad that someone up the ladder decided he could still fly. He felt like an enormous weight had been lifted from his shoulders. In fact, he felt so good, he invited Slade to have a beer with them.

Reluctantly, the Navy commander sat down. "I shouldn't be seen drinking with you guys," he said, eyeing the busy bar at the other end of the club.

"Relax, Commander," Ryder told him, motioning the waitress to bring three bottles of beer.

"Should I put these on the commander's tab as usual?" the waitress asked Ryder point-blank. Luckily the comment went right over Slade's head.

Woody saved the day by flashing out a five-dollar bill and pressing it into the waitress's hand.

Once she had gone, Ryder leaned over to the Navy officer and asked, "OK, Slade, why did they do it?"

"Do what?" the man replied.

"Put me back in the saddle again," Ryder told him.

Slade sipped his beer and shook his head. "You know better than to ask me that, Captain."

"Come on, Slade," Ryder insisted. "This isn't True Confessions. Just give me your guess. Why would the Navy tell everyone I was eating peyote with Charlie Manson in a flying saucer in the desert one day then let me climb into a $30 million F-14 a week later?"

"Because they're fucking nuts, that's why," Woody put in.

Slade filled his beer glass and downed it all in one gulp. "Look, the Navy didn't ask you guys to come here," he said. "The Air Force *sent* you here."

"Well, look at the stats," Woody told the man. "It's going to be embarrassing if two Air Force jocks win the scoring trophy this class. That will make quite a story for *Stars and Stripes*."

Ryder took a swig of beer and said, "Funny that you should bring that up, Captain Woods. I just happen to know a very pretty woman who works for the *Stripes*. She'd love to print that story."

Slade shook his head. "Stay cocky, wise guys," he said

sarcastically. "Brag your asses off to the whole base. But see all those guys over at the bar. When you *lose* that trophy, you'll have every one of them chewing on your asses until the day they ship you out."

Both Ryder and Woody laughed out loud.

"Then what are *you* going to do, Slade?" Ryder asked. "Put in for subs?"

Slade smiled as he drained the last of his beer. "Nope," he said. "The day you guys ship out, I'm getting a five-day pass, I'm flying to DC and I'm gonna find the shine-ass lieutenant responsible for getting me mixed up with you guys in the first place and I'm gonna punch his lights out."

Ryder and Woody were laughing so hard, tears formed in their eyes.

"But I'll answer your question, Ryder," he said, getting up to go. "You want to know why they're keeping you on?"

"Sure," Ryder answered.

Slade looked him straight in the eye and said, "Because I hear you're expendable, Captain . . ."

Ryder reached down and switched on his cockpit radio set, then called into the microphone, "Ready back there, Wiz?"

"Let's do it . . ." Woody answered. "I'm green on everything back here."

Ryder called Miramar tower for final clearance, which he received. Seconds later they were rolling down the runway.

"Boot it, Ghost!" Woody yelled as the F-14 streaked down the asphalt strip.

Ryder obliged by kicking in the 'Cat's powerful afterburner. Instantly the fighter shot forward and lifted off. Ryder coolly eased back on the controls and put the airplane into a steep climb.

"Yeah, Ghost!" Woody was yelling in the jumpseat. His enthusiasm level always went up five notches upon take-off. "Back in the saddle again. Let's show these swabbies how you really fly one of these birds!"

Ryder eased the controls forward and leveled off at ten

thousand feet. He was sick of simulators. *It was damn good to be really flying again.*

And this was to be the most pleasant of flights. An orientation flight. Translated: a joyride. A half-hour freewheel designed to get Ryder used to flying the 'Cat again. It was coming back to him very quickly.

They flew west, then north, about 100 miles out over the ocean, cruising at 550 knots. It was a beautiful California summer's day. That meant the beaches would be crowded.

Ryder guided the Tomcat toward the east then banked to a southerly heading as soon as he spotted Newport Beach.

"We'll fly over all the clutch beaches and scenery this heading," Ryder called back to Woody, easing the 'Cat into a slight dive.

"Roger, Ghost," Woody replied. "There's Laguna. I know a waitress there. Doheny Bay. San Clemente."

By the time they reached Oceanside, the F-14 was flying at a thousand feet and cruising at four hundred knots. Even at that height and speed, they could pick out the bikini-clad girls from the one-piecers.

Ryder lowered the aircraft to seven-fifty. "Give the taxpayers a look at what they're paying us for," Ryder said.

The F-14 streaked down the coastline, steering in and out to keep up with the coastal terrain.

This is what I love, Ryder thought. God help the person who would ever try to take this away from me . . .

They were over La Jolla when Woody came on the line.

"Hey, Ghost," he said. "What do I see down there, about a mile off shore, three ahead."

Ryder banked the F-14 to get a better view. "Is that the admiral's admin ship?" he asked.

"The admiral's yacht," Woody corrected him.

"Out for a sail," Ryder continued. "No doubt getting his mind off all the pressures of running Fightertown."

"Buzz those jerks!" Woody said suddenly.

"Hey, Wiz, calm down, will you?" Ryder told him. "My first time up and you want to buzz the goddamn admiral's boat? They'll bounce me for sure . . ."

"Are you kidding me?" Woody said. "You're golden man. We both are. This is your ticket. If they didn't bounce you for not playing good boy scout in the desert, they ain't going to bounce you for anything!"

Ryder admitted it was tempting. He knew that Navy jets routinely buzzed anything Army or Air Force and had been doing so for years. The year before, in a very famous buzzing incident, five F-4s from a Naval Reserve group buzzed the Army team during practice for the big Army-Navy game.

Like the little devil on Ryder's left shoulder, Woody was back on the line. "Don't you get it, Ghost?" the Wiz said. "They'll think we're Navy. Two Swabbies up from Top Gun. They'll go crazy when they see a Navy plane buzz a Navy ship. The admiral will want a piece of every Navy guy's ass from here to Annapolis!"

"Yeah," Ryder said cautiously. "Until he finds out it was us."

"And what are they going to do?" Woody asked. "Call off Distant Thunder?"

Screw it, Ryder thought, it was just too much to resist. He checked for any traffic in his area. Finding none, he banked F-14 and brought it down to twelve hundred feet, switching on the plane's high-imaging, look-down radar. The white admin ship—actually a converted minesweeper—came out clear on the scope. It was dead ahead, puttering along innocently, two deep-sea fishing rods conspicuously dangling over the back-side.

"Gone Fishing," Ryder confirmed.

He pulled the F-14 up and around. From his altitude and the wind heading, he knew that they were in perfect position to sneak up on the ship.

"OK, Woody, this is your call," Ryder radioed back. How low?"

Woody thought for a moment. "Rattle the porthole windows," he replied. "But don't break 'em."

Ryder brought the airplane down to two hundred feet. So low, the Tomcats sound waves were being instantly muted by the wavetops.

"They'll never hear us," he said as he gunned the 'Cat.

The fighter's mighty twin engines let out a tremendous roar. They were up and over the admin ship in under two seconds. They could see some of the people on board instantly hit the deck. Ryder thought he also saw a bait bucket go over the side.

He did a quick roll then put the 'Cat into a wicked near to vertical climb. They disappeared quickly into a convenient cloud bank.

"Mission accomplished," Ryder said, after leveling off. "I'm sure the admiral is on the phone already . . ."

"Thanks, Ghost," Woody replied. "I feel much better now."

10

An hour later, Ryder and Woody were sitting in two squeaky chairs outside of Slade's office, eavesdropping on the verbal exchange going on behind the Navy commander's closed door.

No sooner had Ryder put the F-14 down when they received a message via the Miramar traffic controller: Slade wanted to see them—*immediately*. They had already concocted a story to cover the buzzing: The admin ship appeared as if it was "adrift, in trouble." They just went down for a closer look—"as a favor." It was simple, direct. And they knew no one would believe it for a second.

By the time they had reached Slade's office, the Air Station Commander for NAS Miramar had already arrived. The ASC was the Admiral's top henchman—the high-level stooge who would chew ass whenever the admiral wasn't available to do it himself.

Now, they could hear the ASC ripping Slade up, down, and sideways.

"Slade is getting it through both tubes," Ryder said, picking out key phrases. Over and over they heard the ASC shouting: "buzzing," "Admiral's ship," "Air Force guys," "your responsibility," "misuse of Navy property" and "I don't give a damn how good they are," and "I don't give a damn about the program."

It went on for five full and furious minutes, the ASC reiterating the same charges, over and over. They didn't hear Slade say a word.

Then, mercifully, it was over. The ASC stormed out of Slade's office and bolted right by Ryder and Woody without giving them so much as a huff. He was out of the Ops Building in a matter of seconds, leaving a trail of steam behind him.

Ryder and Woody each took a deep breath and walked into the Navy Commander's office.

"You wanted to talk to us, Slade?" Ryder asked as they both sat on the couch across from the Navy man's desk.

Slade looked up at them. The color was just starting to come back to his face.

"When are you guys going to learn?" he asked.

"Learn what?" Ryder asked.

"Learn that the admiral has enough pull to have you both cleaning windshields in Iceland," Slade said.

"What did we do now?" Woody asked innocently.

"Don't bullshit me, Woods," Slade said angrily. "Where do you guys get off buzzing the admiral's fucking admin ship?"

There was an uneasy silence. Ryder felt his eyes wandering. The walls of Slade's office were covered with photographs of Slade climbing into or out of every jet the Navy had employed over the past twenty years. It reminded Ryder that although Slade was their den mother, he was also a pilot. And judging from the many commendations that hung next to the photos, he was a pretty damn good pilot at that. For an instant, he was sorry that Slade had to take the brunt of the chewing out by the ASC.

He decided not to even attempt the cover story. "OK, we couldn't resist it," he said. "You know that the Navy never passes up a chance to buzz the Air Force, or the Army for that matter. We were just doing our bit to even things out . . ."

70

"Oh, I see . . ." Slade said sarcastically. "You were just evening things out?"

He slammed his fist on his desk. "For Christ's sake, don't you guys realize what is at stake here? Do you have any idea how important all this is?"

Slade instantly knew he had said the wrong thing . . .

"*No, we don't* . . ." Ryder found himself almost shouting. All of a sudden, things came into focus. Distant Thunder. The nonstop training. The bizarre incident in the desert. The rumors that he was either nuts or on drugs. What *did* it all mean?

"How the hell would we know how important *anything* around here is?" Ryder said angrily. "No one has told us! We've been breaking our asses, flying four times the number of scramble missions, plus keeping up with the classroom stuff. On top of that, I have to live with the thought that just about everyone around here thinks that I'm either on drugs, or crazy or seeing UFOs. You name it.

"So at this point, Iceland is starting to sound pretty good . . ."

Ryder's argument suddenly made sense to Slade. He knew the misplaced pilot was right. The Air Force officers had been through three months of grueling training—and had performed damned well. So well, they were about to steal the Top Gun trophy from the Navy. Yet, because of the strict clamp on the whole Distant Thunder program, neither pilot—nor anyone else he knew at Top Gun—had a clue as to what the Air Force guys were training for.

Slade looked up at them, his demeanor having just done a 180 snap right. "OK," he said, his voice back under control. "I've got to go to an instructor's briefing. You guys lay low for a while. And whatever you do, avoid the admiral."

With that, he calmly put on his aviator's cap and left.

"Well, you sure told him!" Woody said, surprised that so many of Ryder's points had hit home.

"Yeah, I guess I did," Ryder said.

Slade was sitting alone in one of the Top Gun classrooms.

When he had been told about the briefing, he had just assumed that he was one of many asked to attend. But now, it was just himself . . .

He was beginning to wonder if he had had the wrong time or place when the Group Commander walked in. Slade snapped to attention as the man quickly strolled to the front of the classroom. A civilian, dressed in a conservative three-piece suit, accompanied him.

"Relax, Commander Slade," the GC told him. Two Marine guards were stationed at the back of the room. The GC gave them a signal and both immediately left, locking the doors behind them. This done, the three men sat at a table off to the side of the classroom.

"Thank you for coming, Commander," the GC said politely, as if Slade actually had a choice. "Before we start I just want a word with you on Security.

"Certain points we are about to discuss involve the Distant Thunder Project. So anything you hear in this room today is to be considered Top Priority Classified. You should not repeat it to anyone. Any questions?"

Slade had none.

The GC continued. "As you know, we are participating with Air Force Red Flag in a joint exercise a week from tonight. Grade point totals accumulated during the Red Flag exercise will be added to the overall point totals for the entire Power Projection course. So, the Red Flag exercise will be a kind of final exam for our pilots. The trophy will be awarded shortly thereafter. And, if I'm not mistaken, it looks like the two Air Force pilots are going to win it. Is that correct?"

"Yes, sir, it is," Slade answered.

"OK," the GC continued, "what I asked you here for is to discuss where these two Air Force pilots are going after they complete the course here."

Slade was totally surprised. Why would they be telling him this?

The GC read his mind. "I have no idea why you specifically are being briefed on this, Commander," the senior officer said. "All I know is that the admiral was told by a Defense

Department official to brief you on a new shoot-kill/score system which will have a special importance for Distant Thunder."

He turned to the civilian.

"This is Crandall Cunningham," he said by way of introduction. Slade and Cunningham shook hands. "Mr. Cunningham represents a major entertainment company whose name, we really can't reveal. Let's just say that Mr. Cunningham's company makes the most famous amusement parks in the world."

Amusement parks? Slade thought. What did this have to do with Distant Thunder?

The GC went on. "Mr. Cunningham has been cleared for certain aspects of Distant Thunder and he is going to explain this new simulated combat system to both of us.

"So without further squawk from me, I'll turn this little meeting over to Mr. Cunningham."

"Thank you, sir," Cunningham started off, reading from a pack of prepared index cards. "Your GC was right: my company and the US military have always had a very friendly, professional, if quiet relationship. We consider it our civic responsibility to assist our government, although for reasons I'm sure you can understand, we do ask that you refrain from mentioning our company's direct participation in this project."

Beside the table was a TV and a VCR hook-up. Cunningham leaned over and pushed the start button on the VCR and suddenly the TV screen came to life. After a burst of static and five seconds of a color bar, the videotape began.

The first image was that of three F-15 Eagle fighters flying in formation.

Cunningham began his narration: "This video was shot three weeks ago by our camera crew at Red Flag Nellis. They were flying in a Lear chase plane, following this three-ship flight of Eagles, out over the Nellis testing range.

"These F-15s are fitted with new simulated weapons system pods. You can see them under both wings and on each wing tip. These Eagles are being vectored toward a three-ship from the

Nellis Adversary Tactics Group flying F-5s. The F-5s are also fitted with our new system.

"Now, instead of explaining what our new system does," Cunningham said. "I'm just going to quiet up and let you see for yourselves."

The tape continued, showing the three F-15s peeling off and diving. They were over rugged, desert terrain which was in much abundance near Nellis. Using a zoom lens, the video camera spotted the three F-5s flying low over the desert valley. The camera followed the F-15s as they dove toward the Soviet-marked F-5s.

Suddenly, there was a flash of flame under the wing of the lead F-15 . . .

Jeesuz, Slade thought, *he's shooting a real missile at them* . . .

The instructor watched in a kind of confused horror as a missile the size of a AIM-9 Sidewinder streaked away from the F-15 complete with the authentic whooshing noise the firing pilot hears. Moments later the missile impacted on the side of the trailing F-5, a ball of red-and-orange flame erupting just behind the right wing. The sound of a large explosion filled the room.

Slade felt his psyche had just been thrown a curve ball. It appeared he had just witnessed the one hundred percent destruction of an American plane and pilot.

But as they followed the action, they saw that the ball of flame disappeared as quickly as it had come. A brief puff of smoke also quickly vanished. And the F-5 was still there.

"What the hell is this?" Slade said involuntarily. "He nailed that guy . . ."

The videotape rolled on. The '15s were lining up on the two other F-5s. One Eagle pilot was so close, he opened up with his cannon. Just as with the apparent missile launch, Slade saw a stream of yellow and red spew out by the F-15, again accompanied by the authentic whirring noise of an F-15 cannon being fired.

A brief chase followed until the F-5 pilot jinked when he should have juked, moving right into the path of the cannonfire. Impact points could be seen on the F-5, flashes of light perforating its entire tail section.

But again, seemingly miraculously, the flashes ceased, replaced by brief puffs of smoke. And the F-5 flew on.

The camera then concentrated on one of the third Aggressor airplanes. Its pilot had managed to get on the tail of an Eagle. Just as before, Slade saw and heard a missile fire out from underneath the airplane, streaking to its target and impacting with smoke, fire, and sound. And, just as before, the smoke cleared and the F-15 flew on, apparently unharmed.

The six airplanes then formed up, split off, and departed the area, thus ending the videotape.

The tape ended. Cunningham was wearing a Cheshire cat grin.

"Well, I hope I can tell my boss that you two gentlemen were impressed," he said, barely able to talk through his glee.

Impressed, they were.

"What you have just seen is called the Advanced Tactical Airborne Combat Computer-Projection System," Cunningham explained. "It was developed by our studio special effects unit working closely with Navy and Air Force personnel, under a secret program code-named "ZOOT." This tape is a brief demonstration of what this new Zoot system can do. I'm sure you'll agree it's quite an advance over the present TACTS simulated weapons system."

TACTS was another buzzword around Top Gun. It was the catch-all phrase for the conglomeration of computer-commanded sensors, data pods, and graphic displays that made ACM at Top Gun the big video game it was.

Cunningham continued. "This new Zoot system was five years in the making, gentlemen. Everything you just saw on that videotape, pilots will experience in their cockpits. The sights, the sounds—*everything* will be right there. I might add that the Zoot is just as effective in simulated ground attack modes. Either way, it is the closest, the most realistic simulation of aerial combat ever devised."

The GC and Slade nodded with approval. Both Navy men knew that their fighter jocks would immediately get off on the sights and sounds of aerial combat. The old "Con Kill" buzzers

75

which had previously indicated targets hit had just become obsolete.

Cunningham then launched into a lengthy explanation of what made the Zoot tick. It was all done by mirrors— *holographic* mirrors. Using laser-generated 3-D holographic projections from previously stored computer commands, Zoot could mimic missiles firing and the cannonfire. Specially synthesized sound effects accounted for the audible explosions. And of course, the computers kept a running talley of who hit who with what and what "damage" was sustained. "Acceptable damage" would allow the stricken plane to continue in the dogfight, although some of its avionics would click off. "Maximum damage" meant the aircraft was dead, and all but the vital avionics would shut down, forcing the pilot to return to base. Best of all, both the attacking pilot *and* the prey saw and heard what they would normally experience during actual combat.

Cunningham wrapped up his briefing by saying, "It will be a pleasure to work with you gentlemen over the next few months."

But Slade wasn't listening. He knew the Zoot was brilliant. Yet somehow, he couldn't help thinking he'd heard of the device before.

Then it hit him . . .

Ryder! He has seen this in action, he thought. Out in the desert during his survival exercises. The pilot had said that he witnessed a dogfight in which the opponents were apparently shooting at each other. Yet, no one was shot down.

Christ, Slade thought. Maybe Ryder didn't go sun crazy after all . . .

11

The E-2C Hawkeye was barely off the ground when the discussion began.

"How in hell could this have happened?" the assistant secretary of defense asked.

The four officers sitting around the fold-down table were silent. They were the same men who had participated in the previous airborne conference.

"What was that pilot doing out there?" the Defense man continued, his temper barely under control. "Right on the edge of the Deep Zone?"

"He was picked up right on the edge of the Deep Zone," the admiral said defensively.

The pilot they were discussing, Captain Ryder Long, was the same one who had buzzed his admin ship. During the previous airborne conference, they had just heard that the Air Force pilot had had "a bad trip" on his survival exercise. Now word of the specifics of what Ryder saw out in the desert had reached the desk of the assistant secretary.

"Our survival exercise areas are selected by computer, based on terrain, isolation factors, and probable climate conditions," the admiral continued. "The information was punched into the computer and those were the coordinates that came out."

"Are you blaming it on a computer snafu, Admiral?" the assistant secretary asked.

"No," the admiral replied, rubbing his bald head. "What I'm saying is that Captain Long was dropped off at a location that had been cleared by our Miramar computer. But as you know, those computers have no access to the Distant Thunder program. Therefore, our computers now had the idea that a Zoot air exercise would be taking place over China Lake that night."

The Air Force colonel spoke up. "I think the question here is: has the project been compromised in any way?"

The admiral shook his head. "No, I don't believe so. Long is due for orientation in Zoot within the week anyway."

"But, more critical, how about his interaction with the Airborne trooper?" the Defense man asked. "If they talked about anything in depth, this pilot, Captain Long, could know more than he should."

"I can assure you my guy didn't say a word," the Army general said. "He's been in Deep Training for months and his unit has been previously involved in everything from Seaspray to Task Force 160. He knows how to keep his mouth shut."

"But does the Air Force guy know how to do the same?" the Marine general tossed in.

"Captain Long is a highly qualified pilot," the Air Force general said quickly. "So much so, he and his partner are going to take the Top Gun trophy . . ."

Score two points for the Air Force.

"Flying skills have very little to do with *security*, General," the admiral shot back. "In fact, to be frank, your Captain Long has been a pain in the rump for us ever since he came to Miramar. He's been involved in several altercations with the other Top Gun pilots and has displayed an overall rebellious attitude during his training. If he were a Navy pilot, he would have been history long ago . . ."

The Air Force general started to speak, but once again, the man from Defense had to act the part of referee.

"Gentlemen," he said forcefully. "We all know that everyone involved in Distant Thunder was selected according to a certain . . . well, *profile*. We also were aware going in that disciplinary problems were a possibility with some of these individuals.

"But the bottom line here is it makes no difference what these pilots do. They are under a lot of stress now, and they haven't seen a third of what's in store for them. Plus, they have no idea what they've got into."

"Then why don't we just *tell* them," the Air Force general cut in. He had been in favor from the beginning to tell the pilots all aspects of Distant Thunder. "After all, it's their lives that are involved. They have a right, if not the need to know . . ."

"No . . ." the assistant secretary said emphatically. "The President and the secretary have been over this several times. And, they still agree that the number one priority is Security. It cannot be compromised. I don't have to remind you what would happen if word of this leaked out. We can't run the risk of one of these pilots spilling information to anyone. Family, girlfriends, *anyone*. The program depends on it."

There was a brief silence, the only noise being the constant hum of the Hawkeye's engines.

"What does this Captain Long *think* happened to him, Admiral?" the assistant secretary asked.

Once again, the Navy officer rubbed his bald dome. "Well, I'm sure he believes what he saw. And it will especially click into place when he gets his Zoot training. But we've tried to downplay the whole thing. Our intell boys spread the word that he was under some kind of drug . . ."

"Well, that will really help his career," the Air Force general said, his voice angry with sarcasm.

"That will be enough . . ." the assistant secretary said, signaling the meeting was coming to a close. He turned to the Marine general and said, "Please have your men keep a close eye on Captain Long. Report any unusual activity directly to me."

"Yes, sir," the Marine Corps general nodded.

12

The "Scramble" portion of their training now over, Ryder and Woody drew a dawn flight the next day. They took off in F-14 VF-333—their usual airplane—just twenty minutes after sunup.

Monitoring the special Top Gun frequency, Ryder followed

his vector toward a point over Brown Mountain, a mile-high mesa in the middle of the China Lake Range. They were on a so-called combat air patrol exercise, or CAP, which meant they were to stop any "intruders" from entering the immediate airspace.

"Bandits, Ghost," he heard Woody report just moments after they arrived on station. "Two . . . nope, three of them. My gear says they are A-4s. Nine miles straight ahead. At 14,000."

"Roger," Ryder answered, immediately climbing and increasing power. He heard the F-14's variable-sweep wings automatically move back to a 50-degree angle. He checked his airspeed. It was just moving past 550 knots. He was a notch under 19,000 feet.

"OK," Ryder said, peering out through his HUD, "I got a visual on these guys. How's the weapons check?"

"I got all green," Woody reported.

"Hang on then, partner," Ryder then warned him. "Let's keep that batting average at one thousand . . ."

"Roger, Ghost," Woody called back. "My sunglasses are down . . ."

Ryder flipped his shades down too just as he put the 'Cat into a screaming, twisting dive. "Fight's on . . ." he said.

The lead A-4 was by them in a flash, flying dead level, obviously working on a missile sighting for the F-14. But Ryder's controlled, spiraling plummet made for a very bad target.

The second A-4 passed right over them, its pilot also reacting too late to counter Ryder's dropping maneuver.

"Ride it out Ghost, my man!" Woody yelled into his microphone loud enough to cause Ryder's ears to buzz.

Stay cool. Stay tight.

"OK, that was Moe and Larry," Ryder yelled back to Woody. "You got the third stooge?"

"Roger, Ghost," the call came back immediately. "He's diving right at us. Check eleven o'clock!"

Ryder glanced up and saw the A-4 coming at them almost out of the sun. He instantly put the F-14 into a snap 180 left, twisting right over the top and recovering at fifty-five hundred feet. The A-4 twisted in also. But the snappy little bugger of a jet couldn't match the maneuverability of the modern Tomcat.

Ryder yanked back on the controls. The F-14's wings instantly went back to full wing sweep. Suddenly the big fighter was delta-shaped, all the better to dogfight with.

Ryder felt the *g*s increase on his chest as he put the F-14 over the top and started yet another screaming dive. He hadn't flown like this in nearly two weeks and his tolerance for high *g*s was low. Still, he closed his eyes briefly and let the feeling pass through him. He'd been here before. Nothing had changed . . .

When he opened his eyes, the tailpipe of the third A-4 was right in his sights at zero-angle.

"I don't know how you do that," Woody called ahead to him. "But you sure as hell do it good . . ."

The A-4 pilot was caught totally by surprise at Ryder's unorthodox maneuver. Now he tried his best to get away.

"Missile one, away!" Ryder called out, launching an imaginary Sidewinder at the Skyhawk.

Instantly the cockpit was filled with the gratifying sounds of the "kill buzzer."

"Iced!" Ryder called out. "Sorry, Curley . . ."

He pulled the F-14 up on to its ass and climbed, pushing the throttle to full military. He did a quick slide flip and they could see one of the A-4s above and banking toward them, going into a dive to build up some knots for his attack.

"Tighten your belt, Wood Man," Ryder called to his partner.

"Smoke 'em, Ghost!" Woody called back.

The attacking A-4 pilot saw the Tomcat turn over on its back and level off—*completely upside down.*

What the hell is he doing? the Skyhawk jockey thought.

He found out soon enough . . .

Suddenly the F-14 was heading straight for him, still upside down. The Tomcat's maneuver startled him so, he forgot about taking a shot at the '14. He was quickly concentrating on getting out of the way of the oncoming fighter. He ducked—putting the Skyhawk into a last-second dive. He turned and was startled to see the F-14 pilot had followed him down, coming over the top and placing himself right on the A-4s tail.

"Jesus Christ," the A-4 pilot muttered, trying to shake the gyrating Tomcat. "Who is this guy? Flash Gordon?"

The next sound he heard was the "low warning tone," followed quickly by the "you've been killed" tone. The F-14's simulated missile had nailed him in less than three seconds. The A-4 pilot wagged his wings in recognition and pulled up on his stick, shaking his head. "How the hell did he do that?" he wondered as the F-14 streaked by him.

"Where's the third bandit, Woody?" Ryder called back, putting the F-14 into a long, wide-out bat-turn.

Woody peered into his APG-65 digital-mode radar. "He's hiding, Ghost . . ."

"Not for long . . ." Ryder said, continuing the miles-wide turn.

He slowed the F-14 down to a 330-knot crawl and threw the Fuel-Mixture switch to high. This caused the 'Cat to start spewing two long gray trails of smoke.

"Ah, Ghost, my man," Woody said in admiration. "The old smoke-'em-out play."

Ryder gave Woody a thumbs-up signal over his shoulder and put the Tomcat into a slow climb. A large cumulous cloud loomed straight ahead, poking along at about fourteen thousand feet. Ryder steered the F-14 right for it.

"This guy is good," Woody radioed ahead, peering at his empty radar screen.

"Probably a lifer," Ryder said, checking over his head through the clear canopy. There was no sign of the third Aggressor. He twisted around in his seat to see the now miles-long trail of gray smoke.

They were about three miles from the cloud when Woody spotted him. "Here he comes!" the Wizzo yelled. "Hard by three o'clock! At 11,500 feet. Piling on the knots!"

"I see him," Ryder said, quickly getting a visual on the streaking Skyhawk. He knew the Aggressor pilot had had no problem spotting him with the long trail of smoke behind the 'Cat.

Suddenly, the low-warning buzzer started to hum in the F-14's cockpit. "He's got our range, Ghost . . ." Woody reported cautiously. "He's setting us up to fire . . ."

"Roger, partner," Ryder answered.

Just then the F-14 entered the cloud bank. Suddenly they were totally enveloped in white mist. Ryder immediately moved the Fuel Mixture lever back to its normal position. The 'Cat instantly stopped spewing smoke.

"He's coming in . . ." Woody reported as he watched the A-4 bank right and follow them into the cloud.

"I hope he's wearing his rubbers . . ." Ryder said.

Just ten seconds later the A-4 Aggressor emerged from the cloud bank, intent on firing at the smoking F-14 before its pilot put out an "equipment down" call, thus terminating the fight.

But the Tomcat was nowhere to be seen . . .

Suddenly, the A-4's low-warning buzzer came on. The pilot twisted around in his cockpit to see the F-14 was right on his tail. Somehow the Tomcat pilot had maneuvered the fighter to come out of the cloud bank *behind* him.

An instant later, the kill-tone echoed through the A-4's cockpit . . .

The engagement over, the F-14 moved up beside him. He saw the pilot and radar officer flash him two thumbs-up signs. He gave them a "what-the-hell" wave; he knew the F-14 jockeys were damn good pilots to pull off a stunt like that one. They flew side by side for several moments, then the 'Cat roared off, two flashes of light bursting out of its tailpipes indicating its afterburners had just been booted on.

Who the hell are those guys? the Skyhawk pilot wondered as he turned for home.

Ryder barreled the 'Cat right across the Miramar main runway, snapping a 180 turn left at 4*g*s for good measure.

"Break some glass . . ." Woody called ahead.

Ryder intended to. They had just iced three Aggressors and

he sure as hell was going to let everyone on the ground know about it. Leveling off right over the flight line, he quickly snapped a lightning quick victory roll. The quick cockscrew maneuver made him feel lightheaded, but he welcomed it—for lack of a better term, it was a "natural high."

He circled the field and came over the flight line again, cracking off a second perfect victory roll. He could see people on the ground looking up at them as he streaked past. His body started to tremble with a pleasantly nervous rush. He hadn't felt this good in what seemed like a long, long time. The bizarre experience in the desert had drained him physically, but also emotionally. While he never once questioned what he actually *saw* out there, he knew the mind was threatened ever since with demons. Self-doubt. Paranoia. Self-consciousness. It was a constant battle to keep them at bay. The weapon he employed was the sheer joy of flying a $40 million kick-ass jet fighter.

He came around a third time and snapped off his final victory roll. Woody was applauding and yelling into his microphone as usual and Ryder felt a new strength run through him. There were those on the ground that thought he was crazy—the Air Force outsider who got hooked up with some weird characters in the desert then tried to bullshit the brass about it. Let them think what they want. But he was not about to let them forget who was the best pilot presently in residence at Fightertown.

"Take that, you fucking swabbies!" Woody yelled out as Ryder pulled out of the third pass and buzzed the tower for good measure.

Their balls-out demonstration over, Ryder drifted in for a perfect landing. He was at last beginning to feel like himself again. Even the ground crew—Navy personnel all—were impressed.

"Heard you got three today, Captain," the crew chief said after Ryder rolled the big 'Cat up to its hardstand. "How'd the bird work?"

"As advertised," Ryder told him as he and Woody climbed out of the F-14. "Lot of Air Force guys would give a month's pay to fly one of these . . ."

84

"Well, this one is going in the shop right now," the chief told him. "Complete tear down . . ."

The statement surprised Ryder. He and Woody had been riding the same 'Cat—VF-333—for the past two months and they had come to like it a lot. Now the "tear down" order meant they were going to completely disassemble the airplane then put it back together again. Hardly routine stuff.

"Is this some kind of manufacturer's special maintenance check?" Ryder asked him.

The crew chief shrugged. "Beats me," he said as he blocked off the F-14's wheels. "They got a special crew coming in to do the work. You guys will have a new bird next time you go up . . ."

Ryder filed the information away under "very unusual," a particular memory bank that was getting crowded . . .

13

It was nine o'clock that evening by the time Ryder arrived at the OC. The neon, chrome, and glass bar was already filled with horny white-uniformed Top Gun jocks and the usual gang of accommodating town girls. Ryder felt only slightly out of place in his Air Force blues—he had gotten used to sticking out a while ago.

He scanned the place and spotted Woody at the far end of the long bar, waving wildly to him. He was not alone. His librarian friend from San Diego was snuggled up next to him; one of her girlfriends was hanging nearby.

"Girls, this is my main man, Ghost," Woody said by way of introduction. The Wiz then introduced both women, but Ryder didn't hear their names too clearly. He was too busy trying to keep his eyes in his head and his tongue in his mouth.

Both of the women were *beautiful*—blonde, tanned, and wearing slinky things. California beach bunnies of the first degree. He could feel his hormones kick into afterburner.

Woody saw his reaction and couldn't keep the smile off his face. "Here's the game plan, girls," Woody said to them. "We'll have a few cocktails here, maybe dance a little, then we sneak back to our quarters for a *very* private party."

The list of activities was met with a chorus of approving "Ooooos" from the girls. Woody gave a stage wink to Ryder, then ordered a round of drinks.

The librarian's name was Karen and she had an envelope for Ryder.

"I did some further research on Military Unit Names and Badges," she told him. "I found something that might help you."

Ryder took a healthy swig of his bourbon and ginger and opened the envelope.

Inside were several Xeroxed pages with a cover sheet entitled Civilian Irregular Defense Groups, or CIDGs. Reading by the glaring neon bar light, Ryder saw the document detailed the CIA's training of Laotian and Vietnamese tribesmen in the early 1960s before the war in Southeast Asia heated up. Special units of Green Berets had been sent to the area to organize the tribes into guerilla militias with the hope of beating the Viet Cong at their own game. These same Green Berets also secretly worked closely with the Royal Laotian Army and were in fact fighting alongside them as early as 1961.

Ryder wondered where all this was leading to until he turned to the second page. It contained three grainy color photographs of members of these Special Forces' units in various acts of training the CIDG soldiers.

It took a few moments for it to sink in—then he realized that all of the Green Berets pictured were wearing blue scarves . . .

"*Jeesuz*," he whispered softly. Suddenly, he wasn't aware of the chattering hubbub of the bar.

He read on. One of the photo captions said the blue scarf was worn by certain CIDG unit advisers to distinguish them from other groups. It went on to identify the Americans wearing the blue scarfs as belonging to the 15th Special Forces Group out of Fort Bragg.

Woody was next to him, reading over his shoulder.

"Fort Bragg?" the Wiz said. "Isn't that an Army Jump School?"

"It sure is," Ryder confirmed. He knew the famous 82nd Army Division trained at Fort Bragg. And the 82nd was an *Airborne* division.

He looked up at Karen. "Was there anything else on this 15th Special Forces Group?"

She nodded, though somewhat uncertainly. "Yes, there was," she said, retrieving yet another document from her purse. "But, I don't know if this is good or bad news."

She gave Ryder a single sheet of paper, a photocopy like the others. It was a page from an index of Military Units, a kind of "where are they now" listing. Karen had circled the brief paragraph on the 15th Special Forces Group.

Ryder read it over twice and slowly pounded the bar twice. *"Damn!"* he said under his breath, handing the page to Woody.

Woody read it out loud: "In February of 1962, the 15th Special Forces Group jumped into combat at Nam Tah, Laos, with members of the Royal Laotian 55th Parachute Battalion. A three-day battle with a division of Communist Pathet Lao troops ensued during which the Laotian 55th Battalion suffered extremely heavy casualties. A classified number of 15th Special Forces Group personnel were killed in the engagement, reducing its effectiveness as an operating unit. In March of 1962, the 15th Special Forces Group was disbanded, its colors retired, and its surviving members absorbed into other units."

"Wow . . ." Woody said softly. "These guys were history more than twenty-five years ago."

Ryder nodded. "And knowing the Army, it's unlikely they would reactivate a secret unit like that. Especially one that was wiped out years before anyone thought Americans were getting killed in Indochina."

Ryder drained his bourbon and ordered another round of drinks.

Karen noticed both pilots' moods had suddenly turned glum. "I hope you guys tell me someday why you're so interested in soldiers wearing blue scarves," she said.

Woody gave her a reassuring squeeze, saying, "It's Top Secret, babe."

Just then, Ryder felt a hand on his shoulder.

"Hey, shit-mover . . ." he heard a voice behind him say.

Ryder turned to see it was the Top Gun jerk called Panther. The man was drunk as usual. Behind him were five other Navy pilots, each one affecting the standard white-uniform-trussed, crewcut-sunglasses-at-night look.

"A lot of people thought that was a stupid-ass stunt you pulled over the field today," Panther continued.

Ryder turned back to his drink. He was in no mood for this.

"Hey, I'm talking to you, Hot Dog," the Navy jock persisted.

Ryder eyed Woody, who was already moving Karen and her friend on the other side of him where they'd be safe. His eyes said: *Stay cool. Stay tight.* Woody nodded.

"What's the matter, 'weak dick'?" Panther singsonged. "Can't face a real pilot?"

Ryder slowly spun around on his stool. He looked at the man. He was younger than Ryder, about the same size and weight. "Where's your monkey and white cane?" he asked him.

Woody laughed out loud, but Panther didn't get the joke right away. When he did, he instantly whipped off his mirrored-lens sunglasses.

"Do we have to kick your ass again?" Woody asked, moving toward the man. As soon as this happened, Panther's gang moved in closer, too. People in the immediate vicinity started to sense that trouble was brewing. Ryder noticed out of the corner of his eye that two Marine guards were lurking nearby.

Ryder turned to order another bourbon when he saw Panther's left arm moving up. It had a drink in it and Ryder quickly surmised that Panther—having been soaked in the earlier fight—was planning tit-for-tat retaliation.

Ryder decided to go preemptive. He caught the man's left wrist just as it was about to hurl the drink in his face and deflected it. The contents of the full glass of liquor and ice flew through the air, unfortunately drenching both Karen and her girlfriend.

"You fucking asshole!" Panther cried out, Ryder's grip on his wrist feeling like a tightening vise.

"Nice talk in front of the ladies . . ." Ryder said, letting go of the man's wrist and grabbing his shirt collar in the same movement. With lightning-quick speed, he yanked the man down, causing him to crack his forehead on the edge of the bar. Panther immediately crashed to the floor. Ryder never left his stool.

Woody was up and over in a second, intercepting the first punch thrown by one of Panther's clone buddies. An upper cut stopped the man in his tracks, knocking him backward. A third Navy jock threw a punch which grazed Woody's shoulder. The Wiz came back with a left backhand, slapping the man so hard, the noise reverberated throughout the bar.

Ryder was up and ready to take on the next guy—a tall, muscular black man who looked to be the toughest of the bunch. One of Ryder's saloon tactics axioms popped into his head: *When in doubt, hit the big guy in the face.* He did just that, shattering the man's sunglasses at the loss of a chunk of his own knuckle skin. The man returned with a massive black fist that Ryder just barely deflected away from his left ear. Ryder retaliated with an over-around left which caught the man square on the jaw. It was like hitting a chunk of cement, but it sufficiently staggered the man long enough for Ryder to grab him around the neck and fling him into a table full of innocent bystanders.

Ryder turned to see that Woody was in the process of hurling one of the chrome bar stools at the legs of the remaining two Navy guys. One of them jumped, the other didn't. The heavy stool caught the slow one right on his kneecaps; the snapping noise sent a shudder down Ryder's spine. Woody then leaped forward and quickly two-punched the last Navy guy standing.

"Not bad," Ryder yelled to his partner. They had dispatched the Navy jocks like so many bowling pins.

That's when Ryder felt someone grabbing his shoulder. He spun around, a balled fist ready. It was one of the Marine guards.

Ryder hesitated, his fist drawn back and cocked. Punching out the Navy pilots was one thing; swinging at a Marine was another.

The Marine also stopped short, *his* fist reared back, waiting to spring. He was an enlisted man. Taking a swipe at Ryder would be tantamount to striking an officer.

They squared off for a few seconds that seemed to go by in slow motion. The immediate area of the bar where the fight was going on had been cleared of all noncombatants. A crowd of onlookers—just about everyone in the bar—was gathered a safe distance away. There were upturned tables, broken chairs, and spilled drinks everywhere. A half dozen bottles on the other side of the bar had somehow managed to get broken. Despite the skirmish, the bar's pounding dance music recording kept right on blaring.

All the while, Ryder and the Marine stared at each other, wondering what to do.

Panther made up their minds for them . . .

The man had recovered from his unfortunate meeting with the bar rail and, head down, threw a rolling block into both Ryder and the Marine. All three of them went down in a heap, taking out yet another table as they fell. They were immediately gang-tackled by two of Panther's recovering buddies, their combined weight adding to the crush.

The scene reminded Ryder of his days back in college football during a fumble recovery. Before the refs could break it up, everyone in the pile would wildly start punching anyone in a different uniform. The Navy pilots had apparently played football, too, for they were mercilessly pounding away on both Ryder and the Marine guard.

Then Providence came to Ryder in the form of a discarded Budweiser bottle laying nearby. He reached over and grabbed it and then started flailing away—over his head, behind his back, at his feet—figuring that any blow that landed would strike an enemy.

His actions caused the three Navy pilots to stop tackle punching and by that time, Woody and the other Marine guard were pulling bodies off of him. More Marines had appeared by this time and as soon as Ryder got to his feet, order had been restored.

The first person he saw after getting to his feet was the captain of the Marine guard.

"Feeling our oats tonight, Captain?" the Marine asked him.

"You should ask those movie stars the same question, *Captain*," Ryder told him, massaging his battered fists.

The Marine officer quickly questioned one of the Marine guards who was involved in the fight. The jarhead did his duty and told the officer that the Navy pilots instigated the brawl.

"All right, Captain," the Marine officer said, turning back to Ryder. "Do you wish to file a report on this? Name names?"

Ryder looked at the six-pack of ruffled Navy fliers. "No," he said. "Save the Navy the trouble . . ."

The Marine captain looked around the bar. The 150 or so people in the place were still standing around, wondering what would be next. The OC was not a stranger to occasional tussles. But this fight had been a doozy.

"OK, fun's over . . ." the Marine officer called out, adding completely out of the blue, "One round of drinks on the house!"

That's all the crowd needed. Things were back to normal in a nano-second.

The Marine looked at Ryder, Woody, and the two girls and said, "You guys might want to bring your dates somewhere else . . ."

Woody looked at Karen. She and her friend Wendy were soaked through with Panther's thrown drink.

"Let's go girls," Woody said with a wink. "We've got to get you out of those wet clothes . . ."

*   *   *

91

A half hour later, the four of them were back at their pilots' quarters, which Woody had officially renamed the "The Sin Bin."

Before leaving the OC, Ryder had successfully negotiated with the bartender to "borrow" a fifth of Scotch and a bottle of white wine. It was completely against regulations to take liquor from the base bar—but then again, so was having civilian personnel in a military housing unit. It made no difference to either pilot. They were strangers in this strange land. They realized long before that very few of the rules applied to them. And the ones that did, they routinely broke.

While Ryder spent several minutes trying to track down four clean glasses, Woody had retrieved several towels for Karen and Wendy to use, secretly dampening them first. The last thing he wanted was for the women's dresses to dry.

Finally they all sat down in the center living area of the housing. Ryder courteously poured out drinks for everyone— Scotch for Woody and himself, white wine for Karen and Wendy.

Between sips of their drinks, the girls attempted to dry off their dresses.

"This is hopeless," Karen finally said. "I have to get out of this . . ."

Woody looked at Ryder and gave him a covert thumbs-up sign.

"Well, let's go to my room and see if there is anything that I have that will fit you . . ." Woody said in mock seriousness.

With that, Karen and Woody disappeared into his room, leaving Ryder and Wendy to their own devices.

She looked at him with feigned innocence. "I'm wet, too," she cooed.

Ryder smiled. "I know I don't have anything that will fit you," he said, barely containing himself. "But that doesn't mean we can't take a look . . ."

He walked her to his room and closed the door. Then he grabbed her and kissed her, hard on the lips. He felt her moist body press against his. She felt wonderful and smelled sweet.

She stood back and slowly undid the straps on her dress. It

slid off her to reveal a see-through white-lace bra and panties. Ryder felt a breath catch in his throat. She was absolutely gorgeous and deliciously uninhibited.

She sat on the edge of his bed and said, "Now all you've got to do is keep me warm . . ."

Ryder couldn't help but stare at her breasts. They were perfectly shaped. "Grab-able" was the first word that came to his mind.

"Do your duty, Ghost," a tiny voice inside him said.

Yes, he thought as he reached for her, he was *definitely* feeling better . . .

14

It was 0930 the next day when Ryder somewhat groggily lifted off from Miramar and headed off for the China Lake range.

Both he and Woody were grateful that their flight would not involve heavy Air Combat Maneuvering, better known as ACM. Despite the bravado lifestyle affected by most fighter jocks, high-speed, high-altitude flight after a night of drinking was usually an uncomfortable experience. It had to do with the amount of carbon dioxide in the flier's body and how the CO_2 reacted at various heights. Heavy duty ACM after a night of ten to twelve beers had made many a fighter jock vow to jump on the wagon—usually only temporarily.

But today all Ryder and Woody had to do is practice inflight refueling procedures, a relative breeze compared to the high-g jinking of the simulated Power Projection dogfights. They hoped to get the mandatory three "in-flights slurps" under their belts and be back at the base by noon.

The night before had proved to be very pleasant for both.

The fistfight turned out to be anticlimactic compared to the night Ryder had spent with Wendy. She had no hangups, long a problem with the women he chased back at the C-130s base in Wisconsin. She was lovely, bright, friendly, and *very* versatile. He could still feel the love-soaked haze surrounding him as he steered toward the north and China Lake.

But, despite Wendy's lovely presence, Ryder had had a strange dream. Almost identical to the one he had in the desert shortly before meeting the mysterious Trooper Simons, he dreamt he was walking in the desert with a blond woman, one even prettier than Wendy. They were just talking, but again, it seemed like Ryder had known this woman all his life.

The dream had been so vivid that when he woke up that morning, he embarrassed himself by calling Wendy "Maureen."

"'Maureen'?" she said, just a little indignant. "Who is Maureen?"

Ryder shook his head and answered truthfully, "I don't know . . ."

They were flying a different F-14, this one borrowed from the reserve squadron always on hand at Top Gun. Although there were minor variations in the cockpit of this particular airplane—it was slightly older than their regular hot rod—the fighter flew perfectly.

Yet, it didn't have the "feel" Ryder had nurtured with VF-333. Although all jet fighters are sophisticated multi-million machines, each one was nevertheless an individual. Each one had its own "touch." Its own response and its own peccadillos. Ryder's 333 'Cat had a great feel—sometimes it seemed to move the right way even before he jinked the control stick. They worked well together and it bothered him that the airplane was being torn down. With their Top Gun training being completed in less than a week—and the uncertainty of what lay beyond—Ryder had sadly resigned himself to the fact that he'd probably never fly old 333 again.

But for the routine air-refueling exercise, this airplane

would do . . .

Stopping for gas in mid-air was one of the marvels of modern jet flight. The F-14 held 16,000 pounds of fuel on take-off, allowing for a typical weapons load. How long that amount of fuel could keep the fighter flying depended on whether it was simply traveling from one point to another conserving gas, or involved in a fuel-guzzling knifefight at twenty thousand feet. In either case, fuel was the lifeblood of the airplane and pilots were like misers when it came to gas. Every gauge in the multi-instrument cockpit could go on the blink and not upset the jet jock as much as losing his fuel load indicator.

That's where in-flight refueling came in. Airborne tankers—converted Boeing airliners for the Air Force, smaller KA-3 Whales, and A-6 Intruder aircraft for the Navy—roamed the skies during various exercises, waiting to service thirsty aircraft. Just as long as a pilot could link up with an airborne tanker, the time he stayed in the air was open-ended.

Ryder restudied the prearranged vector points and called back to Woody to keep an eye out for the tanker. He raised the 'Cat to fifteen thousand feet, the assigned height for mid-air refuelings at Top Gun and put a call out to the Whale tanker crew. He got them on the second try.

Working with the navigator of the KA-3 Whale, Ryder directed the F-14 to the intercept, a point right above the Argus Range in the China Lake range. The area was not too far from where he'd spent his hellish survival exercise.

His mind flashed back to the information that Karen had provided him the night before. On one hand he now knew that at one time, theirs was an Airborne unit that wore blue scarves as their unit emblem. On the other hand, he now knew the unit—which originally held probably no more than fifty men—had been wiped out in Laos many years before. What was the connection? Or was there any? He fought a sudden temptation to get down on the deck just for a few minutes and look around for any evidence of wayward Airborne troopers. He knew it would probably be useless—the desert in this part of California was so vast, an entire army could be hidden away very easily. As could a few squadrons of black-painted F-5s for that matter.

Another, stronger call from the Navy tanker jolted him back to reality.

"Flight one-seven, do you copy?" he heard the voice in his headphones say.

"One-seven here, I copy," Ryder responded. "I read our merge in about a minute . . ."

"I got them on the screen, Ghost," Woody reported. "You should get a visual in a few seconds."

Ryder pushed the F-14's throttle ahead and felt the airplane buck slightly as their airspeed increased. He shook his head— the 333 would never have acted like that!

He looked up through the canopy and finally spotted the Naval Reserve Whale, flying about four miles ahead of them and a half mile above.

"I see you, Delta Five," Ryder radioed the tanker pilot, using the Whale's call name.

"Boom section deployed now," the Whale pilot radioed back.

Ryder moved the 'Cat up and behind the aerial tanker, watching the long fuel hose start to ooze out of the KA-3's right wing. On the end there was a device that looked like a perforated lampshade. On the right hand side on the 'Cat's cockpit was a nozzle which led into the fighter's gas tanks. It was the old male-female hook-up—an "Adam and Eve" to Navy fliers. With correct mid-air maneuvering, the male organ-shaped nozzle would fit into the boom's "love hole" receptacle. Once the connection was complete, the fuel would drain from the Whale to the Tomcat.

Ryder nuzzled the F-14 up to the boom that seemed to be hanging in mid-air. Up a little. To the left, a bit. Down a hair.

"Foreplay! Ghost, *Foreplay!*" Woody yelled from his backseat.

Ryder eased the nozzle into the boom and heard the reassuring thud of the locking system. The F-14 and the KA-3 were now officially consummated.

Ryder heard the fuel start to rush into his tanks and watched as the fuel gauge indicators rose accordingly. At a preassigned limit, he called the Whale pilot. "First connect complete . . ." he said.

"Roger, one-seven," the Whale pilot replied. "Disconnect . . . three . . . two . . . one . . . Now!"

Ryder heard the boom lock release and the lampshade unhook from the '14's nozzle. The exercise called for three connects—the first one had gone off without a hitch.

The second connect, this one completed by Ryder approaching the Whale in a descent, also went well. But just as they were lining up for the third connect, Woody suddenly broke in on the cockpit intercom.

"Hey, Ghost . . ." the Wiz called ahead. "You won't believe this, but we got four bandits coming up on us, moving at the speed of heat . . ."

"What?" Ryder replied. "This altitude is closed to ACM . . ."

Per the engagement rules at Top Gun, the area below ten thousand feet—known as the Hard Deck—was off limits for training dogfights. Besides the built-in safety factor—it didn't take long for a supersonic jet to plunge a mere ten thousand feet—the two-mile buffer zone was usually reserved for noncombatant aircraft such as the Whales, E-2C Hawkeyes, and other administrative aircraft.

"They're grouping up in attack formation, Ghost," Woody continued. "Twenty miles dead behind us . . ."

Ryder immediately called ahead to the Whale pilot and asked if he was expecting five additional aircraft for refueling exercises. The pilot quickly came back with a negative. At that instant, Ryder broke off the third connect. Whether the four-ship formation was off course or not, mid-air refueling was a delicate procedure that could be dangerous in a crowded sky.

No sooner had the Whale banked away than the four bandits came into visual behind the F-14.

"Jeesuz, I think they're 'Cats . . ." Woody yelled into his microphone.

Ryder immediately snapped to his left to get a look at the four airplanes.

"They're F-14s all right," Ryder called back to Woody.

"And they do look like they're about to engage . . ."

No sooner had the words left his mouth when they both heard not one, but *two* low-warning tones start up.

"Christ, two of them have got a missile lock on us!" Woody yelled.

Something is very wrong here, Ryder thought. Could the attacking pilots be mistaking them for other aircraft they were supposed to engage? But who ever heard of four Tomcats wanting to mix it up with another, clearly *non*-Aggressor F-14? All without warning?

He didn't have time to figure it out—he was getting the hell out of the way of the attacking 'Cat's missile sights.

"Hang on, Woody!" he called back to the pit. Then he slammed on the jet's air brakes, at the same time putting it into a tight-ass 360.

The maneuver nearly ripped the skin off their faces, but it had the desired effect. They were suddenly on the tail of the lead F-14.

Ryder instinctively squeezed the cannon trigger and quickly raked the airplane with simulated fire. Not a kill-shot; more like a knock on the head.

Then, he pointed the F-14 straight up and booted it. He was disgusted for a second when the replacement plane actually chugged twice before the engines kicked in at full military power.

"This goddamn rent-a-plane is a shitbox . . ." he cursed.

Nevertheless, they climbed. Past twelve thousand, fifteen thousand, eighteen thousand, up to twenty-one thousand feet. The second low-tone faded away, meaning the attackers had lost their radar lock-on—at least temporarily.

"Two of them followed us up," Woody reported. "They're right on our ass . . ."

Ryder looped the 'Cat over and leveled out at 21,500. He tried calling back to the pursuing 'Cats but got no reply. He immediately punched up the special Top Gun ACM frequency—perhaps someone there would know what the hell was going on.

But all he got was static . . .

"Jeesuz, those bastards are jamming us . . ." Woody called forward.

Ryder couldn't believe it. The pursuing F-14s had set their Electronic Counter-Measures systems on high, making it impossible for him to call Miramar or anyone else. The tactic was effective but very much against regulations.

"These guys are crazy," Ryder told Woody. "They're breaking every rule in the book . . ."

He put the 'Cat into a screaming dive to further elude the Tomcats, but was startled to see two of the other strange F-14s were rising up to meet him.

Ryder booted his replacement 'Cat and heard its engine cough, twice. "Jeesuz," Woody called ahead. "This thing even has problems going downhill!"

Ryder calmly watched the two fighters streaking up to meet him. One broke off, but the other appeared to be aiming right for him—almost steering *into* a collision course .

"This is going to be close . . ." he called back to Woody.

Ryder's airplane was traveling too fast to make any radical turns, so he simply flipped the 'Cat over sideways and squeaked right past the ascending fighter. The maneuver caused him to pass "canopy to canopy" with the '14, the same one he'd "shot at" seconds before. It was as close as he'd ever come to a mid-air collision. Yet as the two Tomcats flashed by each other at supersonic speeds, Ryder's quick eyes were able to catch a glimpse of the crew in the nearest fighter.

He recognized the pilot instantly . . .

"Panther . . ." he whispered bitterly.

"I don't believe this guy," Woody said, after realizing who was leading the four rogue F-14s. "They'll bust him down to paint-scrapper if we report this . . ."

A sudden, disturbing thought popped into Ryder's head. "Will they?" he asked. "Whose story are they going to believe? Ours or theirs?"

Ryder knew that the Navy's jealousy over the Air Force's lead for the Top Gun trophy knew no limits. This action could simply be back-dated as a routine exercise—and who would the Navy brass want to believe? Its own pilots or two troublemaking AF officers, one of whom had already communed with weirdness during his survival exercise? If they bitched loud enough, a board of inquiry would be set up, witnesses would be called, testimony taken. But the final decision would come down to Miramar's overall commander, the admiral whose admin ship they buzzed just days before.

"Would I be sounding too paranoid if I said that I've got a feeling we might have been set up?" Ryder called back to Woody as they pulled out of the screaming dive. Coverups were a way of life in the military.

"I got to admit I smelled the same rat . . ." Woody replied. "If Panther boy can beat us out here—it will make up for our kicking his ass last night."

Ryder knew they had two choices. Cut tail and run, get back to Miramar and kick up a fuss.

Or . . .

"Put your sunglasses down, partner," he said, yanking back on the controls and steering toward one of the four fighters. It's High Noon . . ."

Woody screamed with delight. "Yes, my man! Let's kick ass!"

Ryder smiled as he ceremoniously flipped down his sunglasses. Woody's verbal explosions helped pump him up. And the enthusiasm was contagious. The Wiz was like a one-man cheerleading squad. Ryder knew he couldn't ask for a better partner.

Ryder preferred a more celebral but no more effective approach. With computerlike speed and efficiency, before each engagement he would review the six golden rules of dogfighting:

Never take your eyes off your enemy—because if he's good, he ain't going to stop watching you.

Make sure you are holding a good hand before you start shooting—God put the sun in the sky simply to allow jet jocks to use it as cover.

Don't shoot until you see the whites of his eyes—(or: Don't go long distance if you can make it a local call); translation: if the missile don't work you want to be close enough to nail him with the cannon.

Once you start shooting, don't go half-ass—follow-through is just as important in ACM as it is in baseball, basketball, hockey, and sex.

Always get on your opponent's ass—no jet fighters have guns in the rear.

And finally: *If the enemy dives at you, scare the shit out of him by turning and meeting him head on*—this tactic will quickly separate the men from the boys.

"OK, Wood Man," Ryder said. "We got four of them. Let's start the simultaneous track. Keep continual on our six o'clock. Weapons status as available . . ."

"Roger, Ghost," Woody replied, flipping all the necessary switches on his AGM radar set. The device had the ability to track as many as twenty different targets from as far as 100 miles away. It sounded like a long distance, but at supersonic speeds, a hundred miles between closing jet fighters could seem downright cramped . . .

Ryder was already planning his strategy. He had to get the advantage on them—whether by hook or crook. And there was one way he could get a head start . . .

"What the hell . . ." he said as he dove down past the Hard Deck, leveling out at a shallow twenty-five hundred feet. "If they can bounce us while we've stopped for gas, we can slide under their skirts . . ."

"All's fair . . ." Woody agreed.

"OK, partner," Ryder said, "let's go cold for a while."

With that, Woody quickly shut off the F-14's radar. To a novice it would have seemed to be an odd thing to do. But radars were strange devices—they were actually the Catch-22 of modern ACM. They were essential to track your enemy. But when your radar set was burning, it emitted such an electronic "signature" it helped your enemy track *you*. So, although with their radar turned off, Ryder and Woody wouldn't know where Panthers' gang of four were, it would make it nearly impossible for the Navy pilots to find them.

Ryder drove the F-14 at full military power, weaving by the occasional mesa and tall hills, until he was at the very edge of the engagement area.

"OK, Woody, take a look . . ." Ryder called back to the Wiz.

The radar warmed up quickly. "They're looking for us," Woody reported. "But they're still way up there. They've split up. Two pairs."

Ryder smiled. Panther, thy ego has doomed thee, he thought. The Navy pilot had committed a cardinal sin of ACM. By splitting his forces, he had weakened the whole.

"OK, go cold," Ryder told Woody. "We're climbing . . ."

He lit the bird's afterburners and put the nose up. He grimaced as the engine once again hesitated before kicking in, but soon enough they were ascending rapidly.

"Warp One!" Ryder called out as they passed Mach 1, the speed of sound. They climbed out of the Hard Deck and were back up at fighting altitude in no time.

"Switch on!" Ryder called back to Woody as they passed eighteen thousand feet.

"We're hot," Woody reported momentarily. "There's two of them in the neighborhood, at fifteen thousand and dropping. Fifteen miles out, backs turned to us."

"OK," Ryder replied. "Back to cold . . ."

It was just 10 A.M. and the sun was at about seventy degrees. Ryder snapped the F-14 right and put the sun to their six o'clock. He raised the F-14 just a little, then slowly turned it down into a dive. Off in the distance he saw two of Panther's F-14s tooling along, no doubt searching for them with their look-down radar scan.

He increased the angle of the dive and booted up the throttle. He felt the *g*-forces increase, rippling his face and chest and causing his speed jeans to go into action.

"Weapons?" he called back to Woody.

"'Winders are hot," the Wiz reported. "Cannon checks out . . ."

"OK, partner," Ryder said, deciding to depart from the normal procedure. "*You* fire it when ready . . ."

Woody didn't miss a beat. "My pleasure," he called back.

They were now just a half mile from the trailing F-14. Ryder could almost read the thoughts of his Wizzo.

5 . . . 4 . . . 3 . . . 2 . . . 1 . . . Fire!

Sure enough, Woody squeezed the weapons release button and an imaginary AIM-9 Sidewinder streaked off the F-14's weapons pylon. An instant later, Ryder's HUD screen went red indicating a direct hit on the "enemy" Tomcat.

"Bull's-eye, Woody," he called back to the pit. "Nice shooting . . ."

Meanwhile the victim's wingman had detected their presence and banked hard right to escape. No such luck.

"Stay on him, Ghost!" Woody was yelling.

"I'm with him," Ryder said as he matched the fleeing F-14's every move.

"Radar-lock on, Ghost!" Woody yelled after a harrowing thirty-second chase. "Grease him!"

Ryder squeezed the weapons release button and knew another make-believe AIM-9 was on its way. Again, the HUD lit up red. Another 'Cat out of the fight.

Ryder pulled up beside the second long enough for Woody to give the finger to the defeated pilots, then he booted in the afterburner and roared away.

"Panther, this is Mad Max . . ."

"Go ahead, Max," Panther answered his wingman.

"Surfer and Snowman are out of it," Max reported somewhat hesitantly. "They're returning to base . . ."

Mad Max, the black pilot who was involved in the OC brawl the night before, knew Panther wasn't going to like the news.

"*Damn* . . ." Panther said. He knew his Pitman didn't have Ryder and Woody on his AGM. "Does your back-seater have a fix on those guys now?" he asked, checking with Max.

"That's a negative, Panther," the answer came back. "We got 'No Joy' on them for the past two minutes. They must be jinking their radar set. They bounced Snowman and Surfer out of the blue."

Panther swung his Tomcat to the east, then headed south,

his wingman Max on his left wing. Both pilots and their Pitmen were scanning the sky for Ryder's aircraft.

"Those gomers are out here somewhere . . ." Panther said to his backseater.

They twisted to the west, then back north, both airplanes completing an eighty-five-mile wide circle. Still nothing.

"Maybe they passed Bingo," Max radioed over. "Bingo" was the jet fighter equivalent of running on empty—the gas gauge is on "E."

"That's a negative, Max," Panther answered. "They were practicing fuel-ups earlier. They've probably got more gas than . . ."

Panther's words caught in his throat. Directly above him, way high up, he saw a black dot.

"Hold it . . ." he called over to Max. "What the hell is this?"

It was getting closer . . .

"Jeesuz," he called back to his Pitman. "You got that on radar?"

"Negative" came the reply. "Whatever it is, it's way up there . . ."

The two F-14 crews watched as the object hurtled downward. It was spinning, as if out of control. But it wasn't dropping straight down—rather it was moving as they moved, as if to force a collision.

"That's them!" Panther's pitman reported as his AGM picked up a substantial blip. Max's pitman reported a similar ID.

"God," Max exclaimed. "They must have climbed to about seventy thousand feet and flamed out!"

Panther couldn't believe how fast the out-of-control F-14 was traveling.

"He's never going to regain it," Panther whispered to himself. Suddenly he knew he could be in a lot of trouble. Although the Air Force pilots would never believe it, Panther had forced this unauthorized fight on them. Now it looked like the AF guys were in *Deep Sierra*—Top Gun jargon for "deep shit."

"*Bail out!*" Panther yelled, as he watched the wildly

spinning F-14 plunge further. "Hit the loud handle!"

No sooner had the words left his mouth when his low warning indicator started humming. In less than two seconds the F-14 had regained control and was now heading right for the two Navy airplanes, barely two thousand feet above them.

"Jesus Christ break off!" Panther yelled to Max. "He's firing on us!"

With that Panther broke his aircraft quickly to the left, cursing himself for being mesmerized by the plummeting F-14. The 'Cat had been falling so fast and behaving like it was in trouble, the last thing he suspected was the Air Force pilots would shoot on them.

But, they did . . .

"They got me!" Panther heard Max say. His wingman had broken too late and Air Force guys had put an imaginary missile right into Max's tailpipe.

A second later, his own "kill tone" also started blaring. He too could not escape the Air Force pilots' electronic air-to-airs.

Now Panther was boiling. "Stay in it, Max!" he yelled as he dove toward the 'Cat. The AF guys had embarrassed him the night before. He was about to let it happen again.

Max shrugged and followed Panther down. It was a violation of the Top Gun rules to reengage after being "hit." But this was an unauthorized fight anyway—so what was the difference?

Suddenly a new voice came on their intercoms.

"F-14s, this is Delta-2 leader," the voice said harshly. "Please report your status . . ."

Ryder was just pulling out of his "out-of-control" dive which had bagged him, Panther, and his wingman when he heard the voice. He looked up and saw a gray-schemed F-18 flying at about twelve thousand.

"That looks like a Marine instructor craft," Woody called up to Ryder as they leveled off at ten thousand.

"This is VF-106," Panther radioed the F-18. "Status is ACM . . ."

"Is this an authorized fight, VF-106?" the F-18 instructor asked. He had been watching the battle on his radar and had noted its irregularities.

Panther hesitated, then answered, "No, sir . . ."

There was a brief silence as the Marine jet circled the battle area, then its pilot spoke once again, his voice even harsher than before: "Return to base . . ." was all he said.

15

Ryder and Woody didn't say a word during the debriefing in the Group Commander's office. They didn't have to—as soon as they all landed and reported to the GC, Panther and Max really admitted they were guilty of an "unauthorized ACM exercise." After that, it was the GC who did all the talking.

When he was through with them—a fiery ten-minute dissertation on Top Gun's engagement rules—Panther and Max slinked out of the debriefing unit, each man's record bearing a hefty "black hole"—a demerit so serious that restitution was nearly impossible.

Ryder and Woody also got up to leave when the GC asked them to hold up a moment.

"You officers should know that we try to discourage personal rivalries here for obvious reasons," the GC said. "But despite the circumstances of what happened out there today, that Marine instructor told me you guys did some great flying."

Both Ryder and Woody started to thank him when the officer quickly saluted them and barked, "Dismissed!"

Once outside the debriefing room, Ryder and Woody shook hands and headed for the OC. "No way are they going to let Panther qualify for the trophy," Woody said, exuberant that they had knocked off the Number One Top Gun pretty boy. "What a jerk, thinking he could jump us like that . . ."

Ryder nodded. He was more impressed that they had

knocked off a total of four Navy aircraft, although he was sure the victories wouldn't count toward the trophy.

"All we got to do is pay attention and not screw up during Red Flag and we ice that trophy," Ryder said.

Suddenly a mysterious cloud called Distant Thunder washed over both of them. They had no idea where they were going after they "graduated" from Top Gun immediately following the Red Flag exercise.

"What the hell are we going to do with the trophy once we get it?" Woody asked.

Ryder shrugged. "Beats me . . ." he said, his voice trailing off.

They downed a half dozen beers at the OC then headed back to their quarters just as it was getting dark. The next day was a down day; the following night, Red Flag would take place. Both pilots were very aware that they would engage in one last Top Gun ACM bout.

After that, there was only uncertainty . . .

Both pilots were exhausted and were intent on sleeping right through to morning. Yet when they reached their quarters they found four men were sitting around the cafeterialike table.

Ryder's first impression was that the men had a strange look about them—they were out of place. One man wore a beard and was of dark complexion. The three others were Caucasian, but still looked slightly odd. Yet all four were wearing the same kind of blue flight suit that he and Woody were assigned.

One of the men, a stocky, red-faced man, saw their bewilderment and rose to introduce himself.

"Captain Averill Lancaster here," he said. "RAF Squadron Number 61. Didn't they tell you we were coming . . . ?"

"No one tells us anything around here," Ryder said, shaking hands with the man. Woody did likewise but not before sniffing the pan full of home-fried potatoes and gravy simmering on the unit's stove.

"I would like to properly introduce you to my friends here,"

107

Lancaster told them. "But I'm afraid I only just met them myself . . ."

One of the other men stood up. He was tall, thin, and wore a nearly skinhead haircut.

"Lieutenant Robert Chauvagne . . ." he said, shaking hands with Ryder and Woody. "French Armée de l'Air."

Another man stood. He was slightly smaller than the Frenchman, rock-jawed, serious, and wearing longish blond hair.

"Captain Heinz Reinhart," he said, nearly crushing Ryder's fingers with a viselike handshake.

"Luftwaffe?" Ryder asked him.

The man hesitated, then nodded and managed a weak smile. "*Ja . . .*" he said. "Special Air Tactics Squadron."

The remaining pilot also rose.

"Captain Raj Sammett," the bearded man said, shaking hands. "Royal Indian Naval Air Force."

"Well this is a regular United Nations meeting, ain't it?" Woody said. "Mind if I steal some chow?"

Lancaster nodded. "Yes, by all means, help yourselves, gentlemen . . ."

Both suffering from beer-induced empty stomachs, Ryder and Woody ladeled out portions of potatoes and gravy and took their places at the table.

"Are you all here to attend the next class of Top Gun, Captain?" Ryder asked. He knew that the Navy regularly invited allied nations to send their best pilots to work out at Miramar. As his Top Gun class had only a few days to go, he assumed the foreigners were signed up for the next power projection course.

The man shook his head. "No, not exactly," he said. "In fact, I have just completed the RAF version of this magnificent school. Back in Bristol, actually . . ."

Chauvagne nodded. "Me, too," he said between bites. "Top flight training school. Off Corsica. The food was terrible . . ."

Ryder looked at the German. "You, too, Captain?"

The German officer nodded briskly, then got up to refill his plate. Sammett did likewise.

"Well, this *is* strange," Ryder said, while wolfing down the plain, yet tasty fare. "If you guys aren't here for Top Gun, what are you here for?"

Chauvagne looked at Lancaster and laughed.

"Well, Captain Long," Lancaster began. "It seems that none of us really know. We have all been tapped by our governments to come here and take part in a special mission of some sort. Very hush-hush."

Ryder and Woody looked at each other, then Ryder asked, "Does this 'special mission' have a name?"

All four men seemed to nod in unison. Sammett was the first one to speak. "It is called *Im-py-rat-ta Mong Doo-ya.*"

Lancaster laughed again and said: "I don't pretend to know Hindu. But I believe that translates roughly into *Distant Thunder . . .*"

16

Quickly, one by one, the jet fighters lifted off into the late afternoon, turned to the northeast, and roared away.

There were F-18s, F-5s, A-4s, and many F-14s. The pilots of Top Gun—jocks, instructors, and Aggressor pilots alike—patiently waited for their time to take off. It took nearly two hours to launch the hundred or so fighters, plus dozens of control craft, E-2Cs, tankers, photo recon airplanes, and admin aircraft. Throughout the operation, the slow, dramatic beginnings of sunset bathed Miramar in streaks of red and orange. These hues, mixing with the bluish flare of jet exhaust and the ever-present smell of JP-8 jet fuel, turned the Naval Air Station into a kind of ethereal world. And the helmeted pilots—warriors for the New Age—looked like visitors from another planet.

It was the night of Red Flag . . .

Ryder and Woody, still saddled with their replacement Tomcat, were among the last pilots scheduled to take off. Sitting on the taxiway, waiting for their turn, both men were silent—alone with their thoughts. Woody was thinking about Karen, the librarian, and the exciting, blissful nights they'd been spending together. Over and over, he kept asking himself: Could this be the real thing?

Ryder also spent some time thinking about women—but in his case, there were two of them. One was Karen's friend Wendy, who he was getting very attached to. She was real—flesh and bones, all in the right places. But then there was this other woman—the woman in the desert, who he had dreamed about again the night before.

But the uncertainty of what lay ahead—not just in his love life, but for his life in general—now sat in his stomach like a lead weight. Where would he be a week from now? It seemed like such a simple question—yet he had no answer for it. And that was the difference.

The events of the recent past ripped through his consciousness in a blur. Their entrance to Top Gun, the automatic "outsider" status and the "don't you forget it" attitude of the other Top Gun jocks. The blistering work schedule. The barroom brawls and the sweet nights with Wendy. His strange, nocturnal encounters with his "Dream Girl." The intense trophy competition. The strange episode in the desert and the irreparable damage to his psyche and his reputation that resulted. The frustrating search for the trooper in the blue scarf.

And behind it all, the lurking, ominous shadow of Distant Thunder . . .

Ryder's thoughts were jerked back to the Real World when he heard a heavily accented Cockney voice break in on his intercom. It was the RAF pilot Lancaster, conversing with the Miramar tower on his launch procedure. Neither he nor Woody had seen much of the foreign pilots since they all met at the quarters. There had been no further discussion of Distant

Thunder; no talk at all about why an international group of pilots was being assembled for the special mission. The foreigners had apparently spent the past two days in isolation, going through a rapid-fire orientation course on the Navy's Fighter Weapons School. So Ryder and Woody were only mildly surprised when they were told the international pilots would be participating in the Red Flag exercise.

The Englishman got his clearance and rolled in front of Ryder and Woody on his way to launch, giving them an enthusiastic thumbs-up as he passed by. Lancaster was flying up front in an old but respectable F-4 Phantom wearing Naval Reserve markings. Sammett, the Indian Ryder had briefly glimpsed earlier in the day wearing a traditional Sikh turban was riding backseat in the lovable "Double Ugly."

Ryder watched the venerable F-4 rumble by—it would undoubtedly be the only "Rhino" in the exercise, at least on the Navy's side. A pang of sadness shot through him. It happened every time he saw a Phantom—his father was flying an F-4 when he was lost over North Vietnam . . .

Next in line was Chauvagne, piloting an F-5 on loan from the Aggressors and hastily painted all white. He, too, waved to Ryder and Woody, and they saluted the foreign pilots in return.

The next aircraft to pass them was an A-4 Skyhawk with the German, Reinhart, at the controls. The man didn't even look their way never mind offer them a comradely wave or thumbs-up. Ryder wasn't surprised—Reinhart oozed Prussian authoritarianism. Even in their brief first meeting, Ryder sensed a distinct unfriendliness about the man—a closed-off, tight-lipped militaristic kind of dude that promulgated the stereotype of the jack-booted German.

Yet Ryder had to keep reminding himself that Reinhart, too, was a member of this very exclusive Distant Thunder club. The American pilot shook his head—how would this man's actions, as well as the other foreign pilots, affect his life in the near future?

Ten minutes later, Ryder and Woody were cleared to

launch, their cranky Tomcat nearly flaming out on take-off.

They formed up with three Top Gun instructors flying A-4 Aggressors and headed northeast. For the exercise, all of the Navy's Aggressor aircraft had a set of zebra stripes on their wings, tails, and fuselage in order to distinguish them from the Air Force's similarly camouflaged Aggressors.

The late-afternoon sky was crystal clear and a new moon was rising early. The four airplanes cruised over the California deserts toward the edge of Nevada to the place where Red Flag would be fought. Officially it was known as Nellis Air Force Weapons Testing Range. Ryder had never been over the range before—most of the time it was strictly off limits to all aircraft both civilian *and* military.

But that didn't stop all the wild rumors that the Top Gun pilots had heard about the place . . .

Unofficially, the pilots called it War Heaven. Like China Lake, the thousands of square miles of War Heaven were wired with sensors, simulated SAMs, moving and stationary targets, yet it outdistanced China Lake in respect to bulk of equipment and state-of-the-art technology. So elaborate a video war game was War Heaven they said, that China Lake looked like a 1950s-style pinball game in comparison.

That War Heaven was a battleground for both airborne *and* ground forces was a badly kept secret—the Air Force and the Army shared this top-secret playground. The scuttlebutt said the range was the scene of huge simulated battles—both on land and in the air—that rivaled in size and scope, actual engagements fought in World War II. The place was supposedly a general's wet dream—studded with all kinds of hot-shit weaponry, both simulated and real. Everything from laser-guided howitzers to ground-based Star Wars equipment. Supposedly there were secret airfields, exotic SAM sites, and training camps for CIA officers as well as other intelligence operatives.

It was like another world, said the few who had been there and dared to talk about it. And their information was sketchy—even during exercises like Red Flag, more than ninety percent of the place was still off limits.

112

By the time Ryder's flight reached the designated ACM area, the massive dogfight was already going full tilt. Even from fifty miles out, he could see the flaring of jet pipes and the ghostly contrails of the spinning jet fighters lighting up the dusk.

On the ground he knew for this exercise it was the US Army against the Marine Corps. Sure enough, as they drew closer, he could see tanks, APCs, trucks, and other vehicles moving everywhere, bathed in the light of simulated, but very realistic-looking "flash" explosions.

It was all being controlled by top officers who were orbiting the battle area in the array of E-2C and AWACS control aircraft. They would direct the planes in the air and the troops on the ground. No one would move without the right word from them. Appropriately enough they were nicknamed "Voice Above."

It was an incredible sight. Even though he knew it was all make-believe, the battle scene still sent a shudder through Ryder.

The closest there is to the real thing . . .

The radio was a nightmarish symphony of calls going back and forth between flight leaders and their wingmen:

"Watch my tail!"

"Bandit on your six o'clock!"

"He's firing!"

"Fox One away! Fox Two away!"

"This sounds like a real 'furball,'" Woody called ahead to Ryder, using the Top Gun lingo for an enormous if chaotic dogfight.

Ryder radioed back: "One hundred of them against one hundred of us. I hope there's someone left for us to pick on."

Suddenly an outside voice broke in on their intercom.

"F-14, one-niner-zero, this is flight leader," the lead instructor in the A-4 called over to Ryder. "We have been asked by Voice Above to provide ground support and suppression for our Marine brothers. Suggest you freelance for a while."

"Roger, flight leader," Ryder acknowledged as he watched the A-4s peel off and head for the desert floor.

113

Once again, Ryder and Woody were left alone.

"I'm glad I'm not superstitious," Woody called ahead to Ryder. "If I was, I'd say that it's more than a coincidence that we're going into this thing without a wingman . . ."

"Knock twice when you say that, partner," Ryder called back.

He, like Woody had his suspicions. They were among the last to take off, and inserted into an A-4 flight that certainly must have been prepared for being called in for air cover. Going into ACM—even the simulated kind—without a wingman was suicidal. A wingman's function was to protect the flight leader's vulnerable six o'clock position. Now, with no one to watch their rear end, they were in danger of being bounced even when they were bouncing someone else. It did have all the makings of a plot—a last ditch one to bust their lead in the Top Guns at Top Gun race.

"This would be a hell of a way to lose that goddamn trophy," Woody said.

"Screw 'em," Ryder said. "We've been without a wingman on more than half our hops. If they want to be infantile and make us lose our perfect batting average, I say let 'em try! At least we'll go down fighting . . ."

"I like that kind of talk, Ghost," Woody replied with a laugh.

Ryder booted in the F-14s afterburner and streaked into the heart of the battle. For the next ten minutes, the darkening sky was a blur of Air Force F-16s, F-15s, F-5s, and even a few of the original swing-wing F-111s on one side, F-14s, F-18s, and Zebra-striped A-4s and F-5s on the other.

Ryder's computerlike mind was running at 110 percent. Calculating dive rates, shooting angles, the 'Cat's speed compared to the "enemy." Woody was hovering over AGM radar set—the gizmo that made the F-14 was a very formidable fighter in the waning light. Like a real Tomcat, it could see at night. Ryder let Woody guide him to all possible bandits, interspersing his reports with various weapons status checks. All the while, they were being squashed by the alternating positive and negative g-forces, their speed jeans working

114

overtime as Ryder steered the F-14 through the ever-darkening sky.

In the massive air battle, both pilots knew no one was working so together as they were. The resulting confidence—even cockiness—gave them the mandatory shot of aggressiveness needed for successful ACM.

And their trademark teamwork paid off once again. They quickly dispatched two low-flying F-111s, and caught an F-15 who had come down to help. Heading for higher altitudes, they faced off with a pair of F-16s—nailing one and allowing the other to escape with a barrage of simulated cannon shells ripping across its tail.

"Fly this motherfucker, Ghost!" Woody would yell every other thirty seconds.

Ryder was getting caught up in the delirium. All I want to do is fly, he thought.

Suddenly a mysterious voice came across their intercom.

"F-14, one-niner-zero," the monotone speaker called—Ryder knew instantly that it was Voice Above. "Red Flag engagement control here. Vector to Delta-Zebra-Romeo. At fourteen thousand. Orbit and prepare to intercept."

Ryder let the orders sink in for a moment. That vector was miles away from the simulated dogfight.

"Engagement Control?" he called back. "Do I confirm Delta-Zebra-Romeo?"

Voice Above quickly confirmed the order with a curt: "Confirmed . . ."

Ryder had no choice but to acknowledge and bank the F-14 toward the assigned area.

"I told you, Ghost," Woody came on the intercom. "They *are* trying to get rid of us. Get us out of this furball and let the Navy guys chalk up some wins."

"Maybe," Ryder answered, as he headed for the very outer fringe of the predetermined ACM area. "Maybe not . . ."

They arrived at their ordered station within a minute and a half. They were not surprised to find there were absolutely no other aircraft in the area.

Ryder put the F-14 into a tight orbit, feeling mildly

ridiculous flying in circles, alone, while the lights and flashes of one of the largest mock air combat exercises were still visible in the distance.

They orbited in silence for several minutes. Then, Woody suddenly came on the line. "Got a bandit, Ghost," he said excitedly. "Wait . . . two of them. Still sixty miles out, but closing fast . . ."

"Where they coming from?" Ryder asked, leveling out the aircraft and doing a quick check of his weapons status.

"Believe it or not, Ghost, they're coming out of the north," Woody reported. "Out of the battle area . . ."

Ryder banked the F-14 to the north. Who the hell is flying down here from the north, he thought. The ACM had been going balls out for nearly fifteen minutes. The rules said that every airplane that was to be engaged in the mock air battle was already on station before the refs called "Fight's on!" By injecting more aircraft at this point would be a nasty example of dirty pool.

"Christ!" Woody yelled into the intercom. "There's three more with them. And there's another four!"

"What the hell is happening here, Wood Man?" Ryder said. "What kind of bandits are we talking about?"

Woody pushed a few buttons and worked to get a cross-section reading on the lead bandit.

"They've got to be F-5s . . ." the answer came back. "But they're emitting, and it's strong . . ."

That was strange. As good as the plucky F-5 was, very few of them carried anything more than the most rudimentary radar systems. Some of the Navy F-5s carried no radar at all. Yet Woody was picking up strong radar signals from these mysterious aircraft.

"Ghost! I got a total of fourteen targets!" Woody yelled out. "And they're reading on us . . ."

"This is giving me the creeps," Ryder said, more to himself than to Woody. Luckily the 'Cat's AGM could track as many as twenty-two targets at once. But the problem was, there was no way they could handle all the approaching aircraft. Yet his orders from the "Voice Above" was to intercept.

Suddenly, he got a visual on the incoming aircraft. In the dusk sky the first thing that appeared were their tail and navigation lights. But that was enough. He knew right away that he and Woody were in all kinds of trouble. Trouble of getting bounced. Trouble of ruining their perfect score. But, most damaging, trouble of letting such a large force get through and possibly blowing the entire exercise in favor of the Air Force. They'd never let them hear the end of *that* back at Top Gun—he was sure that charges of collusion would be rampant before they even landed.

"*Jeesuz, here they come!*" Woody cried out.

The next thing they knew, they were faced head-on by more than a dozen F-5s.

Ryder put the Tomcat into a wicked dive and avoided getting bounced in the opening seconds.

"Give me targets, Woody!" he yelled out, banking the 'Cat hard left, then lifting into a true vertical climb.

"OK, Ghost," Woody continued. "There's the second last guy in line. Up at 14,500. He doesn't see us . . ."

"Roger," Ryder called back, steering the F-14 to a good shooting position. "Maybe we can pick at the rear and knock a few off before they reach the big fight . . ."

"Sunglasses down!" Woody yelled.

"Roger, sunglasses down," Ryder answered.

He was up and on the F-5's six o'clock in a matter of seconds. "Fox One away!" he called out, launching an imaginary Sidewinder.

"Hit!" Woody called back, watching his AGM simulator screen.

The kill was confirmed by Ryder's up-front HUD hardware.

Ryder watched the "dead" F-5 quickly bank away and head back toward the north. "That was almost *too* easy," he radioed Woody.

"They're turning on us . . ." Woody reported.

Ryder wasn't surprised. Their eliminating one of the F-5s had tipped their position to the other thirteen. He expected several to turn back and engage them while the body of the force would head straight for the air battle.

117

"How many coming our way?" he asked the Wiz.

"Oh, God . . ." he heard Woody say. "*All* of them . . ."

"What?"

"All of them, Ghost!" Woody said, his voice rising an octave in excitement.

Things were starting to click in Ryder's mind and he didn't like the result. If all the opposing jets were turning to meet them it could only mean one thing: these party-crashing jet fighters were not intent on joining the battle.

They were after him and Woody . . .

17

It was like a nightmare . . .

Within seconds, Ryder and Woody had no less than four fighters on their tail, wildly firing simulated missiles and cannon shells. Ryder was performing every trick in the book just to keep flying. Suddenly four other mystery jets were attacking him head-on. When he dived away from them, it was only to find two more fighters rising to meet him.

"*Jeesuz*, Ghost, what the fuck is happening here?" Woody yelled out. "We got so many close-in bogies, the AGM is about to blow a chip!"

Ryder managed to bank away from the two climbing fighters and found himself momentarily on the tail of a single bandit. He bravely squeezed off an imaginary missile, which missed. But he knew it had come close enough to set off the mystery fighter's low-warning tone.

But then, as if in retaliation, he suddenly had five of the fighters firing on him from five different directions.

"These guys are nuts!" Woody yelled out as Ryder did a snap 180 to get out of harm's way. They were suddenly eating

118

about six gs, but after he completed the maneuver he was astonished to see that three bandits had jumped on his tail immediately after he leveled off.

"Boy, if we ever needed a wingman . . ." Ryder muttered.

Suddenly his radio crackled, "F-14, one-niner-zero, bank left!"

The voice was vaguely familiar; the advice was well intentioned. A mystery fighter had pulled up underneath Ryder's tail and was beaming in on his six o'clock. Ryder banked the F-14 left, his teeth involuntarily gritting with the force of the gs.

The mystery jet streaked by—followed in close pursuit by an F-4.

Ryder couldn't believe it. "Well, I'll be damned . . ." he said.

"It's that Redcoat in his Rhino!" Woody roared.

Both Air Force pilots were elated—Lancaster had taken the heat off them for an important moment or so, long enough for them to get their shit together.

They watched as the RAF pilot popped the F-5, sending the mystery fighter into a controlled spin and out of the action.

"Phantom, this is F-14 one-niner-zero," Ryder radioed Lancaster. "We owe you a beer . . ."

"The pleasure was all mine . . ." Lancaster called back. "*Both* Mr. Sammett and I will gladly collect."

But now the mystery jets were regrouping and Woody was again calling out some bad numbers.

"Six about to punch us, Ghost!" he yelled. "Dive, baby, dive!"

Ryder knew his Wiz well enough to let the bottom drop out when the man said dive. He put the 'Cat into a screecher, shaking the half dozen bandits and spinning away to the periphery of the action. That's when he saw two more fighters heading his way from the south.

"Who are those guys, Wiz?" he called back to Woody.

"ID coming up," Woody replied, then saying after a pause, "Could be help. Looks like a White Five and an A-4."

A white F-5 and a Skyhawk?

119

"Could it be our exchange students?" Ryder asked Woody, climbing once again into the swarm of mystery jets.

Five seconds later, they were just below the path of the two incoming F-5s.

"This is Lieutenant Chauvagne here, F-14, one-niner-zero," a familiar, French-tinged voice came over. "You need assistance?"

At that moment the French pilot's F-5 streaked by, followed closely by Reinhart's A-4.

There were still twelve mystery fighters somewhere out there, but Ryder could feel a shift in the ethers. He was also starting to put some pieces together. Maybe this separate ACM *was* part of a larger design.

"Phantom, this is F-14," Ryder called over to Lancaster. "Were you vectored here?"

"That's affirmative, F-14," the reply came back.

"Also here," Chauvagne jumped in.

Nothing came over from Reinhart, but Ryder didn't expect the man to be gabby in the middle of this sideshow furball.

"Should we pair up, Captain Ryder?" Lancaster called over.

"Always good to have a wingman . . ." Ryder started to say.

But then something out of the corner of his eye caught his attention . . .

It was one of the mystery jets, flying out on the periphery, almost as if to avoid the action.

"Woody, where's that guy going?" he called back to the pit.

Woody checked the AGM. "Looks like he's trying to beat it out of here . . ." the Wiz reported.

Ryder banked toward the fighter in question. "Got a read on him, partner?" Ryder asked.

There was a slight pause, then Woody replied, "There's something funny about that guy, Ghost . . ."

"Funny, how?" Ryder wanted to know.

"I think he joined this party late," Woody replied. "I don't think he's part of the original gate-crashers. Maybe he's a control ship . . ."

That's all Ryder needed. Something inside him was saying that he should follow that airplane. He called Lancaster.

"Phantom, suggest you and Chauvagne join up. Do what you can. We're in pursuit of the bandit up at 15,600, heading north."

"That's a roger," Lancaster came back. "You'll be out on the fringe of the battle area, F-14 . . ."

"I won't tell, if you don't," Ryder said, booting in the F-14's afterburner.

With that they streaked after the mysterious fringe fighter. Suddenly one of the hunters had become the hunted.

"He's running, Ghost!" Woody called up.

"I see him," Ryder replied, keeping one eye on the fighter's running lights, the other on the bandit's electronic image projected on the 'Cat's HUD. "Keep me up to date. What's his read?"

"This guy is really funny," Woody came back. "I'm picking up an emission, but it's crackling. Like he's carrying some strange equipment on board."

Another piece just fit in.

"He's leaving the combat area right . . . now!" Woody reported. "We'll be out of bounds in fifteen seconds . . ."

Screw it, Ryder thought. He opened the F-14's throttle.

"Something's strange here, Wiz," he called back. "I'm chasing this guy. You coming?"

"If you got a hunch, partner, I wouldn't miss it for the world" came the reply.

Ryder smiled. He knew they were both risking it. Traveling out of the prescribed combat zone could lead them into trouble with both the Top Gun and the Nellis people. But his body was absolutely tingling.

This wasn't a hunch. This was a goddamn premonition!

He strained the Tomcat for all its power, knowing all along that the big engines were greedily sucking up the precious jet fuel by the second.

"We'll be past bingo in forty-five seconds," Woody reported. That was the fuel red line at which they would have to turn back to reach Miramar safely.

Ryder angled the F-14 up on the fleeing fighter. Slowly he inched up closer. Close enough now to see the fighter's tail clearly. The pilot started a few slight jinks in a pale effort to shake the F-14, but to no avail.

"Either he's a shitty flier, or he's past his bingo," Woody observed.

"Probably both . . ." Ryder replied.

Now he saw his chance to pull even with the fighter.

"We'll be past bingo in fifteen, Ghost," Woody reminded him.

"Just a little farther . . ." Ryder said. He strained his eyes to get a make on the airplane. Woody was doing the same thing on his AGM.

Suddenly, they both reached the same conclusion . . .

"Jeesuz!" Woody yelled out. *"That ain't no ordinary goddamn F-5!"*

That's right, Ryder thought to himself. He knew exactly what kind of airplane it was. Suddenly a great weight was lifted from his shoulders. He wasn't crazy after all.

He smiled and pushed his intercom button. "That, Wiz, old buddy, is one, very black, F-5 . . ."

"Jeesuz, Ghost," Woody replied. "Like the ones you saw over the desert?"

"The same," Ryder said.

They streaked along in silence for nearly a minute, chasing the airplane to the north.

Woody was the first to snap out of it.

"Ghost, we are way past bingo," he reported. "We got to turn back . . ."

"We can't turn back," Ryder radioed back. "This guy can provide a lot of answers . . ."

Woody cut him off. "Ghost! We're running out of gas!"

". . . I've got to see where this guy is going," Ryder protested, cursing his dropping fuel indicator needle.

"Hey, Ry," Woody broke in with a low, authoritative voice. "Let him go, *man* . . . we got to get back."

Ryder would look back on it as the first time Woody had addressed him by his given first name. That's how serious it was. And he knew the Wiz was right.

"OK, Captain Woods," he called back, taking one last look

at the fleeing black fighter. "Let's go home . . ."

Slade was the first person Ryder saw as he pulled the F-14 up to its hardstand. Night had fallen by this time and the flight line was bathed in eerie glow of portable arc lights. Theirs was the last of the Top Gun jets to be recovered from the Red Flag exercise.

"What was going on out there, Long?" Slade asked him before he was even off the F-14's access ladder. "We were supposed to link up . . ."

"You probably know more about it than I do, Slade," Ryder told him, peeling off his flight helmet. "We were vectored by Voice Above to a fringe area and jumped by a wolfpack of F-5s. If the UN didn't show up, we would have been eaten alive . . ."

Slade shook his head in disbelief.

"Hey, Slade," Woody said, climbing down from the 'Cat's rear seat. "We iced four bandits in the big fight and one out on the fringe. That makes five."

"So?" Slade said.

"So," Woody continued. "That means your precious goddamn Top Gun trophy is on its way to the Air Force Academy . . ."

Slade was getting mad. "I got nothing to do about that, Woods," he said sternly. "I don't know what they are going to count as 'official kills.'"

"I knew it," Woody said, squeezing out of his helmet. "The Navy is gonna fuck us over . . ."

"I said I got *nothing* to do with any of it, Woods," Slade said, his face turning red. "I'm just interested in why we didn't link up and what went on out in the fringe. Nothing more."

The Navy officer turned back to Ryder. "You got anything else to report, Captain?" he asked.

Ryder looked him straight in the eye. There was no way he was going to tell the Navy officer about the mysterious black jet. "No," Ryder replied. "Nothing else . . ."

Slade was quiet for a moment. Both men were thinking about just what the other *really* knew.

123

"Head for debriefing," Slade said. "Tell *them* Voice Above vectored you to the fringe."

With that, Slade walked away from the flight line, quickly disappearing into the shadows.

Unlike Slade, the Navy debriefing officers appeared not to care about the strange air battle out on the fringe. They simply reviewed the action against the F-111s and the F-15 early in the fight, plus the single F-16 Ryder and Woody managed to bounce. Throughout the hour-long debrief, nothing was said about the black F-5, which suited Ryder fine. He knew what he had seen—and now he had a witness in Woody. But he wasn't about to spill it all over Fightertown.

At the end of the meeting, Woody asked if they would be credited with tapping the fringe F-5. Typically, the debriefing officers simply shrugged and said it was not up to them. The action had been picked up on the TACTS equipment—but whether it would count in their overall total was out of their hands.

It was all academic anyway; both Ryder and Woody knew it. Panther—who was still awaiting a date for his disciplinary hearing—had accounted for three Air Force jets during Red Flag. That was good, but not good enough to knock Ryder and Woody out of the top for the trophy running. Unbelievably, the Air Force pilots had passed through the famous Top Gun with a perfect record.

"This calls for a celebration," Woody said after they left the debriefing room.

"It's a double celebration, partner," Ryder said as they stripped off the last of their flight gear and automatically steered toward the OC. "We taught the Swabbies how it's done and I've got proof positive that I'm not nuts. There *are* funny black F-5s flying around out there."

Woody shook his head. "I always believed you saw what you said you saw, Ghost," he said. "But it's just funny to see it with my own two eyes . . ."

Ryder slapped his friend on the back and said, smiling, "I

know the feeling, pal . . ."

Fifteen minutes later, they were at their regular out-of-the-way table at the OC, plowing through a second round of drinks. The place was more crowded than usual—many of the pilots who had taken part in Red Flag were at the bar, reliving the electronic dogfight.

"It's got to have something to do with Thunder," Woody said, lowering his voice a notch.

"The Black Jets?" Ryder asked, then nodded. "I'm sure of it now. But how does it tie into what I saw that night out in the desert?"

"Beats me," Woody said, draining his second drink in record time, simultaneously ordering another. "It seems the more we find out, the more complicated it becomes."

"OK, let's look at the facts," Ryder said. "We got black F-5s—belonging to who we don't know—flying around out in the Nevada desert. We got some Airborne trooper from a unit that was wiped out in Laos in 1962, playing psychedelic Boy Scout out on China Lake. We got four guys from four different countries, suddenly whisked into Top Gun, two days before the biggest ACM exercise of the decade and it's they who save our asses when we're jumped by some bandits."

"And don't forget they took our F-14 away from us, for a strip down," Woody threw in.

Just then Lancaster and Sammett walked in. Ryder flagged them over to the table.

"Just wanted to thank you, Captain, for the assist out there," Ryder said. "I believe we owe you guys a drink?"

Lancaster smiled. He was your atypical Englishman. Handsome. Rugged. The sophisticated warrior. "A big glass of Yank beer would do it . . ."

Woody was already motioning the waitress over. "I, too, would like beer," the turbaned Sammett said.

The drinks properly ordered, the four pilots began to talk in hushed tones. Lancaster asked how Ryder and Woody came to be involved in the project and they quickly gave him the rundown. Ryder told him just about everything . . . except about his survival exercise gone awry.

125

But the Englishman surprised him.

"I heard about your bizarre experience in the desert, Captain," he told Ryder.

"I, too," Sammett added.

"Officially or unofficially?" Ryder asked.

"Quite unofficial, I assure you," Lancaster replied. "And quite by accident. We were in here last night. Snooping around, drinking your dreadful American gin. We overheard several pilots talking about it."

The waitress arrived with their drinks. Ryder quickly took a healthy slug from his bourbon and ginger. "Well, Captain, I won't bore you with the details now."

Lancaster smiled. "If it's one-tenth of what I heard last night, I'm sure it won't be a boring tale."

"Make a good book someday," Woody said.

Lancaster took a swig of his beer, winced, and wiped his mouth. "You know, it is very curious," he began. "The way you blokes were called into the project, called in from flying, shall we say, less glamorous aircraft. It's not too far removed from how I was tapped."

"How so?" Ryder asked, very interested.

"Well, I've found it to be very strange that of all the RAF top guns, I was the one selected for the project. I'm far from a typical RAF lifer. I don't have the best service record."

Ryder had to laugh. "None of us do," he said.

Lancaster then went on to tell his story. He had got into a "bit of a stew" several months after the Falklands War. It seems that he was flying a recon mission along the Argentine coast when his RF-4 Phantom sprung a bad fuel leak. "Love that airplane," Lancaster said between sips of his beer. "But the fuel system isn't worth a plug!"

He was forced to hit the silk and was quickly captured by the Argentine Navy. "The Wogs accused me of espionage," Lancaster said with a laugh. "Which was quite true, of course. I was snapping their coastal defense. Part of a plan in case we had to go back and teach 'em a lesson a second time."

"The Empire never sleeps, eh?" Woody said.

"Never is right," Lancaster continued. "They threw me in

126

prison. A horrible place. Filled with political prisoners who had been there for years. I knew that the RAF would never admit that I even existed, and the Argies never got a word out of me, so I just assumed that I would languish in that hell forever."

"So what happened?" Ryder asked, swishing some of the bourbon around in his mouth before swallowing.

"I still don't know, frankly," Lancaster said. "I got sprung. One day I was in. Next day, a couple of Swedes from the Red Cross pick me up and I'm on a plane to London, by way of Rio. I was in hospital for two days, then they told me about Thunder."

"Interesting . . ." Ryder said. He thought his being plucked out of cargo-plane obscurity was a strange story.

"I, too, was in jail," Sammett spoke up in his Indian singsongy voice. "I was arrested by my government just because I was a Sikh. I had no trial. No defense. No lawyer. I was in jail for life. Then one day, American diplomat comes. Then I am free! They fly me to American aircraft carrier—Marines carrier actually. With Harrier jumpjets. I practiced for six weeks, then came here."

"They didn't exactly pick the cream of the crop for this mission, did they?" Woody said.

"How about the Frenchman?" Ryder asked Lancaster.

"Very interesting, that chap," the Englishman said, taking another gulp of beer. "He was fighting Kaddafi's troops in Chad, or so he told me. He was part of a kind of French Foreign Legion for pilots."

"Foreign Legion *Air Force?*" Woody asked.

"Yes," Lancaster answered. "French pilots who might have gone astray at one time and rather than face discharge or even prison, they volunteer to do all the dirty work.

"Apparently Chauvagne was a wild one. A good pilot, though."

"How about 'Adolph?'" Woody asked.

"Reinhart?" Lancaster said. "Your guess is as good as mine. I'd like to write him off as typically German, but who knows? He did very well in that spat against those bloody F-5s, though. Got two of them, with no help from us. God knows what he has in his past. But he's a hell of a flier, he is . . ."

Ryder drained his bourbon and called for yet another round. Pilots from different countries, jailbirds or close to it. Flying fools by the sounds of it. Gathered together for a secret mission? What the hell was going on here?

He wondered if anyone really knew . . .

18

More than two thousand miles to the east, in the offices of *The Washington Post*, Senior Editor Jim McCarty was wondering the same thing . . .

The rapifax machine next to his desk finally stopped whirring. It buzzed once then automatically shut off.

McCarty, a twenty-year veteran of the *Post*, picked up the two pages that had been transmitted from the newspaper's London correspondent. The printout paper was thin and filmy and very hard to read. McCarty immediately copied the pages on the Xerox, making them slightly easier to read.

The fax-message contained two brief news stories, clipped out of English-language newspapers from France and Germany. One was dated a month earlier; the other was only two days old. McCarty read both stories twice, then reached for his telephone and called his associate national affairs editor.

"Vic, can you come in for a minute?"

McCarty then lit his pipe, took an extra long drag, and read the stories a third time. By the time he had finished, Vic Tolosko was sitting in his office.

"What do have, Jim?" Tolosko asked.

"Could be a wild one," McCarty said. "Or it could be nothing. I just wanted to bounce it off you if you had a few minutes."

Tolosko glanced at his watch. It was nearly midnight—his shift was nearly over. "Sure," Tolosko said, lighting up a Lucky Strike. "What the hell . . ."

"OK," McCarty said, relighting his pipe. "I just got these two stories from Phillip in London. I asked him to be on the lookout for these and, sure enough, he came up with them.

"This first one is from the English edition of *Le Monde*. Datelined Paris. Headline reads: French Air Force pilot killed in Chad fighting.

"'Captain Robert Maurice Chauvagne of the French Armée de l'Air was killed yesterday when his jet was downed by a Libyan surface-to-air missile while supporting Chadian ground trops.

"'Chauvagne's Mirage fighter-bomber was lost in fighting forty-five miles west of Habre, in the northwest part of Chad. The area has been the scene of recent fighting between loyalist Chadian troops and Libyan-backed Chadian rebels.

"'A spokesman said that a special French Army reconnaissance team tried but failed to recover Chauvagne's body.

"'Chauvagne had just recently been called up to active duty. His unit reported to Chad only three weeks ago.'"

"Is he the first French pilot killed in the fighting?" Tolosko asked.

"Possibly," McCarty said. "But that's not why I think its unusual. Let me read you this second story."

McCarty refilled his pipe again and quickly lit it. He cleared his throat and began reading again:

"Dateline Reihm, Federal Republic of Germany. The newspaper is *The Daily Signal*. Headline reads: Son of famous Luftwaffe pilot killed in auto accident.

"'The son of World War II fighter ace Manfred Reinhart was killed in an auto accident on the Autobahn yesterday. Heinz Reinhart, 28, was alone when his late-model sports car hit a bridge abutment 20 miles outside of Reihm last night.

"'Reinhart's car was traveling at a high rate of speed when the accident occurred, police said. The car was totally engulfed in flames when police arrived and there was no attempt to pull Reinhart from the wreckage.

"'There were no witnesses to the accident. Police said Reinhart was an instructor pilot for the German Air Force.'"

Tolosko glanced at his watch again. "Two pilots killed in a month. Is that really unusual? Those guys lead a dangerous life."

McCarty nodded. "Oh, I agree," he said, reaching into his desk for a file. "But, listen to *this* story. I took it from our foreign readers' service file about two weeks ago:

"The New Delhi Urja News. Obit page. No headline.

"'Sammett Gindu, arrested three years ago for crimes against the government committed during the Sikh insurrection in Bengal, was found guilty and executed by a firing squad at New Delhi's military prison today. Sammett was a pilot in the Royal Indian Navy before his arrest.'"

"Those Indians are either crazy or stupid," Tolosko said, crushing out his cigarette. "I don't think pilots in India are exactly a dime a dozen. Sounds like they wasted a pretty valuable individual."

"Yes, but do you see something here? Or is it just me?" McCarty asked.

Tolosko lit another Lucky. "Maybe . . ."

"Let me read on," McCarty said, retrieving another story from the file. "From the London *Daily Sun*. Last Wednesday. The headline says: RAF pilot's body returned by Argentina.

"'The body of Royal Air Force pilot Group Captain Averill Lancaster arrived at Heathrow Airport late last night, the last casualty to be returned home from the Falklands War. A small group of ceremonial guardsmen braved the rain to assure the proper military honors were served for Lancaster, whose reconnaissance aircraft was crashed off the coast of Argentina several months after the hostilities with that country ended in 1982.

"'A spokesman for the Argentine Foreign Ministry said Lancaster's body had been interred at a military cemetery since the incident.

"'The Argentine government claims Lancaster was on a spy mission when he was killed. Only recently did the British Foreign Affairs Office enter into secret talks with the

Argentines for the return of the body, sources said. A spokesman denied that the British government had acknowledged that Lancaster was on a spy mission when he died, although he confirmed that Lancaster was on active duty with an RAF reconnaissance wing stationed on Ascension Island at the time of his death.

"'An RAF spokesman said a private burial is planned.'"

Tolosko got up and poured out two cups of coffee from McCarty's personal Proctor Silex.

"It's getting a little more interesting," he said, passing one cup to McCarty.

"OK, fifth story," McCarty said. "We carried it just two days ago. Eastern edition. Actually an Associated Press story. Dateline: Nellis Air Force Base, Nevada. Headline: Two Air Force pilots killed in accident.

"'Two pilots for the Military Airlift Command were killed when their trainer jet crashed and burned near Nellis Air Force Base in Nevada yesterday.

"'Air Force officials would release no other details other than the names of the pilots, identified as Captain Ryder Long, 30, and Captain Dennis J. Woods, 29.

"'The officials said the cause of the accident is still under investigation. Dental records were used to identify the bodies.'"

Tolosko took a swig of coffee as McCarty relit his pipe.

"Spooky," Tolosko said. "But what do we have, exactly?"

McCarty shrugged and leaned back in his chair. "Five pilots, all killed within two weeks of one another. Nothing more than that, really. Except . . ."

"Except what?" Tolosko asked.

McCarty got up and closed the door to his office. Although it was midnight, the newspaper's copy room was bustling with activity.

"These two Air Force guys," he said, rereading the story. "It says they were part of the Military Airlift Command."

"So?" Tolosko asked.

"I was in the Air Force and I know a little about their command structure," McCarty said. "The Military Airlift

131

Command is the branch of the Air Force that hauls around cargo, drops paratroopers, flies generals home for Christmas, things like that."

"And?" Tolosko asked, getting up to refill his coffee cup.

"And these two Air Force captains were killed at Nellis, flying a jet trainer," McCarty said.

"Is that unusual?" the young editor asked.

"It might be," McCarty replied. "Why were MAC pilots flying a jet trainer at Nellis? The only reason jet trainers are used is to train fighter pilots."

"Well, maybe these two guys got transferred or something," Tolosko said.

"Again, maybe," McCarty said, sipping his coffee. "But they were both pretty old for fighter pilot training. You're an old man at thirty in the Air Force. If you ain't flying the fastest airplane at twenty-three or twenty-four, you're probably going to be flying cargo airplanes until you get smart and get a job at TWA or someplace. Plus Nellis is not a base for MAC."

Tolosko rubbed his chin and said, "So, we got five pilots dead, two of them Americans who were not flying a cargo airplane, but a jet trainer. Is that all?"

"I don't know," McCarty said, rubbing his balding dome. "That and the fact that none of these bodies are, shall we say . . . recoverable?"

"It would be pretty way out if they were all connected," Tolosko said. "Really spy novel stuff, Jim."

McCarty nodded. "Yeah, probably. But I got a hunch."

"Well, put someone on it . . . ." Tolosko said.

McCarty frowned and adjusted his glasses. "Well, maybe I will."

Tolosko got up to leave. "Who you got in mind?"

McCarty banged his pipe against his well-worn ashtray. "I don't know," he said. "Maybe 'Legs.'"

"Oh, God . . ." Tolosko said with a laugh. "Do you really think she can handle it?"

McCarty got up and put on his coat. "Listen, Maureen is a very capable, well-educated reporter," he said with a mild grin. "She told me so herself the other day."

"I don't doubt she did," Tolosko said.

"Plus, her old man's been flying a desk at the Pentagon for years," McCarty continued. "He can probably lead her to some good contacts."

"What difference does that make?" Tolosko asked. "Every guy who sets eyes on her wants nothing else but to get her in the sack . . ."

"That's just it," McCarty said. "People seem to want to spill their guts to a beautiful young woman. I've seen you do it on several occasions."

"Well, she's so goddamn beautiful, it can work against her . . ."

McCarty put on his hat and turned out his office lights. "We'll see . . ." he said.

19

It was one A.M. and the crew chief had just finished off the last cup of the fourth pot of coffee.

"How much longer, Thomas?" he called out to his lead mechanic.

"At least another two hours, Chief," the reply came back. "Then we still got to paint them over."

The crew chief decided to make yet another pot of coffee. They'd probably be needing it. There were eight men crawling over the three F-14s in the otherwise darkened hangar. They'd been working since four that afternoon. And with at least three more hours of work ahead of them, it was turning into a marathon twelve-hour shift. The problem was, the work on the F-14s had to be completed—and the airplanes aloft—before sunup.

They'd been at it for two weeks now and the job had been a

133

pain in the ass. Typical work orders he could do. But this one had been everything but typical. It had involved some reconfigurations on the trio of F-14s normally used for Top Gun training. First of all, all the normal attachments needed for external mid-air refueling were replaced with a different and frankly less efficient design. That only had taken two working days for each Tomcat.

Next, the points for carrying external fuel tanks under the wings were also removed. In their stead, additional hard points for carrying extra ordnance were attached. Then, key points on the undersides of both jets were being reinforced with a new kind of lightweight armor plating.

Then, a group of mechanics from God-knows-where showed up the night before and changed out all of the avionics in the F-14s cockpits. New, apparently secret instruments and software were installed.

While all this was going on, all three jets underwent engine change-outs. The usual Pratt & Whitney TF-30 engines were replaced by a new, very classified GE jet engine that the crew chief had never seen before. But the new powerplants apparently delivered so much thrust—maybe more than 30,000 pounds each—400 separate points along the fuselages had to be reinforced so the air frame could take the strain.

Last of all, his instructions were to paint over all lettering and emblems on the airplanes. When the job was complete, no one would know that these F-14s were once known as VF-201, VF-297 and VF-333 . . .

The chief knew better than to ask questions as to what it was all about. And the changes that were needed on each airplane weren't all that unusual. In fact, most of these things the chief had been asked to do before.

Except for the new cockpit guts and the order to paint over the US insignia and all references to the US Navy. Those were new ones on him.

PART 2

War Heaven

20

It was exactly midnight . . .

The C-130 Hercules roared down the runway and took off into the ink-black sky. The specially installed jet thrusters on either side of its fuselage kicked in and rocketed the big airplane into a steep and noisy climb.

It was the last place Ryder wanted to be. He was still drunk, the result of yet another marathon booze-up session at the OC. His spirits had been high—according to plan, he and Woody were to receive the Top Gun trophy at class graduation the next day, a "Navy-eats-crow" ceremony he was looking forward to.

But he, Woody, Lancaster, and Sammett had hardly made it back to the barracks when a Navy captain arrived and told them they were moving out. Each was given a set of US Marine Corps fatigues, a pair of paratrooper boots, and a jump helmet. They were told to get ready in a hurry. Within ten minutes they were transported to a dull-black camouflaged C-130 waiting on the isolated admin runway at the far end of the base. Its engines were already turning when they arrived.

A single dim light was burning inside the hold when the four pilots climbed aboard. Inside they found Reinhart, Chauvagne, and a very unhappy-looking Commander Slade. Oddly, no one from the C-130's flight crew was on hand. A single cargo pallet, covered by a black tarp and bound with heavy rope, sat in the middle of the hold.

As soon as they were all aboard, the door had closed automatically behind them and the C-130 started to move. They had immediately strapped into the row of canvas jump seats that ran along the wall of the plane and held on tight for

137

the typically rough jet-assisted take-off.

Ryder was the first to notice that all the windows in the cargo compartment were blackened over.

"I don't like the looks of this," he whispered to Woody who was sitting on his left, pointing out the opaque windows.

"I guess they don't want us to know where they are taking us," Woody answered, noting the door to the pilot's compartment was also locked.

Ryder looked down at Slade who was sitting at the end of the row. He looked like his dog had just been run over.

The plane continued its steep, noisy climb for a full minute. Finally the jet-assists kicked out and the plane leveled off.

"Hey, Slade, where the *hell* we going?" Ryder yelled to the Navy officer over the roar of the big plane's engines.

Slade didn't even turn his head. "I have no frigging idea!" he yelled back. "Just shut up and enjoy the ride."

"Man, is he hot . . ." Woody said. Even in the dim light of the plane's hold they could see Slade's trademark forehead vein bulging.

"We're really up there," Lancaster said to Ryder as they heard the hissing of the compartment's air pressurization system snap on. "At that rate of climb, we're probably up to 35,000 already."

Ryder nodded. It was highly unusual for a C-130 to fly that high. But by this time, he was taking everything that was "highly unusual" about this operation to be the norm.

Ryder tried to guess their direction. He could feel the C-130 bucking a slight head wind. That could indicate they were flying west, meaning the Hercules was out over the Pacific.

But then, as if the pilot had read his mind, the C-130 dipped into a left-hand bank and held there.

"We're circling," he said to Woody.

"Yeah, I can feel it," the Wiz replied. "Wide out, too."

The ride got more turbulent as the Hercules continued to arc. Then the big plane leveled off and flew straight again. Ten minutes later, it went into another circle. Then it leveled off again. After a while, Ryder knew it was useless trying to figure out what the hell was going on.

He looked down the row of pilots, their features distorted slightly in the low-power red light. Slade was sitting still, his eyes straight ahead—Ryder imagined he could see steam coming out of the man's ears. Obviously this midnight express was a surprise to him too.

Next to him was Sammett, head bowed, softly murmuring something, probably his prayers. Beside him was Chauvagne, eyes closed, head back—it appeared that the Frenchman was fast asleep.

Next to Chauvagne was Reinhart, sitting ramrod straight, jaw locked, fists clenched, his eyes flashing back and forth. He knew the mysterious flight was just killing the German. For someone who was obsessed with being in control at all times, a trip to nowhere was an all-out assault on his Prussian psyche. The man looked terrified.

Serves you right, you fucking Nazi, Ryder thought with a bourbon-induced smile.

Directly to his left, Lancaster was taking the ride as well as could be expected. "Nothing they do surprises me anymore," the Englishman said several times in full Cockney. "Of course, I'm still half cut. Maybe this isn't happening."

Ryder laughed again. He knew being drunk this high could have its ill effects, but he was beyond caring at this point.

The military had him—and all of them—by the balls. They were puppets, knotted up in the twisted strings of some generals and admirals somewhere. He knew it was the price he had to pay . . .

All I want to do is fly . . .

They continued the bizarre flight pattern for more than two hours. Circling. Flying level. Circling again. For most of the time the five men sat without talking. Ryder had long since given up trying to calculate where they were going. He was concentrating on keeping the contents of his stomach—at least a dozen drinks and a few bowlfuls of pretzels—inside him where they belonged.

Another hour went by. Ryder could feel the plane's frequent

arcs were getting bigger. The air was a little rougher. Could be heading south, he thought.

Another ninety minutes passed. The plane came out of a circle and leveled off, this time slowing its airspeed. Ryder heard the distant whine of another plane's engines. He could feel the pilot's maneuvering the C-130 back and forth, up and down. Then he felt a slight jolt from the front of the plane. It could only mean one thing: They were refueling in flight.

He turned to tell Woody, but his partner had either nodded off or passed out. The Wood Man had been fueling up with gin and tonics and that was a bad combination at 35,000 feet. Ryder looked around and saw that Reinhart and Slade were wide awake.

The C-130 flew straight and level for a few minutes, then the sound of the other airplane's engines started to fade. Minutes later the Hercules began its circling motion again.

"Screw it," Ryder thought, taking off his helmet and closing his eyes. It was probably four in the morning by this time. He knew he'd never be able to figure it all out—he hadn't figured out a single thing since the whole crazy trip began months ago. So why bother? He put his head back and eventually dropped off to sleep.

The next thing he knew, Woody was shaking him awake.

"Up, Ghost," his partner was saying. "We're landing . . ."

Ryder was wide awake in two seconds. The others were also up and alert, fastening on their helmets and tightening their seat belts. The C-130 was descending—sharply. The scream of the engines filled the compartment as the big plane spiraled downward. The equipment pallet started shaking violently. They could hear the Hercules' fuselage creaking under the strain. Veteran pilots though they were, the quick drop alarmed them.

"What the hell is going on, Commander Slade?" Reinhart finally yelled out, his face as pale as a ghost.

"Shut up, Reinhart!" the Navy officer yelled back. "Just stay buttoned in . . ."

Still the C-130 plunged, the whole plane bucking and snapping with frightening regularity. Sammett was now praying openly and loudly. Even Chauvagne looked slightly ruffled.

"They're grotty," Lancaster said. "God, did they put us through all this just to kill us?"

Ryder tried to stay calm. If it wasn't for the racket of the plane's four big engines, he would have been convinced they were crashing.

Suddenly, with a shriek of its engines, the C-130 pulled up. Its airspeed dropped in a jolt. Ryder knew the pilot had just engaged the plane's airbrakes. Seconds later, the familiar clang of the landing gear being lowered echoed in the compartment.

But despite the din, Ryder's acutely sensitive hearing picked up another sound. This one was coming from outside the plane, probably on the ground near their intended landing spot. It was an odd noise—a methodical thumping sound.

A chill went through him. The sound was somewhat familiar. Is that . . . *gunfire?* he thought.

The next thing he knew he was slammed against the wall of the plane. The C-130 had touched down and bounced. The engines were now crying as if in pain. The big plane hit again—this time even harder.

"What the hell are they doing!" Ryder yelled to Woody over the racket. Still, above it all, he could hear the regular *thump, thump, thump.*

Finally the Hercules hit a third time and stayed down. They could hear the pilot screech on the brakes, the big cargo plane fishtailing as he did so. The combined noise was ear-splitting.

Suddenly, the C-130's big rear door began to open, although the plane was still rolling. The pallet's rollers were unhooked automatically and off it went, landing hard on what Ryder could now see was a very dusty runway.

Slade was up and out of his harness.

"Let's go!" he yelled. "Unhook and get out . . . now!"

In an instant the six men were up and out of their restraints. The C-130 had slowed to a halt, but Ryder could tell the pilot was not going to stop the plane completely for very long. The engines were going full blast, kicking up a whirlwind of dust. Off in the distance the thumping sound was joined by a

141

frightening, familiar cracking noise. It was small arms fire.

No doubt about it, Ryder thought as he moved toward the open cargo bay. Mortars and rifles. They were definitely being shot at.

"Stay down!" Slade yelled as he reached the open door. Suddenly he was out and running on the runway. Sammett went next, followed closely by Woody. Chauvagne stopped only long enough to adjust his helmet strap, then he too plunged down the ramp.

Reinhart was next, but he hesitated. He could see explosions going off at the far end of the runway, as well as clumps of sand being thrown up by gunfire.

The German started to say, "I refuse to go!" But he was interrupted by a hard shove from Lancaster. Both of them spilled down the cargo ramp and onto the runway.

Ryder was the last to go. He ran down the ramp in a crouch and reached Lancaster and Reinhart, who were trying to disengage themselves from a sprawl.

Ryder lifted Reinhart up and pushed him toward a grove of trees that he spotted on the far side of the runway. The others were already running toward the potential hiding place, the dust being kicked up by the C-130's propellers giving them some cover.

Ryder then helped Lancaster to his feet and they both ran quickly toward the trees.

Although there was mass confusion all around him, Ryder nevertheless was able to take in his surroundings. They were on a small landing strip in the center of a valley. Mountains surrounded them on all sides. But the place was anything but peaceful—mortar rounds were going off at both ends of the runway, and bullets were flying every which way above their heads.

He took a quick look over his shoulder toward the field on the other side of the runway. There he could see the distinct muzzle flashes of the guns firing at them. Farther beyond he saw the long looping arcs of the mortar shells.

He had no idea where they were—the valley had a slight desert look to it and the air was hot and stale, yet the field was somewhat lush with tall, green weeds. He also had no idea who was firing at them. Surely they were not in the United States, he thought. His closest guess was El Salvador? Or even *Nicaragua?*

He and Lancaster reached the grove and jumped into a ditch that surrounded it. Slade, Sammett and Reinhart were all huddled together at one end, hands over their heads. Woody and Chauvagne were at the other. He and Lancaster joined them.

Despite the incoming hostile fire, Ryder couldn't help but look around the small airfield. There were three small buildings about a hundred yards from their position and a smaller shack beside them. A wind-sock and pole stood alone about twenty feet from the shack, then a barracks-style building was located fifty feet beyond that. It looked like something out of a 1930s Captain Midnight episode.

In the meantime, the C-130 was turning around, its engines screaming, the small dust storm still being kicked up behind it. They heard the pilot gun the engines and begin his take-off roll.

Jesus Christ, Ryder thought. The fuckers are leaving us here . . .''

Suddenly Reinhart jumped up and started to crawl out of the ditch.

"Come back!" he screamed at the departing C-130. "Come back, you sons of bitches!"

Chauvagne was just able to grab the German's leg before he made it out of the ditch.

"Get back here, Kraut!" the Frenchman yelled as he dragged Reinhart back into the ditch.

A particularly loud volley of gunfire whizzed over their heads. About a dozen mortar shells landed out on the runway in quick succession. There was dust and smoke and pandemonium everywhere.

The C-130 roared down the dirt runway and lifted off. It gained altitude, swung up and around and flew right over them. Ryder saw the pilot wag the wings ever so slightly.

"You motherfuckers!" he screamed as he watched the C-130 turn south and disappear over the horizon.

*   *   *

High above the airfield, beyond the sight of those on the ground, an E-2C Hawkeye slowly circled.

Inside, the Air Force general and the admiral were sifting through a ream of computer printouts. Suddenly the on-board intercom crackled. It was one of the Hawkeye's pilots.

"Message, General," the pilot said. "Punch in channel two, then hit the 'Scramble' button . . ."

The general did as instructed. He heard five seconds of static then a voice came on the other end.

"They are on the ground, sir," the voice said. "Apparently, everyone made it."

"Thank you," the general replied.

21

The shooting stopped after twenty minutes . . .

A few mortar rounds crashed down at the far end of the landing strip, scattering another cloud of dust. But suddenly the mortars stopped too.

Then, there was silence.

"Don't you have a goddamn gun, Slade," Reinhart yelled down the ditch to the Navy officer.

Slade ignored the German. He was too busy keeping his eye on the field. He was fully expecting a rush from the enemy hiding in the tall weeds. Obviously, someone fucked up big time here, he thought.

"Look, Slade," Reinhart snapped, his voice rising in alarm. "They will attack us soon. There must be a hundred of them . . ."

"If there *are* a hundred of them, what the hell do you want a gun for?" Lancaster yelled, lifting his head to look out on the field where the gunfire had come from.

"To blow his own brains out like any good German," Chauvagne added.

Reinhart's face went red with anger. "It's more honorable than surrendering, like any good Frenchman!" he screamed.

"All of you, shut the hell up!" Slade yelled above the shouting.

Ryder was ignoring the argument. His senses were tingling. Something was wrong here. He could *feel* it in his bones.

He moved over beside Woody. "Hey, partner," he said in a whisper. "This is kind of funny here."

"You mean the fact that we are about to be killed?" Woody said, delivering the line like any good straightman.

"No," Ryder said. "I mean that gunfire has stopped *too* quickly."

"You lost me, Ghost," Woody said, strapping down his helmet a little tighter.

Ryder began again. "What I'm saying is, if there were a hundred bad guys hidden over there, it's kind of unlikely they would all stop firing at once, even on command."

"Well, maybe they're efficient commies," Woody replied.

Ryder continued. "Plus, with all the racket, not a single bullet came anywhere near us."

It was the same with the mortar fire. Although barrage after barrage had come crashing down, no shell landed closer than a hundred yards of them. Were these unseen enemy soldiers such bad shots?

"Long," Slade suddenly yelled from the other end of the ditch. "You got the Ted Williams eyesight. What do you see out there?"

Ryder popped his head up. The field was completely still. He carefully scanned it left to right. If there were soldiers out there, they were experts at playing possum.

"It beats me, Slade," Ryder said, keeping his eye on the field. "They may have withdrawn. Maybe they got tunnels or something. But nothing's moving out there now."

They waited in silence for another five minutes. Still nothing happened.

Slade finally eased himself up, looked around, then said,

"OK, Long, Woods, Lancaster, and me are going to crawl over to those hangars. If we can get in, we'll have better cover . . ."

"You're *leaving* us here?" Reinhart started to protest.

"That's right," Slade shot back at him. "Stay down and don't make a move until I tell you to."

"If you abandon us now, Slade, you will be deserting your post!" Reinhart yelled. "If we get out of this, I'll see to it that you are court-martialed!"

Slade looked him straight in the eye and laughed.

"Now, the rest of you stay low," Slade said. "Long, Woods, Lancaster—let's go . . ."

The four men ran in a slow crouch toward the hangars. No one fired at them. They reached the buildings and pressed themselves up against the wall for cover.

"OK, Long," Slade said. "You stay here. Me, Woods, and Lancaster will check out the other one." With that, the three men moved away.

Ryder was alone with his thoughts for the first time since the rather bizarre landing. Just what the hell *was* going on here? he asked himself. Where were they? Central America? Why were they here? They had been warned that they would be put through some very strange roll-outs in the course of their training. Was this just another one?

He kept his eyes glued to the field in front of him. Still nothing moved. The sun was climbing in the sky. It was getting hot—tropics kind of hot.

The questions continued. Were they actually supposed to land in a secured area? Did something get screwed up? Maybe a C-130 filled with Marines would come bouncing in at any minute. Or maybe their drop-off pilot would call in an air strike? Or maybe they would soon be massacred. Did Slade *really* know what was going on?

"Long!" Slade's call interrupted his thoughts.

He looked up to see the Navy commander motioning him toward the second hangar. He crouch-ran to the building and found Lancaster in the process of picking the old lock that held the door together, using his nailfile as a tool.

"This place looks like it hasn't been open in years," Woody

said, quickly surveying the rundown structure.

Ryder looked the building over. Its architecture looked like bad Mexican, circa 1930. The building was constructed out of corrugated tin. Scraps of old posters—some in English, some in Spanish—were plastered on the doors. An ancient Coca-Cola ad—its paint worn and peeling—dominated its northern side. A nest full of extra-large-sized hornets guarded its southern corner.

"How about it, Lancaster," Slade asked the Englishman. "We in or what?"

"This is most unusual," Lancaster said. "This place is a bloody antique and yet the lock is strong enough to hold the Queen's jewels."

"Well, shit, man, get on with it, will you?" Slade said, nervously eyeing the field. "Whoever's out there got to be watching us."

"Are you sure about that, Slade?" Ryder asked him suddenly.

"What the hell's *that* supposed to mean, Ryder?"

"You know what the hell I mean," Ryder said. "I think you've been in on this game from the beginning. What the hell *is* going on here? A loyalty test?"

"How the hell would I know?" Slade said heatedly. "I'm just as much in the dark as you are!"

Ryder looked at him. The man seemed to be genuinely concerned. Was he telling the truth? Was he in the dark? Or was he just a very talented liar?

The minor confrontation was cut short as Lancaster finally popped the lock. "Success!" he said with the slap of his hands.

The four of them grabbed the rolling-type door and pulled at once. Ryder found it to be surprisingly heavy and difficult to move. They finally managed to roll it back only to get a cruel surprise.

"There's another fucking door!" Woody cried out.

Sure enough, there was a heavy steel door hidden behind the tin.

Before Ryder could answer, he heard yet another sound.

"Another airplane coming!" he said.

147

They all looked to the southeast, just in time to see another C-130—this one painted all green—lumber over the airstrip and turn out over the field. The airplane's landing gear was down.

"Jesus, they're going to land!" Woody said. "Maybe it's the cavalry!"

"This place is getting very busy all of a sudden," Ryder said.

Suddenly, they heard the gunfire start up again. It was at full intensity in a matter of two seconds.

"Here we go again!" Slade said, ducking beside the building for cover.

Ryder then heard the telltale noise of mortar shells being launched. He counted to three and then saw a barrage of six shells explode at the far end of the runway.

By this time, the C-130 had turned and was coming in, its pilot jigging and jagging to avoid the groundfire. He had to make a last-minute maneuver to avoid hitting the equipment pallet dropped off by their C-130, then bounced twice before settling down on the landing strip. All the while the air was filled with whizzing bullets and the sound of the mortar shells exploding.

The C-130 screeched to a halt and its cargo door flipped down. Suddenly a group of men—Ryder estimated their number at about two dozen—ran out and instinctively sought the cover of the tree grove.

"Who the hell can these guys be?" Slade asked.

"They ain't Marines . . ." Woody said, noting their distinct lack of weapons.

"Well, they're getting the same welcome reception as we did," Ryder said. "So I'd guess they're on our side."

By this time, Reinhart, Sammett, and Chauvagne had joined them at the hangar.

Suddenly, Ryder heard yet another sound in the din of battle.

"Artillery!" he yelled.

His eyes caught sight of four puffs of smoke coming from the mountain to the west. Seconds later, four shells went screaming over their heads, landing some two hundred feet

148

beyond the hangar with four, earthshaking crashes.

"Those are high-powered shells!" Slade said, covering his ears as the explosions rocked the ground around the hangar.

"Whoever they are, we've got to get those guys in here!" Ryder yelled to Slade, pointing to the two dozen soldiers now occupying the tree grove.

Without a second's hesitation, Ryder was running at top speed back toward the tree grove. Mortar shells were still crashing at either end of the runway, and a rain of bullets was flying over his head. Out of the corner of his eye, he saw four more puffs of smoke on the side of the distant mountain. Immediately four more artillery shells crashed down in back of the hangar, almost exactly where the previous rounds had landed.

Ryder reached the grove, startling the twenty-four men seeking refuge there. All of them were wearing the same kind of Marine Corps fatigues that he and the other pilots were wearing.

He immediately spotted a young, kid-faced guy who seemed like the group's commanding officer and duckwalked over to him.

"Who the hell are you?" the officer asked him.

"I should ask you the same question . . ." Ryder said, as they both instinctively ducked at the sound of a mortar explosion out on the runway.

"We're the 1245th Specialized Aircraft Maintenance Group . . ." the officer shouted over the noise. "I'm Lieutenant Moon . . ."

"Air Force?" Ryder asked. "From where?"

"That's . . . classified!" the captain said.

Despite the dangerous confusion all around him, Ryder had to smile.

"Well, *I'm* 'classified' too, sir!" Ryder said, shaking the man's hand. "Captain Ryder Long. They just dropped me and seven others into this hell soup ten minutes before you arrived. Believe it or not, we're right out of Top Gun . . ."

"Top Gun?" Moon said, looking at him quizzically. "I thought Top Gun was strictly Navy . . ."

149

Ryder smiled again and said, "It's a long story . . ."

Just then Moon's C-130 roared away.

"*Jeesuz!*" Moon yelled, as he watched the C-130 climb into the sky. "There goes our ticket out of here!"

Four more artillery shells screamed overhead.

"Who the hell is doing all this shooting, sir?" Moon asked Ryder.

"Your guess is as good as mine, Lieutenant!" Ryder said, ducking as another shell exploded nearby.

"Well, as soon as those guys on that mountain get their range finder working, they'll chew us up alive . . ." Moon yelled, looking up and down the trench at his men.

"We got some better cover over there," Ryder said, pointing toward the steel-line hangar.

"Lead the way, sir!" Moon told him, yelling, "OK, guys, let's make for that building. Two at a time. Go! *Go!*"

It took less than a minute for the entire group to make it to the side of the first hangar.

Ryder quickly introduced Moon to Woody, Slade, and the rest. The side of the hangar was now the scene of some confusion itself. The pilots and the members of the 1245th were pressed up against the steel wall, covering their ears from the racket.

"We were dropped in here without warning, just like you," Moon was telling Slade. "We've been training for some kind of highly classified mission for about four months. Then, they wake us up in the middle of the night, throw us on the Herc, and here we are . . . wherever the hell 'here' is."

Suddenly, all the shooting stopped once again. Just like before, the cease-fire was instantaneous.

"Oh, God, they'll probably come right at us now," Moon said.

"Don't be too sure," Ryder told him. "We've been through this before."

That's when Ryder decided to test a theory.

"The hell with this," he said. While the others watched in astonishment, Ryder calmly started walking toward the runway.

150

"Hey, Ghost!" Woody yelled to him. "No time for a stroll . . ."

Slade was more emphatic.

"Long, get your ass back here," he shouted. But Ryder kept on walking.

Something was wrong here, Ryder could feel it. With all the artillery fired, mortar rounds and bullets whizzing about, nothing so much as a BB had come anywhere near the pilots, the C-130s, or the members of the 1245th. Even blind men could shoot better than that.

His theory was a dangerous one: that whoever was shooting at them were deliberately missing them.

Now he would have to put the theory to the test . . .

He walked out onto the runway and stopped. It was deathly quiet, only a warm breeze rustling the tall grass in the field.

He walked to the far edge of the landing strip to the border of the field. Still nothing happened.

He took a deep breath and then stepped right into the field. If anyone was going to blow his head off, this would be it. He gritted his teeth and waited.

Nothing happened . . .

After counting to ten, he walked into the field. Cautiously he made his way through the thin, high grass. He stopped to pull a strand and examine it, hoping it would give a clue as to where the hell he was. It didn't. The brownish-green color looked tropical to him, but botany wasn't one of his strong suits.

He walked twenty steps farther before a glint of metal caught his eye. He froze. It was about ten feet off to his right, near a mound of dirt. The slight reflection looked too much like it was coming from a gun barrel. He crossed his fingers, hoping his theory would hold true.

Slowly, he moved toward the mound. He could see a slight wisp of smoke rising above it, adding more evidence that a gun was sticking out of the small earth works. He took a deep breath and came within three feet of it.

He peered through the grass . . .

It *was* a gun. An M-16, to be exact. Complete with a laser-sighting device attached to its snout and what looked like some

151

kind of miniature radar range finder hooked into its stock. The rifle's magazine was missing and in its stead was a belt of ammunition and an automatic feeder. The entire gun was resting on a small swivel tripod, similar to what a photographer might use in the wild.

Behind the gun ran a tangle of wires which led to a black box that was partially buried into the side of the mound. What looked like an automobile battery was buried next to the black box. Beside it, was a third box, this one painted gray and supporting a small radio antenna.

Ryder couldn't help but laugh out loud. The setup was both insidious and ingenious. He was sure all the guns that had fired at them from the field looked just as this one did. Wires, bullets, range finders, battery, and a radio antenna. Each round had been directed by a laser beam, using the mini-radar to swivel the gun and indicate its target. The continuous firing commands were undoubtedly sent via shortwave radio.

No wonder no one was hit—it was never intended that anyone should be. He had been right: the guns had been fired by experts.

But no human fingers pulled the triggers. The guns were actually fired by robots . . .

He walked back to the edge of the field and out onto the landing strip. Woody and Slade had dared to walk as far as the center of the runway. The others were sticking close to the hangar.

"Long, you are one crazy-ass fool!" Slade told him when they met in the middle of the runway.

"Very brave, Ghost," Woody said with a smile.

"Robots . . ." Ryder said, holding up the black box he had kicked out of the mound. "We've just been witness to the most elaborate shooting gallery I'd guess was ever built."

He quickly explained to them what he had found in the field and how he felt the automatic barrage had managed to miss them all.

"The mortars? The artillery too?" Slade asked.

Ryder nodded. "The mortars, yeah. Artillery, who knows? But those rifles out in the field are all programmed to hit

152

predesignated targets in areas close enough to rattle us, but far enough away so we wouldn't get even a flesh wound."

Woody was bewildered by it all. "But who set all this up?" he asked.

"Believe me, partner," Ryder told him, "Everything I saw was made in the USA. I'm positive of it."

He turned to Slade. "Any ideas, Commander?"

Slade shifted uneasily. "How the hell do I know?" he said for what seemed like the millionth time. But deep down, he had his suspicions.

"One thing's for sure," Woody said. "We've been set up . . ."

"We *sure* have," Ryder said confidently. "And we fell for it like a bunch of rubes."

"Well, I'd say we're one step ahead of them," Ryder continued confidently. "We now know that anything they send at us will just be fireworks. Pop-guns. A lot of smoke and flash powder. This has got to be part of some kind of very elaborate battlefield simulator. And they're trying to psych us out of our pants."

Just then he heard a low, dull rumbling noise.

"Jeesuz," Woody said, looking around for the source of the noise. *"Now* what?"

Slade saw them first. "Look!" he cried out, pointing toward the east.

Ryder whirled around to see two dark specks heading toward them, each one only two hundred feet off the deck and trailing a plume of dark smoke behind it.

"Christ, are those F-5s?" Slade yelled out.

"They are," Ryder said, focusing in on the approaching jets. "Aggressors, maybe . . ."

"Aggressors?" Slade said, not quite knowing what to do. "What the hell are the Aggressors doing here?"

"You mean, wherever 'here' is . . ." Woody said.

The two jets were now only a mile away and coming fast.

"Let's take cover . . ." Slade said, turning toward the hangar.

"What *for?*" Ryder asked, never taking his eyes off the

fighters. "Didn't hear me? This is all a joke. It's a gag—another training exercise. These guys are just here to spook us . . ."

Slade and Woody weren't listening. They were too busy running toward the hangar.

Ryder waved them off and turned back toward the approaching jets. Both F-5s were now just fifty feet off the deck and bearing down on him as he stood in the middle of the runway. What's the worst thing they can do to me? he thought as the fighters screamed in on him. That's when he noticed both airplanes were completely painted in black . . .

"Fuck you guys," he said defiantly, determined not to move an inch from his spot. "You're not gonna rattle me . . ."

That's when he saw both planes drop a silver canister. Each one split just twenty feet in front of him, instantly releasing a white cloud of smoke.

He didn't even have time to put his hand to his nose.

His throat was instantly aflame. His nostrils burned and started bleeding. His eyes stung so badly his vision got cloudy, then quit altogether. If he had had anything in his stomach, it would have been all over him by this time.

The next thing he knew he was flat on his back, looking up as the two F-5s passed over him. He felt their hot jet wash. The runway beneath him shook with the ear-splitting screech of fighters' engines.

"Fuckers just gassed me . . ." he thought.

He tried to roll off the runway and out of the cloud of gas, but he quickly discovered that he couldn't move.

The last thing he remembered was seeing the two jets wag their wings as they streaked off to the west . . .

22

It was dusk before Ryder woke up . . .

At first he had no idea where he was. His head was spinning dizzily, his temples throbbing with pain. His eyes were watering and his throat and nostrils felt scorched. An enormous bruise on his back hurt from where he hit the runway.

With a major effort, he opened his eyes to see Woody standing over him.

"Jeesuz! . . . *what happened to me?*" he said, just barely above a whisper.

"You were gassed, partner," Woody said, dipping into a slight bow. "Gassed by your friends, the Aggressors. You have been out for hours . . ."

It all came rushing back to him. The robot guns. The black F-5 Aggressors. The exploding gas canisters . . .

"We were starting to get worried about you," Woody said, coming down into a crouch beside him and handing him a canteen. "You took a mugfull of knock-out gas."

Painfully, Ryder managed to turn his head. He was propped up against the first hangar. His fatigues were ripped and torn in several places, and he could feel blood oozing from a small cut on the back of his head.

"Who else got hit?" Ryder asked, taking a greedy swig from the canteen.

"I got a snoot," Woody told him. "Lancaster, Slade. We ran to drag you off the runway. The rest were able to cover up and get away."

Ryder tried to get to his feet, and failed miserably. His head went into a 9 *g* tailspin before he got to one knee.

"Hey, Ghost, take it easy," Woody said, helping him back down. "You took enough of that snuff to knock out a battalion. You've got to stay horizontal for a while."

Just then, Slade appeared over him. "Still with us, Captain?" he asked.

Ryder gamely nodded, wiping the gas-induced tears from his

eyes. "You didn't bring a six-pack with you, did you, Slade?" he asked. "My throat's kind of dry . . ."

"Well, there just might be a six-pack out there, somewhere . . ." the Navy officer said.

With great effort, he was able to turn his head. To his surprise he saw the runway was now covered with supply pallets similar to the one that had dropped out of their C-130.

"Jeesuz!" Ryder said. "Where'd all *that* come from?"

"You've been missing quite a party," Slade told him.

Just then, they heard the unmistakable noise of an airplane approaching. Ryder managed to lift up his head long enough to see a C-130 appear out of the dusk, its nose, wings, and tail illuminated by a variety of navigation lights.

The Hercules dipped low over the base and roared in, barely twenty feet above the airstrip. Suddenly a parachute appeared from the plane's rear and a large pallet flew out, landing on the runway with a loud thud. The C-130 pulled up, circled the base, then disappeared to the south.

"Wow . . ." was all Ryder managed to say.

"They've been dropping stuff like that every ten minutes for the past five hours," Woody said.

It was all too weird, dreamlike. Ryder still tried to get his bearings, reorientate himself with the surroundings. Above him the stars were out. He could hear much activity going on at the front of the hangar. The mechanics from the second C-130 were busily going in and out of the place.

"You got the hangar door open . . ." Ryder said to Woody.

"That we did," his partner replied. "A few hours ago."

"Anything of worth inside?" Ryder asked, finally steadying himself against the building.

Both he and Slade laughed.

"I guess you could say that . . ." Woody said.

Ryder's brain still felt like it was swimming. He *felt different*.

"We've got a couple surprises for you, Captain," Slade said with a sly smile. "In fact, there's someone here I think you've met before."

"What the hell you talking about, Slade?" Ryder asked, trying and failing once again to prop himself up on his elbow.

156

Suddenly he was staring up at a familiar face. His vision was still fuzzy but he could see it was a young man, dressed in Army fatigues, helmet firmly strapped on. The man looked very familiar, but Ryder couldn't quite place the face.

That's when he saw the soldier was wearing a blue scarf around his neck . . .

"Simons . . ." Ryder gasped. "Bo Simons . . ."

"Hello, Captain," the man said calmly. "How you feeling?"

Ryder felt a jolt of excitement run through him. "Hey, Woody, *this* is the guy in the desert. The guy that . . ."

Woody held up his hand and said, "We know all about it, Ghost . . ."

"That's just one of the few surprises we've got for you, Long," Slade told him. "Do you think you can get to your feet?"

Ryder tried to shake the cobwebs from his head. "Yeah, I'll give it a try . . ." he said.

Woody, Slade, and Simons all helped him to his feet. Things were coming back to him, albeit *very* slowly.

When he was finally able to stand on his own, he managed a painful stretch.

He took another look around. The sleepy airstrip was now a bustling mini-base. The mechanics were busily unstrapping equipment from the air-drop pallets and hauling the booty off the runway. Portable lights were burning away at various points around the area. A small radar station was operational, its diminutive dish spinning rapidly. A larger satellite communications station was being assembled nearby. He even saw what looked to be a portable mess tent had been set up.

"This is all crazy," he said to them. *"Where the hell are we?"*

The three men looked at each other. Finally it was Woody who spoke. "We're in heaven, Ghost," he said. *"War Heaven . . ."*

Slade saw his reaction and said, "The best is yet to come, Captain . . ."

They guided him around to the front of the hangar. He was still woozy—his head clouded in disbelief that the Aggressors had actually gassed them and that so much had changed on the

157

ground since he received the airborne Mickey Finn.

After this, he thought, nothing could surprise him.

That's when he looked into the hangar.

"Christ Almighty!" he blurted out. "How the hell did *they* get here?"

Inside the old, dilapidated hangar sat three beautiful, unmarked F-14s . . .

"There they go again!" someone yelled.

Ryder turned away from the F-14s to see members of the 1245th pointing up to the sky. He looked up and saw what they were so excited about.

High above him he saw four jet fighters heading north. At least two of them were F-5s—he could tell by the tone of their engine noise and their navigation light arrangements. Then he saw three groups of lights coming out of the west. They were white and amber and moving much slower.

"What's going on?" Ryder asked.

"Just watch . . ." Woody told him.

The two sets of aircraft were about three miles apart when the fighters started gyrating in all directions. Suddenly Ryder saw a beam of light flash out from one of the F-5s and impact on the side of the approaching aircraft. In an instant a sharp, loud crack was heard. The "explosion" was so bright he was able to see that second set of aircraft were actually B-1s . . .

Within seconds the sky was filled with flashes of light streaking back and forth between the aircraft. By this time everyone at the base had stopped whatever they were doing and were watching the fantastic aerial display.

"This is better than the best fireworks display . . ." Woody said.

"Biggest goddamn video game ever!" Slade shouted with unheard-of enthusiasm.

Ryder was speechless.

"Simons!" he finally managed to say. "This is . . ."

Once again he was stopped in mid-sentence. "I know, Captain," the young Airborne officer said to him. "This is what you saw that night."

158

Ryder felt a burst of anger well up inside him. His target was Slade. "So much for peyote trips in the desert, Slade!"

"Sorry, Captain," the Navy officer said to him, never taking his eyes off the incredible special effects air battle going on above them.

"*You knew?*" Ryder asked angrily.

Slade turned and looked him straight in the eye. "Yeah, I knew . . . I was told, but not until afterwards," the Navy officer told him. "But you got to remember: what you saw out there that night was more classified than the President's ICBM go-codes. That's why the Airborne guys had to get you out of there and we had to go with the 'he-was-doing-drugs' cover story."

Slade then quickly told him about the briefing he'd attended on the holograhpic battle simulators.

Ryder looked back up at the dogfight and shook his head in disbelief. The air battle—the lights, the missile trails, the lifelike explosions and associated noise—defied description, other than looking like an incredible living cartoon . . .

"Out of this world, isn't it, Ghost?" Woody said to him, the Wiz following every movement of the dogfight. "Only could the people who brought you the most spectacular amusement parks in the world could pull this off . . ."

"It cost more than a billion dollars," Slade said with a sigh. "The most secret undertaking since the boys at the Manhattan Project built the bomb."

Suddenly the air battle was over. The B-1s turned and streaked off to the east; the F-5s retreated to the south.

"OK, show's over!" Ryder heard someone yell nearby. It was Lieutenant Moon, leader of the 1245th. Instantly, the mechanics went back to unpacking the pallet gear.

Ryder pulled Woody aside. "Hey, partner," he said under his breath. "I need some straight shooting. What the hell is going on here?"

Woody smiled. "Sorry, Ghost," he said. "This must be quite a rush for you . . ."

Ryder nodded, massaging his sore neck. "To say the least . . ."

"Let's get some chow and I'll try to fill in some of the

159

blanks," Woody said.

Ten minutes later, Ryder was looking at a plastic camouflage plate full of food.

"Is this steak?" he asked Woody as they took their places at one of the dozen cafeterialike tables.

"Sirloin," the Wiz told him. "Prime cut . . ."

Ryder sampled the pile of vegetables. "This stuff tastes like it's just been picked . . ."

"Everything they dropped to us was fresh," Woody said, buttering a hot roll. "Thank God, some of Moon's guys knew how to set up and use the stoves."

"We didn't eat this good at Top Gun," Ryder said, savoring a piece of sirloin.

"That's for sure," Woody answered. "Whatever is going on here, they didn't scrap on the chow. In fact, we had mesquite chicken for lunch . . ."

Ryder still felt like he was in dreamland.

"What *is* going on here, Wiz?" Ryder asked him. "Any idea at all?"

"We know a little," Woody said, methodically cutting his steak into long, thin strips.

"Well, come on," Ryder said impatiently. "Let me have it . . ."

"Well, as you know, they started dropping in supplies right after you got conked," Woody said between bites. "Simons and his CO showed up some afterwards. Bunch of them came across the field waving a white flag, if you can believe it. Their boys took out all of those robots guns, while Simons and his boss paid us a visit. They're the ones who told us we were in War Heaven. We're actually up in the north-easternmost of the range. You can't get a more restricted area than this one, partner."

"But there's nothing out here for at least a hundred miles . . ." Ryder said.

Woody smiled. "According to Simons and his CO, that's not exactly true. This place is a playground—an amusement park for soldiers. Look at the rifles you found in the field . . ."

It was true, Ryder thought. The elaborate robot-aimed guns

were frighteningly real.

"That whole show was a simulated 'opposed landing,'" Stick continued. "Including the gas attack. Of course, I don't think they expected some crazy ass to stand right in the middle of the target area."

Ryder had to laugh about it now, although his nostrils and throat still felt like someone took a blowtorch to them.

"Can you imagine anything being more authentic next to the real McCoy?" Woody asked.

Ryder shook his head between mouthfuls of the delicious meal.

"Well, this place has special effects like that all over," Woody said. "The artillery. The mortars. That video game in the sky just now. And God knows what else . . ."

"Incredible" was all Ryder could say.

"Brought to you by those wild guys at the Pentagon Psych-ops unit, and paid for by the generous taxpayers of the USA," Woody said, ladling out some mushroom gravy. "Slade said it cost a billion dollars. I think that's the low-ball estimate."

"OK, so we know *where* we are," Ryder said. "Now, do we know *why* we are here?"

Woody shrugged. "Part of the training," he said. "Simons' OC told Slade that this is where the military has been training for secret ops for years. Started back when they tried to rescue the Iranian hostages. Remember that? The crews trained here for weeks, then they went over there and fucked it up royally. After that, the Pentagon said never again. 'We want our special forces trained in such realistic conditions that they'll feel the fire on their asses when someone shoots at them.' So, they've been working on this place ever since."

"And we're here to train for Distant Thunder?" Ryder asked.

"Your guess is as good as mine," Woody said, finishing the last of his steak. "Just because they've plopped us down in this place, they've haven't been exactly running at the mouth talking about what comes next . . ."

Ryder thought for a moment, then said, "Those 'Cats, in the hangar. I didn't get a chance to look them over . . ."

"They're beautiful, Ghost," Woody said, his face brightening. "They've been reworked to the Max. New engines. Armor plating underneath. New in-flight fuel systems. And, they're carrying those holographic-imager guns. 'Zoot-shooters' is what Simons said they call them."

"What about Simons?" Ryder asked. "Where does he fit in?"

Woody shrugged again. "Beats me," he said. "He ain't talking much. He's with a regiment of Airborne guys, been operating over here for months. However, he did tell me he's part of the 15th Special Forces Group."

"So they weren't wiped out entirely as a unit in Laos in 1962?" Ryder asked.

"Well, yes and no," Woody said, lowering his voice a little. "The 15th was reactivated, just awhile ago. But get this for a twist: Simons' old man was with the original 15th. He went down in Laos with the rest of them."

"What?" Ryder was surprised.

"Straight poop, Ghost," Woody told him. "Simons was a jabeep sergeant down in Texas somewhere, working communications when he got transferred—in the middle of the night, yet. Next thing he knew, he was training for Airborne. Then they gave him a blue scarf, made him an officer, and he's been out here ever since."

"This 'middle of the night' stuff sounds very familiar," Ryder said, finishing his meal with a roll and butter.

"Amen, brother," Woody said. "In any case, Simons and his CO are dropping by tomorrow. Giving us a briefing. Then I guess we get to work."

"Work?" Ryder said, as they got up to leave. "What kind of work?"

"What else do you think they do in War Heaven, pards?" Woody said with a grin. "Play guns . . ."

23

It was Saturday morning and the parking lot at the Pentagon was only half full.

The guard at the north gate couldn't take his eyes off the woman who had pulled up in the old, battered Volkswagen. She was beautiful . . .

"Maureen O'Brien to see the counsel general," the guard heard her say. She was flashing some kind of ID—maybe from *The Washington Post*—but the gatekeeper's eyes were zeroed in on her legs, revealed to the thigh courtesy of her innocently hiked-up skirt.

"May I go through?" she finally asked the guard.

He immediately snapped out of his stupor. "Yes, ma'am," he stammered. "Go right ahead . . ."

She pulled up as close to the massive building as possible and parked the VW. Several minutes later, she was flashing her ID to a Marine guard stationed inside the building's north lobby.

"Do you have an appointment, miss?" the courteous Marine asked. He too was taken by her outstanding beauty.

"Not exactly," Maureen told him. "But could you call up to his office and tell him his daughter is here?"

The Marine was soaking in her hour-glass shape, the smartly cut blond hair, perfect skin, beauty queen looks, and smart, attractive clothes.

He knew he could get in trouble fraternizing but he couldn't resist. "Excuse me, ma'am, but has anyone ever told you that you look just like . . . ah, what's her name now? In that rock band, she sings with her sister. One's blonde, one's brunette . . . I know all their songs by heart . . ."

Maureen smiled at him. "Yes," she said shyly. "I know who you mean. People have told me I look a little like her."

Ten minutes later, she walked into her father's massive office. He was the Pentagon's top lawyer—a military equivalent of the US attorney general. His office was a cluster of law books and mementoes from his thirty-year career.

"Hi, Counsel," she said, kissing him on the cheek. He was a tall, strapping man. She was his only daughter and even he was struck by her beauty. Since her mother died four years before, she was all he had left.

"This is a surprise, Moe," he said, as they sat on his office couch. "What's new at the paper?"

"Nothing much," she said, taking off her beret-style hat. "I think they won a couple Pulitzers last week. But nothing close to what I'm involved in."

"Honey, be patient," he said. "You've only been there for four months . . ."

She lit a cigarette and retrieved an ashtray from his desk.

"They've given me what could be a hard-core assignment, Dad," she told him. "But I'll need your help . . ."

He immediately went on guard. "What kind of help?" he asked.

"I need information on two pilots who were killed out near Las Vegas a few weeks ago," she said. "Some kind of training accident."

"Well, did you call Nellis Air Force Base?" he asked. "The Public Information Officer would have the details."

"I've already called him," she said. "Twice. He's not giving out anything other than the names and ages of the pilots."

General O'Brien frowned. He could see where the conversation was leading to. "Why is it so important?" he asked. "Does your editor think they were killed flying a Stealth jet or something?"

"No," she said. "Not that. He's just working a hunch and I can't tell you all the details. I'd just like to know a little more about the accident."

"Well, what can I do?" he asked, knowing the answer.

"There must be some kind of more detailed report on them here," she said. "I mean, the Nellis PIO won't even release the names of next of kin. That's strange, isn't it?"

He rubbed his chin. "It's *unusual,* but not unheard of."

"Could you find someone I could talk to here?" she asked, her voice softening a bit. "Or some kind of a report I can peek at?"

He shook his head. "The answer is no," he said emphatically. "I knew it would come to this someday. I still think those bastards at the *Post* only hired you because you are my daughter. They think they've got a goddamn pipeline into this place now."

She smiled. "Oh, Daddy. So what? I'm not the first person to get hired because their father was a big shot. This might be a good story, for me, for the paper."

"But suppose it's classified, Moe?" he asked, mildly irritated.

"Daddy," she said, crushing out her cigarette. "You know I wouldn't go with anything that would be damaging. To you. To anyone. I'm an Army brat. I bleed red, white, and blue. Besides, for some reason, this pilot—Ryder Long—he seems familiar to me somehow."

"Sure," he said in resignation. He was quiet for a moment. He couldn't believe that the years had slipped by so fast. It seemed like only a year ago that she was sifting through twenty-two invitations to her senior prom. Now she was working him over for classified information to print in the newspaper that was universally hated by everyone at the Pentagon.

"I'm sorry, honey, but there's not much I can do to help you," he said, standing up.

"Oh, that's OK," she said. She hugged him tightly and whispered "I love you" in his ear.

He hugged her back. He had five months to go before retirement. He had to tread lightly.

"I'll call you Monday," she said. "Maybe we can have dinner?"

He looked at her one last time and shook his head. Her mother was a beauty, but Moe was *gorgeous*. He was proud his genes had at least *something* to do with it . . .

After she had gone, he locked his door and went over to the large safe in the corner of his office. He worked the combination and opened the heavy door. Then he reached inside, fingered through a few dozen files until he found the one he wanted.

It was marked "Project Distant Thunder."

24

Ryder woke up the next morning feeling like a million bucks . . .

Although he had been knocked out for nearly ten hours, he was grateful for a good night's sleep. He had bedded down in one of four bivouac tents dropped by the C-130s and set up by Moon's men. But the sleeping quarters were hardly the old cot and steelwool blanket of the old days. Rather, each person had his own cubicle, separated from the others by opaque plastic sheeting. Each cube had a lamp and two electrical outlets. The beds consisted of a fold-out spring and a roll-up/roll-down mattress that Ryder was sure was filled with duck feathers. At the end of the large tent were ten portable sink-john-shower combinations reminiscent of toilet facilities in a Winnebago. There were even facilities to clean their uniforms, as well as an extra change of clothes for everyone.

Ryder was blown away by how elaborate everything was. And it was all quite proletarian—the pilots slept in the same sized cubes as Moon's enlisted men.

He met Woody and Lancaster in the mess tent and stuffed himself with Eggs Benedict, fresh-squeezed orange juice, and sweet rolls. They lingered over coffee until one of Moon's men appeared with the news that Simons and his commanding officer had arrived to give the pilots a "what's going on" briefing.

The three pilots walked across the small camp to the shack which was rechristened as the Operations Building. On the way they could see that Moon's men had succeeded in opening the second hangar. A quick look inside and they saw the building was filled to the roof with tools and equipment needed to keep jet aircraft running, as well as auxiliary generators, portable batteries, and a workshop. Moon's men were already working on the lock of the third hangar.

They filed into the Ops Building and found Chauvagne, Reinhart, Sammett, and Slade were already there, as was Moon and two of his sergeants. A dozen or so folding chairs had been set up for the briefing. Simons was in the process of setting up a schoolhouse-style blackboard while the CO—a tall, John Wayne lookalike named Major Maxwell—sat by calmly, smoking a huge cigar.

Once everyone was settled in, Maxwell stood up and introduced himself.

"Welcome to War Heaven, gentlemen," Major Max began. "I hope you have recovered from the shock of being dropped in here, without warning. But, as you'll find out, this military reservation is so secret, that any advance notion that you would wind up here would be dangerous to maintaining the security of this place."

He waited for the preamble to sink in, then continued. "The reason we are here, gentlemen—most of us anyway—is Project Distant Thunder. We will not get into the specifics of the operation until later on. We *are* here to train for the project. We *are* here to learn not only how to be better soldiers but also how to be self-sufficient—a crucial element to the success of Distant Thunder. The best way to understand War Heaven is to think of it as a kind of Top Gun that involves all of the aspects of ground-air attack operations. Just like at Top Gun, some of the people here are instructors; some are students. You, gentlemen—and I—are here to learn.

"I can guarantee that you will be surprised by what goes on here in War Heaven. Maybe even shocked. It is what the Pentagon likes to call 'total environment training' or what some of our people call 'deep training.' Just like at Top Gun, only two percent—a very select group of individuals from various covert military units—ever come here.

"This environment is set up in such a way that no one

person—not I or you and anyone assigned here—ever knows everything that goes on here or why. Not everything you will experience here will have a ready explanation. In fact, the place is actually run by three Cray supercomputers, each one capable of handling one half billion computations *a second*. These computers control everything except the weather. They are programmed with one idea in mind: to make War Heaven as close as possible to actual combat—that is, to make it *unpredictable*."

Maxwell relit his cigar and turned to the blackboard.

"Now," he continued, "they say you can't tell the players without a scorecard. So here's the current War Heaven line-up. Counting your unit, there are currently five groups training here. Each unit is either in training for some aspect of Distant Thunder or is serving as instructors for that training."

Maxwell wrote five words on the blackboard: "Blue," "Gray," "Green," "Aggressors," and "Spooks."

Maxwell continued. "Let me begin with my own unit, the 15th Special Forces Group, otherwise known as the Blue Army. We are a small airborne regiment, two battalions or about 1,800 men. We have a small complement of airlift, old Hueys mostly, some Cobras. So if you see any choppers flying around, you know it's probably us.

"The Gray Army is a small infantry brigade, present strength is approximately 4,000 men. They have some transport, but for the most part, they are foot soldiers. Their specialty is large unit assaults and they are damned good at it.

"The Green Army—they're all jarheads, by the way—is a reinforced mechanized regiment, presently carrying about 2,500 men. They are equipped with transport, plus M-1 tanks, APCs, mobile artillery, and howitzers. They specialize in simulating opposed launchings, so you will not be surprised to learn that your reception yesterday was courtesy of the Greens. And we were nice enough to capture all that equipment away from them."

Maxwell paused to catch a breath and light up another stogie. Everyone in the audience was totally fascinated.

"Next come the Aggressors, of which I can tell you very

168

little other than they are about a squadron and a half in strength. They drive F-5s and A-4s and are all painted black.

"The Aggressors are well named. They are drawn from the best instructor pilots from Top Gun and Red Flag. They are tough. Uncompromising. And they are *your* Number One Enemy."

There was a slight murmur from those gathered.

"Which brings us to the Spooks," Maxwell said. "And that's your designation."

Maxwell then nodded to Simons, who passed out a crudely Xeroxed sheet to everyone. The sheet contained a somewhat complicated graph and listed all five War Heaven groups. Beside each name was a list titled "Advantages" and "Alliances."

"These are the rules of the game," Maxwell said. "The supercomputers spit these out regularly, basing their calculations on millions of bits of information. Now I know these rules will be confusing at first. But I also guarantee that you will know them by heart within a week.

"The idea here is to practice skills and get points. Each unit is assigned a certain number of merits for carrying out a successful operation. The exact merit rating system is very complicated, but as an example, a three-gun artillery barrage by the Grays on the Greens might be worth ten points. A successful guerilla style hit-and-run raid might be worth fifty points. An all-out infantry assault would get as many as five hundred points; a close-coordinated, combined air and ground attack could go as high as seven hundred points.

"Each unit is expected to garner some points each day—just to keep everyone on their toes. Those being attacked can also get points for a successful defense, if one is appropriate.

"Any questions?"

Sammett raised his hand. In broken English he asked, "How is score kept? Who watches battles?"

"The Referees," Maxwell answered. "They are everywhere. You'll see 'em from time to time, riding around in white jeeps, or flying white aircraft, Lear jets, mostly. They keep an eye on specific things. On occasion, you might be called on to help one

169

of them out. Give him a ride or use of a radio or whatever. Sometimes, we have to drop what we are doing and lift them somewhere in a chopper. Let me tell you this straight: Never refuse to help one of the refs. It's against the rules and it will cost you points. This is because they are also in charge of providing security for War Heaven. Any intruders, the refs have to deal with them. So remember, no matter what the circumstances, help out when they ask.

"Also, whether you know it or not, this place is wired up the yin-yang. There are sensors and microphones planted everywhere, and TV cameras hanging off of every tree, ledge, mesa, pole, you name it. Plus you'll get used to seeing a lot of Hawkeyes flying over. They also help the Refs keep an eye on things.

"Any other questions?"

Chauvagne raised his hand. "What happens if a group gets no points, say over a certain period of time?"

Maxwell smiled. "Well, then, your unit has flunked the course, my boy," he said. "You're mustered out of here as quick as you've seen any military organization move.

"We had an Army Engineers unit in here last month, training for some special mission in the Carribean. They never got their act together. Never got the hang of thinking for themselves, of finding a way out of their problems. The Grays leveled them in a week. Those troops—or ex-troops I should say—are all clerks up in the Great Lakes now.

"Does that answer your question?"

Chauvagne nodded. Translation: Fuck up and they would all be back into military limbo . . .

Major Max took a long puff on his cigar and continued. "OK, now for weapons. First, my Blues. As I said, we have a small airlift capability. We are also equipped with a number of simulated weapons, just as all the groups are. Our arsenal, if you will, consists of Zoot Shooters, some Flashers, which are super-bright phospherous charges and Supertears, that is, highly concentrated tear gas bombs.

"Besides Zoot Shooters, the Grays carry Flashers and Powder Puffs. Puffs are bombs containing everything from sneezing powder to powerful skin irritants, which we call The Crabs, for obvious reasons. The Grays have been known to use Stink Bombs on occasion, and believe me, the Stinks are very appropriately named.

"The Grays are also very sneaky. They are well trained in boobytraps, sniping, and infiltration.

"Because the Greens are allowed so much firepower, they use a variety of shells. The most important are their Thunder bombs, which are a variation on the old 'airburst' bombs of World War II. These are very loud explosions, which can have you hearing bells for a week. They also use lightning bombs, which are super-Flashers. These bombs are so bright, they can blind you temporarily. The Greens also use some Supertears and Zoot Shooters."

Maxwell looked out on his audience. "Everyone still with me?" he asked. There was a smattering of head nodding.

"OK, the Aggressors," he continued. "They are the real bastards. They are allowed to carry everything from Supertears to Stink Bombs to Crabs. Plus, I think you are all well acquainted with their use of sleeping gas, or 'Z-Gas' as we call it. The Aggressors also carry Puke Gas which is self-explanatory and 'Hal-Lou,' which, I'm afraid to tell you, is a gas that causes hallucinations."

Someone in the audience whistled the opening bars of Taps.

"That's right," Maxwell said. "These Aggressors are tough—they make most of the instructors at Top Gun look like schoolgirls."

Woody reached forward and nudged Slade on the shoulder. "You gonna take that, Slade?" he asked.

Slade ignored him. He was too busy wondering how the hell he got roped into this mission in the first place.

"Now, as the Spooks, your weaponry consists only of Zoot Shooters and Supertears. I know it sounds like you will be outgunned, but that's what the computers have given you. If you ask me, it's an attempt to toughen you up, and to make you think. You'll have to create your own advantages. Never forget that."

Maxwell relit his cigar for the final time and began again.

171

"You now have a rundown of the weapons. Now let's go over the alliances:

"First, the Grays are allowed to attack us, the Blues, and you, the Spooks. They can not attack the Greens.

"The Aggressors can attack anyone. The bad news is that the Grays frequently ally themselves with the Aggressors. The rules here at War Heaven allow the individual commanders to link up with other units on occasion. Again, the idea is to create an atmosphere of unpredictability.

"The Greens can attack anyone. They are like freelancers, they roam the whole range because they are so mobile.

"Now, my group, the Blues, are allowed to attack both the Grays and the Greens. But we will not attack you Spooks. This is why I am here today. In many cases, we will be working together, because, frankly, we are the smallest, least-equipped units. The only ace we used to have in the hole is that we could call on a squadron of B-1s—the ones you saw here last night. Well, I was told this morning that the B-1s have been withdrawn. So, it's just us girls. I'd like to think our alliance will be one of cooperation and dedicated to using our brainpower. We'll need it.

"Any questions?"

Woody raised his hand. "Yes, sir," the Wiz said. "Just what do we do now?"

Maxwell smiled and relit his cigar. "Well, we are supposed to operate as independent units. So, I believe Commander Slade should assume command, as I believe he is the highest-ranking officer. I will leave this rather large rule book in his care. Then, I suggest you work on getting those F-14s turned over . . ."

No sooner had Maxwell stopped speaking when they heard the scream of jet engines. In a second, all of those assembled were up and out of the Ops Building just in time to see a single A-4 swoop down low over the base. The group stood helpless as the Skyhawk released a large single silver canister which exploded just to the far side of the runway.

"Freaking Aggressors!" Maxwell said, as he calmly wrapped his blue scarf around his mouth and nostrils. "I told you they were sneaky."

The Skyhawk was gone in a flash. Meanwhile the smoke rising from the exploded canister turned into a slightly yellowish cloud. Those unfortunate enough to be near the runway when the A-4 came in were now running from the scene, holding noses. Some made it; others didn't.

Those closest to the cloud immediately fell to their knees and started coughing violently. A brief sharp wind—probably caused by the jet wash of the A-4—came up and blew most of the gas out over the field, away from the base. All of the men affected—about a half dozen—were from the 1245th. Immediately Moon ran from the Ops Building toward his fallen men.

Major Max had seen it all before. "CZ gas . . . ." he said, sniffing the air. "Cyanphozogene or Supertears, a very concentrated type of tear gas."

"What will happen to them?" Slade asked Maxwell.

"They'll be hurting for a while," the Blue commander said. "CZ attacks the mucous membranes. Makes your eyes water and your lungs turn inside out. They'll be hacking for a couple hours."

Ryder looked at Woody. Both pilots were bewildered by the swift attack.

"They've got to be kidding . . ." Woody said.

Ryder shook his head. "I hope I packed my gas mask," he joked darkly.

"This is *absurd*," Reinhart said loudly. "Bombing your own men?"

Maxwell lowered his scarf long enough to light his cigar. "Now don't be too hard on them, Captain," the Blue commander said. "That flyboy just taught us all a lesson."

"Such as?" Chauvagne asked.

Maxwell exhaled a long cloud of cigar smoke. "Such as, what would have happened if this was a real war and that was a five hundred pounder full of napalm?" he asked. "Time to get some kind of Early Warning System set up or those bastards will be sneak-smoking you around the clock."

Maxwell nodded to Simons and the Airborne lieutenant immediately climbed into the all-blue jeep and started its engine.

173

"As I said before, gentlemen," Maxwell smiled. "Welcome to War Heaven . . ."

25

"These look like upgraded F-14Ds," Ryder said, sticking his head into the tail pipe of one of the hangar Tomcats. "New engines, new avionics, more weapons points."

"Hey, Ghost!" Woody yelled as he climbed up into the cockpit of another Tomcat. "Take a look at this bird."

Ryder approached the craft and ran his hand along its fuselage. It *felt* familiar. He climbed up the access ladder and peeked inside the cockpit. Within a second he knew he was looking into a very special airplane.

"This is the old 333 . . ." he said. "It's been upgraded and dinked with, but I'd know this baby anywhere."

Woody clapped his hands in excitement. "Great!" he said. "I love this airplane . . ."

"Roger," Ryder said. "This is the one *we're* flying."

He climbed down and inspected one of two of the Zoot Shooter, hanging underneath the F-14's wing. He half expected to see a logo with a mousehead on it, but all that was painted on the innocuous-looking holographic projection unit was a series of numbers. He walked underneath the wing and tapped on the airplane's belly fuel tank. It was empty.

Suddenly he was struck with a thought. "Where the hell do we get the gas for these things?" he called up to Woody.

Sitting in the cockpit, Woody shook his head. "You know, it never crossed my mind before," the Wiz said. "There's certainly no JP-8 tanks anywhere here."

Ryder had walked to the nose of the airplane by this time and was inspecting the unusual-looking in-flight refueling nozzle

174

right next the canopy. A light went off in his head.

"If there's no fuel around," he said. "They must want us to take these up and refuel in the air."

"Good thinking, partner," Woody said, climbing out of the rear seat of the 'Cat.

"Yeah, 'good thinking,'" said Slade, just walking into the hangar. "But we got a problem . . ."

Ten minutes later, Ryder, Woody and Slade were out walking the length of the runway.

"Damn!" Ryder swore, reaching the end of the airstrip. "It's too goddamn *short* to handle a F-14."

"This doesn't make sense," Slade said. "What the hell would they drop us here for, with all the comforts of home and two jazzed-up F-14s, and with an airstrip that's a thousand feet too short for takeoffs?"

Both Ryder and Woody shook their heads. Suddenly it was very quiet at the small base. The only noise was a methodical pounding of Moon's men working on popping the superlock holding the doors of the third hangar together.

This is getting crazier by the minute, Ryder thought.

26

Nellis AFB

Maureen never even considered stopping by one of the casinos in Las Vegas. She rented a car at McCarran Airport and immediately drove the fifteen miles out to the sprawling desert air base called Nellis.

It had been a sudden trip—a hunch she got after visiting her father. She knew how the military worked. She had been persistent in her questioning of the Nellis PIO, a second lieutenant named Haas. If something *was* unusual with the deaths of the two pilots, then Haas now knew that she was so tipped. A typical military coverup would then be set into motion, one that would eventually drape itself in a blanket called National Security.

But Maureen knew it took time to build a stone wall. She decided to fly out to Nellis immediately, on the hopes of buttonholing the Nellis Public Information Officer before the No Comment game plan went into motion. Besides, the *Post* had a liberal expense account policy and this would be her first trip out of DC on assignment.

She pulled up to the base main gate and encountered two black-bereted Air Policemen.

"I'm here to see Lieutenant Haas," she told them.

One of the guards leaned down to her car window. She was wearing a simple white blouse but had taken the precaution of unbuttoning her top three buttons.

"Is he expecting you, ma'am?" the guard asked her, his eyes immediately drawn to her cleavage.

"No," she said, instinctively twisting a strand of her long blond hair. "But could you call him and tell him Maureen is here?"

The Air Policeman did as he was told. Twenty minutes later, Lieutenant Haas walked into the main gate's reception area.

She introduced herself and immediately saw Haas start to blanch.

"I'm sorry you came all the way out here, Miss O'Brien," Haas, a man of prematurely gray hair, said. "But I told you all I know over the phone."

"I understand, Lieutenant," she said. "But is this all the information you know or is it all the information that the Air Force will release?"

The question gave Haas some pause. He'd dealt with the press before, but certainly never one so . . . so beautiful. But her question told him she was zeroing in on something.

"It's all the information I have *at this time,* Miss O'Brien," he told her.

Just then, two jet fighters streaked over the base and right over the reception area, banking into a final approach for landing. The strange markings on the airplanes caught her eye.

"Those airplanes, Lieutenant?" she asked. "They almost looked like Russian MiGs."

Haas smiled. "Actually, they are F-5s, Miss O'Brien," he said, hoping the subject was changing. "They are attached to our Aggressor Squadron . . ."

"Aggressor?" she asked.

"Yes, ma'am," Haas answered. He could talk all day to her about the Aggressors. "They are airplanes painted to look like Russian fighters that we use to help train our regular pilots in how to counter Soviet tactics."

"Well, I find that very interesting," she said.

He gave her a look up and down. He couldn't pass up this opportunity. "Well, Miss O'Brien, so your trip out here won't be a total waste, would you like a tour of our Aggressors Facility? It might make for an interesting story . . ."

She didn't hesitate. "I would love to," she said, smiling.

27

Ryder knew it was the hottest part of the day. Probably close to ninety-five degrees, he estimated. The sun was beating down on the small, shadeless base unmercifully. Ryder was sweating up a storm as he worked with Moon's guys in trying to unlock the third hangar.

"This is a motherfucker, Captain, sir," Moon's sergeant, a guy named Bronco, said. "Whoever sealed this shut didn't want anyone getting in here very easily."

Unlike Hangars 1 and 2, which featured combination locks

177

that were opened after an hour or so, they found out that besides the superlock on Hangar 3, the building had also had its doors welded shut.

Ryder took his turn with the small jackhammer. They'd been pounding the door welds for more than three hours and were little more than cutting halfway through. He could only hold the electric hammer level for two minutes. After that his hands would go numb and he would have to hand the hammer over to one of Bronco's men, who would do their two minutes and then pass it on to the next man.

The hangar was larger than the other two and was set apart from the rest of the buildings at the airstrip. It also appeared to be the newest structure, the other buildings seemingly authentic leftovers from a landing strip built decades before.

It was soon Ryder's turn to use the hammer again and he attacked the welds with a zest born of frustration. They couldn't launch the F-14 and were therefore quite helpless. The third hangar was the only mystery left uncracked at the airstrip and perhaps whatever it contained would help them out of their dilemma.

Suddenly, the artillery started up again. Three shells crashed down at the far end of the strip, causing a trip of very bright flashes.

"Jeesuz, they're firing on us again," Sergeant Bronco said.

"Those are flash bombs," Ryder said, recalling Maxwell's briefing earlier in the day. "Small ones, I would guess."

Woody appeared, holding a pair of binoculars. He handed them to Ryder and pointed to the mountain ridges to their west where the firing was coming from. "That's the Gray Army up there," Woody told him.

Sure enough, Ryder could just barely see the small figures of the artillerymen moving in silhouette across the ridge. They were firing three 50mm standard field pieces. A small gray flag fluttered close by the big guns.

Three more shells came crashing in hitting the same area well away from the populated part of the base.

"They're shooting for points," Ryder said. As Maxwell had explained, the separate units in War Heaven received points for various types of actions. The Grays were lobbing in the small flashers just to add to their scorecard, just like the Aggressor A-4 that dropped the Supertears earlier.

Three more shells crashed in, causing the sudden bright flash and starting a minor grass fire about a half mile from them. Even though they all knew the Grays were just shelling them as harmless harassment, the sight and sound of the flasher shells crashing in was still somewhat unnerving.

"We've got to find a way to shoot back at those guys," Ryder said to Woody, handing the binoculars back to him. "If we don't start getting points, we'll be out of here and all this bullshit we've gone through will have been for nothing."

His own comment struck deep within him. Maxwell said that if you are mustered out, you are thrown into some crappy military job, relegated to spending the rest of your service life in limbo. The thought struck fear into Ryder's heart. Despite the craziness first of Top Gun and now of War Heaven, he had to admit it was exciting. He couldn't imagine going back to flying C-130 Humpers, or worse.

It was his turn on the jackhammer again. He attacked the welded door with renewed ferocity.

All I want to do is fly, he thought.

It was nine o'clock later that night and Ryder was trying to sleep.

He lay on his bunk inside his plastic cubicle, listening to the whirring sound of the jackhammer in the distance as a night shift continued the attack on the third hangar door.

In the next cubicle he could hear Sammett softly praying. Beyond him, Reinhart was loudly snapping the pages of an instruction manual that arrived with the base's portable radar unit. Radar was one of Reinhart's specialties, he had told him, and, although the unit was up and running, he was determined to learn every last detail about the instrument.

A mild smell of incense drifted through the tent—Sammett had somehow smuggled some in and he was burning a stick before retiring. The unmistakable sound of cards flipping on solitaire was coming from Slade's billet. There were no sounds at all coming from the cubes of Woody, Lancaster, or Chauvagne.

Ryder was restless. Although he had put in a full day's work under the hot desert sun, he just couldn't convince his body that it was time to sleep. One reason was his mind was going overtime. The same questions kept flashing by: Why put us here with two F-14s and a too-short runway? The airstrip base was obviously meant to be a forward airstrip, a launching point for attacks on the Grays and the Aggressors units. Yet how could they possibly complete that mission, if they couldn't get airborne?

He took the problem to the next logical level. If the reason they were at the small strip was to prepare for Distant Thunder, could that mean they would encounter similar obstacles once Distant Thunder got underway? Would the runway be too small then too? Would they be placed on a hostile, isolated environment like this?

What kind of supplies would they have once they deployed for Distant Thunder? Certainly *not* the excellent food they were eating at the airstrip mess tent. (Roast chicken had been the tasty evening meal.) Maxwell had mentioned nothing about resupply at the base. Right now they were dependent on whatever the C-130s had dropped to them the day they landed. What if no more came? What happens if the base ran out of food?

Or suppose the Aggressors decided to launch an all-out gas attack on them, using Puke and Hal-Lou bombs? The place would be incapacitated for days. Their tenure could end as quickly as it began—and with no points to show for it.

No wonder he couldn't sleep—he felt like he had the weight of the world on his shoulders. *Think it out* is what Maxwell told them. But he imagined his brain was already starting to hurt, he was thinking so much.

And off in the distance the droning whir of the jackhammer had finally stopped. The crew had ceased work for the night trying to open the door of the mysterious third hangar.

He welcomed the silence and closed his eyes. Memories of

180

Wendy—the girl he left behind at Miramar—pleasantly drifted into his mind. But then another question popped into his head: If he somehow passed the rigors of War Heaven and went on to the undoubtedly dangerous Distant Thunder, would he be with a woman—*any* woman—ever again?

He must have drifted off eventually, because when the explosion rocked the base, he had been in the middle of a dream about the woman in the desert . . .

He was up and on his feet in a second, pulling on his Marine Corps utilities with one hand and tugging on his combat boots with the other. He heard similar confused movement in the other cubes.

"Ryder, *what was that?!*" Sammett yelled over to him.

"I don't know, Sam," he answered, strapping on his helmet. "But it sounded bigtime . . ."

He was out of his cube and running toward the front of the large tent, stopping to pound on Woody's front flap.

"Wiz, let's go!"

Woody was out of his cube in a second, although he'd barely fallen into his clothes and boots.

Just then, a second explosion went off . . .

"Come on, partners," Woody said, retrieving his helmet.

Together they ran from the tent and spotted a high spiral of flame coming from the mess area.

"Jeesuz! They hit the goddamn mess tent!" Woody cried out as they ran toward it.

Ryder scanned the sky for telltale streaks of incoming artillery but was relieved to see none. If it had been an artillery shot, it would have landed dangerously close to the base personnel's sleeping quarters. Of all the things he had to worry about, he didn't want to add the thought of *actually* getting killed in War Heaven to the list.

They reached the mess tent which was now completely engulfed in flames. Slade ran up beside them, along with the other pilots, Moon, and some of his men.

"Thank God, no one was inside there . . ." Moon said.

"It wouldn't have went up if there were," Slade said. "But what about your sentries, Lieutenant?"

Moon quickly looked around and didn't see a trace of the five men he'd assigned to night watch.

"Look, over there!" Ryder yelled out, seeing a crumpled form near the second hangar.

They ran to the spot and found one of the sentries, bound, gagged, and groggy.

It was a guy named Riley. "Looks like he's been drugged," Woody said. "You can almost smell it on his clothes."

Ryder did notice a faint, sickly sweet smell in the air. It was the same smell that had permeated his lungs after he had been knocked out by Simons' Airborne troopers during his ordeal in the desert.

Moon ordered several of his men to comb the base and find the four other sentries, and the group returned to the scene of the fire.

"Who did it and how?" Slade asked, summing up everyone's thoughts.

"It wasn't an artillery or a mortar shot," Moon said, putting forth Ryder's earlier observation. "They would have been risking lives."

"And we would have heard an aircraft," Woody said.

"I'd say it was guerillas," Ryder offered. "They came in, overpowered the sentries, made sure the mess tent was empty, and blew up the goddamn thing . . ."

Ryder's theory proved correct as Moon's men appeared with two more of the missing sentries.

"What happened?" Moon asked one of them.

"I'm . . . I'm not really sure, sir," he answered, holding his head. "Someone jumped me from behind, sprayed some gas up my nose, and, next thing I knew, I'm in dreamland."

The fire had died down enough for Ryder, Lancaster, Slade, and Woody to approach the charred wreck that was all that remained of the mess tent.

"A total loss, I would guess," Lancaster said with classic understatement.

"Our gourmet service didn't last long, did it?" Slade said.

182

"Jeesuz, all that food, gone," Woody whispered. "What will we eat?"

Slade shrugged. "Got no answer for that one now," he said.

"Perhaps Maxwell can help us out?" Lancaster asked.

"Maybe," Slade said. "I'll have to check the rule book for that one."

Just then, Ryder spotted a pair of wires on the ground near the burned-out tent. He walked over and retrieved them.

"Blast wires," he said. "Electrical cables for detonating explosives . . ."

"So it was a guerilla attack," Slade said, looking over the wires.

Just then one of Moon's men ran up. "Sir! You've got to see this," he said excitedly.

The small group followed the running guard across the base, to the far edge of the runway. Using a high-powered flashlight, Moon illuminated first the guard, then the last of his missing sentries who were just coming to. Beside them, tilting slightly into a small ditch, was a jeep.

Ryder quickly put the pieces together. "Looks like your boys put up a fight, Moon," he said, helping one of them to his feet. There was a confusion of tire tracks in the immediate area.

"Looks like two vehicles came in," Woody said, examining the tracks. "The sentries saw them, had a fight before they were overpowered."

Moon approached the second sentry, still lying on the runway. "How you feeling, Markellis?" he asked the man.

"Fine, sir," the sentry answered a little slowly. "Bastards came up on us real quick, sir. There were about twelve of them, in a jeep and a truck. We fought 'em, sir. But there were too many of them."

"That's OK, Markellis," Moon said. "You done good. They took off without their vehicle."

Moon climbed into the jeep. "And they left the keys."

"Will it start?" Slade asked.

Moon turned the key and Ryder saw a puff of smoke come out of the tailpipe. "It's quiet running," he said, lifting the hood. "I'll bet they muffled the engine and tailpipe somehow."

Sure enough, upon lifting the hood they saw that the motor was indeed running and that most of the engine was surrounded by a cloth packing material of some kind.

"A perfect desert guerilla vehicle," Lancaster said. "Quiet enough to sneak up on your enemy, make the hit, then disappear . . ."

"Pretty obvious who did this," Moon said, noting the all-gray paint job on the vehicle.

Ryder nodded and said, "Well, thanks to your guys, we got some transport now. This will come in handy."

"What are you thinking, Long?" Slade asked.

"Well, they just iced our food supply," he began. "But we got one of their vehicles. I think we should go for a ride when it gets light, do some recon, and find one of their camps . . ."

"Then what?" Lancaster asked.

Ryder started to answer but Woody beat him to it. No matter; they were both thinking the same thing.

"We blow one of their buildings," Woody said with a grin. "And we steal some of *their* food. Right, Ghost?"

Ryder slapped five with Woody in their old ritualistic fashion, and said, "My thoughts exactly."

28

The sun was coming up on the Gray Army's forward base, causing a change in sentry shifts. The base was small and temporary. Just three tents, six vehicles, a few mobile artillery pieces, a communications set and canteen truck—all painted gray.

There were twenty troops assigned to the base, under the command of two officers and a sergeant. Their primary task was mobile artillery strikes. But they also provided reconnaissance duties for the Gray's huge main base thirty-five miles to the southwest and served as a launch point for special Gray Army guerilla teams.

The night before, just such a hit team left the base for the first-ever strike on the War Heaven newcomers, the Spooks. The guerillas passed through the base on their return, reporting their objective had been hit, but that they had lost one of their vehicles in the process. It wasn't clear at the time whether points would be deducted from the guerillas' strike as a result of losing their jeep.

The small base was coming to life now. New sentries were posted within the barbed wire compound. The day's duty would involve dispatching three of the mobile field pieces to the mountain ridge overlooking the Spooks' base. From there the Gray crews would launch twenty-four laser-targeted flasher shells at the Spooks, just as they did the day before.

However, the first order of business for those just rising was to do their morning calisthenics then eat breakfast.

"When was the last time you did jumping jacks first thing in the morning?" Ryder asked Woody, handing him a pair of binoculars.

He, Woody, and Moon were perched on a small hill about a mile from the Gray's forward base. They had been watching the position since before sunup, using the left-behind jeep for their transportation.

"These guys are pretty cocky," Moon said, taking the spyglasses from Woody. "They set up only five miles from us."

"Yeah, they might know something we don't," Ryder said. "They must have been tipped somehow that we can't launch our aircraft."

"Plus, Maxwell must have been right about the unspoken agreement between the Grays and the Aggressors," Woody said. "These guys would be crazy to sit out in the open like this if they weren't in cohoots with the Aggressors."

"Good point, Wiz," Ryder said, taking the glasses back for one more look. "They haven't got any antiaircraft weapons that I can see."

"What now, Captain?" Moon asked Ryder.

185

"I say we divert around these guys and see what's up thataway," he said, pointing to the south. "If I remember the layout of this place, we are at the northeastern edge of the restricted area. That would seem to indicate that the main strengths of the other groups are to the south."

"Sounds logical," Woody said, moving back toward the jeep. Each man had taken the precaution of wearing his Marine utilities inside out. Oddly enough the inner linings were gray. The jeep was gray and they hoped the combination would make anyone seeing them from a distance think they were part of the Gray Army.

They pushed off, swung a wide arc around the small Gray base and headed south. Moon was behind the wheel, Ryder was beside him with Woody stretched out in the back. The terrain in the northern Nevada desert changed frequently from hard, arid flats to weedy field similar to the one near their airstrip.

As they drove along they could see that Maxwell had been right when he said War Heaven was wired. Not a mile went by when they didn't see some kind of sensor apparatus, wire cables, or mini-radio antennas. They didn't see many trees, but the ones they did—Joshua trees mostly—wore a TV video camera and an antenna they knew was used to transmit the video images back to some unknown receiving station to be monitored by the War Heaven refs.

They drove another twenty miles, when Ryder suddenly heard something.

"Hold it . . ." he said urgently to Moon, who immediately applied the brakes. "Listen . . ."

Woody and Moon listened.

"Hear it?" Ryder said.

They listened harder.

"Coming from that direction," Ryder said, pointing due south.

They waited a moment, then Woody said, "Shit, I hear it . . ."

Moon was looking at them quizzically when the sound finally reached him. It was a low, dull rumbling. Almost like a freight train moving in the distance.

"What is it?" he asked.

"There's two of them" was Ryder's cryptic answer.

"At least," Woody confirmed.

Moon got the message just then. "Shit, airplanes?" he asked. "Aggressors?"

"Yeah, sounds like they've just taken off," Ryder confirmed, looking around them. "And we ain't got a pebble to hide behind."

He was right. They were traveling across a high, but barren patch of desert. They closest thing for cover was a small mesa at least three miles away.

"What do we do, coach?" Woody asked. "Punt?"

Ryder put his mind into fifth gear. "No," he said. "Let's try the Statue of Liberty play. We'll find out once and for all if the Grays and the Aggressors are playing footsies . . ."

They started driving again, not fast, not slow. The idea was to look normal. Within a half minute they spotted the jets coming up over the southern horizon.

"They're F-5s . . ." Ryder said, focusing in on them with the binoculars. "Judging from the dirt in their wash, they've been airborne for less than a minute."

Dirt in the wash. The amount of black smoke coming from a jet fighter's tailpipe. It got cleaner the longer the bird was in the air. Dirty wash meant the airplanes had just taken off. This also meant their base was nearby.

The black F-5s were over them in thirty seconds. They didn't wag their wings as they passed over the jeep at about 1,200 feet.

"That's a bad sign," Ryder said as the jets screamed overhead.

"Maybe we should have waved . . ." Moon said.

"I feel like some guy dressed as a native trying to fool Jap Zeroes off Guam or something," Woody said.

"Yeah, I saw that movie, too," Ryder said, never taking his eyes off the jets.

Just then, first one then both jets broke off to the left and went into a 180.

"Damn!" Ryder cursed. "They're coming back to take another look . . ."

187

"Maybe they're not linked with the Grays after all . . ." Woody said.

"Or maybe they're looking for the missing jeep?" Moon said.

Ryder saw the jets turn again, making their maneuver a complete 360-degree circle. "Whatever they're into," he said, "here they come again. Let's stay cool. Ignore them . . ."

The F-5s screeched in on them, flying at no more than 500 feet this time. As they passed over, they both tipped slightly, giving the pilots a better view of the ground below.

"Fuck you!" Ryder yelled out, saluting as the jets went over. "Fuck all you guys . . ."

The two jets appeared to slow briefly after passing over, as if the pilots were deciding on coming back for another pass. Five tense seconds went by. But in the end, the F-5s booted it and kept on going.

"Whew . . ." Woody said.

"Yeah, we're rid of them," Ryder said. "But I'll lay a hundred they're on their way to gas the airstrip."

"Damn!" Moon muttered.

"Nothing we can do about it now," Ryder said in resignation. He looked to the direct south. A faint wisp of the jet's light gray trail still pointed toward their takeoff point, somewhere past the small mesa.

"I vote we go find their base," Ryder said.

29

Maureen was awake and packed by nine o'clock, out on the road by ten.

She was able to keep the rent-a-car, thanks to the rental car place owner, a guy named Joey who never, ever let his cars—

Empire Cars, the Best in the West!—leave the Vegas area. Joey took one look at Maureen and had immediately changed his policy. She was heading for San Diego; it would be quicker to drive then try to book a flight, and Joey was going to let her rent the car for as long as she wanted.

Her mind was racing as she headed toward the highway. Her tour the day before of the Aggressor Squadron's facilities had been a smart move. She endured lengthy explanations of how an F-5 looks and acts just like a Soviet MiG-21 long enough for Haas to reveal to her the Aggressor pilots had just finished a major aerial exercise. It was against the Navy's well-known Top Gun squadrons, and judging by Haas' lack of braggadocio when discussing the exercise, she guessed the Air Force had gotten the worst of it.

But it wasn't the fact that the Aggressors had just fought the Navy in a huge mock aerial battle that fascinated her. It was that the exercise had taken place on the same day as the two Air Force pilots had been reported killed. Haas never made the connection; she had. Before leaving, she had innocently asked him if all the Aggressor pilots had returned safely after the exercise. He confirmed they did. She concluded his not mentioning again that the two pilots were reported killed on that day was an error of subconscious omission on his part. Surely it would have stuck out in his mind and he would have reinforced it with her. Or at least that's what she thought her old college psych professor would have said. In any case, she had another hunch.

She pulled onto the well-traveled Route 54, hoping to make LA by noontime and San Diego by nightfall. With luck she'd be able to get into NAS Miramar the next morning.

30

"There they are, the dirty bastards," Woody said.

They were looking down on the Aggressors' base, a fairly small setup that utilized the hard dry surface of a long-ago dried-up salt lake as its runway.

"I counted four airplanes," Ryder said, looking through the spyglasses. "Counting the two that are out, that would make it a squad deployed here."

"Four operations buildings," Moon said, writing it all down in a small notebook. "Five vehicles, including a water tanker. Two engine starters, one radar dish, one satellite dish, and a radio shack."

"Estimate about forty-five people in all, I'd say," Ryder added. "And at least one of those buildings is holding their supply of gas."

"How about those weapons around their perimeter?" Woody asked. Sure enough there were four SAM-style mobile units at each corner of the base.

Ryder took the glasses from him and studied the weapons. "I don't know what the hell *they* are," he said slowly. "Some kind of Zoot Shooter SAMs, maybe."

"Interesting that they have weapons to defense an air attack," Moon observed.

"That's true," Woody said. "Maybe they're smarter than the Grays."

"Or maybe they're just being cautious," Ryder said. "I wonder what the rules say about shooting troop helicopters? If the Blue Airborne guys decided to chopper in and attack, maybe these guys can zoot-shoot the Hueys and that way make them turn back . . ."

"It's a possibility," Woody said. "Of course, just about everything is a goddamn possibility out here."

Just then, they heard a familiar rumbling noise again. It was the two F-5s, returning from their strike.

The jeep was under better cover this time, out of sight from the fast-moving jets. They watched as each F-5 banked sharply and landed on the steel runway. A dozen or so ground personnel appeared and immediately started servicing the aircraft.

"Well, I've seen enough," Ryder said, wondering what their own airstrip would look and smell like when they returned.

They took a few more notes then retreated back to the jeep.

"What's our gas situation?" Ryder asked Moon.

The lieutenant tapped the jeep's fuel gauge and the needle moved to a point between a half and a quarter. "Enough to get back," Moon confirmed. "Some left over for a short ride later . . ."

They moved out, retracing the route they'd taken. It was just eleven in the morning, but Ryder felt as if he had already worked a full day. It was getting hot and he was getting thirsty. And hungry. Then he remembered that all of the airstrips' food had gone up in smoke. He wondered if the C-130s had dropped any while they were gone.

They were back up on the high plain when they first spotted the trouble. Or it spotted them.

Not a mile away, flying low were two Cobra gunships. And they were heading in their direction.

"These guys have got to be Blues," Ryder said. A quick sight through the binoculars confirmed this; the Cobras were painted all blue.

"If they're Blue, they're all buddies," Woody said, quickly adding, "But we're dressed as Grays . . ."

"And Blue attacks Gray," Ryder said, watching the choppers draw closer. "Better boot it, Lieutenant . . ."

Moon immediately complied, flooring the jeep and almost knocking Woody overboard in the process.

"We'll never outrun them!" Moon shouted over the wind.

"I know," Ryder yelled back. "But at least we'll be a moving target . . ."

Suddenly there was a streak to their left and what *looked and sounded* like an explosion. Yet it was gone in a flash—no dirt was kicked up, no smoke remained.

"What the hell was that?" Moon yelled.

"It must have come from a Zoot Shooter," Ryder shouted,

turning just in time to see the lead Cobra fire another shot. Just like the holographic dogfights he'd seen before, a very authentic-looking TOW missile appeared in a flash from underneath the chopper, with a very real-looking smoke trail behind it. This time there was a simulated explosion off to their left. The flash was bright, the noise like thunder. Yet they were completely unaffected and the image disappeared in less than a second.

"*Jeesuz*, this is fucking *weird!*" Woody cried out, expressing their universal feeling. The explosions were so real, they gave Ryder the chills. It was hard to believe they were just holographic projections—high-tech cartoons.

"Keep going!" he yelled to Moon, who looked as if he had no intention of slowing down. "I think if they hit us, the jeep will shut down . . ."

"Oh, great!" Woody moaned loudly. "That's a long fucking walk back!"

Moon drove like the devil. He had plenty of room to maneuver and was therefore able to keep up a wild zigzag course. Ryder and Woody were hanging on for their lives and doing their best just to stay inside the roofless vehicle.

All the while the simulated explosions were going on all around them. The "explosions" were as intense as a hundred flashbulbs going off at once. The noise was so loud, their ears began to hurt. And the Blue pilots were persistent.

"This is fucking nuts . . ." Ryder said to himself.

They were coming to the end of the high ground. Now Moon would have to maneuver the jeep down into a long gulley, wide out around the Gray's artillery base and head for home.

If they lasted that long . . .

Moon pushed the jeep into third gear and slowed down, unintentionally causing the two Cobras to overshoot them. Using the opportunity, he gunned the jeep down into the gulley and stopped it pressed up against the rocky ledge that formed one of the gulley's sides.

The Cobras quickly found them and fired two more simulated missiles each. Even though the explosions were still frightening, the rocky ledge prevented the missiles from getting a direct hit on the jeep. The Cobra pilots, knowing they'd been outsmarted, buzzed the gulley angrily, before finally flying away.

"Yikes, that was close . . ." Woody said. "I think . . ."

Ryder knew what he meant. The seemingly harmless attack had left all three of them nervous wrecks. Perhaps there was a subliminal psych-out element in the simulated explosions. Something that triggered a fear of death deep down inside a person that just could not be convinced the attacks were just "cartoons." Thunder and lightning were relatively harmless, but they still managed to scare the shit out of lots of people when they occurred.

Once they were sure the Cobras were gone, they set out again, Ryder once again catching himself thinking that there might not be any food for them when they got back.

31

The E-2C Hawkeye climbed to 12,500 feet and started circling. Inside, the four general officers waited as the assistant secretary emptied the contents of his briefcase on to the fold-down table. Then the meeting began.

"Gentlemen," the assistant secretary started grimly. "I'm sorry to report that the situation is deteriorating rapidly. Our latest satellite photos have shown an alarming build-up just over the past week and a half. The President and the secretary have been meeting around the clock with the Joint Chiefs. They are all aware of this latest development."

He paused to let the bad news sink in. Then he passed out two photographs to each man.

"As you can see, these individuals have been taking precautions to hide their activities from the air," the assistant secretary explained. "The first photo was taken ten days ago. You can see several structures are clear in the photo with several more under construction.

"The second photo was taken day before yesterday. Please notice that the key structures are now camouflaged, and the ones being constructed are nearing completion."

The four officers studied the photos grimly.

"It's amazing they could have moved forward so quickly," the admiral said. "They must be working day and night . . ."

The Defense Department official nodded. "We theorize they are indeed working twenty-four-hour shifts, but they have also increased their labor force substantially."

The Air Force general noticed one building in the most recent photo that was conspicuously *not* camouflaged. "What is this building?" he asked, pointing out the structure to the undersecretary. "They seem to be purposely leaving it uncovered."

"We noticed it, too," the assistant secretary replied. "DIA analysis thinks its the prison . . ."

"*The bastards* . . ." the Marine general said. "They know the Big Bird is going over every twelve hours. Yet they're covering everything but that . . . that hellhole."

"It's the only thing they want us to see . . ." the assistant secretary said, studying the photo, his voice almost a whisper.

The men didn't speak for a full five minutes. The only sound was the constant hum of the Hawkeye's engines.

Finally the man from Defense broke the silence. "What this means, gentlemen, is that the training schedules will have to be accelerated. I think you can see by these photos that we have no choice . . ."

All four officers nodded.

The assistant secretary picked up a single sheet of paper marked Top Secret. "This report says that the equipment is all working fine and that the training schedule for the ground forces seems to be moving along well," he said, scanning the page.

"The Blue and Gray armies are in fine shape," the Army general said.

"As is the Green Army," the Marine general added.

"The Aggressors are also performing well," the admiral said quickly.

The Defense Department man nodded, then turned to the Air Force general.

"I understand the Spooks are in place now," he said to the officer. "Any problems in the command transition?"

"No sir," the Air Force general replied. "None at all."

The assistant secretary was secretly relieved. As soon as the international group of pilots was airlifted into War Heaven they had passed out of the control of the Navy and into the control of the Air Force. Thankfully, there seemed to have been no hang-ups in the switch-over.

"They have been down for two days," the Air Force general continued. "They've been briefed on the rules of War Heaven and have seen some limited action. But all in all, they seem to be, shall I say, *adapting?*"

"Have they scored any points yet?" the undersecretary asked.

"No," the Air Force general answered. He had been hoping the question wasn't going to be asked. "But we must remember they've only been down forty-eight hours and they are still new to it all."

"So they are not yet operational . . ." the assistant secretary said.

The Air Force general frowned. What did they expect? "That's correct, sir," he finally answered.

"Maybe their training could be accelerated," the admiral offered.

The Air Force general shook his head. "No," he said emphatically. "We've laid out their training pattern to the last detail. It's important that it proceed at its own pace. If not, the whole idea of their being self-sufficient goes down the drain . . ."

The assistant secretary ran his hand through his hair. He was caught between a rock and a hard place. On one hand, the Distant Thunder participants had to complete all of their training before being deployed. On the other hand, the situation was deteriorating so rapidly, it could explode—literally—at any time.

"All right, General," he said finally. "The training schedule will stay intact for now. Please just keep me posted daily—if not hourly—on their progress, especially when the Spooks start scoring points."

"Yes, sir . . ." the Air Force general answered.

32

"We got good news and bad news," Slade told Ryder. "Which do you want to hear first?"

Ryder, Woody, and Moon had just returned from their harrowing patrol. They were somewhat relieved to see that there were still people working at the airstrip as they drove up. The F-5s they'd seen had indeed attacked the base with Supertears. But the airstrip's small radar unit had picked up the Aggressors and all the personnel had taken cover before the first canister was dropped.

Now, as they climbed off the captured jeep, Slade looked tired and haggard. Yet he was wearing the slightest trace of a smile.

"Bad news first," Ryder said, taking a swig from his canteen.

"It's actually a double whammy," Slade said, boosting himself up onto the hood of the jeep. "We have absolutely no food. And no water to spare, so watch it on that canteen, Long.

"Part Two: Maxwell was here, and according to the rules, he can't give us any food. Plus, he says that there won't be any C-130 drops until . . ."

"Until what?" Ryder asked anxiously.

"Until we score some points . . ." Slade said.

Ryder was taken aback. "What the fuck are they doing?" he

asked. "What are we? Pavlov's dogs? Do a task, make points, get food?"

Slade could only nod. Woody and Moon were also very surprised at the news.

Ryder was getting hot. "How can they expect us to score points if we can't get the frigging F-14s off?" he asked heatedly.

Slade looked at them and his thin smile returned.

"Well, that's the good news . . ." he said, wiping his brow. "We got the third hangar open."

Ten minutes later, Ryder was staring into the open third hangar, his mouth wide open in astonishment.

"*Jeesuz Christ!*" was all he could say.

"Can you believe this?" Slade asked.

Already, Moon's men were shuttling equipment in and out of the large hangar. Ryder saw Lancaster, Sammett and Chauvagne were prowling through the building. Even Reinhart was on hand, supervising a crew of Moon's mechanics.

"Is all this equipment what I think it is?" Ryder asked.

"It is . . ." Slade confirmed. "We've been going all over it since we finally busted through about two hours ago."

The booty inside the hangar was divided into two neat sections. The first section, taking up space on the left side of the building, consisted of a half dozen Zoot Shooter SAM sets, plus a number of smaller weapons and what looked to be two dozen small generators to power the simulated guns. Instantly, Ryder knew that once the equipment was set up and working, the Aggressors could never strike at the airstrip again without getting some return defensive fire.

But it was the equipment on the right side of the building that amazed him.

"It's a goddamn field catapult . . ." he said.

"That's right," Slade confirmed. "It's in about two thousand pieces right now."

"Can your guys put that thing together?" Ryder asked Moon as he studied the myriad of pumps, snag wires, electrical cables, and water tanks.

Moon shook his head. "At first it looked like a hell of a job," he said. "But they left behind some pretty detailed instructions. Plus, what choice do we have?"

Immediately, Moon waded into the hangar and started getting his men coordinated. "First thing we do is take inventory of every box," he said to his sergeants. "Then get me your top six mechanics. If they are airmen, tell them they are now corporals. Corporals are now sergeants. You guys are now master sergeants. Now let's get going and figure out how to build this *mutha* . . ."

Ryder had to shake his head in admiration for Moon. The little man was certainly a take-charge kind of guy. Ryder was certain it was no coincidence that Moon had been assigned to the airstrip.

Ten minutes later, Ryder and Woody were in the Ops Building, giving Slade a report on their recon mission.

"We got a Gray artillery base just five miles from here," Ryder said, drawing a rough map on the blackboard. "Then there's an Aggressor base about twenty miles to the south. That's where the F-5s that attacked you launched from."

"You mentioned you ran into some Blues?" Slade asked.

"That's putting it mildly," Woody said.

"Two Cobras spotted us about fifteen miles out," Ryder explained. "They thought we were Grays and they didn't stop long enough to let us explain. I swear I lost about a third of my hearing because of their Zoot bombs. You can't imagine just how realistic those things are until someone is shooting them at you."

Slade took it all in, then said, "Well, I think you'll agree that our number one problem is food right now."

"Nothing left from the mess tent?" Woody asked.

"Morsels," Slade said. "Maybe a half meal for each guy and that's stretching it."

"Christ, it's going to take us, shit, how long to put up that catapult?" Woody said. "It would have been hard enough to do if we were well fed. How long is it going to take when everyone is hungry?"

"If we set up the Zoot SAMs first," Slade said. "And we score some hits on some Aggressors, we may get points that way."

"But how many?" Ryder asked. "That's the important question. If I read the scheme of things around here, I don't think hitting two F-5s will give us enough points to feed thirty people for very long."

Ryder returned to the idea he had the night of the Gray guerilla attack. That was, to take the offensive. "There was a canteen truck at that Gray base . . ." he said. "Maybe Maxwell can lend us a few guys and . . ."

Slade held up his hand. "Forget it," he said. "We can't work with Maxwell until we score points."

"Says who?" Ryder asked.

"Says the rule book," Slade said. "I've been reading this bastard and it's got to be the most confusing, typically military pencil-pushing bullshit I've ever run across. But it is quite clear on how War Heaven units can act together. It states specifically that each of the cooperating units have to have scored points before linking up."

"Talk about Catch 22!" Woody said.

"Maxwell compared it to a pick-up basketball game," Slade said. "You know, both teams have to 'break ice?'"

"So, we'll just have to go after the Grays ourselves," Ryder said calmly.

"Just us against them . . ." Woody said.

"Got to be," Ryder answered. "We know it was those guys who shelled us yesterday and probably the day we landed. I won't be surprised if they open up again today."

"So?" Slade asked, his voice going dry.

"So, while they're busy popping us," Ryder said, "we go grab their food."

"Just like that?" Slade asked.

"Well, we got to plan it down," Ryder said. "A lot of it will depend on if Moon's guys can get one of those Zoot Shooters up and working."

Slade shook his head and asked skeptically, "Then what?"

199

"Then we move the goddamn thing over to their base," Ryder said, getting exasperated. "And blast the bastards!"

"It's five miles away!" Slade said, his voice rising.

"What's the alternative, Slade?" Ryder asked him sharply. "We cry uncle and they ship us out to parts unknown. Me and Woody will be back to flying toilet paper to Japan again and you'll be flying a goddamn desk in Michigan somewhere."

Slade's face went red with anger.

Ryder continued. "Look," he said harshly. "We were put here to think. *To think*, Slade. We've got to be innovative. Take risks. Act on our own. Why the hell do you think they're not dropping us steak and eggs every morning? It's because wherever the hell we're going after this place, we probably ain't gonna get anything dropped to us at all!"

"So since when have you become a mind reader, Captain?" Slade shouted at him.

"You don't have to be a mind reader to figure it out, *Commander!*" Ryder said firmly. "They drop us here, feed us top shelf grub, and in one blast—*poof!*—our chow is gone. They put us on an airstrip with two hotshit F-14s and a runway that can handle C-130s and Piper Cubs and that's it, then suddenly, when we use our heads and bust the third hangar, we find our answer, the catapult. Now I think someone is sending us a message . . ."

Slade folded his arms across his chest and asked testily, "Which is?"

"Which is 'learn how to be on your own, guys,'" Ryder said, the anger evident in his voice. "Because where we drop you next time is going to be a very lonely place. And you'll still have a job to do . . ."

The tension in the Ops room was so heavy, Ryder thought the roof would cave in.

"Look, Slade, I know you're in charge here," Ryder said. "Just by an iota, but you're still top cat. But we got to work together on this, man. I say, let's give it a try. So what if we fail. What happens? No one gets killed. Who knows, maybe we get points for just trying it? In any case, we're sure we ain't getting anything for *not* trying."

Slade shook his head, then finally said, "OK, Long. Get it together. Plan it. Get Moon involved. Go and do it. But if it doesn't work . . ." his voice trailed off.

"OK, Slade," Ryder said, his voice calming down. Once again, he felt sorry for the Navy officer. He was thrown into this totally without his consent. "Don't worry," he told him. "We'll bust ass the rest of the day and all night on it. *We'll make it work*."

33

The Officer's Club at Miramar was crowded as usual. Although it was only just noon, the dark neon-glo bar was elbow to elbow with Navy pilots and sun-dressed young women.

Maureen O'Brien sat alone at a corner table, taking it all in. She had had no trouble getting through the main gate—the guards apparently waved through every girl who showed up dressed to kill. She had already told herself that this wouldn't be an official visit—no interview with the PIO, no tour of the flight line. Any information she got here, it would come from "unofficial" sources.

A waitress brought her an iced tea. "Waiting for someone, honey?" the older woman asked, writing out her bill.

"Not really," Maureen answered. "I just heard this was a nice place to have a drink. Meet some Top Gun guys."

The waitress laughed. "Well, there they are," she said, motioning toward the crowded bar. They are here, day and night. You're a pretty girl. Go get 'em!"

Maureen laughed a little. She liked the waitress. "It's strange my being here," she said. "I guess you could say I'm from an Air Force family."

The waitress smiled. "Really?" she said. "My third husband was in the Air Force . . ."

Maureen couldn't resist the next question. "Is this place strictly Navy?" she asked.

The waitress nodded. "It is now," she said.

"Oh, were there Air Force people here before?" Maureen followed up.

"Just two guys," the waitress said. "They were here until about a week ago. Nice guys, too. Never found out their names. Big tippers, though. They didn't get along with the Navy. No sir."

"What do you mean?" Maureen asked.

"Well," the waitress said, sitting down at the table. "I hear the Air Force guys beat out all of the Navy jocks. You know, for this Top Gun trophy they hand out? You saw the movie, honey, didn't you?"

Maureen nodded.

The waitress continued. "Well, when the Air Force guys looked like they were coming out on top, some of these Navy brats got all upset. They had a fistfight in here one night, honey. Talk about the movies! It looked like something from a movie all right—a cowboy movie!"

"Boys will be boys" was all Maureen could think of saying, adding, "Where are these Air Force guys now?"

The waitress shook her head. "Oh, they're gone . . ."

"Gone?" Maureen asked, a nervous bolt running up through her. "Dead?"

The waitress laughed. "Oh, no, honey," she said, getting up to leave. "They've moved on. Reassigned I guess. It was kinda odd that they were here in the first place. You know, Air Force at a Navy base. Like oil and water. They don't mix."

Maureen nodded. She felt she was on the right track, but she knew she couldn't throw an intense question at the waitress without raising the woman's suspicions. Maybe she could snoop around the personnel office later.

"Who won the fight?" she asked quickly.

The waitress laughed again. "Depends on who you talk to, honey," she said. "Why not ask that boy over there? He was in the middle of it . . ."

She was pointing to a Navy pilot sitting alone at the very end of the bar.

"Plus, he could use a pretty girl like you to cheer him up," the waitress said in a whisper. "He didn't make the grade, like the others did. Had some problems with his officers or something. Anyway, they're making him go through the whole thing again, the poor guy."

"Well, thanks for the tip," Maureen said. "He looks kind of cute. Do you know his name?"

The waitress thought for a moment, then said, "I'm not sure, but I think they call him 'Panther.'"

34

It was noon, the next day, and, as usual, the Nevada sun was beating down unmercifully.

The entire group of airstrip personnel was gathered in the cryptic Hangar 3. Ten of Moon's men, Moon himself, Woody, and Ryder were dressed in their Marine utilities, everyone else was stripped down to their skivvies and boots.

Most of the men were tired. The Aggressor F-5s had attacked them late the day before, depositing six canisters of irritating pepper gas along the runway. Unlike Supertears, the Pepper lingered in the air and caused itching to both the skin and throat. Earlier in the day they had been shelled heavily from the ridgeline, most likely by the same Gray force. Between the attacks and the 1245th's attempts to sort out the components for the catapult, it had been a very trying twenty-four hours.

Everyone was also hungry. They were all doled out small portions of the food and water that survived the guerilla attack, but it amounted to little more than a half a cup of food per man.

Nevertheless, Moon's men were able to assemble one of the ZootSAMs they had found in Hangar 3. It turned out to be an ungainly thing, not meant to be mobile at all, with not one, but two portable generators needed to make the contraption work. The entire base was treated to a test firing shortly after dawn. It took a few attempts, a few adjustments to the power supply, and many consultations with the extensive yet detailed instruction manual, but they finally got the thing to fire.

It was a fascinating device. In all appearances, it looked similar to a Roland Air Defense battery. But instead of missiles mounted on its launcher, there were four holographic projectors. After the several failed attempts, Moon adjusted the correct knobs and pushed the firing button. Instantly, the projector emitted an intense beam of light while a loud whooshing noise was heard. In a second, what looked exactly like a six-foot-long surface-to-air missile streaked away from the launcher and rocketed into the sky. It exploded ten seconds later, having found no compatible target.

To a man, the group was stunned. The sight, the sound, even the heat from the device was so lifelike it was frightening.

Now the ZootSAM had been mounted on the captured jeep. But a problem had arisen earlier. The jeep had very little gas left in its tank. Certainly not enough to drive the heavy ZootSAM to the Gray base and back. It left them with no other choice but to push the jeep to the target.

Ryder and Woody waited for Moon to end his pep talk to the 1245th men who would remain at the base. He asked them to work their asses off getting the catapult parts in order and ready for assembly, a task assigned to all but two of those staying behind. The remaining pair would start work on assembling the second ZootSAM, with Slade and the other pilots assisting.

Their final words with Slade had been brief. The Navy officer mumbled, "Good luck." Ryder told him the best luck they could get was that the Grays would commence their daily shelling on schedule. This way, the attackers would know that the Grays forward base would be nearly deserted.

With that, the raiding party set out. Drawing lots, the first man jumped in behind the jeep's steering wheel, and put the vehicle in neutral. The other fourteen men—Ryder, Woody, and Moon included—got behind and along side the jeep and started to push.

It was a grueling trip. There was no water, no shade, no relief from the relentless sun. The ZootSAM weighed nearly a ton and much of the terrain was either rocky, uphill, or both.

They were about two miles out when Ryder, scouting up ahead, spotted a small convoy of Gray trucks coming in their direction.

"They're still a mile off," he reported back to the group.

"They've got to be heading up to the ridge," Moon said. "There must be a pass around here someplace."

"We'd better divert anyway," Ryder cautioned.

They were at the top of a rise, which flowed down into a small valley, bordered by a good-sized hill. "If we can get down into the valley, and squeeze that hill, they'll be far on the other side of us. Then we can circle the hill and keep going."

"OK by me, Captain," Moon said. "But I think we might want to start the engine for this one. Make it a little easier on the guys."

Ryder and Woody both agreed. "Shit, yes," Ryder said. "Use some gas . . ."

Moon jumped in behind the wheel of the jeep and started it up. Carefully, with his men on either side steadying the ZootSAM, he drove the vehicle down into the valley, along the side of the hill, and up the other side.

Ryder and Woody went on ahead to scope out the top of the rise on the other side of the small valley. Reaching the summit they found themselves peering out onto a much larger valley, one bordered by a mountain range some ten miles away.

The first thing Ryder saw was a large convoy of tanks, making its way across the valley about four miles from their position.

"Green Army," he said to Woody. "Thank God they're moving away from us."

Ryder scanned the rest of the valley and was surprised to see what looked like a small town located right in the middle of the vast open range.

"Well, look at that," he said, handing the spyglasses to Woody.

"What the hell . . ." Woody exclaimed, giving the binoculars back to Ryder. "It looks like something out of *Shane*."

It was true. The little town was nothing more than five store fronts located on one side of what looked to be a well-worn street. Several vehicles were parked in the street, though, and that was the strangest part of all.

"There's two Blue trucks down there," he said to Woody. "And a couple of Gray trucks right next to them. There's even a Green APC down there."

"What the hell is going on?" Woody asked. "I thought all those guys were supposed to be enemies. What are they all doing parked next to each other? Trading war stories?"

Ryder didn't have any answers as to what the situation in the small town was. And he didn't have time to think about it now.

Moon pulled up in the jeep and they quickly showed him and the others the small town in the distance. Then, they pushed on.

Two more hours passed, and the hot, gritty work of pushing the jeep continued. Finally, somehow, with the officers and the enlisted men working together, they made it to the rise overlooking the Gray's camp. Just as Ryder hoped, the base was nearly deserted.

"OK," Moon said. "Now what?"

Ryder took in the situation. The artillery pieces were gone, of course, as were three of the support trucks. All that remained was what looked like a fuel truck, another jeep, and the canteen truck.

"What's the buzz, Ghost?" Woody asked.

Ryder thought it over then laid it out for them. "OK, we know if we go down there and they zap us with Zoot rifles, we're out of action, for what? Is it twenty-four hours?"

"I think the rules say thirty-six hours," Moon said. "And the enemy can hold you for even longer. And they can interrogate you."

"OK, whatever," Ryder continued. "So we've got to sneak up on them. Surprise them."

"Sure," Woody said. "How?"

"Well, we fooled those F-5s yesterday," Ryder said. "They thought we were Grays."

"Yeah, but they were way up and traveling fast, Ghost," Woody said. "These guys will know who we are before we get through the gate."

"That's all we have to do," Ryder said. "Get to the front gate. Then, let go with the SAMs. Your guys rush in, and maybe we have a fistfight . . ."

Both Woody and Moon shrugged. "I can't think of a better plan," Woody said.

"Neither can I," Ryder admitted.

"What the hell is that?"

The Gray soldier in charge of the canteen truck saw the jeep approaching. At first he thought the all-Gray vehicle was part of the artillery platoon returning early from shelling the Spooks. But then he saw the ZootSAM on the back of the jeep and knew the vehicle wasn't from the artillery team.

The jeep was moving slowly down the hill, sputtering as if it were running out of gas. The three men inside the jeep were waving at him like they were old friends. The whole thing had an odd look about it. He thought of reaching for his ZootM-16, but finally decided not to.

He walked to the unguarded front gate and waited for the vehicle to rumble down the hill. Maybe these guys were guerillas, he thought.

Three seconds later, he knew he'd fucked up . . .

There was a sudden flash from the ZootSAM. The Gray soldier froze in place—the simulated missile streaked right toward him. He blinked, then opened his eyes just as the projection was right in front of him. He thought, I'm gonna die . . . But then, weirdly, the holographic image passed right through him, continued on hitting the main operation building head-on with the sound of a tremendous "explosion." The noise was deafening, the flash hurt his eyes.

"Jesus Christ!" he cried out. "What the fuck is going on!?"

Suddenly he was grabbed from behind and pulled down to the ground. Next thing he knew he was flat out on his back, looking up into the faces of three soldiers.

He tried to shout out, but one of the soldiers put a hand over his mouth.

"Who are you guys?" he managed to ask.

"Shut up," the soldier told him.

Just then the jeep rumbled by. Another ZootSAM went off, hitting the base's small radio shack, knocking out the radio. At least a dozen soldiers were now running into the compound, picking up Zoot rifles along the way. He heard another ZootSAM go off, then there was silence.

The soldiers got him to his feet and pushed him through the gate. He saw the other eight Grays lying out in front of the command hut, facedown and spread-eagled. Amazingly, the mysterious troops had come in and taken the base in less than a minute.

The Gray soldier shook his head as he joined his comrades on the ground. "I wonder if we'll lose points for this?" he thought.

35

It was getting late . . .

Slade was wondering just what the hell was happening with Long and the raiding party. By his estimation, they were more than two hours late in returning.

He briefly considered sending out a party to look for them, but just as quickly decided against it. Most of the available men were either working on the catapult or the ZootSAMs. Reinhart and three others were out in the field looking for something—roots, plants, small animals, anything—that might help feed the airstrip's personnel. It was hot and Slade knew no one felt like working. But he also knew that keeping the men busy would take their minds off the fact that no one had eaten anything substantial in almost two days.

The steady *thump-thump-thump* of the Gray's artillery barrage continued unabated—it had been going on for nearly two hours now. The flasher shells crashed down with clocklike regularity a half mile away, always landing in the same general area, an incredibly scorched piece of earth just off the far end of the runway. Although it was harmless, Slade found it impossible to ignore the barrage, such was the frightening glare of the flash and the ear-splitting sound of the explosions. The effect was nerve-wracking.

The Navy officer was manning the airstrip's radar set while the others worked. The screen had been absolutely clear for three hours and he found the hypnotic effect of watching the screen's bar spinning only increased the painfully empty feeling in his stomach.

Suddenly, a blip showed up on the edge of the screen. He centered the indication and boosted the set's power for a clearer definition. Just then a second blip appeared. Both were heading right for the airstrip.

Slade knew immediately that it was the Aggressors. Their two-ship attacks were becoming as frequent—and as predictable—as the Gray's routine afternoon shelling.

"Damn!" he cursed, knowing that the assembly of the airstrip's ZootSAMs was nowhere near completed.

He called out to two of Moon's men nearby and they quickly spread the word that an air attack was imminent. All of the strip's personnel would head for Hangar 3—the designated air raid shelter.

But just as he was about to secure the radar set he felt a chill run through him. Suddenly two more blips had appeared on the screen, followed by two more. These aircraft were also heading right for the airstrip.

"Six of them?" he whispered. Right then he knew this wasn't going to be another routine air raid.

He secured the radar set and ran across the runway, looking for the foraging party. After several tense seconds he spotted them—just barely—in the tall grass more than a quarter-mile away.

He tried yelling, but the loud blasts of the Gray's artillery barrage drowned out any hope he had of the men hearing him. Plus, the sound of the approaching jets was beginning to fill the air.

Slade had two options—take off into the field and warn the men or head for Hangar 3 and hope the foraging party would have enough sense to stay low when the air raid began. For some reason, he felt it was his duty to be with the men in the field. Without a moment's hesitation, he plunged into the tall grass and started toward them, moving as fast as he could.

Meanwhile the men of the 1245th and the foreign pilots were struggling to get not only themselves but also the equipment back into Hangar 3. They didn't want the Aggressors pilots to know they were putting together the ZootSAMs before they had a chance to fire at them and score points.

But in their haste to move one of the SAMs, a brace was knocked over and the whole setup was sent crashing to the ground. Now, men who were already safe inside the hangar had to come out and pick up the dozens of pieces that went scattering about. Hot, thirsty, and famished, the men went about the task as if in a fog. They were reaching the end of their limits.

Just then, the full-throated sound of the attacking jets exploded through the valley.

The first two aircraft—F-5s—roared in as a few of the 1245th men were still scrambling about near Hangar 3. The jets quickly dropped one canister apiece of Supertears, then streaked away. Two men were caught flush by the concentrated tear gas; they immediately dropped to the ground in pain.

Several would-be rescuers ran out of Hangar 3 to help the stricken comrades only to see two more aircraft—this time, A-4s—flash in and drop two red canisters each. These exploded in a puff of crimson powder. Right away, those at the airstrip knew the bombs didn't contain Supertears . . .

Slade knew it, too. He was halfway across the field when the second pair of jets came in and he turned just in time to see the red cloud rising over the airstrip.

By this time the men in the foraging party had spotted him and were moving in his direction.

"Red gas, Commander?" Reinhart asked as they met.

"I think it's Crab Gas," Slade said. "Super-itching powder . . ."

The Navy officer tried to keep track of all the attacking jets. The two F-5s who had come in first were circling around and positioning themselves for another run. This had never happened before—in the past, the jets had quickly dropped their loads and left. The second two-ship flight was circling high overhead, as if they were looking for targets of opportunity. The third pair of fighters—also F-5s—was flying low at the southern end of the valley, loitering for a chance to strike.

He and the foraging party agreed to stay low to the ground and slowly make their way back to the airstrip. He hoped they could reach the edge of the runway and bolt for the Hangar between runs of the attacking craft.

Suddenly he heard an ungodly screech. He turned to see one of the A-4s was bearing down on them at full speed.

"Get down!" he screamed, but it was too late. The Skyhawk streaked in, released its payload, and was gone in a second.

The canister fell ten feet from their position and exploded. They were instantly covered with sickly blue gas. Slade was horrified as he struggled not to breathe in the substance. But it was no use—he felt as if someone had kicked him square in the stomach. His throat suddenly swelled up, his hands and legs went stiff, and his head was bolting with pain.

He turned to look at the others. Two men were doubled over, violently dry-heaving. Reinhart was completely white and also

211

doubled over in pain. The fourth man looked to be unconscious.

"Puke gas . . ." Slade said to himself. "The bastards hit us with puke gas . . ."

Slade felt his own stomach start to flip. In a second he, too, was dry heaving. Off in the distance he saw the second pair of F-5s were attacking the base. The two A-4s had regrouped and they were streaking in on the base also. The sound of jet engines—evil, dastardly screams—filled the air. He felt like the world was crashing down around him.

"This . . . is . . . *crazy,*" he gasped between heaves.

He tried his best to stay upright, to stay conscious. He watched as the jets repeatedly pounded the base with a variety of Supertears, Crab Gas, and Puke Gas. Within a minute, the airstrip was enshrouded in a misty, blue-pink vapor that he knew even the huge doors of Hangar 3 couldn't completely keep out.

Suddenly one of the A-4s streaked right over them, its pilot undoubtedly checking to see if the puke strike had been effective. Slade was horrified to see the Skyhawk turn and bank back toward their position.

"God, he's coming back again," he thought. "The bastard is just trying to rack up fucking points . . ."

Slade was more nauseous than at any time in his life, his worst hangovers included. The other four men were writhing on the ground, making sickening gurgling sounds. At that moment, Slade was certain another puke bomb would kill them all . . .

He wanted to yell to the others to hold their breaths, but he couldn't speak. He sucked in as much air as he could and watched helplessly as the A-4 bore down on them.

Suddenly there was a burst of light, and an ear-splitting explosion. Slade managed to look up at the A-4 just as it was about to release its bombs to see a wash of flame splash across its fuselage. The A-4 immediately pulled up and went into a vertical climb. It flipped over, then leveled out and beat a shaky retreat. It happened all so quickly, Slade wasn't sure what had happened.

"What the hell was that?" Slade heard himself say, before passing out.

He was unconscious before he realized someone had hit the Skyhawk with a ZootSAM . . .

They found Slade, Reinhart, and the others an hour after the air raid had ended. All five were unconscious and severely dehydrated when the search party brought them in. The first person Slade saw upon coming to was Ryder.

"What the hell happened to me?" Slade asked, his voice barely above a whisper. His mind was a complete blank.

"Nothing a ton of Bromo-Seltzer won't handle," Ryder told him.

Slade was gradually coming out of it. His stomach was aching, his head pounding. Yet he knew he was safe.

He got up on his elbow to see they were inside Hangar 3. The rest of the airstrip personnel was seated on the floor all around him, happily *eating*.

"You guys . . ." Slade mumbled. It was coming back to him, albeit slowly. "You knocked off the Gray base?"

Ryder smiled and nodded.

"You got food?" the Navy officer asked.

"We got some food," Ryder confirmed. "Not much. They were almost as low as we were . . ."

Slade pulled himself up into a sitting position. The way his stomach felt, the last thing he could think about was food.

"You guys iced that Skyhawk?" he asked, holding his head.

"That was us," Woody said, joining the conversation. "Got an F-5, too."

"Everyone OK?" Slade asked them.

"A few guys are still sick," Ryder told him. "Between the puke gas, Crabs, and Supertears, you guys got walloped. But everyone is coming around now. How about you?"

Slade rubbed his aching belly. "I feel like I drank a gallon of shitty Scotch."

Ryder shook his head. "You look like you drank *two* gallons," he said. "Believe it or not, the best thing to do is get

213

some chow into your stomach."

On cue, one of Moon's guys appeared with a half a plate of beef stew and a small tin cup of water. Slade took one look at the food and felt his stomach flip again.

"Close your eyes and take just one bite," Woody said. "After that, you'll be OK . . ."

Slade forced down a spoonful of the stew, coughed once and took a swig of water. He was sure he'd upchuck. But a few seconds passed and gradually his head started to clear. His stomach stayed down and the color came back to his face.

"The patient is responding, Doctor . . ." Ryder said to Woody.

The Wiz smiled. "Yeah, another success story," he said.

"How much chow were you able to get?" Slade asked, downing another spoonful.

"Next to nothing," Ryder said somberly. "Just enough to give everyone a half portion. Plus, we got eight more mouths to feed."

Ryder pointed to the eight gray-uniformed soldiers sitting near the door of the hangar.

"Prisoners?" Slade asked.

"We brought them with us," Ryder confirmed. "Anything in the rules about getting points for POWs?"

Slade took his third and final spoonful of stew. "I'll check," he said.

The Navy officer scraped up as much of the remaining gravy as he could, licking his spoon clean. "Hell of a lot of trouble to go through for a few morsels," he said.

Ryder nodded. "We've still got a lot to learn about this place," he said. "But the important thing is that we took innovative action and it was successful. Plus, we bagged two Aggressors. That's got to be worth something . . ."

The meager meal was over quickly and the airstrip personnel went back to work. It was almost evening, yet the remaining ZootSAMs still had a while to go before they were ready.

Ryder and Woody went all over the captured canteen truck

they'd taken from the Gray base. It had provided the raiding party with wheels back to the base, allowing them to arrive in time to end the air raid. But now its gas tank, like that in the captured Gray jeep, was nearly empty.

"Add gas to our shopping list," Ryder said, dejectedly.

That's when he heard a low drone off in the distance.

"*Listen,*" Ryder said. "What's that?"

Woody listened and heard the dull sound. "Could it be?" he asked.

It was nearly sundown and the Nevada sky was awash in brilliant red. Together they scanned the crimson sky.

"There it is!" Ryder said, pointing to the south. Sure enough, way off, an aircraft was approaching the airstrip.

"Prop job," Woody said. "It's got to be a Herc . . ."

Others at the airstrip now heard the airplane approaching and were gathered around Ryder and Woody, full of anticipation.

Their score: One Skyhawk. One F-5. One forward artillery support base captured. Eight prisoners taken. How many points would that add up to?

"Now we see the payoff," Ryder said to himself.

36

"Hello, Jim?" the long-distance voice asked. "This is Maureen . . ."

"It's about time," McCarty, the editor, answered. "Where the hell are you?"

"I'm at Miramar Air Station, in San Diego," she told him. "You know, 'Top Gun?'"

"Top Gun?" McCarty was surprised. "That's Navy . . ."

"I know," Maureen told him.

"I thought you were in Vegas?" McCarty said, "at an *Air Force* base."

"I was," she said. "But I followed a lead here and what a lead it was . . ."

She was sitting on the edge of her hotel bed, sifting through the fifty pages of notes she'd written out in the past day.

"I ran into a Top Gun pilot out here," she began. "If you can believe it, he flunked the Top Gun course. Not because he wasn't a good pilot. But because he pulled some crazy stunt right before he was supposed to graduate."

"Let's make sure we're still talking about the same story," he said. "What does this Navy guy have to do with two dead Air Force pilots?"

"That's just it, Jim," Maureen said. "They're *not* dead. At least they weren't the day Nellis put out that crash story."

"How can you be so sure?" McCarty asked. He was fumbling with his pipe, trying to get it lit while taking notes at the same time.

"Because this Navy guy spilled it to me," Maureen said. "In fact, the reason he flunked Top Gun was because he got into some kind of unauthorized dogfight—or whatever you call it— with these two Air Force pilots, Ryder and Woods. They were like rivals of his. Inter-service stuff. You know, boys will be boys.

"Apparently these two Air Force guys were assigned to Top Gun as part of a secret project. They beat out all of the Navy pilots. One of them, Ryder, had a very bizarre experience in the desert during a survival exercise, but I can tell you about all that later."

McCarty was trying to get it all down.

"I went to the personnel office here," Maureen continued. "And for the price of a hamburger and a cup of coffee, I got ahold of personnel files on both Air Force pilots."

"But how did you know to go to Miramar in the first place?" he asked her.

"Because the PIO at Nellis told me about this big aerial exercise that the Air Force and the Navy fought against each other," she answered. "It's called Red Flag. Simulated stuff,

216

you know? These Air Force pilots were flying on the Navy's side, like kind of a final exam. And they were the best pilots of them all. They won every dogfight they were in. In fact, they were supposed to win the Top Gun trophy out here, and believe me the Navy people were really upset about that!"

"When was this Red Flag exercise?" he asked.

"That's just it," she answered excitedly. "It took place two days *after* the Air Force said these guys died."

McCarty was beginning to smell a coverup.

"So what happened to them?" McCarty was becoming very intrigued.

"This pilot told me they just disappeared," Maureen answered. "The night before they were supposed to accept the award, they were flown out of Miramar. No one has seen them since."

McCarty tried to put it all together. "OK," he began. "The Air Force says two of its pilots died in a crash, but a flunked-out Navy pilot claims same two pilots were really training at Top Gun and disappeared the night before they were supposed to win the Top Gun trophy."

"That's it, so far . . ." she confirmed.

"So far?" McCarty asked.

"Yes, Jim," she said. "I'm saving the best part . . ."

He was almost afraid to ask. "Which is?"

He heard her laugh a little then say, "Which is that two days before Red Flag, four other pilots were flown into Miramar, given a crash course and then flew in Red Flag."

"So?" he asked.

"So, this Navy guy told me these new pilots disappeared the same night Ryder and Woods did," she told him. "Along with the toughest flight instructor there. A guy named Slade."

"And that's the best part?" McCarty asked.

"No," she said. "The best part is that these other pilots weren't Americans."

McCarty felt like he was about to hit pay dirt.

"Where *were* they from?" McCarty asked, looking for his Dead Pilots file.

"France, Germany, India, and England," she answered in

217

measured tones. "If you look in your file, I think you'll find you have their obits, too . . ."

37

It was just before sunrise the next day when the C-130 dropped the eighth last cargo pallet at the airstrip. The airplanes had been arriving all night, one every two hours, dropping food and equipment into the Spookbase.

Two men were watching the activity from the mountain ledge looking down on the airstrip.

"That's eight . . ." one of the men, a major in the Gray Army, said, indicating the drop in a small notebook.

The other man was punching in numbers on a hand-held computer. He was a captain in the Aggressor squadron. "Eight drops," he said, entering his latest data. "Eight-thousand-pound pallets. That's just under four tons.

"They won ten points each for the two airplanes. Twenty points for capturing Charlie Base. Five for taking the prisoners and another five for innovation. That's forty points."

"Forty points for four tons," the Gray major said. "Two hundred pounds for each point. Pretty good . . ."

The Aggressor pilot nodded. "Yeah," he said. "The kick is they probably don't realize just *how* good."

They didn't . . .

The War Heaven "points-for-supply" system was simple to anyone who had ever bet a football game. Each day, the Cray Supercomputer that was the mind and soul of the ultrasophisticated simulated battleground not only controlled the War Heaven's seven and a half million components—it also set the odds for the success and failure of each of the range's current participants every day. It was these odds that determined how

218

many points each participant could score in their daily actions. How many points each unit scored determined how much equipment and chow each unit received.

So the Cray Supercomputer was really War Heaven's giant bookie.

It had determined that the odds of the Spooks countering the six-aircraft Aggressor air raid had been very high. Knowing ahead of time about the planned air raid, as well as every other major action in War Heaven, the Cray had heavily favored the Aggressors in the match and made the Spooks the underdogs in the action—understandable as they were the new kids in War Heaven.

But the Spooks beat the odds and won the match. The biggest asset had turned out to be their strategy: Before they attacked the Gray base, they had quickly assembled one of the ZootSAMs. This not only helped them capture the base, it also, unwittingly, put them into a position to surprise the attacking airplanes and get two quick scores and break up the air raid. It had been an intangible that the Cray hadn't foreseen and therefore the supercomputer scored it as Innovation. For the action, the Spooks had won five innovation points—like extra points kicked after a touchdown. So, while the Aggressors were able to gain a total of thirty-five points for their effort—based on number of bombs on target, time over target, and so on— the supercomputer had determined they lost it, 40–35.

"And the spread was twelve points," the Gray Major continued. "They did good."

The Aggressor pilot had to agree. Although his base would receive 5,600 pounds of equipment, he knew the loss against the Spooks wouldn't soon be forgotten.

"And they don't even have their airplanes up yet," he said.

"What's next?" the Gray Major asked, lighting a cigarette as he continually scanned the Spookbase with his spyglasses.

"We got to talk about it," the Aggressor pilot answered. "Once they find out that catapult goes together as easy as an erector set, they'll be up and flying."

"Three days?" the Gray Major asked. "Four, maybe?"

"I'd say three," the pilot determined. "They'll spend half of today just opening their packages . . ."

The Gray Major thought a moment. "Can you hit them again inside in the next forty-eight hours?"

The pilot shook his head. "Depends on what we get on our drop," he said. "We're low on fuel, batteries, and ordnance."

The pilot took a swig from his canteen. It was filled with orange juice. Then he asked the Gray Major, "How about you guys? Can you launch some kind of a ground assault?"

"Maybe," the officer answered uncertainly. "We'd have to ask for more people from HQ. If they say yes, it'll take a day for them to move up here. Getting them into position and all the logistic bullshit will take another half day. It might depend on whether you guys can give us aircover. If the Blues caught us moving like that, without air support—they could really screw us up."

"Possibly," the pilot said. "But remember the Spooks got two of our airplanes. An A-4 and an F-5. Direct hits, too. Their avionics are locked for a week. So we only got four birds. And the Spooks have at least one ZootSAM, probably more . . ."

He took another swig from his canteen, then said, "Plus, I think my HQ is going to want to bounce the Greens soon. We need points and we haven't touched those guys in two weeks."

"We need points, too," the Gray Major said. He knew that Gray HQ was planning a large-scale major action against the Blues within ten days.

Suddenly the pilot had an idea. "How about this," he said. "You need points, and so do we. Let's bounce the Greens together. Score heavy. Then use the shit to bounce the Spooks before they get their catapult working."

"Where can we hit the Greens so easily?" the Gray Major asked.

The pilot smiled. "Do you think we fly all those recon missions for nothing?" he asked. "For the past week we've been tracking one of their scout columns up on the very north edge. Six vehicles. Two M-1s, two APCs, a Bradley, and a jeep."

"So?" the Gray Major asked.

"So, they've discovered Smiling Jack's . . ." the pilot said.

The Gray major caught on right away. "OK," he said with a smile. "I'm starting to like it . . ."

38

Lieutenant Moon stretched out the measuring tape and drove a wooden stake into the dirt airstrip.

"OK," he said to the eight-man work detail. "Start digging right here. Two point five feet across, five point three feet down . . ."

Sergeant Bronco, the man in charge of the work detail, nodded. "OK, guys, get to work . . ."

The eight men with shovels started digging, their first few spadefuls lacking the slightest hint of enthusiasm.

"Are you certain that your people have checked the rulebook?" one of the shovel brigade asked.

Moon smiled at the man. He was dressed, like the seven others, in the uniform of the Gray Army.

"Yes, they did," Moon lied. "It clearly says prisoners of war can be used for work details."

The questioner shook his head and mumbled, "Fuckin' crazy place . . ."

Ryder was standing nearby watching. The whole airstrip was in much better spirits this day. He could feel it. He knew it had a lot to do with the fact that they were also all well fed, thanks to the booty dropped to them during the night. With the arrival of each C-130, the place erupted with cheers. They had fought the good battle and they were being rewarded. There was nearly a thousand pounds of food alone, plus much-needed fuel, oil, batteries, and the other necessities of running the small operation.

Ryder felt good, he had to admit it to himself. They were learning how to play this real-life video game. And he knew the other units were getting to know it.

He walked over to Moon.

"What's our clearance beyond the ditch, Lieutenant?" he asked.

"We'll have about fifty feet, sir," the man answered, adding, "though I think we'll have to put a couple generators out there somewhere . . ."

"Won't make any difference," Ryder said, looking at the

empty ground and imagining how the catapult would fit in. "If we come off that ramp and don't hit our airspeed, we're going down . . . *hard.* At that point it won't make much difference if he hit a couple generators on the way."

Moon nodded. "That's what I thought you'd say, sir," he said.

They had figured out the secret of the catapult just before midnight the night before. While the C-130s were dropping them their payoff, Moon, Ryder, Woody, Slade, and Reinhart had sweated over the catapult's technical manual wondering just how the hell it went together. Ryder arrived at the solution first. He theorized that the catapult went together in the easiest possible way—not always the most logical engineering way of doing things, especially in the military. After another hour they had discovered that, simply put, the pieces fit together as quickly as "Put Piece A into Slot B." By following this assemble pattern, the more complex components of the catapult would fall together.

However, it took some innovation on Reinhart's part to come up with a way to provide power—and, just as important—steam to the giant slingshot. Reinhart devised a system where the heat coming from the operation of the electric motors could be captured and used to heat the water to make the needed steam. This way the catapult actually powered itself. A pipe carried the compressed steam through the trench to the T-Bar which would hold the F-14 at three points along the fuselage. The steam would rapidly "evacuate" the pipe, carrying the T-Bar and the F-14 with it. Ryder knew it would have to hit a speed close to 120 mph for them to launch.

The men of the 1245th were busy putting the catapult components together, under the very watchful eye of Reinhart. Sammett, Chauvagne, and Lancaster had each taken over assembly of the remaining ZootSAMs. Slade would help Moon with the "engineering." That left Ryder and Woody to figure out all the other problems. The first one was water.

"We'll need more water than we got now," Moon told Ryder. They received 140 gallons on the latest drop and all of that would be used keeping everyone from going thirsty.

"How much?" Ryder asked Moon.

The smallish young man shrugged. "Hundred gallons could do it, if we're careful," he said.

"Where the hell we going to get a hundred gallons of water in the middle of the desert?" Woody asked.

Ryder thought a moment, then said, "We could start looking in that town we saw yesterday . . ."

Moon nodded vigorously. "Good plan, Captain," he said. "I've been wondering about that place. Greens just leaving the place. Blue and Grays parked everywhere. Kinda crazy, too. A town out in the middle of nowhere . . ."

"What do you think is going on there, Ghost?" Woody asked.

"Beats me," Ryder said. "But I think we should go and find out."

The first thing Ryder heard was the piano . . .

Someone was playing honky-tonk. It was coming from what looked like a saloon located in the center of the five-storefront town. Outside the bar, Ryder counted two Blue jeeps, one Gray APC, and at least a half dozen Green vehicles, including two M-1 Abrams tanks which were parallel-parked directly in front of the building.

"Quite a crowd for this early in the morning," Ryder said, passing the binoculars to Woody.

They were a half mile away, their jeep pulled behind a rare desert boulder formation.

"What could the story possibly be here, Ghost?" Woody asked, keeping his eyes glued to the spyglasses. "Here we are, getting conditioned like mice in a lab to attack the Grays, the Aggressors, and they're trained to bounce us. Yet here *they* all are, partying in the middle of War Heaven. And before noon yet!"

"Who knows what the hell is really going on?" Ryder asked the rhetorical question of this and every other day in War Heaven. "I say let's just stroll in there like we own the place. Feel our way around. If they don't have any water to spare,

223

maybe someone will know where we can get some."

"I'm with you, partner," Woody said as they jumped back into the jeep. "We're Air Force guys wearing Marine Corps clothes, driving a Gray Army jeep, trying to get water to launch our Navy jets . . ."

"You see?" Ryder said as they drove toward the town. "We'll fit right in around here . . ."

The piano playing turned out to be a record, but the saloon was authentic enough.

Ryder and Woody parked their jeep beside a Green Army APC and walked through the swinging saloon doors. There were about fifty people inside—most of them soldiers, with a few mysterious-looking civilian types. A dozen tables, a well-worn bar, and a large liquor supply comprised the place. The air was thick with cigarette smoke and the smell of booze. Over the bar was a rather crudely painted sign which said: "Welcome to Smiling Jack's." Next to the bar was a set of stairs that led up to the second floor.

No one paid them much mind when they walked in. Not at first anyway. They saw a few card games were in the works, as was one game of darts. In the far corner, two men were shooting eightball on an ancient pool table.

Everywhere, soldiers of the Gray, Blue, and Green armies mixed freely.

"Well, this is weird . . ." Woody said after his eyes had adjusted to the dimly lit interior. "Now what?"

"When in Rome . . ." Ryder said, moving toward the bar.

The bartender didn't give them a second look. "What'll it be, guys?"

"Two bourbons," Ryder said.

Woody poked his elbow. "I hope this is on you, Ghost," the Wiz said. "'Cause I ain't got no money. I ain't even got a wallet."

Ryder did a quick self-frisk. He, too, was broke.

The bartender poured out their drinks and passed them to Ryder. "Charge to . . . ?" the barkeep asked.

"Charge?" Ryder repeated the question.

"Yeah," the bartender said, taking in their uniforms. "What are you guys? New Grays?"

Ryder shook his head and took a sip of his drink. "We're Spooks . . ."

The music stopped. Suddenly it seemed like everyone in the place was looking at them.

"You guys *really* Spooks?" the bartender asked.

Ryder nodded nonchalantly.

The bartender simply shrugged, and noted the drinks on a ledger kept next to the bar's circa 1950s cash register. The roomful of people went back to whatever they were doing.

Ryder was taking his second sip from the drink when a man in a Gray Army uniform sidled up next to him.

"Spooks, eh?" the man, a sergeant, said. "You guys flying yet?"

Ryder looked at the man and shrugged.

The Gray soldier shrugged himself. He ordered two beers, took them, and left without another word.

A soldier from the Green Army was the next one to approach them. "Hey, Spooks . . ." he said in a friendly if slightly low voice. "Nice job greasing that Gray artillery base the other day."

Once again, Ryder didn't speak; the man got his drinks and left.

"Figured it out yet, Wiz?" Ryder asked Woody.

"Yeah, sure . . ." Woody said.

Ryder surveyed the room. He spotted a table with three Blue Army soldiers sitting at it.

"Let's go talk to these Bluecoats," he said, pointing to the table. "They're supposed to be our allies, right?"

Woody nodded. "Last time I checked," he said.

They walked over to the table and Ryder spotted the senior officer in the trio. The man was a captain, possibly a chopper pilot.

"Captain Ryder Long, Air Force," he said. "This is Captain Woods."

The man stood and shook Ryder's hand. "Captain Esposito," the man introduced himself. "Lieutenants Carter and Ruggeri."

Everyone shook hands.

"Sit down, guys," Esposito said. "First time in here?"

Ryder nodded. "Yes," he said. "In fact, we only found out about this place yesterday."

Esposito nodded. "Well, it takes awhile to find your way around Heaven," he said.

"You guys are in choppers?" Woody asked.

The three men nodded. "We're part of a Huey squad," Esposito said. "We're Major Max's aircrew."

Ryder nodded. "Yeah, the major was part of our welcoming committee."

He sipped his drink and gave the place another onceover. He reminded himself that the plan was to go with the flow and see what happened. Their first priority was to look for a water supply. Their second task was to pick up any information that might prove useful. Woody was playing along.

"So," Ryder said. "Big crowd here this morning, eh?"

All three Blue officers looked at him. He could tell by their quizzical looks that he had said something screwy.

"Well," Esposito said. "We're waiting . . . just like you guys."

Ryder and Woody looked at each other and each gave a slight shrug. "Actually, we're looking for some water, Captain," Ryder said.

"Water?" Esposito asked. "You ain't got water at your base?"

"We do," Ryder said. "But just enough for drinking and so on. We need a lot more, for reasons we can't really get into. Do you know where we could get about 250 gallons?"

Esposito shook his head slowly. "Water is like gold out here on the range," he said. "Especially up here in the North. You'd be better off going down South. Maybe you can work a deal down there with some other Blue forces. Do you have anything to trade?"

Ryder thought a moment. "Maybe," he said. "But getting down south is the problem. We got two vehicles and not enough gas between them to get a quarter of a tank."

Esposito rubbed his chin. "Let me think about this for a moment," he said. "You guys need water and you also need transport. Now I know you also did a nice job on that Gray base the other day and that you popped two Aggressors. So you must have got a nice drop after that, right?"

Both Ryder and Woody nodded. They could tell Esposito was a born wheeler-dealer.

"Tell you what," the Blue officer continued. "When I get back to my base, let me talk it up. Maybe we can chopper you guys to our main base down South and you can arrange to get your H2O."

"What do we bring to the party?" Ryder asked.

Esposito shrugged. "Maybe you slip us one of your ZootSAMs," he offered, lowering his voice. "You know, *very* quietly. We don't have any up here and the Aggressors know it.

"Now if we had one, they'd go apeshit if we popped them, especially in a match where we're underdogs. We get our In-No points and it would keep them off our backs for a while."

Ryder let the proposed deal turn over in his mind. A ZootSAM for 250 gallons of water. In War Heaven, anything was possible.

"We'd have to clear it with the others at the airstrip," he said.

"Absolutely," Esposito said with the air of a man who'd made many similar deals. "Talk it over. Give us a call on the radio. Be discreet. We'll fly over and work out the details."

It was a start, Ryder thought. "OK, Captain," he said. "We appreciate the offer."

"Got about a minute to go, Captain," one of the Blue officer's lieutenants efficiently reported.

Esposito immediately signaled the bartender to pour out another round, including refills for Ryder and Woody.

"Best to get the drinks beforehand," Esposito explained.

The other two Blue officers nodded knowingly.

The drinks arrived and Esposito offered a quick toast: "To success!" he said, quickly touching everyone's drinks glasses.

"Ten seconds, sir," the lieutenant checked in. All three Blue

227

officers adjusted their fatigues and their hands brushed their hair. Ryder noticed that everyone in the bar was now turned and staring at the top of the stairs. The bar's second story appeared to contain a number of rooms. There were many doors all marked with apartment numbers. Rooms for the help? Was this really an old motel? Was everyone waiting for a floor show?

What the hell, Ryder thought. Whatever was happening at the bar, it was about to commence in ten seconds.

He gave Woody a quick look, then he sipped his drink, leaned back, and waited with everyone else.

Suddenly the door nearest the top of the stairs burst open. Those gathered in the bar instantly broke into a hearty applause. The taped honky-tonk music kicked back up again.

Out from the room came first one, then two, women. They were dressed like saloon girls in a cowboy movie: short, one-piece low-cut outfits, black net stockings, high black heels. Both women were extremely attractive—in a sleazy sort of way.

As the first pair made their way down the stairs, two more similarly dressed women came out of the room, followed by two more. Then two more.

Another door near the top of the stairs opened and a trail of women started flowing out of a second room. Each one was as beautiful as the next. The place was quietly going nuts.

By this time, the first contingent of women had reached the barroom floor and were quickly mingling with the patrons. Neither the women nor the soldiers they were entertaining had any self-conscious compulsions. The soldiers immediately started thrusting their hands down the fronts of the women's outfits, an act that usually met with a playful squeal from the women in hand.

It was like something from an X-rated movie. "Does this happen every day?" Ryder asked the Blue captain.

"Every day," Esposito answered. "But only after noontime. That's the rule."

The women kept coming, as many as fifty in all, one for each soldier in the bar. Eventually five women had made their way to the table, quickly finding available laps.

Woody didn't hesitate to grab his showgirl. Neither did Ryder . . .

"What's your name?" Ryder asked the woman as soon as she was down on his lap and comfortable.

"Sandy," she said with a thoroughly professional smile. She was gorgeous. Brown hair, cut shag, blue eyes, nice bum.

"My name is Ryder," he said. "Can I talk you into going back to my place?"

She laughed again. "My place is closer," she told him, taking his hand and gently placing it on her right breast. "It's right upstairs. Do you want to see it?"

Woody leaned over after getting a similar invitation from his lap bunny. "See ya, Ghost," he said.

Woody and his friend got up and headed for the stairs. "Take notes . . ." Ryder called after him.

"Come on, Ryder," Sandy urged him. "I got a bottle on ice."

Ryder turned and looked at Esposito. He, too, was getting ready to go upstairs.

"Captain?" Ryder said, stopping him momentarily. "Should I know what's happening here?" Ryder asked.

"We're in Nevada, Captain," Esposito said. "Two things are legal in Nevada: gambling and . . ."

"Cathouses," Ryder said under his breath. Ryder looked around. The place was emptying, all of the patrons paired off and moving up the stairs. He had never seen the art of getting laid be more organized.

"Don't worry, Captain," Esposito told him. "You're in a demilitarized zone. Everyone in War Heaven considers Smiling Jack's as an open city. Neutral ground. Don't worry about it . . ."

Ryder nodded. That was enough for him—for the moment. Sandy was pulling toward the stairs. "Just one more question," he said to Esposito. "Who pays for the young ladies' time?"

Esposito laughed and gave him a stage wink. "Uncle Sam does, of course . . ." he said.

39

The telephone answering machine clicked twice, beeped, and started replaying a message:

"Hello, Daddy, it's me. I got to talk quick to get everything in. I was in Las Vegas but now I'm in San Diego but I'm heading back toward Vegas again to someplace called the Weapons Range. You remember those two Air Force pilots who were reported killed? Well, I've been told they took part in some kind of training exercise two days after . . . that's right, after . . . their airplane supposedly crashed. I was able to get their personnel files from here after I bribed a woman in the personnel office by buying her lunch. Oh, maybe I shouldn't tell you that. Oh, well, this might turn into a big story. There are also some foreign pilots involved somehow. I've got to go now. I hate talking into these machines. I hope you won't get upset. But this is a good story and I'm just doing my job. I'll call later. Love. Bye."

General O'Brien switched off the answering machine and sat quietly for a few moments. He was angry. Why did his own daughter have to get mixed up in this?

He reached for the telephone and dialed a special access number. The phone on the other end rang twice before a secretary answered.

"This is General O'Brien," he said. "Can I speak to the assistant secretary, please?"

Ten seconds later, the assistant secretary was on the line.

"I'm sorry to bother you sir," O'Brien began. "But we have a problem."

"What kind of problem, General?" the defense official asked.

O'Brien took a deep breath, then said, "I have reason to believe that Distant Thunder might be compromised . . ."

There was a stark silence on the other end. Finally the voice said, "Compromised by whom?"

O'Brien took another breath and said slowly, "By a member of the press . . ."

There was another long silence, then the assistant secretary said, "Please be in my office in ten minutes, General . . ."

40

Two Aggressor F-5s flew low over Smiling Jack's, shaking the saloon to the rafters just as Sandy was reaching her third climax.

She collapsed back onto the bed, her face flushed with delight, breathing heavily. She quickly regained her composure and curled up in Ryder's arms.

"I've never been with a pilot before," she confessed. "Can you tell me what an afterburner is again?"

Ryder smiled. "Some other time," he said.

The room was matchbox small—a bed, a light, a dresser, and a door. That was it. He had lost track of the time—the session with Sandy being a sweet and refreshing surprise. It had given him a new appreciation for the old term of "cleaning your pipes."

But he knew it was time to get going . . .

Ryder nuzzled her lovely breasts one more time for luck, then got up and put on his pants.

"Please come back sometime, Ryder," she said sincerely. "I have fun with the other boys, but I like you . . ."

He looked at her, invitingly naked on the bed, clutching a pillow. She was probably no more than twenty or twenty-one.

"I like you, too," he said, finding the words came out easier than he expected.

A strange thing had happened to him during the lovemaking session: he had opened his eyes once, and in the dim light of the room, imagined for a moment that he was with the woman he'd been dreaming about—the woman in the desert. He had

231

blinked quickly and was somewhat reassured that when he opened his eyes again, it was Sandy's face he was kissing. It had been a weird, yet somehow, pleasant fantasy.

Five minutes later, he was back downstairs. Woody was sitting at the bar, swigging a beer, waiting for him.

"Well, that was . . . *interesting,*" Woody said.

Ryder nodded. "Real enlightening," he said.

They headed out to the jeep. Other soldiers had drifted out into the small dusty main street and were in the process of starting up their various vehicles.

"Every time I think I've seen it all this place gets stranger," Woody said as they watched the two Green M-1 tanks pull away and rumble down the street. The four other Green Army vehicles were following close behind. The Blue soldiers also mounted up and moved out in the opposite direction. The single Gray vehicle was already gone by the time they came out.

Ryder's lovemaking session with Sandy hadn't been entirely fun and games. He was able to get some information from her about the small town and Smiling Jack's. According to Sandy, the town was less than a year old. Like the buildings at the airstrip, it had been constructed to *look* old. Smiling Jack, she said, was a former CIA man. He was called out of retirement to run the bordello when the Central Command of War Heaven decided that its soldiers needed some kind of release—top secret R&R—from the constant war-gaming. But the Command knew they couldn't let all of the War Heaven participants loose in a big city, especially like Vegas. The danger to the classified integrity of the place would be horribly jeopardized. So they built the small town and installed the bar and cathouse. The girls were all hired from Vegas in what must have been some recruiting drive. They were all checked out medically, given psychological tests and those that passed were given loyalty oaths. Apparently Uncle Sam believed the old saw that no one can keep a secret like a hooker.

"It's amazing," Woody told Ryder as they pulled away from

the town. "The government running a brothel right in the middle of the most restricted military base in the world. Can you imagine what would happen if a story like that made it into the newspapers?"

Ryder agreed. "A major scandal. Senate hearings. Special prosecutors. Someone goes to a country club jail for eight months. Books. Movies. A miniseries."

They were about a half mile away from the town when they heard a tremendous explosion.

"*Jeesuz!*" Woody yelled, pointing back toward the town. "Look at that!"

Ryder immediately stopped the jeep and turned to see what Woody was talking about.

He saw the wispy remains of a simulated explosion on the road leading south out of the town. Then there were three more blasts in quick succession.

Ryder quickly had the spyglasses out and up to his eyes. "It's the Green Army column," he told Woody. "They're getting bounced . . ."

"By who?" Woody asked. "I don't hear any artillery or airplanes . . ."

Ryder saw that the half-dozen vehicles in the Green column had stopped dead in the road. He could see troops sitting very still on the vehicles, almost as if the slightest movement would set off another explosion.

"I'm not sure," Ryder said. "But I think someone mined that road . . ."

"Zoot*mines*, too?" Woody asked.

Ryder didn't answer. He heard aircraft. "F-5s, coming in," he said.

"There they are!" Woody said, making out two black shapes in the cloudless sky.

Sure enough, two Aggressor jets swooped in on the stranded column and began raking it with Zootcannon fire.

"And what the hell is this?" Ryder asked, handing the glasses to Woody. Ryder had spotted first a few, but now many, ground troops moving in the desert near the stricken Green vehicles.

233

"Gray troops . . ." Woody said. "Bastards must have mined the road and hid and waited. While the Green boys were getting laid, the Gray guns were laying a trap . . ."

"And coordinating it with the Aggressors," Ryder added, watching as the F-5s relentlessly pounded the Green troops. "Talk about getting caught with your pants down. The Grays probably had a spy at Smiling Jack's, waiting to give a signal when the Greens moved out."

The Green Army troops offered little resistance in the battle. Ryder knew the Zootmines had most likely knocked out key elements of their vehicles, making it impossible for them to move or fire back. In real life, in a *real* battle, the column and all of its troops—caught unsuspecting and out in the open— would have been quickly destroyed.

They watched as the advancing Gray troops peppered the vehicles with Zootrifle fire, the small, bright sparks against the Green vehicles indicating simulated bullet hits. The engagement was over quickly. The Gray soldiers disarmed the Greens and led them away. All the while the F-5s buzzed angrily overhead. The Green vehicles were left behind, but Ryder was sure this was only temporary.

"Fifty bucks says the Grays will have those vehicles in their camp and repainted by sundown," he said.

Woody nodded. "And the Hercs will be dropping manna to them all night."

Ryder started the jeep and they set out for the airstrip once again. "How many points do you get for an ambush?" he wondered.

41

The E-2C Hawkeye was barely airborne when the Air Force

general began talking. He was tired, as were the three other officers on board. But he had just received two pieces of news from Washington—both of them bad.

"I just got off the horn with the assistant secretary," the Air Force general told the others. "And he is not happy. The situation at the target is getting worse. Plus, we have a possible breach in the security of Distant Thunder . . ."

The Air Force general let the information sink in before starting again.

"Apparently a reporter from *The Washington Post* has put some things together," he said. "Somehow the *Post* gathered all the obituaries for the Spook pilots. Then they sent this woman reporter out to check on our pilots, Ryder and Woods. She was at Nellis the other day, then headed for Miramar. Now she's heading back toward Nellis."

"How much does she know?" the Army general asked.

"We can't be sure," the Air Force officer replied. "But apparently she talked to one of the Miramar pilots. Just our luck he was a disgruntled guy who didn't pass the Power Projection course. He told her all about Long and Woods and how they nearly won the Top Gun trophy . . ."

Suddenly all eyes were on the admiral.

"It's not the Navy's fault that the Air Force sent us two hotdogs," he said in his own defense. "They were cocksure and made a big flap. They were in brawls every night. That pilot Long who got lost in the desert was also the talk of the base. Then they made a big deal about this trophy. Anyone at Miramar would have remembered them. They were too high profile from the beginning."

Despite his quick ass-covering, the admiral knew that one of his Navy pilots squawked and he knew he would be in for some heat. He vowed to shit-can the pilot responsible.

"How were we first informed about the reporter?" the Marine Corps general asked.

The Air Force officer shook his head. "Apparently she is the daughter of one of the general counsels at the Pentagon," he told them.

There was an audible gasp from the other three officers.

"Don't jump to conclusions, gentlemen," the Air Force officer warned them. "The general is being interrogated right now. And his career is undoubtedly ruined. But he was the one who personally called the assistant secretary about his daughter and that she was sniffing around. He turned his own kid in, apparently after she called him from Miramar."

"So what should we do about her?" the Army general asked.

The Air Force officer shook his head. "We really have no choice," he said slowly. "As you know, the referees in War Heaven also handle the security there. They have been alerted. They'll have to deal with it."

There was an icy silence inside the cabin.

"You mentioned more problems at the target?" the admiral said, switching to unpleasant topic number 2.

The Air Force general nodded grimly. "Yes, I'm afraid so," he started. "The assistant secretary has seen the latest KH-12 photos and they are not good. The entire facility is very close to completion . . ."

The three other officers were astounded. "Including the launch pads?" the Marine general asked.

"Yes, including the launch pads," the Air Force general confirmed. "We have no idea how they did it. But they did. And that means we have to accelerate our response. The assistant secretary wants the first ground units deployed within the week."

Now there was a stunned silence in the cabin.

"A week?" the Marine general asked. "That will be sending those men to their deaths!"

"If we don't do it, half the population of this planet will be sent to their deaths!" the Air Force general shouted.

The officers went silent again. Each man felt as if the events were moving too fast for them to keep up.

The admiral pounded his fist on the table. "How could they possibly finish that facility in a matter of a week?" he shouted. "They obviously have been getting some help. And I can guess just where!"

The Air Force officer held up his hand. "No, you're wrong, General," he said. "The assistant secretary has been in touch with the Soviet ambassador and the Chinese ambassador. Both have emphatically denied that there is any kind of collusion."

"How can we possibly trust them, though?" the Army general shot back. "Both have been close to this situation from the beginning. We know the Soviets provided the initial building and scientific materials."

"Yes, you're right," the Air Force officer said, not at all relishing his role as stand-in for the assistant secretary. "But, we all know that it got away from them. It got too hot for them. They couldn't handle it. Remember, they came to us with the location . . ."

"But what's to say they're not two-timing us," the admiral said, bringing up the old argument that had been raging since Distant Thunder was born. "We've given them access to *so much*. What if the *Post* reporter finds out about that!"

"Admiral, please," the Air Force general said sternly. "We can't debate these arguments every time we meet. The course of action has been established by the President. The *President*, sir! We have no choice but to follow it through."

The admiral's face was flushed red.

The Air Force general waited until everyone had regained their composure, then he started again. "The assistant secretary wants a status report on all the ground units in twenty-four hours. He will make the final determination as to whether the units are prepared to go."

"And what if they're not?" the admiral asked, the bitterness dripping in his voice. "What if we send them all over there and they don't take the objective?"

"You *know* the strategy, Admiral . . ." the Air Force general said, anger again rising in his voice. "If the units fail to achieve the objective, then *we* launch an ICBM attack against the facility. Undoubtedly we'll destroy it. But we'll kill a half billion Asians in the process. Does *that* answer your question completely, Admiral?"

"We are sending our men to their deaths . . ." the general said. "And not a single Russian soldier will be anywhere near it. And that facility is right on their doorstep. That's what bothers me . . ."

"It bothers me, too, Admiral," the Air Force general said grimly, his voice almost a whisper. "But we must remember: whether we like it or not, our troops are training for a suicide mission. We can't expect anyone to come back from this, especially those pilots.

"And that's just the way it is . . ."

42

The Blue Army UH-1B Huey helicopter touched down at the Spookbase just after morning chow the next day.

Ryder and Woody had briefed Slade and the others on all aspects of Smiling Jack's and the offer Esposito had made. After some discussion—during which Moon assured Slade that the airstrip could be adequately defended from air attacks with four ZootSAMs instead of the five on hand—it was decided to call the Blues and work out an arrangement.

Esposito flew the chopper in himself. Two other lieutenants were with him, as well as a sergeant/waist gunner. Ryder met the Blue officer as he emerged from the craft and quickly introduced him to all the Spookbase officers.

High above, two smaller helicopters slowly circled the base. "Those are our Cobras," Esposito said, pointing to the attack choppers. "They'll be riding shotgun for us."

Esposito was then shown the progress of work being done on the catapult. Amazingly, the launcher was nearly fifty percent complete, thanks to the simplified means of assembly and the extra eight workers they had gained in capturing the Gray Base.

"You guys got Gray troops helping you?" Esposito laughed. "That's great! You should get some 'In-No' points just for that!"

"I'm sure the Gray command know we have them," Slade told the Blue chopper pilot. "They haven't shelled us since."

"That's because you lose points if you endanger your own troops unnecessarily," Esposito said. "So you guys not only folded up that Gray artillery base, you got some free labor to boot . . ."

Slade hadn't got that far in the rule book. "We plan to return them when the work is through," he said.

Esposito laughed again, then said, "Well, give them back if you want. But make sure you make some kind of a deal and get something in return."

It was time to go. Ryder, Woody, and Lancaster would make the trip. The other pilots planned to fire up one of the F-14s later in the day. Moon estimated that if the needed water could be secured, the Tomcats could be airborne sooner than anyone had thought possible.

The thought excited Ryder as he climbed aboard the Huey. It seemed like he hadn't been behind the controls of an airplane in years, although it had only been a matter of days.

Time moved very slowly in War Heaven . . .

The Huey lifted off with a great gust of wind and dust, climbed and headed south. As soon as they were up, Ryder saw the two Cobras, mean-looking little choppers carrying a wild array of Zootweapons, move up and take their positions in front of the Huey.

"Any SAM or antiaircraft threats they can handle," the waist gunner told them. "But if any Aggressor airplanes show up, we'll have to beat it . . ."

The sergeant went on to explain that if any of the choppers took a Zoot air-to-air missile hit, all but the critical avionics on the stricken craft would shut down. After that, the pilot would have no choice but to land the helicopter and abandon it. Its passengers would then have to hoof it to a friendly area or risk getting captured.

"I think I'd rather get captured if we ever lost the chopper," the sergeant said. "Major Max would put us in anthills if we came back without the bird."

Ryder was strapped into the seat closest to the door and he was enjoying the view. The desert was incredibly vast and diverse. They passed over arid areas as well as short-grassed fields. There were mountains, mesas, and occasional small streams or dry riverbeds.

Every once in a while they would see some movement on the ground. They watched two Gray recon jeeps scatter at the sight of the three Blue choppers. They passed over a concentration of recon Blue forces, holed up on the side of a hill, waiting to attack a Gray Army staging area on the other side. They also flew over a long line of abandoned Green vehicles, probably two dozen in all.

"Aggressors got them," the sergeant told them. "Them and the Grays have been hitting the Greens all over War Heaven in the past few days."

"How come?" Ryder asked, remembering the similar, if smaller, attack he and Woody had witnessed near Smiling Jack's the day before.

The sergeant shrugged. "Who knows?" he said. "The Aggressors and the Grays are always up to something. They're probably going for points more than anything else. It's easy for them to pick on the Greens because they aren't very quick with all that heavy equipment, plus they're the smallest ground force.

"The Grays and the Aggressors make some easy points, here and there and it adds up. They get their drops, they marshal their resources, then they make a major strike like against the Blue HQ or even you guys. They'd get 'In-No' points up the warzoo if they knocked you out before you got your airplanes up . . ."

"It's nice to know we're so popular," Lancaster said.

Ryder nodded. He couldn't help but be amused by the fact that everyone—from waist gunners to hookers—knew more about the goings-on in War Heaven than he did.

They reached the main Blue base within an hour. It was a

massive, sprawling place, laid out in a large star pattern. In the middle of the base there were several dozen helicopters lined up in three neat rows.

"It's an old defensive perimeter system they set up in Vietnam in the early days," the sergeant told them. "Each point of the star has a dozen or so heavy weapons. If a ground attack comes and the enemy reaches the perimeter barbed wire, they are automatically caught in the interlocking field of fire between the two points of the star. It was real effective in Laos and the Central Highlands, so they tell me."

The talk of the Vietnam War reminded Ryder that this Blue Force was actually descended from the destroyed 15th Special Forces Group. He knew that Simons' father had been a member of that ill-fated unit; he wondered if the waist gunner, or Esposito, or even Major Max had had any relatives connected with the 15th. And if they did, was there a connection between them and the ultimate aim of Distant Thunder?

His thoughts were broken when the chopper touched down inside the star-shaped compound. A Blue Army major named Apple was on hand to greet Esposito, who in turn introduced Ryder, Woody, and Lancaster. They quickly retired to Apple's quonset hut quarters where he offered them all an ice-cold beer.

"So I hear you boys need some water," Apple said, retrieving beers for the three Spooks and Esposito.

"About three hundred gallons, Major," Ryder said. "We're trying to get our field catapult working and we need water to make steam."

Apple nodded. "Well, we got some extra water you can have," the small but rugged, ruddy-complexioned man said. "Espo here tells me you'd be willing to part with a ZootSAM in exchange?"

"That's correct, sir," Ryder confirmed. "It is ninety percent assembled right now. Should be finished by the end of today."

"How about a generator for it," Apple asked, opening a beer for himself. "I know those things can take a lot of juice."

"Generator's included," Ryder said, feeling the refreshing cold beer ooze down his throat.

241

"That's great, guys," Apple said, obviously pleased. "I'm glad we can help each other out. You know, it will be a boon for us, once you guys get flying. Those Aggressors have really bounced us around in the past two weeks. They attacked us here with Supertears five days in a row. A few of our outlying bases got the same treatment."

Lancaster quickly told Apple about the combined Supertears-Itch Gas-Puke Gas attack on Spookbase several days before.

Apple was astounded. "They hit you with Puke Gas? Those sons of bitches! They're supposed to use Puke only in very special instances."

"It was a six-plane attack," Ryder said.

Apple nodded knowingly. "Well, they were going for points," he said. "They're planning something. You can smell it in the air. They got two of our choppers just west of here eight days ago. Got another one just three days ago. We didn't recover any of them, plus they captured the pilots, who, if you've gotten that far in the rule book, *have* to fly for them."

"Incredible," Lancaster said.

"OK," Apple said, quickly draining his beer. "Let's go get you that water."

An hour later, the deal was complete. The Blues had cleaned out one of its fuel trucks and filled it with more than 350 gallons of water.

"Don't let anyone go drinking it," Apple told them. "That water will taste mighty oily. But it should serve your purposes to make steam."

The plan was for Ryder and Woody to drive the truck the hundred or so miles back to Spookbase. Lancaster would ride in the Huey and they would be connected by radio. If they ran into any trouble, the Cobras would handle it while Ryder and Woody made a run for it. If it looked hopeless, they would simply abandon the truck, climb into the Huey, and chalk it up to experience.

*   *   *

The first hour of the ride went well. Ryder had steered the moderately sized truck onto a fairly well-paved roadway and they were able to move along at a reasonable forty-five miles an hour. Meanwhile, the Blue choppers were always somewhere overhead, keeping a lookout for any potential troublemakers.

Ninety minutes into the estimated three-hour journey, Ryder got the distinct impression that things were going *too* well.

It turned out to be a premonition . . .

Ryder knew something was wrong the second he heard the truck's radio crackle.

"We got a bit of a problem," they heard Lancaster say calmly.

Ryder grabbed the radio microphone. "What's up, Averill?" he asked, scanning the sky for the Huey.

"We're about five miles ahead of you," Lancaster reported. "We can see a hell of a fight going on about twelve miles north of us . . ."

"Who's mixing it up?" Ryder asked, at the same time trying to imagine an alternate route back to Spookbase.

The radio crackled. "It appears to be Grays against Greens," Lancaster said. "There's a Green armored column pinned down just south of a large mesa. The Grays are firing on it from two sides, and the Greens are firing back.

"We're going up high to get a better look. Back to you in a flash . . ."

"Goddamn it!" Ryder cursed. "We don't have time to screw around with this . . ."

They both scanned the landscape on either side of the roadway. Most of it was fairly barren, but there were gulches and dry riverbeds, obstacles the water truck would have a hard time negotiating.

The radio crackled again. "More bad news, Ryder . . ." they heard Lancaster say. "We've picked up two Aggressors moving this way. Skyhawks. Coming in low . . ."

"Same old story," Ryder said, braking the truck to a halt. "Grays and Aggressors beating up on the Greens."

Woody shook his head. "And everyone in War Heaven

knows they're just stocking up to hit us . . ."

The radio came alive again. "Spooks, this is Espo. I've got to withdraw my choppers until these A-4s clear the area."

"We copy," Ryder said into the mic. "Any suggestions?"

"Stay cool," Espo advised. "They won't go after a small truck like yours. Not when they can rack up points working over some Green tanks. Pull over and wait it out. We'll be back as soon as the air raid is over. Out."

With that, they saw the three choppers link up and disappear over the western horizon. Off in the distance they could hear the sounds of the battle and the racket of the approaching jets. The desert sun was at its highest point and it was getting very hot inside the truck cab.

"Well, we wait it out," Ryder said, wiping his brow.

"Damn," Woody said quietly. "I just wish Apple had given us a few beers for the ride."

"Yeah," Ryder said, dejectedly. "Me, too . . ."

43

Maureen had no idea where she was . . .

She had been driving on the straight-as-an-arrow desert road for what seemed like days. The last human contact she'd had was at a crossroads gas station at seven that morning. Claiming that she was a photographer for *National Geographic*, she had asked the attendant for directions to the Nellis Range. The man first made a crude remark about topless African women, then directed her to the unmarked road a half mile from the station. This led to the Nellis Range, he told her.

The first impression she had was that the roadway was new. The asphalt looked little used, the yellow center line barely faded. Forty miles in, she had reached an unattended guard house with an open gate. A sign nearby simply said: *Restricted Area—Keep Out.* She ignored it and continued on the road.

That had been hours ago. Now she was getting hungry and hot. She'd been driving all night, leaving San Diego in the late afternoon and would soon be tired also. She fretted over not calling the car rental agency—she knew Joey the owner would be mad at her for taking on such an odyssey. But, looking at her gas gauge, she decided the point would probably be a moot one. The tank was down to nearly a quarter, and she had reason to believe that there were not many Sunoco stations in this neck of the desert.

She was lost and she was mad, but not frightened. She had been watching the jets for the past few hours. They were streaking overhead with clocklike regularity, most of them either heading northeast or southwest. She surmised these airplanes were traveling back and forth to the Nellis Range, and seeing them spared her from the overwhelming feeling that she was alone—*all alone* in the middle of the Nevada desert.

Another hour went by. There was a mountain range ahead and she hoped that once over it, she'd find the vast military reservation the Navy pilot named Panther had led her to believe was Nellis Range. But by the looks of her gas needle, even the mountains were too far away.

Don't panic, she told herself as the car kicked, its carburetor drinking the last few drops of gas. This road wouldn't be here if nobody passed this way, she reasoned. Someone would eventually have to come by. Until then she would have to devise a plan. She'd wait. Work on the story, even start developing the lead. Flag down whoever went by, get some gas, resume the journey. She congratulated herself for her self-induced pluck.

If only she had thought to bring some water . . .

At some point, Maureen fell asleep. She had vague, convoluted dreams that somehow involved the "missing" pilot Ryder Long. When she woke up it took her a few seconds to recall the predicament she was in. When she did, a bolt of panic

245

ran through her—had anyone driven by while she was sleeping? Had she missed her chance for rescue? She cursed herself for not raising the hood, or putting on the four-way flashes, anything that would have signaled her distress.

She took a succession of deep breaths and tried to calm down. If anyone *had* driven by, surely they would have stopped. But this reasoning only served to heighten her anxiety. If no one had driven by in hours, then how many people *did* use this road? She quickly did some more deep breaths, telling herself over and over to calm down, be cool, work out a plan.

The sun was now dipping off to her left, giving the mountain range in front of her an off-pink look. It was getting late. Suddenly she realized that she might have to spend the night in the car. More deep breaths. If only she had some water.

44

Ryder wiped his brow with his now-soaking shirt-sleeve. It was hot—probably the hottest day since they had arrived in the desert. He wished he had something to drink—ironic, he thought, for someone driving a water truck. But he had already tried to sip some of the water he was carrying only to find that Major Apple had been right: the water was oily and undrinkable.

Woody was slouched down in the truck's passenger seat, trying to doze despite the continuous booming of Zootbombs. They been waiting out the battle up ahead for nearly two hours and from the sounds of it, there would be no letup anytime soon. The roadway beneath them felt like a small never-ending earthquake, such was the intensity of the simulated explosions. Between explosions, the air was filled with the distinctive zipping sound of Zootgunfire. The flashing of the Zootbombs was also intense—so much so, it began to hurt their eyes and they found themselves having to look away from the battle scene. Neither man had been in *real* combat before but neither could imagine it looking or sounding very much different from the high-tech simulation ahead.

The Aggressor A-4s had remained over the battlefield for nearly thirty minutes, continually plastering the Green column with a variety of Zoot ordnance. Just as Ryder had calculated the Skyhawks were running low on fuel, two Aggressor F-5s arrived to take their place. Since then, there had been a revolving door of Aggressor strike craft; what had started out as a simple ambush had obviously turned into a major action with both sides sticking it out and racking up points.

The bad news was the battle had kept the Blue choppers far away; the last time they'd talked to Lancaster, their helicopter escort was down and waiting in the mountains twelve miles to their west. With so many Aggressor aircraft flying around, Esposito didn't want to risk meeting up with one either flying to or from the battle.

"Those Greens are really putting up a fight," Woody said, giving up on trying to sleep. "Not like that column outside of Smiling Jack's."

"That's what happens when you haven't got laid in a while," Ryder said.

Suddenly their radio crackled.

"Lancaster here," they heard the familiar Cockney voice say. "Sorry, chaps, but Captain Esposito tells me we have to withdraw the helos."

"What for?" Ryder asked, speaking loudly into the radio mic so Lancaster could hear him over the racket of the nearby battle.

"We got a strange call," Lancaster told him. "From the refs. They need some choppers on the western edge of the range. A security problem that has to be handled immediately. The Blues are the only chopper troops in the area. And you'll recall what Major Max told us what happens if we don't cooperate with the refs."

"Well, I'll be damned," Ryder said, not relishing the prospect of waiting out the Gray-Green battle unprotected.

Lancaster continued. "We'll be taking the long way around back to Spookbase once this security thing is cleared up. Esposito hopes you'll understand and he says he's willing to call off the deal for the ZootSAM . . ."

Both Ryder and Woody understood. They knew that Esposito couldn't risk pissing off the refs just for something as pedestrian as moving three hundred gallons of oily water to Spookbase.

"We copy," Ryder called back to Lancaster. "And tell him he still gets the SAM. But please ask him if he has any suggestions as to what we might do?"

There was a burst of static, then Lancaster replied, "Affirmative. He suggests you backtrack ten klicks to a east-west crossroad. Follow to the east to open country, then reroute north again. You'll be passing through empty territory, and you shouldn't run into anyone. You should start to see familiar territory after a couple hours on that north road. I'll inform them of your situation back at the base. Good luck and over . . ."

Ryder immediately started up the truck and began making an eleven-point U-turn.

"It'll be the long way around and we might have to dodge some Grays," he said. "But it sure beats sitting here and cooking."

"I'm with you, Ghost," Woody confirmed.

Ryder gunned the truck back down the road, the sounds of the ferocious battle gradually getting dimmer. By the time they reached the crossroads, they could hear no sounds from the battle at all.

They turned onto the prescribed road and headed east. The sun was going down behind them—it would be dark in a little over an hour. With some luck, Ryder hoped they'd reach Spookbase before 1900 hours.

The moon came up so bright that when dusk fell they found they could drive without using the truck's headlights.

Although they were in unoccupied territory, Ryder felt safer riding without the headlamps.

They reached the north road and steered onto it, bouncing along the rough surface. The sun was long gone and the bright moon was rising quickly in the night sky. Heading due north they noticed the western horizon was a never-ending string of bright Zootflashes. The Gray-Green battle was still going full tilt.

Woody let out a long breath. "You got to admit, despite everything, it's sure peaceful out here . . ."

Ryder was about to agree with him when he saw three sets of lights appear out over the eastern horizon. Woody saw them at the same time.

"They're not Aggressors," Ryder said, noting the wide space between the approaching aircraft's navigation lights. "I think they're Hercs . . ."

"They *are* Hercs," Woody confirmed, using their spyglasses to get a good look at the aircraft. "And they're flying low enough for a drop . . ."

"But this is unoccupied territory," Ryder said. "There's not supposed to be anything—or anybody—out here."

They watched the aircraft turn to a slight northwest heading, then twist back and head right toward them. The lead craft then dipped down and they saw the familiar parachute pallet yank out from the C-130's rear.

"Jeesuz," Woody said. "They're dropping stuff right in the middle of the desert . . ."

"What the hell is going on?" Ryder asked, slowing the truck down to a crawl.

The second C-130 dipped in and disgorged its pallet, pulling up into an engine-screaming turn. The third airplane did likewise, its equipment pallet landing no more than an eighth of a mile off the road from them.

The three Hercules then formed up and quickly roared away, disappearing off to the south.

Ryder stopped the truck completely. They were both silent for a moment, each wondering what to do.

"The way I see it, we got two options, partner," Woody said.

"We can keep on going or we can wait and see who picks up this stuff."

Ryder smiled. This was supposed to be one big War *Game*, right? So why not play?

"I think we have a third option," he said. "I say we go and see what kind of stuff they dropped . . ."

Woody turned it over for a few moments, then said, "Sure, what the hell . . ."

Five minutes later they were making their way down into the roadside gulch and up the other side to where the equipment pallets lay. They were sure no one was coming. The road was so straight and the moon so bright, they knew they'd see any approaching vehicle from way off.

Ryder reached the first pallet and waited for Woody to catch up with his jackknife. The pallet was packed and bound just as the one dropped to them at Spookbase. Ryder estimated each of these pallets weighed close to a thousand pounds.

Woody arrived and was soon cutting away one side of the pallet's heavy rope bindings.

"Do you think these may have been dropped here by mistake?" the Wiz asked as he worked on the thick twine.

"Who knows?" Ryder answered, scanning the road in each direction looking for anyone approaching. "Anything is possible in this place."

Woody finally managed to cut through one rope bind. He made quick work of slicing through the pallet's heavy canvas covering. Underneath they found several wooden boxes.

"Look, there's writing on them," Woody said.

Sure enough, there were sets of numbers stenciled on the side of the box. But it was the writing in the bottom corner that proved most mysterious.

"What the hell does that say?" Woody asked, trying to read the lettering in the moonlight.

"It says: Cartoon Valley," Ryder reported.

"'Cartoon Valley?'" Woody repeated. "What the hell is that?"

"Beats the shit out of me," Ryder said.

"Now what?" Woody asked.

Ryder was playing this one by ear. "What the hell," he said. "Let's bust one of them open."

They pulled the box out, and using the jackknife, pried off the nails holding its cover down. The box itself was heavy and was obviously well packed, indicating something breakable was inside.

"I almost got this cover off," Woody said, springing off the wooden lid just as he spoke.

They both plunged their hands in the box only to grapple with handfuls of packing straw. Finally, Ryder hit something solid.

He reached deep down and pulled it out. It was a clear wrapped package containing circuit boards.

Meanwhile Woody had reached inside the box and grabbed another box, brought it up, and opened it.

"What the hell you got there?" Ryder asked anxiously.

"More high-tech toys," Woody said, inspecting the contents of the box. It was filled with semiconductor chips and wire. "Not exactly your typical CARE packages, are they?"

Suddenly Ryder felt his sixth sense tingling . . .

He spun around and saw a pair of headlights coming from the south.

"Damn, we got company," he said, pointing toward the approaching lights. They were still a good ten miles away. "Time to go . . ."

"What should we do with this stuff?" Woody asked.

"Leave it," he answered. "None of it is any good to us."

The headlights were still three minutes away by the time they reached the truck. Ryder quickly gunned the engine and they were moving within seconds. Only then did they discuss their find.

"What do think?" Woody asked him, as he watched the headlights in the side-view mirror. "Who the hell would be getting all that sophisticated stuff way out here?"

"Beats me," Ryder said. "Maybe there's something out here we don't know about. Whatever the hell 'Cartoon Valley' is."

"Well, those guys coming to pick up this stuff must know," Woody said.

"Yeah," Ryder agreed, tracking the headlights again. "The question is, how do we benefit in finding out where their base is?"

45

The light in Maureen's eyes was so bright, her pupils began to sting.

She was terrified. She had fallen asleep again, this time just before sundown. And again, she had dreams—much more vivid than before—about the pilot named Ryder Long . . .

But now a loud explosion had knocked her awake. Immediately her car started rocking back and forth violently. There were bright lights everywhere, some white, some blinking red. Great clouds of dust were swirling all around her. The noise was deafening.

"*What's happening to me!*" she whispered, trying her best to wake up from the bad dream.

Suddenly there was a loud rapping at her driver's side window. She took a quick look and saw the ghastly image of a man's face appearing in the midst of the lights and dust and noise. She gasped, trying with all her will to fight off the panic.

But she couldn't. It was just too much. She felt herself fainting. Water . . . she thought, slipping into unconsciousness. "If only I had brought some water . . ."

When she came to sometime later, Maureen was surrounded by at least a half dozen men. It was dark and she was laid out on the cold asphalt, a coarse blanket covering her from the neck down.

The men were soldiers, and when she realized this, she

became slightly more at ease. She saw her car, with all its doors open, parked about twenty feet away. Just beyond it, parked in the middle of the road, were three helicopters, their bright searchlights still trained on her rental. It was these machines that had produced the nightmarish wind, sound, and light show earlier.

"Miss?" one of the men was saying. "Can you hear me?"

She nodded weakly.

"You're OK," another man said, his voice carrying a definite English accent.

She was quickly snapping out of it. That's when she saw most of the soldiers were carrying guns.

"You are in trouble, though, miss," the first man said. "Do you know this is a restricted area?"

"I'm . . . I'm a photographer," she told them.

The first man shook his head. "No you're not," he said. She looked up to see he was holding her *Washington Post* ID card.

"OK," she said, finally getting up. "I *am* a reporter. I'm sorry. I took a wrong turn somewhere and ran out of gas. If you can give me some gas, I'll just turn around and leave . . ."

While she was talking, she was taking in everything about the soldiers. Five of them were wearing Blue uniforms and blue scarfs around their necks. The one who spoke in the English accent was wearing a green uniform that she recognized as Marine Corps issue. The seventh man, the one with the ID card, was wearing a strange black-and-white-striped uniform. He almost looked like a football referee.

"I'm sorry, miss," the referee said. "You'll have to come with us . . ."

"For what?" she said in the sternest voice she could muster.

"Well, miss," the referee said. "You're going to be put under arrest . . ."

"Arrest?" she almost laughed out the word. "On what charge?"

The referee looked at her grimly. "Espionage . . ."

This time she did laugh. "You've got to be kidding," she told the man.

He shook his head. "This is very serious, miss," he said.

"You've been apprehended in a restricted area. You should have turned around when you reached the gate and the warning signs way back there."

"But the gate was wide open . . ." she started to protest. But the man was ignoring her.

". . . and you were apprehended with photographic equipment," he was saying. "These are serious charges . . ."

She had had enough. She was still shaking from the rude awakening. Plus she was hungry, tired, dirty, and cold. Time to play the trump card.

"OK," she said. "I'm sorry I wandered onto your base. But I think you'll find that your espionage charge is way out of line. I'm not a spy. In fact . . ." she let the words come out as authoritatively as possible, ". . . my father, General Tom O'Brien is a counsel general at the Pentagon. I think one call to him would . . ."

The referee held up his hand. "We know all about your father," he said sternly. "He's being held on a charge of espionage, too . . ."

46

Ryder walked into the airstrip's operations shack and found Slade asleep at his desk. The small building, like the whole airstrip, reeked of tear gas.

"Slade! *Wake up!*" he said, shaking the man.

Slade woke so quickly, it startled Ryder.

"What the hell . . ." the man asked. "Ryder . . . what's going on? Where the hell you been?"

"We're back with the water, Slade," Ryder said. "Didn't Lancaster get back yet?"

Slade scratched his head. "No, he didn't," the Navy officer

said. "Isn't he with you?"

Ryder sat on the edge of the desk and ran his hand through his hair. "No," he said. "Woody and I drove back in the water truck. Lancaster stayed with the Blue choppers. We ran into a hell of a fight around fifty miles south of here. The Grays ambushed a big Green column, then called in the Aggressors for air support."

"Those goddamn cowboys," Slade said, slamming his fist on the desk. "They're taking the whole thing so fucking seriously."

"Yeah, well maybe they know something we don't," Ryder said.

"So what happened to Lancaster?" Slade asked.

Ryder continued. "We were waiting for the Aggressors to clear the area so the choppers could go on. That's when Esposito got a call to help the referees . . ."

"The referees?" Slade asked. "What the hell for?"

"Don't ask me," Ryder said. "All I know is they took off and left us on our own. They had to go or the refs, you know, like what Maxwell said. It's all in the rule book."

Slade thought for a moment, then nodded. "It is," he said. "I think I read that just yesterday. You lose points if you don't help the refs."

"Woody and I had to drive that frigging water tank halfway across Nevada," Ryder said. "But Lancaster said he'd call in and tell you."

"He might have tried to call us," Slade said. "But we've had it rough here since you guys left."

Ryder sniffed a couple of times. "So I can tell," he said. "What happened?"

"Goddamn Aggressors," Slade said. "They were at us all day. One Crab Bomb attack and a half dozen more with Supertears."

Ryder whistled. "These guys are getting out of hand."

"Well, we got two more of them," Slade said. "Moon's guys got two more ZootSAMs working. The lieutenant himself shot down an A-4 and an F-5."

"That's good news," Ryder said. "We should get some kind

255

of a Herc drop for that . . ."

"We'd better," Slade told him. "We're just about running out of food again. Fuel for the generators is pretty low, too."

"We're going to need every pound of material we can get," Ryder said somberly. "Esposito said the Gray Army are planning a big attack on the Blues. They're going for broke. And the Aggressors will probably throw in with them. That's why they've been picking on the Greens—and us, too—to get cheap points. Then they split the supply drops."

Slade was nodding. "I know. I heard the same thing from Major Max today," Slade said. "They say this will be the biggest fight in the history of War Heaven and there's no way we can stay out of it. The Grays know we'll support the Blues so they're going to do everything to knock us out before we get flying."

He and Ryder headed out of the shack and toward the water tank truck.

Slade was still working the last of the tear gas out of his eyes. "This place gets crazier all the time," he said.

"You ain't heard nothing yet," Ryder told him. "We found a base out there that makes everything else here in War Heaven look like a bad penny arcade."

It took a moment for Ryder's comment to sink in. "What?" Slade asked, completely perplexed.

Ryder continued. "There is a base no more than twenty miles southeast of here. It's built into a valley. It's all desert. But I'll tell you, whoever is operating it can throw a switch and suddenly it looks all green. Like a forest."

"You're nuts," Slade told him. "What did you get hit with, Hal-Lou while you were out there?"

By this time they had reached the water truck. Sitting on its hood was Woody.

They quickly told the Navy officer about the mysterious Herc drop and about looking through the pallet.

"Some trucks arrived and loaded up the stuff," Ryder continued the story. "We followed them. Way the hell over to this small mountain range and into this valley. Out in the middle of nowhere. We were about a mile away when we see this really strange shit happening. One second the valley is

256

desert. The next, it's as lush as a rain forest."

Slade looked at them. "Look," he said, "I have no choice but to believe you. This place is so fucking screwy, I know anything can happen here. But changing desert to jungle with the flick of a switch? That's a little *too* fucking screwy . . ."

"The marking on the boxes we found said 'Cartoon Valley,'" Woody told him. "And the crates were filled with semiconductors, circuit boards. You name it. Stuff you would need to pull off an illusion like that."

Slade could only shrug. "Beats me what it's all about," he said. "But as wild as it is, we can't concern ourselves with it now. I've got something to show you guys . . ."

He walked out toward the darkened runway, Ryder and Woody close behind. The airstrip itself was totally blacked out; the only visible lights were dimmed bulbs attached to the radar and the three ZootSAM launchers.

Slade's first stop was the small radar station which was manned by two of Moon's men.

"Anything on the scope, guys?" the Navy officer asked. The technicians did a quick check. "Nothing, Commander," one reported.

"OK, yell loud if you see anything," Slade told them.

Next, Slade walked toward the control box for the airstrip's high-power portable lights. With the flip of a switch, he turned on half of the bank of fourteen lights. Suddenly the northern end of the runway was illuminated.

And there sat, completely installed and gleaming, the field catapult . . .

47

The Zoot air-to-air missile hit the Huey helicopter with a deafening broadside, its lightning flash blinding the four people riding in its passenger compartment.

RAF Captain Lancaster reached up to his ear just as the holographic image of the explosion was disappearing. He felt a trickle of blood—the explosion had been so loud, it had ruptured a blood vessel in his ear canal.

The woman reporter they were transporting wound up in his lap. The two soldiers sitting across from him were also tossed around as the chopper lurched first left then right.

Up front in the flight compartment, Captain Esposito saw his control panel lights blink off, one by one. He knew instantly what was happening—the black box inside the Huey's control computer, reacting to the Zootmissile hit, was systematically shutting down all but the most essential flight systems. Esposito knew he had to land the Huey—quickly.

"Hang on back there!" Esposito yelled back to his passengers. "We're going in . . ."

Lancaster helped the woman back up to her seat. Her blouse was ripped slightly in the tussle, and the British pilot found himself staring at her very lovely cleavage.

"Thank you," she managed to say, trying to settle down her long blond hair, then adding, *"What the hell happened?"*

Lancaster began to say they'd been hit by a holographic projected missile, but quickly caught himself. He didn't want to be the one who spilled the whole Zoot story to *The Washington Post.*

"Better strap in," he told her instead.

The chopper touched down twenty seconds later. Esposito quickly climbed back into the passenger compartment, checking to make sure everyone was in one piece.

"What happened just then, Captain?" the reporter asked him. "Did we crash?"

Espo also caught on quickly. "Equipment malfunctioned, miss. We'll have to evacuate the craft . . ."

They slowly climbed out of the chopper, Esposito dousing the few lights left on aboard the aircraft. They were in a gully, next to a small forest of desert bush. Yet despite the site's seemingly isolated location, the air was filled with the noise of running machinery.

High above, Lancaster could see a pair of navigation lights circling. He knew they belonged to the Aggressor airplane that had shot them down. He pulled Esposito aside and pointed out the jet's running lights.

"He's got our position already," Lancaster said.

"Son of a bitch flyboy," Esposito said. "Taking out a transport chopper. Those guys will do anything for the points."

The Blue Army captain quickly took stock of the situation, then whispered to Lancaster. The British captain nodded and moved over to keep the reporter occupied.

Esposito gathered his crew around him and said, "We got to watch what we say around the reporter. She's not stupid, so don't give her any condescending answers. Just be polite. Say, 'Yes, ma'am,' 'No, ma'am,' 'I'm sorry I don't know the answer to that, Ma'am.' Got it?"

They nodded.

Just then the sound of the machinery got louder.

Esposito signaled for his navigator and the waist gunner to check out the source of the noise. They scrambled up the side of the gulch—and quickly slid back down again.

"Lot of soldiers right over the hill," the navigator told him, just out of earshot from the rest of the group.

"How far away?" Esposito wanted to know.

"No more than a half klick," the navigator reported. "They're Grays. Some on foot. Some in vehicles. In full battle gear. Looks like a big movement. Maybe two battalions."

"Jesus Christ," Esposito cursed. "We gotta get bounced right in the middle of half the Gray Army. I can't believe they didn't see or hear us come down."

Lancaster was back beside him. "They are moving at night, Captain," he said. "Perhaps this is the beginning of the big battle Major Apple spoke about."

"Just our luck . . ." Espo said, then added, "Goddamn referee. He's back probably sucking up a Bud, and we're playing his go-boys."

They had dropped off the ref back at the Central Command HQ with instructions to move the reporter to Smiling Jack's

259

where they would turn her over to men from the National Security Agency.

Suddenly they heard the roar of a mechanized vehicle. They all turned toward the end of the gully and saw a Gray APC was coming toward them. The vehicle's powerful searchlight was on them in a second.

"Damn!" Esposito said as the APC screeched to a halt. In a matter of seconds they were staring at a half dozen Gray troops pointing ZootM-16s at them.

The navigator moaned. "Major Max is gonna go nuts when he finds out we lost his chopper."

Esposito glanced over at the woman reporter. His heart sank when he saw that she was taking notes.

48

"This is a very serious matter, General," the assistant secretary said. "You have no idea what is at stake here."

"I can only agree with you, sir," General O'Brien replied. "That's why this suspicion of espionage is so absurd. I am an American, damn it. I've served this country loyally for more than thirty years."

They were alone, sitting in the assistant secretary's private office in the basement of the Pentagon. O'Brien had no idea what time it was, but he was sure that it was dark outside. He had talked to more than twenty-two officers in the past twenty-four hours. He had worked his way up through the assistant secretary command staff, to the joint chiefs of staff and now, finally, the assistant secretary himself. Where would it end?

"General," the assistant secretary said. "What would you do if you were in my position? My people would say to me that this wouldn't be the first time a family has gone in for espionage together. Look at the Walker family. How can I explain this to the secretary and he to the President?"

"I've told you, sir," O'Brien said. "I don't know anything about this project, other than it's code name was approved by my office and that it involved some deep training of selected troops."

The assistant secretary lit a cigarette. "Then it's just a coincidence that your daughter is now in custody, after trying to gain access to the most restricted area in the country, with photographic equipment?" he asked in a puff of smoke.

"She's a reporter, for God's sake," O'Brien replied, calmly but sternly. "Have you called the *Post* yet to confirm that she works there?"

The assistant secretary didn't answer . . .

49

"The question is, does it work?" Ryder asked, looking at the in-place field catapult.

It was early the next morning. Already the airbase was abuzz with activity.

"It will work," Lieutenant Moon said in answer to Ryder's question. "All we needed was the water and you got that. We started loading it into the tanks earlier this morning. We've got the generators cranked up and hope to have a full load of steam within the hour."

"Then what?" Ryder asked the young officer.

Moon looked over his handiwork—the catapult was installed in less than thirty-six hours, thanks to the help of the men, the other pilots, and the eight Gray POWs. Moon allowed himself a moment of pride.

"Then we test it a couple times," he answered Ryder. "Then

we launch . . ."

Launch. An excitement was running through Ryder, triggered the night before when he first saw the catapult shining in the glow of the portable runway lights. It was the same feeling he had when he first flew many years ago. All this craziness, all the uncertainty about what Distant Thunder was all about—all of it he put up with simply because he wanted to fly. And *keep* flying. Now, looking to the catapult, he hoped—prayed—he'd be flying again.

"You've done a great job here, Lieutenant," Ryder told him. "You and your men have been outstanding . . ."

"Thank you, Captain," Moon said modestly. "Glad to be part of it . . ."

The lieutenant went back to work supervising the other component of the system, the four heavy gauge wires that would stretch across the runway and watch the Tomcats on landing, similar to recovery on an aircraft carrier. Ryder walked to Hangar One to look over the three F-14s one more time.

The flight hangar had become Reinhart's domain. The unsmiling German pilot had taken over all aspects of the Tomcats' checkout, starting the engines every day, tuning the avionics, and supervising the other pilots and Moon's men in keeping the fighters ready for the day they would actually fly.

And he knew that day could be today . . .

Oddly, Ryder hadn't had that much control with the other foreign pilots since they arrived at Spookbase. It just seemed that everyone had selected his duty to perform and they went about doing it. Sammett and Chauvagne had first worked around the clock on the ZootSAMs and now were helping Reinhart with the weapons systems on the 'Cats. Lancaster—wherever he was—had become an aide de camp for Slade. Ryder and Woody, it seemed, had been destined to be the intelligence officers for the base, a role they fell into just as the others fell into theirs. Ryder couldn't help thinking: Had it all been somehow planned this way?

Reinhart gave him a very businesslike update on the three fighters. All were in good shape—their engines were in top

262

trim, all the electronics were "green." The day before the German had pulled each jet out of the hangar and tested their Zootweapons—Sidewinders and the front cannon. Each time the holographic projection units worked perfectly.

"I can see why the Aggressors are so anxious to keep us grounded," Reinhart told Ryder. "These airplanes are worth three of their F-5s or A-4s. We have the multi-targeting systems, the APG radar, the variety of weapons. The Aggressors drop gas bombs and probably have very weak radar."

Ryder agreed with the German. The balance of power would change if and when the 'Cats got airborne. Besides providing an air cap for the base, and thus interfering if not preventing further air attacks, the F-14s could theoretically go out looking for the Aggressors, challenge their until-now complete dominance of the skies over War Heaven. The Aggressors would have to change their tactics. They would have to be prepared to dogfight. They would have to carry defensive weapons, which would cut down on the number of gas bombs they could carry.

Everything would change if they could only get the F-14s into the air . . .

Ryder was examining the F-14's odd mid-air refueling probe when Slade and Woody walked into the hangar.

"What's up?" Ryder asked them. "Any news about Lancaster?"

Woody nodded. "Yeah," he said, smiling. "And it's Twilight Zone time again."

"We just got a call from a guy at Smiling Jack's," Slade said. "He says *he's* got Lancaster. And he wants to make a deal."

"Smiling Jack's?" Ryder said. "What the hell is Lancaster doing there?"

"This guy wouldn't even ID himself, never mind tell me how our boy wound up in a cathouse," Slade told him. "He just says that he's a go-between and he'll deal Lancaster back to us."

"In return for what?" Ryder asked.

"The eight Gray POWs," Woody said. "It's a prisoner swap . . ."

"Somehow, Lancaster and that Blue chopper crew got themselves captured," Slade added. "I talked to Major Max and he's making a separate deal for his guys. But he's pissed because the Grays won't return his Huey."

"So what do we do?" Ryder asked. "I can think of worse places to be held captive than a cathouse."

"Yeah, we should all be so lucky," Slade said, not forgetting that both Ryder and Woody had gotten their tubes cleaned several days before while on the initial water scouting mission. "But we need the Redcoat back. So I say, let's deal . . ."

Two hours later, Ryder drove the captured Gray jeep into the small town and parked in front of the saloon.

It had been a slow journey. Woody and Slade had accompanied him along with the eight POWs and everyone had to take turns riding on the jeep's hood and tail. This, and the rough terrain, made the five-mile trip a ninety-minute odyssey.

As before, the town was crowded. There was a scattering of Blue Army trucks and jeeps. But what really caught Ryder's attention was the dozen or so Gray vehicles parked out front. Three M-1 tanks, several APCs, two Bradleys, even a mobile howitzer parked alongside the building. All were wearing a fresh coat of Gray paint.

"The spoils of war," Ryder said, touching the still sticky paint on the side of a nearby APC. "The Greens better find themselves some good walking boots."

Woody agreed to keep an eye on the Gray POWs while Slade and Ryder went into the bar to meet the mysterious go-between, a man known only as Jammer.

The saloon was crowded with Blue and Gray soldiers, with the usual scattering of civilian types. The Greens were conspicuously absent. It was past noon, so the girls were already circulating among the troops, pairing off and moving upstairs. Slade was taking it all in with open-mouthed astonishment.

"This is unbelievable," he said as he and Ryder made their way to the bar.

"Yeah, sure," Ryder said, feeling more and more immune to the craziness of War Heaven. "You want a beer, Slade?"

The Navy officer didn't hesitate. "You bet your ass I want a beer," he said, feasting his eyes on a nearby female employee.

Ryder ordered two beers, charged them to the Spooks' tab, then asked the bartender where they could find the man called Jammer.

"Got business with him?" the bartender asked.

"We're here to make a deal with him," Ryder answered, sipping his beer.

The bartender nodded knowingly. Ryder realized the barkeep was most likely a CIA operative; who else could be trusted to pour drinks in a bar such as this? He reached down underneath the bar and came up with a portable telephone. A quick, muted conversation followed, after which the bartender pointed to the upstairs.

"Room 39," he said. "Knock three times . . ."

A quick trip up to the second floor and three raps on door number 39 later, they were greeted by the man called Jammer.

Far from being the wheeler-dealer they expected, Jammer was a small, balding US Army colonel who looked more like an accountant than one of the cast of War Heaven characters.

"Come in, gentlemen," Jammer said, ushering them into the small room. It was exactly the same layout Ryder had seen before in Sandy's apartment, except Jammer had a desk, a reading light, and a telephone.

"You know why we're here, Colonel," Slade told him.

"Yes, I do, Commander Slade," Jammer said. "And I'm glad that you brought Captain Long with you."

Ryder was fairly surprised the man knew who he was.

"We have the eight Gray soldiers outside," Slade said. "Where's Captain Lancaster?"

Jammer pulled a small notebook out of his pocket and ran through a few pages. "Let's see," he said. "The captain is in Room 15. You can go see him, Commander, if you like. And, if

I could have a word with Captain Long?"

Slade looked at Ryder, who shrugged. "I'll go round up Crumpets," Slade said. "I'll be back in a few."

Slade left, leaving Ryder and Jammer alone.

"What's up, Colonel?" Ryder asked the strange little man.

Jammer laughed and motioned him to take a seat. Ryder eased into the desk chair as Jammer sat on the edge of his bed.

"Your name has been coming up a lot lately, Captain," Jammer said. "In the strangest places."

"I guess I don't know what you mean, sir," Ryder said, genuinely mystified. Was there a stranger place than War Heaven?

Jammer rubbed his chin in thought, then said, "There's a young woman here, not one of the working girls, who claims she knows you. Or, more accurately, knows all about you."

"Who is she?" Ryder asked, wondering himself.

"Oddly enough, she's a reporter, Captain," Jammer said, looking him straight in the eye to get his reaction. "A reporter from *The Washington Post* . . ."

"Jeesuz," Ryder said. "I can't believe you let a reporter in here . . ."

"That's just it, Captain," Jammer said. "We didn't. She was apprehended out on the western edge of the range. That's what Esposito's chopper crews were called on to do—transport a referee to pick her up. Captain Lancaster had the back luck to be aboard when the call came in.

"Esposito's Huey was shot down by an Aggressor last night as they were bringing the woman here. He and his crew—Lancaster included—were captured by the Grays and brought here, as was the woman."

Ryder shook his head. "Well, I'm glad to know what happened to them, and that they're all OK," he said. "But what's it all got to do with me?"

Jammer reached into the desk drawer and came up with a manila envelope. The first thing he pulled out was Ryder's last service photo, taken several years before when he first started flying C-130s. Then he retrieved a paper-clipped batch of documents which Ryder recognized as his service file.

266

"The woman was carrying these when we apprehended her," Jammer told him. "She had similar but not as extensive documents on Captain Woods. She apparently picked them up at NAS Miramar. Just walked in and asked for them at the personnel office."

"And they gave them to her?" Ryder asked. "What she do, hold a gun on them?"

Jammer laughed again. "This woman doesn't need a gun," he said.

Ryder was baffled. "I'm sorry, Colonel," he said. "But I'm in the dark about all this . . ."

Jammer was quiet for a moment, then he said, "Captain, I realize that you and the others are being kept in the dark about a lot of things. And I know that your experience here in War Heaven must be bewildering. But I must also say that what we are doing here—what we are preparing for—is of the utmost importance. I cannot emphasize this enough. We, in this country and in fact, all over the world, are facing a crisis of unprecedented proportions. The Cuban Missile Crisis pales greatly in comparison. But just as with that situation, the classified integrity of the preparations to deal with the crisis is *most* essential."

Jammer returned the documents to the envelope and placed it back inside the desk.

"No more than a dozen officers at the Pentagon know what Project Distant Thunder is about," the colonel began again. "Yet, we catch this woman reporter, trying to sneak into War Heaven, with a full dossier on you and Captain Woods, two of the prime components in Distant Thunder. What do you make of all this?"

Ryder shrugged again. "I really don't know, Colonel," he said. "How could I possibly tell someone—anyone—about Distant Thunder when I don't know what it is all about myself?"

Jammer didn't answer.

267

50

Slade found Lancaster lying on top of a bed with one of Smiling Jack's working girls.

"Well, I hope I'm not disturbing you, Captain," the Navy officer said, noting both were fully clothed.

"Not now, Commander," Lancaster answered with a grin. "Your timing is perfect . . ."

The RAF pilot climbed off the bed, gave the girl a peck on the cheek. "Goodbye, my sweet," he said before following Slade out into the hall.

"Well, you've been sprung, Lancaster," Slade told him. "We're giving up the eight Gray POWs for you."

"Sorry for the mess, Commander," Lancaster said. "I know those Gray soldiers were helpful to us."

"Don't worry about it," Slade said. "We're just about through with them anyway. Besides, this will be eight less mouths to feed."

They stopped at the far end of the hall to wait for Ryder.

"My brief capture was not a total loss," Lancaster said. "I've seen and heard many things in the past twelve hours."

"Such as?"

"Such as a massive build-up of Gray troops moving our way," Lancaster told him. "Our chopper was forced down right in the middle of them last night. Before they separated us, Espo and I theorized that the Grays are planning a two-prong attack. The Blue's northern base is one target . . ."

"And we're the other," Slade finished for him.

"Exactly, Coomander," the Englishman confirmed. "When we get back to Spookbase, I can document everything I saw. It may prove helpful."

Just then, the door down the other end of the hall opened and Ryder emerged, shaking his head.

"All through with Mr. Jammer?" Slade asked him.

"Sure," Ryder said. "And he's as screwy as everyone else here."

The trio made their way downstairs and saw the eight former

Gray Army POWs sitting at the bar, with Woody holding down the far end.

Slade quickly explained to them that they were free to go. He was sure that they could catch a ride back to their unit from one of the many Gray vehicles parked outside.

The prisoner exchange completed, the Spook pilots walked out to the jeep. Ryder quickly briefed them on his talk with Jammer about the mysterious woman reporter.

"She's a beauty, I'll tell you that," Lancaster reported. "She was a little batty when we picked her up, but she sprung right back. Was working on her story even as the Grays were moving us to Smiling Jack's. She kept her cool. Didn't say much. Just observed."

"That's all they need," Slade said. "A reporter in the middle of this Fantasyland . . ."

Lancaster laughed. "I don't think they know quite what to do with her," he said. "But she's going to have a crackerjack story when she's through . . ."

With Slade behind the wheel, the jeep roared out of the small town, just as trucks—both Gray and Blues—were driving in.

"Jeesuz, this place is busy," Slade said. "But I suppose that should be expected from the only cathouse within a few hundred miles."

"They also expect a big crowd here tonight," Woody told them. "The bartender told me every time there's a big fight brewing, Smiling Jack's throws a party. You know, like gladiators getting their last kicks. Booze. Food. Girls."

"Incredible . . ." Slade said.

Lancaster was shaking his head and laughing. "You Yanks are really potty," he said. "In England before a big battle they all give you an extra biscuit with your tea."

Slade, Woody, and Lancaster then went on to discuss the various virtues of some of the bar girls they had seen at Jack's. Ryder, however, remained quiet for the entire return trip.

The pilots returned to the base just as Moon was preparing to

269

test the catapult for the first time.

A crowd of base personnel gathered at midpoint of the runway to witness the event. Moon's men checked and rechecked every component one last time. The lieutenant himself was huddled over the catapult's all-important steam boiler, watching a gauge which would tell him when the correct amount of steam had been accumulated.

Finally he called out, "OK, we are at launch pressure."

His men cleared away from the mechanism and Moon calmly walked over to the catapult's control panel. The launcher looked all the world like a huge metal slingshot, the Spookbase's David against the Gray Goliath.

"All clear," Moon yelled out. Then, without fanfare he flipped a switch.

There was a sudden *whoosh* of steam and a loud, metallic bang. The fastening chucks streaked forward incredibly fast, hitting the end bar with another clang. It was over in less than two seconds. Ryder and the others knew by Moon's yelp that the thing worked. There was a spontaneous eruption of applause and cheers.

Moon was beaming. "We'll be able to try a real launch this time tomorrow," Moon proudly told Slade.

Just then, they heard a familiar whine of engines. Off to the south they saw a single C-130 approaching.

"This must be the payoff for icing those two Aggressors yesterday," Slade said. "It won't be much, because the fuckers really plastered us. But at least it will be something."

The Hercules roared in and disgorged an equipment pallet at the opposite end of the runway, far away from the catapult. The big plane circled around, came in and dropped a second pallet, then climbed and disappeared over the southern horizon.

"Two loads," Slade said, watching Moon's men run to recover the pallets. "Just enough to keep us going for another day, maybe two."

"Don't worry, Slade," Woody told him, turning back toward the catapult. "Once we get those Tomcats in the air and scoring points, they'll be dropping to us day and night."

51

The sun was slowly dipping into a brilliant desert sunset as Ryder approached the small town. He was not surprised to see a parade of headlights moving down the main road toward Smiling Jack's. Woody had been right—it *was* going to be a busy night at the cathouse.

Ryder was alone. He knew this mission had to be a solo—not even Woody could help him on this one.

Ryder had spent most of the day simply thinking. Thinking not only about where he was, but also *who* he was. The answer? He was a soldier, but he was also a fairly rational human being. He realized the need for the secrecy surrounding Distant Thunder—even the aircrew that dropped the first atomic bomb was kept in the dark until the deed was done. But he also had to balance certain conflicts within himself. Was this effort—the elaborate war gaming in War Heaven, his extensive training at Top Gun—heading toward a resoundable conclusion? Obviously the stakes were high—he knew this even before his sobering talk with Jammer.

But ever since the whole crazy dream started, he had been getting his information from the sole source: the Military. Do this, do that. Go here. Go there. He obeyed not so much because he was a flag-waving automaton, but because the reward was that he could fly. Fly the most elaborate, expensive, and beautiful jets in the world. He had sold his soul in return for being free—free to soar at 25,000 feet at twice the speed of sound. That's all he had ever wanted. He had no family. No friends outside of the service. No real place to call home. He knew he could drop off the face of the earth tomorrow and who would know? Who would care? He was a loner not so much by choice, but by fate. He had always assumed it would be like this for his whole life. And he had always accepted it as such.

Until today . . .

He didn't really believe in things like ESP, coincidences, synchronicity—his mind was far too technical. He had never allowed it to expand into the realms of imagination to consider what invisible forces were working in the world—if any. But it was his conversation with Jammer that had flipped him. Not about the Distant Thunder, its importance or the importance of keeping the whole goddamn thing secret. It was when the officer had mentioned the woman reporter. Something struck Ryder right between the eyes when he first heard about her, even though Jammer had never even mentioned the woman's name. The message—where did it come from?—hit Ryder so loud and clear, his ears had started ringing and they hadn't stopped since. Lancaster's description of the woman only intensified the feeling. His subsequent hours of thinking—yes, he would even call it meditating—had convinced him of one thing: She was the woman he'd been seeing in his dreams lately.

He knew that he had to meet her . . .

He drove down into the town and found the place was so mobbed he had to park the jeep at the far end of the street. The crowd at Jack's was already spilling out into the street. He noticed mostly Blue and Gray troops, plus a few troops wearing all red flight overalls. Ryder theorized that these men were Aggressor pilots.

He squeezed his way inside the saloon's swinging doors and made his way to the bar. In amongst the crush of drinking soldiers there were at least a hundred bar girls roaming about. As usual, paired-off couples were moving up and down the stairs leading to the second floor. There were three bartenders handling the crowd, and it appeared they weren't even bothering to charge the drinks to the correct units. It was a drinking man's dream—an unlimited open bar.

Ryder managed to flag down one of the bartenders and get a bourbon. As he sipped the drink, he scanned the crowd looking for familiar faces—one of them being Jammer. But the mysterious colonel was nowhere to be found.

Then Ryder got lucky and spotted Sandy, the girl he'd been with on his first trip to Smiling Jack's. She was across the crowded room, snuggling on the lap of a Gray Army captain. After a few moments, Ryder was able to get her attention. She whispered something into the officer's ear, causing him to let out a boisterous "Hot damn!" Then she broke free from him and joined Ryder at the bar.

"I was hoping you'd come back, Ryder," she told him.

Ryder looked at the sweet young thing. He suddenly wished he could bed her on the spot. But he was here for a different reason.

"I need a favor," he said to her. "I need some information . . ."

She looked slightly confused, but said, "I'll try to help."

Ryder bit his lip in thought. He knew what he was about to do wasn't exactly kosher. He also knew that there was a good chance that Sandy, just like all of the other girls at Jack's, was a CIA operative and could immediately turn him in. But his ears were still ringing. He knew he had to go through with his plan.

"The Grays brought a woman here yesterday," he began. "They had captured her along with the British pilot from my base. Do you know who I mean?"

Sandy nodded immediately. "Yes, I saw her," she said.

"Do you know if she's still here?" Ryder asked.

Sandy frowned. "Is she a . . . a special friend of yours or something?" she asked.

"I just have to talk to her," Ryder said quickly. "It's very important, honey."

Sandy looked him straight in the eye. Suddenly the veneer of the bar girl disappeared and the cold hard look of a government employee came over her.

"You know, we can both get in deep trouble if we continue this conversation," she said sternly.

Ryder shook his head. "I know," he said. "But it is *very* important that I talk to her."

Suddenly it seemed like they were the only two people in the room. Sandy brushed back her hair in a nervous indication of thought. Finally she said, "She's still here. Somewhere up in the rooms."

"Is she under guard?"

273

Sandy shook her head. "No," she said. "There's no need for that. Where can she go?"

"How will I know which room she is in?" Ryder asked.

Sandy stayed serious for a moment, then smiled. "She'll probably be in the only room that's not locked . . ."

Five minutes later, Ryder was up on the second floor, after having climbed the saloon's stairs as discreetly as possible. The second story was a labyrinth of hallways and doors. Occasionlly he would meet a happy couple either entering or leaving a room. But he could tell by the sights and sounds within that very few of the rooms were unoccupied.

He started trying doors, hoping that he wouldn't inadvertently burst in on a couple in mid-thrust. Every one he tried was locked. Except one . . .

It was room 53. As soon as he felt the doorknob turn freely in his hand he knew—actually *felt* it in his psyche—that the woman reporter was inside.

He didn't even think about knocking; he simply stepped inside the room and came face to face with the most beautiful woman he had ever seen . . .

"I know you," she said, speaking first with a slightly surprised look. "You're Captain Ryder Long . . ."

"Yes, ma'am," he said.

Ryder felt as if he was living a dream within a dream. It was the woman he'd first met while dreaming in the desert. Good God, his body was buzzing, excited flashes were jolting him in parts of his inner being that he'd never felt before. She was special . . .

"I've been looking for you," she said slowly. "And frankly, I'm very surprised to see you alive."

"Why is that?"

"Well," she said. "Do you know that the Air Force claimed you had been killed?"

He almost didn't hear her. He was enraptured by her presence. It was a feeling that was so new, he was trembling. He knew he was treading on parts unknown.

"Killed?" he asked, shaking his head.

She touched him. She reached over and took his hands and never stopped staring into his eyes.

"They put out a story that you and a Captain Woods were killed in a training accident," she told him. "Your obituaries were printed in my newspaper . . ."

"Really?" he asked, wondering if his sensory tracks were going to overload.

"It's true, I had the obits themselves, but they took them away from me," she said, gripping his hands tighter. "There were other obits for four other pilots from around the world. My editor somehow caught them all. He had a hunch and sent me to follow it up."

She stopped to catch her breath. "I went to Las Vegas and saw the public information officer at Nellis. Then I went to Miramar and talked to a guy named Panther . . ."

"Panther!" Ryder said.

"Yes, he was drunk and told me everything," she continued. "He told me about you and Woods and how you should have won the Top Gun trophy. He told me about your experience in the desert, and about Red Flag and your disappearing, and the foreign pilots and I didn't want to believe for a second that you were dead . . ."

Suddenly she was in his arms, holding him. He was out of it. Nothing like this had happened before . . .

"Well, Maureen, I'm here . . ." he said, hugging her tighter.

The blue Cobra helicopter landed beside the Spookbase Ops building, kicking up a whirlwind of dust as it settled down.

Major Maxwell emerged from the front seat of the attack copter. The small machine was now his only form of transportation since his Huey had been forced down and captured by the Grays.

Slade was waiting in the door of the Ops for the Blue Army officer. Moon and the other pilots, with the exception of Ryder, were on hand. The big John Wayne lookalike swaggered into the Ops Building greeting each Spook officer with a bone-crushing handshake. Then, as always, he took center stage.

"I wish I brought better news," he began. "But I don't. Our scouts have confirmed that a very large force of Gray troops is only about five clicks from here. These are the same units that Esposito and you, Lancaster, saw the other night.

"They are very well equipped. In fact, we've spotted Hercs dropping to them even as they were moving. They and the Aggressors have really plastered the Greens in the past few days. I haven't seen a Green soldier or column in days. So I doubt if they will be a factor in this coming battle."

"When can we expect an attack?" Slade asked. "And how big?"

Major Max shook his head. "Hard to call," he said, through a cloud of cigar smoke. "The Gray commander has three ways to go. Attack our base, full blast. Attack your base, full blast. Or split his force, send a big contingent after our base, then maybe a smaller force against you here. In any case, we should expect that they'll have plenty of air support from the Aggressors."

"We do have some good news, Major," Slade told him. "We hope to launch tomorrow . . ."

Major Max clapped his hands once in delight. "That *is* good news . . ." he said enthusiastically. "If you can keep the Aggressors occupied, you can score some big time points and will certainly help to even things out for both of us."

"What is your strength, Major?" Reinhart wanted to know. "Can you send us troops when the fighting starts?"

Max shrugged, then shook his head. "I can only say that we'll make that decision as the situation develops. Right now, I got a handful of Hueys and some Cobras and I've already been told that I can expect no help from my HQ.

"Now, I can lift a fairly large force if we had to, but most of my guys will be in the trenches surrounding our base. As it is, we'll be outnumbered at least six to one."

"Why are they doing this?" Slade asked. "The Central Command, I mean. You guys are an airborne unit. You would think the Command would want you training—and fighting— in airborne assaults and so on."

"Beats me, Commander," the Blue Army major answered.

"We've certainly been practicing for airborne operations. Chopper assaults and so on. Search and destroy, Vietnam stuff. We were scoring big against the Grays until they linked up with the Aggressors.

"But now, for some reason, Central Command wants to see us in a defensive role against a superior force. They want to see how well we can hold a position."

"Could be a good opportunity to make some Innovation points," Woody pointed out.

"Maybe," Major Max said, lighting his cigar. "That's why I want to keep open the option of sending some troops over here. And I hope you guys will do the same as far as air support is concerned."

Slade stood up and shook hands with Maxwell. "You can count on us," he told the major.

Ryder knew it was time to go.

He was lying on the bed, holding Maureen close, while downstairs and in the rooms around them, the noise level of the blowout was steadily growing.

He didn't want to let her go—ever. They had talked for about an hour about the situation, about themselves. She had asked him no probing questions, never once tempting him to betray any secrets about War Heaven or his unorthodox training. And she didn't know anything about Distant Thunder. But then, of course, neither did he.

"This is the craziest thing that has ever happened to me," she said, as he stroked her long blond hair. "I'm sure my editor is wondering where the hell I am. My poor father is probably being given the third degree somewhere, thinking his daughter has ruined his career. I don't even know what happened to my rental car.

"But I do know that this is one of the most peaceful moments in my life. Lying here with you, Ryder."

He kissed her, long and softly. "I have to go," he told her.

She pulled him closer to her. "I'm frightened, Ryder," she said, adding, "And I don't frighten too easily."

"Don't worry, honey," he said. "I'm sure they'll just keep you here for a while, then realize they'll have to turn you loose. But I'd expect they're going to give you a very long lecture about National Security and how you newspaper people are always trying to spill the government's best secrets . . ."

"Oh, I know," she sighed, her hand finding its way to his bare chest. "But they don't frighten me. It's you I'm frightened for . . ."

"Don't worry about me," Ryder said, mustering up some swagger. "I'm a pilot. I'm being trained for a secret mission. This has become my job."

"What kind of a job?" she asked, turning to look him in the eye. "They put out an obituary on you. On all of you. What does that tell you?"

Ryder squeezed her tight. "It's just their way of putting out a cover story, I guess," he answered. "Why, what does it tell you?"

She was silent for a few moments, then said, "It tells me that they're sending you on a mission they don't expect you to come back from . . ."

Ryder knew it was true. He had thought over that aspect more than once. Still, to hear someone else say it was slightly unnerving.

She pulled herself up until she was face to face with him. "I'm afraid that I'll never see you again . . ."

He took her face in his hands and kissed her. "You will," he said as valiantly as possible. "I'm not a romantic, Maureen. Sometimes I wish I was. All I know is that something very special has happened here, with us. I'm not going to let anything get in my way of seeing you—holding you—again. I promise . . ."

He couldn't believe the words were coming from his mouth. He had never said anything quite so sincere to any woman before.

She grabbed him and held him tight. "Please keep that promise . . ." she said.

Looking back on it he realized that getting up and leaving her was one of the hardest things he had ever done. She looked so beautiful, so sweet, he would have liked to smuggle her out of the place and have them run away forever.

He held her for a long time. Then, without another word, he turned and left the room, closing and locking the door behind him.

In the next room over, Jammar removed his earphones and switched off the small tape recorder. Then he reached for the telephone on the room's bedstand and punched in a series of access numbers.

The phone on the other end rang once and was answered by a familiar voice.

"She doesn't know about Distant Thunder," Jammer reported.

The assistant secretary let out a long sigh of relief. "You are sure?" he asked. "Did you catch everything?"

"Yes, sir," Jammer answered. "We had six bugs in her room. Everything they said was picking up. They didn't discuss it. Ryder came through with flying colors. He didn't mention anything she didn't know. In fact, it seemed like they got very romantic in the short amount of time they were together. They were talking like they'd known each other for years.

"But, in my opinion, Ryder passed the gut test as far as loyalty goes."

"That's also a relief," the assistant secretary said. "But getting back to the girl. What exactly does she know?"

Jammer reached over for his notebook. "She knows about the cover stories," he said. "Somehow one of the editors at the *Post* was able to get them all and he got suspicious that six fighter pilots from around the world would all die around the same time. He probably assigned the girl to the story figuring her connections and her father at the Pentagon might help uncover something."

"What else does she know?" the assistant secretary asked. "What has she seen there?"

Jammer flipped through his notebook's pages. "Well, she's seen Blue and Gray troops. She has to know that the helicopter she was on was somehow forced down. She feels like she's been taken prisoner. She's seen everything at Jack's. And, she'll hear an earful starting tomorrow when the final exercise gets going."

The assistant secretary was quiet for a moment. "She's really seen too much already," he said finally. "If we let her out now, who knows what she'll do."

"We can really lay it on her," Jammer suggested. "Maybe hold her father's career up in front of her. Delay or drop any investigation in return for her keeping quiet."

"That scares me," the assistant secretary said. "Only a handful of people know what Distant Thunder is all about, and only a few dozen outside of Nevada know what War Heaven is all about. I'd sure hate to add the name of a *Washington Post* reporter to that list."

"I know what you mean," Jammer said. "But what's the alternative?"

Once again, the assistant secretary was quiet. "I'll have to clear it with the secretary first," the man said. "But I don't think we have any other choice but to send her along when the units deploy . . ."

52

Ryder watched the three flashes streak across the sky and land at the far end of the Spookbase runway.

It was just past midnight. He was still a mile from the base, slowly maneuvering the jeep along the high, rough terrain when he saw the first flasher shells fall on the airstrip. Just as those three landed, he saw three more streaks fired from the ridge overlooking the Spookbase. Three more followed after that. Then three more. The flasher shells were coming in with such regulatiry he knew the shelling was more than the leisurely barrage the Grays used to send over in the afternoon.

No, he knew this time they were serious. The big battle was getting underway.

He gunned the jeep and started racing for the base. That's when he heard a very distinctive whine. He turned to the south to see the running lights of four Aggressor airplanes heading straight for the base.

"Goddamn," he cursed to himself. "They're going to night bomb the place . . ."

As he watched helplessly, the first two F-5s peeled off and began their low-level bombing run. He knew the Aggressor pilots were showing a lot of nerve. The F-5, a fighter, and not a bomber to begin with, was not the ideal airplane to attempt a night mission. It had low-tech radar and just about no infra-red or night vision capabilities.

"How the hell are they going to see where they are going?" he asked himself.

He didn't have to wait long for an answer . . .

Suddenly three more shells were fired from the ridge. But instead of falling as the others did, these seemed to hang up in the air. Ryder had the spyglasses up to his eyes in a second and saw that the Grays were now firing off flasher-style parachute flares. All at once he put two and two together. He was seeing yet another example of Gray-Aggressor cooperation. The flasher-flares were illuminating the entire valley, creating a weird, pseudodaylight. It was a simple tactic: the Grays were lighting up the target for the Aggressors.

The first two F-5s streaked in and deposited a canister apiece on the runway. Ryder could see a hazy green cloud of sneeze gas start to rise from the base. The two jets pulled up cleanly and started a long wide-out around the base.

The second pair of F-5s mimicked their comrades' maneuver perfectly. Both streaked in low, guided by the flare light, and dropped two more bombs. This time Ryder could tell by the cloud these canisters were filled with Supertears.

The first two airplanes came around again. Suddenly he saw a flash come up from the middle of the base and explode just

281

feet from the trailing F-5. Someone had fired a ZootSAM at the bombers and had just barely missed. The sudden antiaircraft fire caused the F-5s to pull up and out of their bombing runs, at least temporarily.

"All right!" Ryder yelled out. "Give it to those bastards!"

The second pair of F-5s bore down on the base but were met with two ZootSAMs. Ryder watched as one of the holographic projectiles arched up and over the airstrip, catching the lead F-5 square on the tail. There was a tremendous flash and the sound of an explosion. It was a direct hit. The F-5 suddenly went vertical as Ryder knew all of the pilot's noncritical avionics were shutting down. The plane flipped over once and then steered back to the south. Scratch one Aggressor . . .

But the attackers were far from giving up.

As Ryder watched, the four F-5s split up and began individual bombing runs. The Gray troops on the ridge doubled the number of parachute flares. The air raid was heating up. Ryder lurched the jeep forward. He had to get to the base.

Lieutenant Moon ran through the cloud of Supertears, a wet hankie over his face. One of the Aggressors' canisters had landed square on one ZootSAM station, incapacitating the crew. Moon was hurrying to their rescue.

He reached the stricken men to find them laid out on the ground, coughing, their eyes bloodred. Suddenly he saw an F-5 streaking across the field and heading right toward him. He hit the deck hard as the F-5 screeched overhead. It dropped a Supertears bomb which landed about a hundred feet away from him. But he knew the pilot's real target was the ZootSAM launcher.

Suddenly, out of the haze of gas, Ryder appeared. In the midst of the noise and confusion of the battle, they shook hands and quickly discussed the situation. Most of the personnel were holed up in Hangars 1 and 3. All four of the ZootSAMs were in action—Slade and Woody were manning one at the far end of the base.

"We've bounced one of them already," Moon yelled over

the racket. "But I'm sure they'll keep this up . . ."

Ryder nodded quickly. "With those Grays pumping out chute flares, the Aggressors can zero in on us all night . . ."

Just then they saw that one of the F-5s was coming back. Without hesitating, they scrambled to the ZootSAM's control panel. Ryder knew they had no time to calculate the firing; a manual aim would have to do. Moon pushed a bank of buttons as Ryder yanked the device around to the opposite direction from which the airplane was heading.

The F-5 streaked over them with a deafening roar. Moon squeezed the ZootSAM's firing trigger just as they saw a small canister fall from the airplane's wing. The holographic missile roared away from its launcher just as they were enveloped in the jet wash of the attacking airplane.

The projectiles landed simultaneously. The canister exploded practically on the Ops Building's doorstep, covering the structure in a bluish-pink haze of Supertears. Meanwhile, Moon's ZootSAM impacted on the underside of the retreating jet, causing an explosion so loud, it sounded to Ryder like someone had set off a blockbuster firecracker right next to his ear.

The F-5 flipped over and went vertical, a sure sign of a missile hit. Both men gave out a victory yell. The Spookbase SAMs had already brought down two F-5s and the attack was less than five minutes old.

Ryder and Moon then pulled the two stricken SAM operators to the relative safety of Hangar 1. Inside, they found the foreign pilots and some of the 1245th men, working on the F-14s even as the air raid progressed.

Lancaster helped bring the men inside. Just then, another F-5 swooped in and deposited a Supertears canister just fifty feet from the building.

"These guys don't give up," Lancaster said to Ryder as he propped up one of the gassed ZootSAM operators.

"This is just a softening up raid," Ryder said, peeking out the hangar door. The Gray parachute flares were dotting the sky and he could see exhaust trails of the attacking jets everywhere. The sky was streaked with the simulated trails of ZootSAMs.

"You need help, Captain?" Lancaster asked. He and Sammett had practically built a ZootSAM themselves and were thus familiar with the device. Ryder was tempted to take them up on their offer, but couldn't.

"No, the important thing is that these airplanes are ready to fly tomorrow," he said. "You'll be all right in here just as long as the place doesn't take a direct hit."

Another F-5 streaked by, laying a canister of sneeze gas near Hangar 3, where most of the base personnel were sheltered. Just then, Ryder heard another type of jet engine, the distinctive roar of an A-4 Skyhawk.

"There they are!" Moon yelled out from the hangar door.

Sure enough, Ryder could see two A-4s circling high over the airbase, waiting for the F-5s to clear out.

"They're going to keep coming at us as long as they can see us," Moon said.

"That's why we've got to take out those Grays shooting off those flares," Ryder said, aiming his spyglasses toward the ridge.

They ducked back inside the hangar as the two A-4s roared in and dropped two canisters each of Crab Gas. Luckily, a fairly brisk wind was blowing through the valley, scattering the gas quickly.

Ryder got an idea. "Maybe it's time to ask a favor from our neighbors," he said.

With that, he was out the door and running to the base communications shack.

Twenty-five minutes went by. The A-4s continually swept back and forth across the Spookbase, dropping combinations of Crab Gas and Supertears. The pesky Skyhawks were flying very low, just eluding the ZootSAMs, being thrown up at them. When the A-4s finally ran low on fuel, they departed, only to have their places taken by two new F-5s.

Ryder watched this portion of the battle from the small communications hut. Suddenly the radio within it crackled to life.

"Spookbase, this is Blue Zebra," the static-filled voice said. "How can we help?"

Those were the words Ryder had been waiting to hear.

"What's your strength and position, Blue Zebra?" he asked into the shack's microphone.

"We are two Cobras, Spookbase," the reply came back. "Approximately twelve clicks north of you . . ."

Ryder did a quick plot in his head, then called back, "Blue Zebra. We are under air attack. The targets are being illuminated by Gray artillery troops on a ridge overlooking our base. Can you turn those lights out?"

There was a blast of static as an F-5 raced over head. "Spookbase, that is a roger to your request," the voice said. "Can you provide us with covering fire against the Aggressors?"

"That's affirmative," Ryder called back quickly. "I'll get to work on that immediately. Good luck, Blue Zebra. We owe you one . . ."

Another fifteen minutes went by. The pair of F-5s was replaced once again with A-4s. But, per Ryder's instructions, no further ZootSAMs were launched.

He was crouched at the centerline of the runway after he, Moon, and Lancaster pushed one of the ZootSAM launchers to the location, using the blazing light of the chute flares to guide them. Ryder was certain that the A-4 pilots, who would soon give up their station to two more F-5s, had informed their comrades that no ZootSAMs had been fired at them in the last quarter hour. He was hoping this would lead the Aggressor pilots to assume that the Spooks had decided to sit back and ride out the air raid.

They just finished calibrating the ZootSAM after the move when Ryder heard the helicopters.

He turned to the northern end of the valley and saw two faint lights enter it, flying slow and low. It was only a quick jog to the radio station.

"Blue Zebra," he called out. "This is Spookbase. Do you have a visual on the target?"

The reply came back quickly. "Affirmative, Spooks," the voice said. "We also copy two A-4s, leaving the area now. Right over us. Right now."

Ryder heard the Skyhawk pilots boot their engines and fly away. So far, so good, he thought. Not five seconds went by when he heard the familiar whine of two F-5s.

"OK, Blue Zebra," he said. "Copy F-5s in the battle area. We'll take care of them."

The chopper pilot acknowledged and signed off. Ryder immediately returned to the ZootSAM, training his spyglasses on the two choppers. As he watched, the two, insectlike Cobras sped up and climbed toward the top of the high ridge. Just then, like clockwork, the two replacement F-5s screeched in dropping additional Supertears canisters down near the unoccupied Hangar 2.

In a way, Ryder was glad to see the F-5s. Because they were notoriously slow fliers at low altitude, they were more vulnerable to the base's ZootSAMs.

Suddenly, Ryder saw first one, then two flashes up on the ridge. The Cobras had opened their attack on the Gray artillery base and it appeared as if they had achieved complete surprise.

Just as Ryder had figured, both F-5s, seeing the Cobras, twisted around and steered toward the action on the ridge. That's when Ryder squeezed the ZootSAM's trigger once, twice, three times.

In sequence, the three simulated missiles magically roared away from the launcher and streaked off toward the F-5s. At the same time, per a prearrangement, Slade and Woody also launched a trio of missiles from their position, as did Moon's men who were manning the two other outlying ZootSAMs.

The sight of a gang of pseudo-projectiles was too much for the Aggressor pilots who immediately took evasive action which led them away from the Cobra attack on the Gray's artillery base.

By the time the jets recovered, the quick, surgical, surprise attack on the Grays was complete. Using ZootTOW missiles, the Cobras succeeded in knocking out the computerized aim and target systems in the Gray's artillery pieces, rendering them useless. Within twenty seconds the entire valley was plunged back into a security blanket of darkness.

53

Ryder and Moon spent the remainder of the night tending to the gassed 1245th men and checking on the base's defenses. Slade and Woody were anchoring the defensive systems at the northern end of the base, just as Ryder and Moon were handling the southern end. In between all this, Ryder was keeping tabs on the preparation of the F-14s.

The early morning hours passed slowly, if quietly. They could see flashes of light on both the southern and western horizons, indicating battles between the advancing Gray troops and the Blue Army's airborne hit-and-run squads. White contrails, left behind by high-flying Aggressor aircraft, crisscrossed the dark sky.

Just before dawn, Woody and Slade were relieved at their ZootSAM post and walked down to Hangar 1 where an impromptu breakfast was being held.

"Tell me this is all a dream," Woody said to Ryder as they took a break to gulp down some K-ration-style food.

"This is nothing," Ryder said, quickly filling him in on Maureen, the obit cover story angle, and his other activities at Smiling Jack's early in the evening. He immediately swore his friend to secrecy.

"Don't worry," Woody said after hearing it all and promising Ryder he would keep it to himself. "Who would believe any of it, anyway?"

The Wiz leaned back against the hangar wall and dozed off,

as did many of those present. But Ryder didn't even think of sleeping—he knew he couldn't if he tried. The adrenaline from the earlier air raid was still pumping through his body, but this was just a secondary intoxicant. It was the thought of Maureen that was keeping him awake and alert.

He walked out onto the runway just as the first streaks of dawn were lighting up the sky. Although he thought that this should be the quietest time of the day, he could still hear the distinct din of machinery, far off but gradually getting more apparent.

He scanned the ridge overlooking the base. In the nether light, he thought he could see shadows, many shadows, moving back and forth. He convinced himself momentarily that it was little more than the early-morning light playing tricks on him.

He walked to the communications shack and quickly monitored all the frequencies used in War Heaven. The entire spectrum was filled with chatter—some of it in code, some of it understandable. Judging from the intensity of the activity, Ryder surmised that the Blues and Grays were battling each other in more than a dozen places. He was suddenly grateful to Major Max for allowing the Cobras to take out the Gray artillery base, when it was obvious that the choppers could have been deployed elsewhere.

Ryder did a quick scan on the base radar system and finding nothing immediate, turned back to scanning the imposing ridge again. This time the dawning sun was brighter and the crest of the ridge was bathed in an early-morning crimson.

In this light, Ryder saw his first definitely distinguishable humans moving across the high ridge. They were in the general vicinity of the Gray artillery base and he theorized that it was a unit sent to retrieve the knocked-out field pieces.

But then he thought he saw more figures moving about on the southern tip of the ridge. And were those others, crawling along its center?

He turned and realized that Woody, Slade, and Moon were just behind him, their eyes fixed on the ridge. It was getting lighter by the second. Things were starting to come into focus.

"I'm getting a very bad feeling about this," Woody said. "I

feel like someone's watching us."

No sooner had the Wiz spoken when the first beam of sunlight emerged and bounced off the ridge. All four men were startled by what they saw.

The entire ridge was lined with troops—hundreds, if not a thousand of them, each one in a Gray uniform. It looked like a scene from a cowboy movie, a swarm of Indians stretching as far as the eye could see.

"Jesus Christ" was all Slade could manage.

"Now I know how Custer felt," Ryder said grimly.

Just then, their concentration was disturbed by the sound of a jet engine firing up. The good news was the airplane in question was one of the F-14s in Hangar 1.

"Now that's a sound I can live with . . ." Ryder said, a jolt of excitement running through him.

Moon was at his side in a second. "Captain Long," he said. "I suggest you and Captain Woods suit up. I think we're ready for a launch . . ."

Ryder and Woody were suited up and strapped into the F-14 when the first artillery shells began to come in.

To everyone's surprise the surrounding Gray Force weren't shooting their usual flasher shells. Instead they started lobbing gas—Supertears, Crab Gas, and Sneezers. The shells themselves were detonating at a height of a hundred feet right over the base. The wind, while not as brisk as the night before, still helped blow some of the gas away. But enough found its way to ground level to make moving about the base very uncomfortable.

Meanwhile, controlled pandemonium had broken out in Hangar 1. Ryder's F-14, the refurbished VF-333, was up and all its avionics were hot. Ryder was shaking slightly; the excitement of the upcoming launch, the rush from the night before, the lingering sweet memory of Maureen all combined to put an electrical charge through him. What a crazy, screwy life I lead, he thought to himself.

He snapped on his helmet and his flight gloves—old friends

he hadn't worn in a while. All the time, the Gray gas barrage was getting more intense. Ryder knew they could probably expect an Aggressor air raid at anytime. *If* the catapult worked and *if* the F-14s were really airworthy, the Aggressors would have a reception party waiting for them.

Everything in his cockpit checked out. He called back to Woody who also reported everything as "green."

Ryder gave Moon the thumbs-up signal. With that, he increased the engine thrust slightly and lifted the brakes. Slowly, the F-14 lurched forward.

"We're moving, pardner," Ryder called back to the pit.

"Seems like a hundred years . . ." Woody replied wistfully.

They wheeled the F-14 out of the hangar and slowly moved out onto the runway. With two of Moon's guys acting as traffic cops, Ryder moved the Tomcat into position over the catapult. The ground crew hooked up the front wheel's T-bar to the catapult shuttle. The airplane was now in the correct position over the catapult's capacity safety valve. This device weighed the jet, and the corresponding number was given to Moon who would make sure enough steam pressure was available to launch the F-14.

Everything was going smoothly when suddenly Ryder realized the Gray artillery barrage had intensified, with a quick six shells exploding right above them.

"They've spotted our roll-out," Ryder called back to Woody.

"The last thing they want is for us to get off the ground," Woody replied. "Maybe we should mask up now, just in case we get any leaks."

"Good idea," Ryder confirmed.

Both pilots attached their oxygen masks and started breathing the F-14's filtered air. Outside the canopy, the entire base appeared as if it was enveloped in a thick London fog. To their credit, Moon's technicians were scrambling around, working the catapult and directing the F-14, despite taking in mouthfuls of the irritating gas.

Right behind them, the second F-14 rolled out, Lancaster at the controls, Sammett in the back. Ryder knew the third airplane, to be held in reserve for the moment, would have Reinhart at the wheel with Chauvagne working the pit.

Another two minutes went by. Ryder concentrated on the F-14's engine trim and rechecked its computer calibration.

Like the field catapult, the airplanes had been improved to the point of simplicity. All of the calibrations proved to be correct, the engines never lost a beat, even the radio was virtually static-free.

Ryder could see Moon's men feverishly working the catapult's steam system and generators. They manually lifted the catapult's blast deflectors, two large pieces of corrugated metal that would take the brunt of the fiery exhaust of the F-14's take-off. Moon himself would serve as the launch officer, the guy who would simultaneously give Ryder the signal to go, while pushing the catapult launch lever.

Ryder studied the terrain ahead of him. It was fairly flat for a quarter of a mile, the landscape broken only by the dozen or so generators in place there. The terrain got considerably rockier around 1,800 feet, then flared up to a slight opposing ridge at about 3,000 feet. He knew the take-off would also be simple— not in its execution, but in its outcome. It could only go one of two ways. They could launch successfully or if the F-14 failed to achieve 120 miles per hour in the first several seconds of flight, the Tomcat would plow into the ground at about 2,500 feet.

"I hope Moon's guys used lock washers on this thing," Woody called ahead to Ryder, referring to the catapult.

Ryder had his eyes fixed on Moon, a slight figure now just barely visible through the haze of gas and the rush of steam from the catapult. The young officer gave him the signal to increase his engine thrust. Ryder tapped the throttle up. He gave another signal to one of his men to increase the catapult's steam pressure.

"You ready, partner?" Ryder asked, starting a countdown in his mind.

"I've been ready for days" came the reply.

Ryder scanned the control panel for one last check. Everything was still burning "green." They were at Go for launch. Just then at least a dozen gas bombs exploded right over the catapult. The Grays were throwing everything at them in an effort to prevent the launch. Moon's men were coughing, hacking, some were vomiting from the intensity of the gas attack, yet they stayed at their stations.

Just then Moon gave Ryder the five-second warning. Ryder closed his eyes for a moment and conjured up the beautiful image of Maureen. Hang on, honey, he thought.

Now his eyes were wide open. Moon gave him the dramatic Go signal. All of sudden there was a huge whoosh of steam and a loud bang.

Suddenly the ground rushed forward. Ryder yanked back on the control stick while booting the airplane up to maximum power. The plane never bucked. The next thing Ryder knew he was looking straight up at a high cloud bank. The catapult had worked perfectly. They had gone from a standing start to 120 mph in 2.2 seconds.

Finally, they were airborne . . .

54

More than 40,000 feet above the Spookbase, an EC-135 AWACs was circling slowly. The military version of a Boeing 707 was crammed with electronic battle management gear all on a direct link with the Central Command's Cray supercomputer. More than a dozen operators sat at control consoles in the body of the aircraft, monitoring the thousands of aspects of the massive simulated battle below.

In the forward cabin, the Air Force general was receiving a continuous flow of reports from the field. Every ten minutes or so, the senior man of the operator corps would enter the cabin and give him a brief battle report.

"Ready for an update, General?" the senior man asked, sticking his head into the cabin.

"Yes," the general answered. "Let's have it . . ."

The senior man took a deep breath and began:

"As expected, lead elements of the Gray Army have come within four kilometers of Blue Base North. The Blues have commenced holding actions along a very flexible line. Some are working, others are not."

"What's happening with the Spooks?" the general asked.

"Well, as you know, they were able to break up the Aggressor's air raid during the night," the man answered. "We don't have any information yet as to how many of the men were incapacitated as a result of the air strikes, if any. A reinforced battalion of Gray troops occupied the ridge to the north of the airstrip and commenced gas shelling shortly after dawn . . ."

Just then, another man stuck his head into the cabin, handed the senior man a slip of paper, then quickly left. The senior man read the message over quickly, then reported it to the general: "We've just received an unconfirmed report that the Spooks have launched . . ."

The general was so pleased he slammed his fist down onto the table. "Yes!" he said. "They're up . . ."

"It's still unconfirmed, sir," the senior man cautioned.

"Well, *confirm* it, son," he half barked at the senior man. "And give me a holler when you do . . ."

The man left and the general immediately grabbed his secure phone and punched in an access number. Two rings later, the assistant secretary was on the line. "We have an unconfirmed report that the Spooks have launched at least one F-14, sir," the general told him.

There was a brief silence on the other end of the line. Then the Defense Department man said: "Thank you, General. I know that is good news for you and for the program. I'll inform the Secretary right away."

55

As soon as Ryder leveled out the F-14, he put it into a tight 180 snap turn and headed right over the base. It was exhilarating to be flying again. He felt free. Free of the craziness of War Heaven. Free of the dread of what lay ahead for Distant Thunder. Free to dream of when he'd see Maureen again.

He brought the F-14 down low and executed three quick barrel rolls above the Spookbase. Despite the speed of the plane and its spinning motion, he could clearly see the base personnel waving and celebrating as they streaked overhead. It was their victory, too. They had fought against heat, hunger, air raids, harassment shelling, and isolation to make the base work and to get the catapult operating. All in all, an outstanding feat.

The aerial cock-strutting over, Ryder steered the powerful fighter around again and headed for the occupied ridge. His first priority was to get an estimate of the number of Gray troops located there. His second one was to let them know that despite their gas attack the Spooks were up and flying.

He brought the 'Cat high over the ridge, the sun at his back. Below he could see a line of Gray troops stretched the whole length of the mile-long ridge. They were equipped with dozens of artillery pieces, plus a few captured Green Army vehicles.

"I'll guess a thosuand guys," Woody called ahead.

"A reinforced battalion maybe?" Ryder replied. "That's a lot of Indians . . ."

He turned the F-14 on its back and looped, feeling a heavy g-force for the first time in a while.

"*Jee-suz,*" Woody moaned from the pit, also feeling the g-force. "I forgot how much fun this was . . ."

Ryder brought the F-14 down low and blasted right over the top of the ridge. Where the Gray troops had simply watched them pass over high the first time, now they were ducking and running in all directions as the 'Cat streaked in low over them.

"Like ants, they scatter . . ." Woody said scornfully.

But both he and Ryder knew they could do little else than buzz the Gray troops and rock them with the occasional sonic boom. The reason was they had no ordnance to drop on them, nothing in the line of gas canisters available to the Aggressors. The only thing they could use was the 'Cat's nose cannon, and that would appear counterproductive.

Just then, Woody came on the line. "We got company, Ghost . . ."

"How many and where?" Ryder asked, checking his weapons supply.

"I read four," Woody replied. "Two F-5s, two A-4s, thirty clicks south. They're wide-out now, but I got a hunch they'll be cornering in any second . . ."

Ryder thought for a moment, then said, "Assuming our Gray friends here have been in contact with the Aggressors and have told them we're airborne, it could be the A-4s are carrying the gas, and the F-5s are riding shotgun."

"I think that's a definite possibility," Woody said, adding, "Gomers now twenty-two clicks out . . ."

Ryder was on the horn to the base. "Lancaster? Do you copy?"

Ryder knew the second F-14, with Lancaster at the helm was teed up and ready for launch.

"Ten by ten" came back the reply. "How's the view up there?"

"Crowded," Ryder answered. "And it's about to get worse. We got a thousand Gray troops up on the ridge. Artillery, plus a few captured Green tanks.

"We also have four bandits out on the periphery, ready to turn for us at any minute."

"We copy, Ryder," Lancaster radioed back. "What's the plan?"

Ryder told Lancaster about his bomber-and-escort theory.

"I suggest you launch and give us a CAP," Ryder said. "We'll go after the A-4s."

"Roger," Lancaster replied. "We will launch within two minutes. Waiting for the steam to heat up a bit."

Just then Slade came on the frequency. "Ryder, can you

give us a fix on those Gray tanks?" the Navy officer asked. "If they have Zoot capability, they could knock out this catapult . . ."

Ryder realized this. Along with every other piece of military equipment in War Heaven, the catapult contained a black "kill box." If the catapult took a Zootcannon shot of sufficient intensity, the kill box would freeze the mechanism immediately, just as the Aggressors' all-but-critical avionics blinked out when they caught a ZootSAM.

"Roger, Slade," Ryder called back. "Back to you in a second."

He turned the F-14 back over the ridge a second time. "Let's count these tanks, Wiz," he called back to the pit.

They streaked over the enemy-held high ground at less than cruising speed.

"I see three in all," Woody said. "One on each forward point . . ."

Ryder relayed the information to Slade. "It's just a matter of time before they start taking shots at us," Slade said. "Somehow we've got to figure out a way to protect the catapult controls or we'll be back to grounded status."

"We can always try to get them with the nose cannon," Ryder said.

The only problem was that the gun's purpose was for dogfighting, not ground support. They would have to be more lucky than skillful if they hoped to knock out the tanks.

Just then, Woody broke in on the line. "Here they come!" he said. "All four of them, just made their turn in. They are now twelve clicks away. Coming up from due north."

Ryder spun the jet around to face the oncoming Aggressors. At the same time he heard the radio chatter indicating the second F-14 launch.

"OK, Lancaster," Ryder called out. "Let's do it just the way we planned it . . ."

The four Aggressor aircraft split into pairs ten miles out from the target. The bomb-laden A-4s reduced their speed and altitude, while the F-5s booted their engines and climbed.

The overall flight commander, piloting the lead F-5, had been in touch with the commander of the Gray troops on the ridge. The subject was the two Spook F-14s that had just launched. Although the two fighters had been in the area just seconds before, they were nowhere to be seen now.

And that made the Aggressor flight commander nervous.

"Delta Two," he called out to his wingman. "Keep your system on open scan for those Spooks."

The Aggressor commander felt an uneasy sensation at the back of his neck—the sixth sense that said someone was watching him. He knew the F-14s were equipped with the highly advanced Hughes AGM, radar, while his F-5 was carrying a far less sophisticated model. With the F-14's "look down" radar capability, the Aggressor pilot was certain the Spook pilots were way up around 40,000 feet, watching him.

"Delta One, this is Fox One Leader," the lead ship of the A-4 two-flight called. "Request clearance to commence bomb run . . ."

The flight commander took one more look around him. He saw no trace of the F-14s.

"Fox Leader, commence bomb run . . ." he said slowly into his microphone.

He saw the two Skyhawks start a wide arc around the back of the ridge, lining up the Spookbase target on a south-to-north heading. The flight commander radioed his wingman as the A-4s completed the maneuver. "Delta Two, still nothing?"

"That's a roger, Delta One," the reply came back.

No sooner had the flight commander acknowledged his wingman's call, when he saw two dark patches of smoke flying low at the far end of the valley.

"Holy shit . . ." he muttered. "It's them . . ."

The Spooks had got the drop on him. He had been searching the sky above them looking for the F-14s. Never did they think the Tomcats would be hiding low.

The flight commander yelled out a warning to the A-4s, but it was too late. Not only had the 'Cats surprised them, one of them was heading straight for the Skyhawks, who, having just completed the longer arcing maneuver, were out of speed and momentum. The second F-14 had flared up and was now in a direct line with the flight leader's wingman.

"Christ!" the flight commander cursed as he banked to cover his partner. "Who *are* these guys?"

The first F-14 barreled toward the A-4s head-on. The Skyhawk pilots, also without the benefit of an advanced radar, were caught completely by surprise. The lead A-4 pilot had to pull up before dropping his canisters over the base—if he hadn't he would have collided with the Tomcat for sure.

The second Skyhawk wasn't so lucky. Trailing his leader by a thousand feet, the A-4 was down and committed by the time he realized the F-14 was coming right at them. As the large profile of the Tomcat raced toward him, the A-4 pilot quickly dropped his load and yanked back on his controls.

To his surprise, the Tomcat pilot executed the exact maneuver, letting the A-4 get slightly ahead of him. The Skyhawk pilot twisted and turned in the vertical, but he couldn't shake the seemingly possessed 'Cat driver.

Suddenly the Skyhawk's low warning buzzer sounded, followed immediately by the high warning—the 'Cat had launched a ZootSidewinder. The A-4 pilot did one last ditch maneuver, but the holographic projected missile, perfectly mimicking a real Sidewinder, rode right up the Skyhawk's tailpipe, exploding with a simulated flash and a loud *bang!*

Immediately the Skyhawk's avionics started to blink out. The pilot found himself in a brief, uncontrolled climb, before leveling out. Then he steered the airplane back toward his base, knowing he had the dubious honor of having been the first Aggressor shot down by another airplane over the restricted skies of War Heaven.

But he knew he wouldn't be the last . . .

Meanwhile, the F-5s were tangling with the other F-14. The 'Cat pilot had already bounced one of the flight leader's wingmen with a six-mile ZootSidewinder shot that took a full minute to impact on the Aggressor airplane.

Now the flight leader was trying to shake the second 'Cat. He did a snap 180 left, followed by a scissor-turn, only to look back and see the F-14 was still right on his tail. The F-5 pilot banked right and put the aircraft into a sharp climb. Again, he saw the 'Cat pilot had anticipated his moves and was still on his tail.

The Aggressor was now intent on escaping. He flipped the F-5 over and went into a high-energy dive. It was a risky maneuver, but he also knew it would take a few seconds for the Spook pilot to turn over the big Tomcat.

What he didn't anticipate was the appearance of the lead F-14, the one who had iced the A-4 moments before. Just as the F-5 pilot was going down, he saw the lead F-14 heading up toward him!

Goddamn, these guys are crazy! the F-5 pilot thought as he yanked back on his controls and banked left at the same time. But pulling out of the high energy dive proved to take just a few seconds too long. He saw the telltale flashes of holographic light coming from the nose of the onrushing Tomcat. Instantly he felt a scattering of dull thuds against his wings and nose. As the F-5 started to slow up and turn, it exposed its defenseless underbelly to the F-14's cannon. The F-5 pilot now felt a hundred thuds against his wings and fuselage. His avionics bank blinked once, then went out. The plane went into a sharp climb, then leveled out.

The pilot grudgingly wagged his wings as he turned toward his base. He was unmistakably dead. The F-14's simulated cannon shots had been right-on . . .

No sooner had the Aggressors left the area when the Gray Army opened up once again with its gas shelling.

Ryder pulled his Tomcat down low over the ridge and buzzed the Gray troops at a height of no more than two hundred feet. The maneuver served only to halt the firing momentarily. As soon as he pulled up and around, the Grays had their field pieces working once again.

He saw the airstrip was once again enveloped in a haze of Supertears and Crab Gas.

"Slade?" he called into his mic. "Are you there?"

His radio crackled, then a coughing, congested voice came

on: "I copy you," Slade replied. "They're really giving it to us. What's with those tanks?"

Ryder flipped the F-14 over and screeched above the ridge again. To his dismay he saw that two of the tanks had been moved forward of their previous positions.

"Slade, it appears they may be moving closer for a shot at you . . ." Ryder reported.

At that moment, Lancaster was in the process of buzzing the ridge. He, too, radioed Slade that he believed the Zoot tanks were about to open up on the airstrip.

"You guys have got to try to take out those tanks," Slade called. "If they hit us, we might as well close up shop . . ."

"I agree with you, Slade," Ryder called in. "But I'm at half fuel now. I'm sure Lancaster is, too. We're gonna waste a lot of fuel trying to bounce the tanks."

There was a short silence on the other end, then Slade said, "We got to risk it. If the tanks get lucky, we won't need the fuel in your airplanes anyhow . . ."

Ryder knew they had no choice. He called over to Lancaster, requesting he stay up top and watch out for any other Aggressors. Then he put the 'Cat into a long turn around the valley.

"Ready to be a shitmover, Wiz?" Ryder asked, using the Navy's often-used derogatory name for Air Force ground support pilots.

"Hey, Ghost!" Woody replied quickly. "I'm all for it. I'm having a ball back here . . ."

"OK, partner," Ryder said, diving down and lining up the first tank. "Hang on . . ."

Ryder switched the gun to its boresight setting, locking the airplane's radar into the cannon's aiming mechanism. A small circle appeared on his HUD screen. He lined up the circle with the tank, counted to three, and squeezed the cannon's trigger. He felt the very realistic shuddering of the Zootcannon going off. The simulated flashes of light spewed out of the nose of the F-14 and streaked toward the ridge, scattering the Gray troopers. He walked a barrage of the projection fire up the side of the first tank, then pulled away.

"I might have hit him," Ryder yelled back to Woody. "But there's no way to know if we got the kill box or not."

"Rake 'em again," the Wiz suggested.

Ryder flipped the Tomcat over and came back at the tank again. This time he held his fire until the HUD circle was dead-on lined up with the tank. He squeezed the trigger and sent a second barrage of simulated fire into the vehicle.

"That one might have done it," Woody said, looking back at the target area.

But just as he spoke, Ryder noticed first one, then two puffs of smoke coming from one of the other tanks. He watched as a barrage of Zootshells streaked over the field and impacted dangerously close to the catapult.

Slade was on the line less than three seconds later. "They're firing on us!" the Navy officer shouted into the radio.

Ryder immediately flipped the 'Cat over once again. "Let me try something . . ." he said to Woody.

He put the F-14 into a dive and lined up on the tank that had just fired. When he reached the critical distance, he squeezed not the cannon trigger, but the Sidewinder release. They both felt the slight bump as the ZootSidewinder growled and roared away, its warhead looking for any target of opportunity.

"C'mon, baby," Ryder urged as he watched the pseudo-missile streak away. "Solve our problem for us . . ."

The warhead apparently found something to its liking in or around the tank. The Zootrocket slammed into the side of the M-1, exploding in a holographic flash.

"Yes, sir, Ghost!" Woody yelled out after seeing the hit. "How to fly this mutherfucker! That tank is dead, dead, *dead* . . ."

Ryder did a wide bank and overflew the target again. He could tell the missile had tripped the tank's kill box, simply because of the crowd that had gathered around the stricken vehicle. Confirmation came when they saw the other two tanks withdraw from the edge of the ridge and head back down to the safety of the rocks below.

"Scratch one M-1 . . ." Ryder said calmly into his mic.

"Great shooting, Long," Slade replied. "Got to be the first

301

tank taken out by an air-to-air . . ."

"They'll be licking their wounds for a while," Ryder said. "Time for us to test that arresting gear."

56

There were two men sitting in the small, obscure office in the basement of the Pentagon, a large video screen before them flickering.

"This has just come in, sir," an Air Force colonel attached to the National Security Agency, said, pushing a videotape cartridge into a VCR.

"And how did we get this?" the other man asked.

"We had to risk sending a SR-71 over the target area, sir," the colonel explained. "We needed higher resolution that the KH-12 satellite couldn't give us. The result is the closest look we've had of the site so far."

"Any chance that spy plane was detected?" the man asked.

"No, sir," the colonel answered. "One thing the people on the ground don't have is ultrasophisticated radar. Our airplane was flying at seventy thousand feet at Mach 4. There's no way they saw us."

"All right, Colonel, start the tape," the man said.

The colonel pushed the VCR Play button and the formerly static-filled screen sprang to life. Suddenly the two men were looking down on a jungle setting.

"This is the area approximately thirty-five kilometers from the site," the colonel explained, using a pointer to indicate spots on the TV screen. "This is the outside ring of the Iron Circle. The valley you can see is the only viable approach to the target from the air. The mountains to each side and to the rear give them an unbeatable natural defense on three of four sides."

302

"Amazing," the man said. "Devilishly ingenious."

"Yes, sir," the colonel answered. He continued. "You will notice these emplacements, sir. First a group of three, then this group of five . . ."

"Yes, I see them," the man said, looking at what appeared to be a series of telephone poles lying side by side. "What are they?"

"Those are part of their first defense line of SA-2 batteries, sir," the officer explained. "They are stationed at the opening of the valley. They are the exact same SAM missiles used against our airplanes over North Vietnam. You see, here are six more sites."

"Incredible," the man muttered. "I would think those missiles would be fairly antiquated by now. I mean, they're at least twenty years old . . ."

The colonel nodded. "They *are* old, sir," he said. "But the technicians have obviously been able to keep most of them in working order."

The videotape continued. Patches of jungle interspersed with SAM sites.

"Notice this ring of ten sites," the colonel said, again using the pointer. "This is the beginning of their second defense line. Inside this area, the concentration of SAM sites increases by a factor of five."

The man clearly noted the increase of SAM-site clearings. The videotape rolled on.

"All right, sir, we're coming up on the third defense line," the colonel explained. "You can see we are close to the center of the valley right there."

The man saw the ridges that served as the walls of the large lush valley. It seemed that every possible square foot of the ridges and the ground below was crammed with SAM sites.

"Good God," the man said. "There must be hundreds of them . . ."

The lieutenant colonel let out a heavy sigh. "There are thousands of them, sir . . ."

The camera now moved across the valley. The deeper the image went into the valley the more SAM sites that were apparent.

"This is almost absurd," the man said. "How could they have come into possession of this many missiles?"

The colonel shook his head. "We have to remember, sir, that during the Vietnam era, the North Vietnamese took delivery on thousands of SA-2s from the Soviets. After the war, when Vietnam and the Soviets solidified their military ties, the Soviets shipped them more sophisticated surface-to-air weapons, like the SA-4 and the SA-5.

"Just like any weapons turnover, the Vietnamese retired their old models and erected the new ones."

"And the old ones were not destroyed?" the man said.

"Apparently not, sir," the officer answered. "The Vietnamese most likely stored them, probably disassembled and crated."

The man frowned. "And have we figured out how this . . . *this madman* got a hold of them?"

The colonel gave an involuntary shrug. "Hard to say, sir. Perhaps he bought them. Perhaps he entered into an agreement with the Vietnamese. He was, after all, a member of their ruling politburo right after the south collapsed."

"But why would Hanoi want to get involved in this?" the man asked, his voice rising in anger. "What can they possibly hope to gain?"

"Again, it's hard to say, sir," the colonel answered. "As you know, we have very little on-ground intelligence in Hanoi. We have no real idea of their involvement or their intentions, other than they gave him all their old SAMs."

A gathering of buildings now slowly came into view on the videotape. It was at the far end of the valley and surrounded by rings of SAMs and other defensive fortifications.

"OK, here's the site itself, sir," the colonel explained, using the pointer. "We believe this templelike building is his headquarters. These smaller buildings may be research housings. These are barracks. And this . . ." he emphasized a tall gray structure on the screen, ". . . is the launch pad."

"Can you freeze that frame?" the man asked. The officer pushed a button and the videotape suddenly stopped.

Through the wavy lines of static, they both studied the structure.

"God, it looks like it's right off of Cape Canaveral!" the man said.

"You are not the first to say that, sir," the colonel told him. "It was definitely constructed using plans for our old Titan launch pads, right down to the booms and safety housing. It was built in an amazingly short amount of time."

"When will it be operational?" the man asked.

"The NSA estimates no more than two weeks, sir," the colonel answered. "DIA thinks even less . . ."

The colonel pushed another button and the videotape resumed playing.

"Here is their big missile storage housing," he said, pointing out a large, tall and thin structure.

"And what is that strange-looking building?" the man asked. "It looks like a big igloo."

The colonel sighed again. "That's their uranium enrichment housing," he said grimly. "And it is probably where the warheads are located. Again, this structure was built in record time, almost as if it was shipped nearly whole."

"And we've confirmed it originated in Tehran . . ." the man asked angrily.

"I'm afraid that is correct, sir," the colonel said. "From the more *radical* elements, shall we say?"

There was a tense silence as the videotape continued.

The colonel then indicated a series of barracks-type buildings. "This is the prison, sir," he said. "Large enough for about two hundred men . . ."

"And the bastards put it right next to the radioactive stuff!" the man said bitterly. "The ultimate hostages!"

The camera moved out of the far end of the valley and to a site about ten miles away.

"Here's their runway," the colonel said. "Their hangars and repair shops. Notice there are a couple of Soviet-built Fitters outside. We've traced them to Libya. They also have aircraft and pilots from North Korea, Iran, as well as Vietnam and other countries."

The videotape ended shortly thereafter and the big screen went back to noiseless white static.

The man put his hands up to his eyes and rubbed them. "All

those SAMs," he said. "It's remarkable that they could have moved them all the way across Asia. Surely they must have done it by night. And it must have taken them years! But how could they do it? There aren't many roads in that part of the world, not roads that can move such equipment anyway."

"Sir, back during the Vietnam conflict, the NVA moved whole divisions with equipment by bicycle," the colonel said.

The man shook his head. "Hanoi. Tehran. Libya. North Korea. And with all those missiles, now I know why they call it Thunder Alley . . ." he said, getting up to leave. "With this information, I can now see why the secretary had asked the timetable to be moved up."

The colonel retrieved the videotape and put it back into its container marked "TOP SECRET."

"Thank you, Colonel," the man said. "Good job . . ."

"You're welcome, Mr. President," the officer answered.

57

The C-130 Hercules swooped down low over the Spookbase and dropped its fourth equipment pallet. Then the big plane climbed and disappeared to the south. No sooner had it gone when another C-130 appeared over the base.

"Jeesuz! Another one!" Slade called out, pointing at the Herc as it dropped down and turned toward the base.

"Central Command obviously liked our performance today," Ryder said, watching the operation.

The equipment drop had been going on for nearly three hours. Nine airplanes had dropped a total of thirty-six equipment pallets, and both Slade and Ryder assumed this tenth plane would drop four more.

"Forty loads," Slade said. "That's more than we got when

we were first dropped here."

"We must have been big underdogs in this one," Ryder said. "Three airplanes iced wouldn't bring us all this. Maybe we got some In-No points for icing those tanks, and launching from the catapult for the first time."

"Whatever happened," Slade said, "this stuff will really help us . . ."

"Not to mention bugging the hell out of those guys," Ryder said, scanning the ridgeline. The Gray gas assault had stopped as soon as the C-130s arrived. Now, he could almost feel the envy coming from the soldiers overlooking the valley. "I haven't seen any Herc drops to *them*."

"Let them suffer," Slade said, watching as the tenth Herc came in and dropped its first pallet.

Ryder changed the subject. "We did pay a price for the fight earlier today," he told Slade. "We used up about half our fuel supply. And I doubt if these Hercs are going to start dropping fuel tanks to us."

They stood and watched the airplane come around three more times, dropping a store of equipment each time.

"That's it, forty . . ." Slade said, as the Herc climbed away.

"Look, he's circling again," Ryder said, keeping his eye on the C-130.

The big plane turned back over the base, but was too high to disgorge an equipment pallet.

"What's he up to?" Slade wondered.

Just then, they saw a small parachute come flying out of the back of the airplane and slowly float to the ground. The C-130 pilot then wagged his wings, climbed, and disappeared over the southern horizon.

Ryder immediately ran over to retrieve the parachute. It was a document satchel, tied with twine and overlapped with packing tape. He used his jackknife to rip open the wrappings and found a sealed envelope inside.

"What the hell is it?" Slade asked as he joined him.

Ryder opened the envelope and found two typed pages. The first one showed a specific list of coordinates and altitudes. The second page was a set of instructions and times.

"Are those what I think they are?" Slade asked.

"I think so," Ryder said. "If I'm not mistaken, these are times and instructions for a mid-air refueling."

"So this is how we'll get our gas . . ." Slade said.

Ryder read the instructions more closely. "Well, that's the good news," he said. "The bad news is this first rendezvous time. It's in the middle of the night . . ."

It was close to midnight when Ryder and Woody took off. The flaring from their F-14 engines lit up the valley with an eerie quick orange glow. As soon as their airplane was airborne, all the lights at the base were extinguished once again, denying targets to the Gray troops that occupied the ridgeline.

Ryder had no idea what to expect once they met up with the aerial tanker. He had noted when they first found the F-14s at the base, the standard navy air-refueling drogue had been removed and a strange, unorthodox drogue put in its place.

He climbed to the prescribed 32,000 feet and headed toward the assigned vector point which was about 150 miles off the coast of northern California. Woody was in back, tuning up the AGM.

"Let me know as soon as you spot something, Wiz," Ryder called back to his partner.

"Getting something now," Woody reported. "Big enough for a KC-135, but it's riding low. Not at the prescribed altitude. I'm calibrating now . . ."

Ryder checked his own auxiliary radar screen and saw the target blip. He turned and moved toward it.

"He's at 29,500, Ghost," Woody told him. "And slightly off the course they gave us. But it's worth a look."

Ryder opened up his throttle and streaked toward the aircraft. Its navigation lights were in sight within a half minute.

Ryder moved up and under the aircraft. It was the size of a KC-135. That exact size, in fact. But, to the surprise of both pilots, they discovered the airplane was actually a Boeing 707, the civilian version of the KC-135.

"That's probably a red-eye flight heading to Los Angeles," Ryder said, clearly reading the TWA marking on the jet's tail.

"That pilot is probably yelling like crazy at us," Woody said, knowing the jet fighter's radio couldn't pick up the civilian's radio transmission just as the airliner couldn't pick up theirs.

"It's good to know that life still goes on," Ryder said sadly. He suddenly felt like he had been on another planet and not just for a few weeks.

It seemed more like forever.

They continued their search for the air tanker, sweeping back and forth over the assigned rendezvous point. Suddenly Woody called ahead, his voice excited. "Ghost! I got him," he said. "Coming in high from the west. He's way up there, a hundred miles out . . ."

Ryder saw the indication on his own radar screen and put the fighter in a wide circle to wait for the tanker.

"Ghost, I know this will sound strange," Woody radioed ahead. "But I'm getting a very funny reading on this guy's radar."

"Funny how?" Ryder asked.

"Funny as in I don't think it was made in the USA," Woody replied. "I'm getting a lock on a SRD-5M 'High Fix' radar . . ."

"'High Fix?'" Ryder said. "Are you getting it on the I-Band?"

"That's a roger," Woody answered.

Jeesuz, what now? Ryder thought. He knew no American-made airplane would be carrying a SRD-5M radar.

That was because the device was manufactured in the Soviet Union . . .

Both pilots watched in amazement as the large airplane's navigation lights came into view.

"Those are *not* KC-135 blinkers," Woody said.

"It's a turbo-prop," Ryder said, drawing the F-14 closer to the approaching airplane. "Can you raise them on the radio, partner?"

Ryder heard Woody try to hail the mystery airplane,

switching radio bands until he hit the right one. All the while the airplane was getting closer.

"No reply," Woody told Ryder.

By this time the two airplanes were flying roughly parallel to each other, about two miles apart. It was a fairly clear night, yet try as he might, Ryder couldn't see any markings on the airplane, nor could he see the airplane long enough to identify its type.

Suddenly the airplane started blinking its navigation lights. Not knowing what else to do, Ryder blinked the F-14's lights in response.

The lights on the big plane blinked again. Then it banked softly toward the Tomcat. For the first time, the pilots got a clear look at the strange airplane.

"Woody, old buddy," Ryder said, not quite believing what he was about to say. "That's a Russian airplane . . ."

There were no markings, no numbers, no big red star on the side of the airplane. But Ryder knew the craft was a Soviet Naval Air Force air tanker. And for some reason, they had been told to rendezvous with it out over the Pacific.

Just then, from a side porthole in the big airplane, they saw a bright, strobelike light begin to flash.

Ryder blinked his lights and pulled back on the F-14's throttle, reducing his speed to match that of the mystery airplane. The light continued flashing, long and short bursts.

"Do you read Morse code, partner?" Ryder asked.

"Affirmative, Ghost" came the reply. "OK. I see: 'H,' 'O,' 'O,' 'K,' Hook."

"Hook?" Ryder wondered. "As in *hook*-up?"

"Worth a try," Woody said.

Then, from out of the rear of the airplane came the refueling hose, its tip illuminated with some kind of green fluorescent substance.

"Well, if that ain't an invitation . . ." Ryder said.

He deployed the F-14's odd-looking fuel drogue, and moved the jet fighter closer toward the fuel boom.

"Hell of a thing to be doing in the middle of the night," Woody said. "Linking up with a Russian refueling plane? Can it get much crazier than this?"

"Don't ask . . ." Ryder said as he gingerly connected the F-14 up to the mid-air refueling boom.

Soon, they could hear the fuel being transferred from the big plane to their tanks.

"Hope it's our brand," Ryder said.

58

Major Maxwell lit his fifth cigar of the night. He knew it would be useless to try and sleep. The racket outside his command tent from the Gray Thunder shells was enough to wake the dead.

Suddenly his radio crackled with static.

"Blue Command, come in . . ." the voice on the other end said.

Maxwell grabbed the mic. "This is Blue Command, go ahead."

"This is Simons, sir, 0100 situation report."

Maxwell grabbed his map and unrolled it. "OK, Bo," he said. "What do you have?"

"We've been forced back another two clicks, sir," Simons reported. "We are now at coordinates Seven-five West, Five Two East . . ."

Maxwell noted the coordinates on the map. The Gray Army was now just three miles from his command HQ. He knew it was just a matter of time before they broke through.

"How are you holding up, Bo?" he asked.

"They've bounced two choppers and got one of our vehicles," Simons said. "But we've been able to knock out one of their tanks.

"We're falling back a platoon at a time, leaving a squad in

each area just to delay them."

"How's your equipment?" Maxwell asked.

"Right now, not bad," Simons answered through the static. "But our generators are getting low on the ZootTOW missiles. The choppers are OK with their Zoot air-to-ground stuff, for now. But there are just too many of these guys. They are very well equipped. We've seen C-130s dropping stuff to them behind their lines."

"What's their strength?" the major asked.

"I'd say we're facing at least four battalions, sir," Simons reported. "We're making the shots, but it seems that every guy we turn back, two guys take his place . . ."

"Any Aggressors flying around?" Maxwell asked.

"Negative, sir" was the reply.

Maxwell relit his cigar. "OK, Simons," he said. "Just keep up the delaying action. That's what Central Command wants us to do. So we'll do it. Call back in fifteen minutes and we'll talk about bringing everyone back in here for the final perimeter defense."

"Roger, sir," Simons acknowledged.

Maxwell wished he had a cup of coffee, or better yet, a very stiff drink. Maybe the Cray supercomputer had gone crazy. Why in hell did it have his airborne rapid assault force fighting a defensive delaying action that was doomed from the start?

High above, cruising the night sky at 52,000 feet, the EC-2 AWACs airplane was closely watching the F-14 on its highly sophisticated radar system.

"They've fueled up and are heading due south, sir," the airplane's chief radar officer said to the general leaning over his shoulder. "We've just sent them the new orders and flight coordinates."

"When will they pass over the Special Range?" the general asked.

The radar officer pushed a few buttons and read a digital display next to his screen. "At present speed and course, in approximately ten minutes."

"OK," the general said. "Have communications call down to the Central Command. Tell them the F-14 is on its way . . ."

"Talk about being out in the middle of nowhere," Woody said, looking down on the barren, darkened desert landscape. "It almost looks like another planet . . ."

Ryder wasn't paying attention.

They had unhooked from the apparently Soviet aerial tanker with no problems and with no direct contact with its crew. The mystery airplane had then turned northward and disappeared, he and Woody chalking up the rendezvous as just another strange incident in the skies above War Heaven.

No sooner had they turned back toward the Spookbase when they received a mysterious radio transmission, ordering them to fly a course which would take them about twenty miles east of Spookbase.

They didn't question the orders. They were now veterans of War Heaven. And Rule number 1 was: "Don't ask questions, because nothing makes sense anyway."

So now Ryder was following the precise course prescribed in the new orders. And even though he was flying the most sophisticated jet fighter ever built, he found his mind wandering back to the lovely Maureen. Where was she now? Was she still at Smiling Jack's? Did she still feel the way he did? Would he ever see her again?

Suddenly, Woody broke into his private thoughts.

"Hey, Ghost!" the Wiz called ahead. "I'm getting something very strange on the scope . . ."

Jolted back to reality, Ryder called back, "What's up? Aggressors?"

"Negative," Woody said. "Very strange ground clutter ahead about twenty miles. Lots of electronic radiation. Infrared stuff. My scope is jumping like crazy."

"Getting any hostile indicators?" Ryder asked, checking the status of his full load of Zootweapons.

"Negative," Woody reported. "Not right at this moment, anyway . . ."

Ryder leveled the airplane off at four thousand feet and strained his eyes to see ahead of him. They were about fifty miles northeast of Spookbase. The location of the ground activity appeared to be a deep valley just ahead of them. Yet it looked as dark as the rest of the landscape.

"You sure your equipment is straight, Wiz?" Ryder called back to the pit. "I can't see anything up ahead that would give off those readings . . ."

"I rechecked everything, Ghost," Woody answered. "It's all coming back to me ten-by-ten, even the back-up decoder. Everything is telling me that valley is hotter than hell with electronics . . ."

It suddenly dawned on Ryder that the valley ahead might be the same one they had seen lighting up several nights before.

"Wood Man, check those coordinates," Ryder asked. "Is it me or are we heading right for that strange place?"

Woody was back on the line in less than fifteen seconds. "You called it, Ghost," he reported.

This was turning into quite a night, Ryder thought. First the mysterious meeting with the Soviet-built, if not Soviet-piloted airplane, and now this.

"Well, I guess we should check it out . . ." Ryder said, noting the area was right in line with the course he was told to follow.

He lowered the airplane further, leveling out at two thousand feet and steered right for the valley in question. If anything the terrain ahead looked darker than the rest of the landscape . . .

They were about a mile from overflying the valley. Yet nothing ahead looked amiss.

Then, suddenly . . .

"Holy Christ! There it is again!"

There was a tremendous flash of light. It was so bright it blinded Ryder. Instinctively he pulled back on the Tomcat's controls and the aircraft started to climb.

Ryder blinked his eyes back into working order. Although he had been somewhat prepared, when he opened his eyes he still couldn't believe what he saw.

Not only had the entire valley become illuminated as if it

314

were daylight—it looked like it was covered with bright green trees, much more vivid, much more realistic than when they had driven nearby the night they saw the mysterious Herc drop.

"This place is incredible!" Woody cried out, seeing the same thing.

They were right over the valley now. What Ryder's eyes were telling him, his brain didn't want to accept. The landscape below looked as lush and green as a . . .

"It looks exactly like a goddamn *jungle*," Woody said.

Ryder shook his head. He could see quite clearly, trees, vines, small fields, even streams. Yet everything was so bright. It looked both *real* and *unreal* at the same time.

"It's got to be some kind of holographic projection," Ryder called back to Woody. "Like a fantastic illusion. That would account for your scope's high readings."

"Well, it's one hell of a trick," the Wiz said as they streaked over the far end of the valley. "No wonder they needed that drop of semichips and circuit boards. Can you imagine what it must take to throw up something like this?"

Suddenly, as if they tripped a switch, the incredible lights in the valley blinked off.

"I guess I thought I'd seen everything," Ryder said. "But that last gimmick took the cake."

He turned the airplane around and streaked toward the valley again.

But this time, nothing happened. The ground remained black and featureless.

"No radiation at all now," Woody reported. "Maybe someone blew a fuse."

They flew over the landscape one more time, and again the illusion didn't appear.

"Well, they wanted us to fly over it," Ryder said. "But I guess it was just for one peek."

He turned the F-14 to the west, toward Spookbase. "Maybe we can get someone on the radio when we land," he said. "Have them explain it to us."

59

Major Maxwell and Bo Simons stood outside the command tent and counted the helicopters as they landed within the Blue Army North compound.

"There's number fourteen and fifteen, sir," Simons said, wiping his brow with his blue scarf. "That should be it . . ."

A thunder bomb went off overhead, followed by two flasher shells.

"God! I'll have no hearing left after this," Maxwell muttered.

There was still about an hour left of darkness. Off in the distance they could see the advance elements of the encircling Gray Army.

"What are our orders, Major?" Simons asked. "Fight to the end?"

The major nodded. "I guess," he answered. "'Hold out until notified' is how Central Command put it . . ."

Two more thunder bombs went off above them.

"How are your troops?" Major Max asked as soon as the noise died down.

"The men are holding up fine, sir," Simons said. "Like always, they're curious as to what we are training for . . ."

"*We* are all curious, Simons," Major Max said. "But remember, 'Ours is not to question why' . . ."

Just then they heard a frighteningly familiar sound.

"Aggressors!" Simons said, pointing to the east.

"Just what we need," Major Maxwell said bitterly. "Quick, sound the air raid alarm . . ."

The two F-5s came in low and fast over the star-shaped Blue Army base. It was just dawn and the rising sun gave them some defensive cover. Below, the pilots could see the Blue Army troops scattering to their positions.

Both airplanes dropped a single canister and roared away. The bombs—containing a mixture of Supertears and Crab Gas—exploded just fifty feet from Maxwell's tent, spraying the immediate area with the abrasive mixtures.

Both Maxwell and Simons put their scarves around their mouths.

"Simons, get that ZootSAM up," the major yelled to him as he watched the two F-5s turn back for another run. "I'm calling the Spooks . . ."

Ryder saw the welcoming lights of the Spookbase blink on.

"Captain Long, this is Moon," his radio crackled. "Ready for the approach?"

"Roger," Ryder answered. "Talk us in . . ."

He switched down the F-14's landing gear and lowered its arrestor hook.

"Hang on, Wiz," he called back to the pit. Then he put the Tomcat into a slow dive, lining up the nose of the airplane with the center of the illuminated runway.

"OK, Captain," they heard Moon's voice say. "Down a little, to your left. Nose down. Nose down. To your left. Left. A hundred feet. Seventy-five. To your left. Fifty. Twenty-five . . . *You're down!*"

The airplane snagged the third arresting wire and screeched to a halt.

"Like getting laid in a tornado!" Woody yelled out, describing the sudden jolting landing.

"No such thing as a bad landing," Ryder reminded him.

They popped the canopy and prepared to climb out when they saw Slade climbing up the access ladder toward them.

"Can you guys launch again right away?" he asked.

"What's up?" Ryder asked.

"Maxwell just called us," Slade said, handing him a canteen filled with hot coffee. "They're really getting plastered up his way. The Grays have him surrounded and the Aggressors are gas bombing their base."

"Where are the other two 'Cats?" Ryder asked, handing the coffee back to Woody.

"They've already launched and they're on the way," Slade told him. "This is the big push, the big Blue-Gray battle and I think we should be involved in it . . ."

"That's what we are here for, I guess," Ryder said, putting his helmet back on. "How have our friends up on the ridge been behaving?"

"Not a peep out of them all night," Slade said. "Makes me wonder if they're really still up there . . ."

Moon's men were scrambling all over the aircraft making sure everything was in working condition. Then they moved the F-14 back over the catapult and hooked it in. Moon gave Ryder the thumbs-up and a few seconds later they were airborne again.

Lancaster turned his F-14 over and positioned himself on the tail of the fleeing F-5. He watched as the crosshairs on his HUD linked. He instantly squeezed his Zootmissile launch trigger and watched the holographically projected Sidewinder flash away and impact on the Aggressor's right wing.

"Good shooting, Group Captain," Lancaster heard Sammett say from the backseat.

"Still more where he came from," Lancaster said. "Do you have another target, old boy?"

Sammett checked his AGM. There were no less than fifteen Aggressors buzzing around the Blue base. Off to their left, Reinhart and Chauvagne had just bounced an A-4 and were working on another F-5.

Up ahead, Sammett saw a pair of A-4s just pulling up from a gas attack on the completely gas-enshrouded Blue base.

He began lining up one of the A-4s when the radio inside their F-14 crackled. "This is Central Command," both Sammett and Lancaster heard the caller say. "Turn immediately to course Seven-Two-Delta-Zero. At altitude 15,500 feet. Await further instructions . . ."

"Did you copy that, Sammett, my friend?" Lancaster called back to the Indian.

"Yes, sir," the pit man answered. "Why would they pull us out, now?"

Lancaster broke off the engagement with the A-4 and immediately turned to the ordered course. "I don't know the answer to that, chum. But go we must . . ."

He put the F-14 into a climb and saw that Reinhart was right beside him. Obviously he had received the same message. Then the British pilot noticed that the Aggressors were also leaving, having formed up and headed south.

"Curious . . ." he said as he upped the Tomcat's throttle.

The two F-14s—as well as all the Aggressor aircraft—were gone from the area when Ryder and Woody arrived ten minutes later.

60

Maureen couldn't sleep. The noise coming from the battle off to the north was so loud, the panes in her room's window were shaking.

At least she *thought* it was a battle. She had watched the bright flashes and columns of smoke rising from behind the hills on the northern horizon all night. Jet aircraft had been streaking overhead since sundown—with each one she had wondered if Ryder was behind its controls.

She had been taking notes since arriving at Smiling Jack's, concealing the documents under her clothes whenever anyone came to her room to deliver meals and so on. She had pages of notations so far, starting from what she heard when her helicopter was forced down and she was transported to Jack's by the Gray-uniformed soldiers, up to what Ryder had told her. Her only conclusion so far was that some kind of incredibly sophisticated war game was going on in the Nevada desert.

But she knew that it was only the tip of the iceberg . . .

It was the recent activity at Jack's that had her most puzzled. Simply put, a group of soldiers—dressed in more standard US Army uniforms—were taking the town down, piece by piece and carting it away in large civilian tractor trailer trucks.

They started the morning before. The soldiers, about fifty in all, had already taken down two buildings at the end of the street and had begun work on the third, working under powerful searchlights.

At this rate, she knew the town—with the saloon included—would be gone in two days.

There was a sudden knock at her door. She quickly stuffed her notes down the back of her skirt and sat on the bed.

The door opened and Jammer walked in, accompanied by a woman who was dressed like a nurse.

"Miss O'Brien," Jammer started. "Let me first tell you that your father has been informed of your stay with us and that he is much relieved. We have also contacted your editor and he, too, is glad you're safe."

"Thank you, Major," Maureen said. "Now when do I get out of here?"

Jammer looked plainly worried. "I'm afraid that isn't going to be anytime soon, Miss O'Brien," he said. "I'm sure you must realize at this point that you have stumbled upon a very highly classified project. I am authorized to tell you that you are one of only a few dozen people who have seen as much as you've seen. Know as much as you know."

"I demand that you release me," Maureen said, her Irish temper boiling over. "I am a citizen of this country. You have no right to hold me against my will."

Jammer shook his head. "But, yes we do," he told her. "The national security of this nation would be jeopardized if we let you go. That is why we can't . . ."

"So what do you intend on doing with me?" she asked.

Jammer turned toward the nurse. "This is Lieutenant Irene Daly," he said. "I'm afraid she's going to have to give you an injection. Something to make you sleep . . ."

Ryder put the F-14 into a low orbit around the Blue Army base, both he and Woody straining to see any activity.

"Where is everybody?" Woody asked, looking down into the haze-covered base.

"Beats me," Ryder answered. "According to Slade they had a battle royale going on up here . . ."

He lowered the Tomcat down to five hundred feet and streaked directly over the base. It certainly *looked* like a battle had just been fought—there were various pieces of equipment strewn about, including several apparently abandoned Huey choppers.

"Looks like the Grays won the fight," Ryder said, buzzing low over the base a second time. A single small Gray Army flag was fluttering over the Blue Army's command tent.

"Now it looks like everyone cashed out and went home," Woody said.

Ryder flashed over the base one more time then turned south. "We can't waste fuel flying around up here," he told Woody. "Maybe the other guys will know something when we get back."

"Spookcase, this is Ryder, come in . . ."

"Still nothing, Ghost?" Woody asked.

"Negative," Ryder answered, his voice betraying his concern.

The F-14 was back over the airstrip fifteen minutes later. They were circling the base, but, strangely, no one was answering their radio calls.

"What the hell is going on?" Woody asked. "They can't all be asleep, unless the Grays hit them with knock-out gas."

"I don't think so," Ryder said, steering the airplane over the ridge. It looked as deserted as the Blue Base up north.

"Central Command knew we were up tonight. I doubt if they would have authorized a sleep gas strike knowing we had to be recovered with help of people on the ground. Even if the Grays attacked and took over the base, they'd still have to illuminate the runway for us."

It was a particularly dark night with no moon, so the whole ridge and valley area was blacked out. Woody had activated the F-14's look-down radar system in an attempt to detect something—any kind of movement at the airstrip. But so far, he'd come up empty.

"If someone doesn't turn on those runway lights, we're going to have to fly around until there's enough light to put

321

this baby down," Woody said, stating their predicament. "Judging from our fuel load, that'll be another ninety minutes from now."

"And we'll waste all the fuel we've taken on," Ryder added. "It doesn't make sense . . ."

He put the Tomcat into another wide circle around the valley. Suddenly Major Max's initiation speech came back to him: "You were put here to think. To adapt. To innovate."

Sunrise was still about forty-five minutes away. "There are no roads around here that I can set down on," Ryder said. "No flat piece of desert that I could be sure we'd get off again."

"Doesn't leave us a whole lot of choice, partner," Woody said.

"We'll have to risk it . . ." Ryder said, turning the F-14 around for an approach. "Besides, I got an idea . . ."

He switched on his powerful nose light and lowered the 'Cat's arresting hook. He was far from being an expert at "hook landings," although the ones earlier had gone off without a hitch. But he knew things could get complicated when you were trying to land a multi-ton fighter on one of four cables that, if done properly, would stop the 'Cat from 120 mph to a dead stand still in two seconds.

"Hang on, *mon ami*," Ryder called back to Woody as he floated the 'Cat down.

When he saw the arresting cables in the beam of the noselight, he quickly punched up the Zootcannon arming system. Squeezing the trigger, he sent a stream of bright holographic images right into the cables. The reflected light was enough for him to aim and catch—although roughly—the third cable.

The F-14 stopped as advertised, but he and Woody almost crashed through the canopy.

"Wow!" Ryder exclaimed. "Are we still in one piece?"

"No such thing as a bad landing, Ghost," Woody reminded him.

Ryder quickly shut off the Tomcat's engines and associated systems. He could hear Woody in the back shutting down the airplane's computer system. Once they were sure the airplane was secured, he popped the canopy . . .

No one came out to meet them and they could see no lights, no evidence of anybody around.

"This is very spooky," Woody said, climbing out of his seat. "Where the hell is everyone?"

They both climbed down out of the big 'Cat, not an easy thing to do without an access ladder. Then, systematically, they searched every building, structure, and the immediate grounds. They found a cup of hot coffee still sitting on Slade's desk. Some of the food was still warm in the pots at the temporary messhall. Even the radar and communications systems were still switched on.

Just then they heard the sound of a helicopter approaching.

"There it is . . ." Ryder said, pointing to the large Chinook-style chopper moving slowly down the valley.

They watched and waited for the chopper. It circled the base twice then set down in the field right next to the runway.

About a dozen soldiers alighted. But they weren't wearing the uniforms of the Blues or Grays.

"I think these guys are referees," Ryder said to Woody as they watched the men approach.

Out of the group of soldiers, one familiar face emerged. It was Jammer.

"Hello, Captain Long," the man said, walking up to them. "I assume this is Captain Woods . . ."

"That's right, Colonel," Ryder answered. "I hope you are here to clear up a few things . . ."

Jammer smiled briefly. "Yes and no," he said, reaching inside his uniform and pulling out an envelope. "I have one last mission for you to fly. The most important mission of all you've undertaken here in War Heaven."

"Sounds serious," Ryder said. "Do you mind if we ask where the rest of our guys are?"

"They're safe," Jammer said. "That's really all I can say. You'll get your answers soon enough . . ."

Ryder and Woody looked at each other and shrugged. Another crazy day in War Heaven.

"As I said, we have one more exercise for you," Jammer continued. "It involves a night launch and these soldiers will help you work the catapult and get off. We'll do a preflight briefing right around 1900 hours . . ."

"We got fifteen hours between now and the next nightfall," Ryder said. "What do we do until then?"

"Sleep," Jammer said. "Get some chow and get some sleep. You'll need a lot of both . . ."

Woody started stripping off his flight suit. "Well, I'm all for sleeping and eating," he said.

"One more thing, gentlemen," Jammer said, opening up the envelope he was holding. "I've been asked to inform you that Central Command has been extremely pleased by the way you performed here in War Heaven. It has been nothing short of brilliant.

"And so, in appreciation of what you have endured, and what you are about to endure, I've been asked to give these to you . . ."

He handed a small packet to each of them. Ryder ripped his open and took out a silver pin. It was a set of wings topped off by a star.

"Congratulations, gentlemen," Jammer said. "You've both been promoted to major . . ."

Both Ryder and Woody were glad to take Jammer's advice. They had eaten heartily of the field rations the refs had brought with them, then they retired to their individual cubicles and slept away most of the day.

A Ref sergeant woke them up at 1800 hours and they ate again. Then they met Jammer in the airstrip's Ops Building.

"All right, men," the man said, unfolding a map on the desk in front of him. "It was no accident that your course after refueling carried you over what we call Cartoon Valley."

"Do you mean that light show about thirty miles from here?" Woody asked. "Good name for it . . ."

"That's it," Jammer answered, indicating a point on the map. "You've probably guessed that the illusion you saw was another example of holographic projection . . ."

Both Ryder and Woody nodded.

"OK," Jammer continued. "That specific site was set up to mimic a target that's halfway around the world. A target whose destruction is, in itself, the object of Project Distant Thunder."

Ryder felt a jolt of excitement rip through him. He sensed that finally the War Heaven training was coming to a climax and they would, for better or worse, be moving on to the real thing.

"Your exercise involves hitting a target at the end of that valley," Jammer said, pointing to an X-spot on the map. "My men have been working all day adapting your F-14 to carry several special air-to-ground Zootmissiles. When the actual mission takes place, you will, of course, be carrying live ordnance."

Jammer rolled up the map and continued. "The coordinates for the target have been programmed into your on-board computer. But, just as in the actual mission, it has to be a manual launch, under hostile fire. That's why we are having this dry run of sorts tonight . . ."

"Under hostile fire?" Woody asked.

"That's correct, Major," Jammer answered. "And that is why we've constructed Cartoon Valley . . .

"When we directed you over the canyon last night, we were studying your reaction profile more than anything else. But suffice to say, only a minimal number of all the holographic projections devices were operating when you saw it."

Ryder and Woody gave each other a sidewise look. They didn't mention that they had seen the Cartoon Valley light up several nights earlier.

"I can't imagine anything being added to that projection," Ryder said.

"Well, there will be," Jammer answered. "It's the simulated hostile fire I spoke about."

Outside they heard the sound of the F-14's jet engines beginning to warm up.

"You and your unit performed remarkably well here," Jammer told them. "Setting up that field catapult, procuring the water, scoring points when you were outnumbered, enduring the gas attacks. All very commendable . . ."

"It was not just us, Colonel," Ryder said. "Our unit— Lieutenant Moon's guys—they did the yeoman's work . . ."

"We are well aware of that, Major," Jammer said. "But you two pilots were the focal point of it all. Even the other pilot teams were never intended for anything but a support or a back-up role should something happen to you two."

"But when are we going to learn what the mission is?" Ryder asked him. "Surely we are at a point in the training where we can be brought into the loop . . ."

Jammer nodded. "Yes, you're correct, Major," he said. "One of our control officers will brief you after this exercise. He will be able to answer all your questions. And more . . ."

61

They launched at exactly 2000 hours. Jammer's refs were as good as Moon's men in operating the catapult and the F-14's launch was the smoothest one yet.

Ryder immediately steered north of the Spookbase, using his flight computer to guide him back to Cartoon Canyon. During the short ride, he and Woody spent the time familiarizing themselves with the new Zootweapons slung underneath the aircraft.

"It appears like it's a very powerful, short-range cruise missile," Woody said after reading the data that had been integrated into the F-14's memory banks. "It's a manual steering device with a warhead that will detonate a hundred feet above the target."

"A down-burst bomb," Ryder said. "Whatever we'll be shooting at, they definitely don't want a scattering of debris."

"OK, we are coming up on the target," Woody said. "Just ahead about twenty clicks. My data says we'll encounter a defensive perimeter at eighteen clicks out. Another at twelve and another at four and in . . ."

"That's a lot of defense," Ryder said. "Better activate the

ground threat warning system, Wiz . . ."

Ryder checked his infra-red scope. The electronic clutter arising from the canyon painted a 3-D outline of the terrain.

He punched his flight computer to the preset attack mode and brought the F-14 down to a thousand feet.

Suddenly Woody was on the line. "Ghost! I'm getting multiple threat warnings."

"What kind of threats?" Ryder asked, holding the aircraft at a thousand feet.

"ZootSAMs," the Wiz answered. "Hundreds of them! The next thirty clicks are loaded with them. Be ready to begin evasive tactics."

"Roger . . ." Ryder answered. He reached down and switched on his electronic countermeasures device. The ECM would serve to jam the electronic signals of the ZootSAMs ahead.

He then threw another series of switches and watched as corresponding lights blinked on within his HUD system. This particular device was a Threat Evaluation Countermeasures system. By using high-speed video resolution, it painted a picture of the canyon and its defensive perimeters. Each ZootSAM site that was emitting, and therefore "detectable," was automatically evaluated and assigned a number on the computer's "value" threat scale. ZootSAM sites that would be several miles from the F-14 when it made its bombing run would be assigned a lesser threat value than ones the airplane would be flying directly over. The intensity of the threat was transferred to a color system. The most dangerous ZootSAM area appeared in bright red. Areas of reduced threat were treated in yellow, medium threats were colored in orange. All Ryder had to do was keep wthin the yellow pathway and follow it to the target. But it was not as simple as it appeared.

"Jeesuz," Woody said to Ryder. "Are they kidding with all these SAM sites? If this is how the actual target stacks up, it's going to get very, *very* hairy . . ."

"I guess that's why we got our promotions, partner," Ryder said.

He brought the F-14 down to 750 feet, using his Terrain Avoidance gear to keep him at a safe height. Suddenly, about fifteen clicks from the canyon, they saw the flash of light, just as intense as the night before.

"That's a hell of a way to say 'Hello,'" Woody said.

When they blinked their eyes back into focus, they saw the elaborate holographic projection had been switched on. What was just seconds before a dark, barren desert landscape now looked all the world like a lush green jungle.

"Arm the weapon," Ryder called back to Woody. He could see the target area at the far end of the canyon. The yellow pathway on his HUD system showed they would have to take a twisting, turning route to safely launch the weapon. No wonder Central Command wanted it all done manually . . .

"*Jeesuz*, Ghost, here they come!" Woody yelled into the intercom.

Just then, the airplane ground threat warning device started ringing. At the same instant Ryder saw what looked to be dozens of ZootSAMs being fired at them.

"Christ!" he yelled back, almost involuntarily. "There are hundreds of them."

The night sky turned into a massive fireworks display. The ZootSAMs flashed up at them, fiery trails marking their paths. Ryder immediately started jinking and juking to avoid the simulated weapons.

"Hang on!" he yelled as he started the jarring evasive maneuvers. Ryder wasn't even thinking as he swung in and out of the SAM paths. He was flying purely on instinct.

He put the F-14 down to five hundred feet causing many of the Zootmissiles to fly above them.

That's when they started picking up the low-level ground-fire.

"We got AAA coming up at us!" Woody yelled out.

"I hear you . . ." Ryder said, putting the F-14 on its right wing. The odd angle gave them a spectacular view of the holographic jungle below. The detail was frighteningly accurate. In one quick glimpse, Ryder saw not only authentic-looking trees, fields, and streams, he could clearly see SAM emplacements, AAA guns, radio transmitters, even World War I-style trenches. And it was all so *goddamn* real. It was more like *being* in a movie, than just watching one.

They continued the bomb run, Ryder moving the F-14 around like some target in a massive video game.

More than once they felt a dull thud coming from underneath the airplane, indications that some of the AAA shots were hitting. Oddly, the hits weren't affecting the avionics of the airplane like usual Zootshots would. They also were blindsided four times by simulated SAMs, near misses, but possibly close enough to damage the airplane had it been actual combat.

Finally, they saw the target indicator up ahead.

"OK, there's the pot of gold," Ryder told Woody. "How's the weapon?"

"All locked on and green," Woody replied. "Ready for launch . . ."

He darted around yet another barrage of ZootSAMs, incredibly dodging them all. At one click out, he launched the weapon . . .

They felt a jarring rumble underneath them as the simulated missile roared away. The preflight data indicated that at this point Ryder was to increase his airspeed and actually overtake the missile, this way not getting caught up in the blast.

He pushed the throttle ahead and continued the nerve-wracking maneuvering. They overtook the holographic missile just as it was beginning its descent to the target.

"Could be right-on," Woody reported, tracking the Zoot-missile on his radar.

Suddenly there were two explosions, just a heartbeat apart. One was akin to dropping a heavy bomb, but the second one was a tremendous blast so powerful, Ryder nearly lost control of the airplane. The first explosion was obviously their Zootmissile going off. The second blast could only have been the simulated result of the target being hit.

"*Jesus Christ!*" Woody yelled out, shaking off the effects of the huge simulated secondary explosion. "What the hell do they want us to bomb?"

Ryder was wondering the exact same thing . . .

They practiced the hair-raising bomb run four times before

turning back to the base. During each attempt Ryder made it a point to memorize each jink, juke, twist, and turn he would have to execute to avoid being hit by the simulated antiaircraft fire. The last run was the best. They were able to avoid just about all the AAA shots and everything but two near misses by ZootSAMs. However, each time the missile made it to the target they were enveloped in the violent aftereffects of the secondary explosion.

"We might have lived through that last one," Ryder said to Woody as he steered back toward the Spookbase. "But that second blast is what bugs me."

Woody agreed. "If we climbed into straight vertical at that point, those SAMs would have us for breakfast. If we go low, the AAA crews will pop us. And we can't generate enough speed after dropping the weapon to get away."

"Typical military Catch-22," Ryder said. Maureen's words about their fake obituaries came rushing back to him. What kind of mission could it be if the military put out fake obits on them? The answer came to him all too quickly: It was a mission they didn't expect anyone to come back from . . .

They landed without incident and immediately met with Jammer in the Ops Building.

"We've just received the results of your exercise," the colonel told them. "Looks good for the first time. The target was hit all four times. Your escape mode was, shall we say, *different* each time, however."

"Meaning we didn't make it every time?" Ryder asked.

Jammer nodded grimly. "That's correct . . ." he said.

"Well, that will come with more practice . . ." Woody said.

"That's the problem, gentlemen," Jammer said. "There is no more time to practice . . ."

Ryder felt the words sting in his ears. "Is that by necessity or design, Colonel?"

Jammer looked at him, wearing a very worried look.

"The necessity of the situation, Major," he said. "The events controlling the timing of this mission are not in our hands. We cannot control it or put it on a workable timetable. It's a situation that is frankly out of control. We have to go in

330

quickly, or it will be too late . . ."

From that point on, Ryder began repeating the maneuvers he knew he would have to perform to carry out the bombing mission—and survive.

"You mentioned that a control officer was to brief us?" he asked.

Jammer nodded. "Yes, and I can't think of a better time than to have him talk to you now."

Jammer picked up the radio mic and simply said, "OK, come on in . . ."

Then he turned back to Ryder and Woody. "Let me explain that a control officer is someone who has been in on the mission's objectives right from the beginning. One of them was assigned to your group."

"You mean, this control officer has been in amongst us all along?" Woody asked.

Jammer nodded. "That's correct, Major," he said.

"A spy in other words," Ryder said.

"Not really," Jammer said. "This particular officer was assigned to your group because he closely fit the profile that most of you did. He fit in. He knew his stuff. He contributed. He helped out you and the rest of the unit when the situation dictated."

Ryder couldn't imagine who the anonymous control officer was. *Everyone* had pitched in at the airstrip. *Everyone* had contributed. Who could it be?

That's when Lieutenant Moon walked in . . .

62

It took a few moments for the initial shock of discovering that Moon was Central Command's spy in the Spookbase, to wear off.

"You make quite a James Bond, Lieutenant," Ryder said.

"I'll take that as a compliment, Major Ryder," the young officer said.

Moon had a four-page document marked Top Secret. It had several photographs attached. He quickly read over the front page, cleared his throat, and began:

"Before we get to the specifics of the mission, let me just say that I know you have both endured a lot of hardship, anticipation, and uncertainty both at Top Gun and here in War Heaven. I think once you see what we are facing, you'll agree that all of it was necessary.

"In a nutshell: the world's nuclear nightmare has come true. An army of terrorists has been able to secure atomic weapons. They have also been able to acquire launching systems for these weapons—systems that while crude are still able to deliver nuclear warheads to just about any spot on earth.

"Our mission—the one we've been training for—is to stop these terrorists before they are able to launch."

Moon stopped to catch his breath and let the news sink in. He couldn't help but notice the stunned looks being worn by Ryder and Woody. Even Jammer, who had heard it all before, looked very nervous.

Moon continued. "This clandestine ICBM base is located in one of the most inhospitable places on earth. It is in the middle of the Keng Hkam valley in eastern Burma. In case you don't realize it, that part of the Burmese wilderness is basically a hotbed of anarchy. There is no governmental control there or in many other places in Burma. The local Burmese natives call the location of the ICBM base the Iron Circle. This is because it has tremendous defense in depth. The people in charge of the Iron Circle have raised an army of thirty thousand men, bandits and rebels mostly. They are tough, well trained, well paid, and utterly vicious. They have bought up many weapons on the black arms market and, most important to you, they have come into possession of thousands of Vietnam War-era SAMs . . ."

"Did you say 'thousands?'" Woody interrupted.

Moon nodded solemnly, then continued. "I will anticipate two questions. One, who is behind this clandestine base?

Gentlemen, you will probably be shocked to learn that the perpetrator is none other than Colonel Toon . . ."

Toon? Ryder couldn't believe it. Toon was the legendary North Vietnamese pilot who was supposedly shot down during the war. His name, even among the pilots at Top Gun, was spoken with a certain amount of reverence.

"Yes, we have confirmed that Toon is indeed alive," Moon continued. "Somehow, he's been able to draw in a number of individuals and governments hostile to the US and incorporate them into his plan, which, by the way, he views as his destiny. To rid the world of the 'impure,' as he calls his enemies.

"Question Number Two: How did Toon amass such power? At some point during the late 1970s and early 1980s, Toon and his entourage took up residence in the Keng Hkem valley. He hired local bandits, using money gained from growing opium. These bandits gradually—but quietly—expanded their sphere of influence in eastern Burma. The government—which in itself is a very strange mix—had neither the ambition nor the manpower to take on Toon's boys. So they proliferated. They in fact began their own government. They collected taxes from the natives, drafted soldiers, printed money, and set up a bartering system.

"It was from this power base that Toon very discreetly started buying up components to build a nuclear warhead. He did most of this work through intermediaries. And it's my sad duty to tell you, gentlemen, that it wasn't all that hard for Toon's go-betweens to deal with respectable people in respectable governments, like Germany, Pakistan, Sweden, and Japan. He also had many contacts with less-than-desirable governments like East Germany, Libya, Iran, North Korea, and, of course, Communist Vietnam.

"Through almost a decade and a half, Toon was able to assemble his nuclear components while at the same time gathering together a mass of conventional weapons that rival those of the majority of nations on this earth."

Ryder had a question. "Did the Russians have anything to do with this?"

Moon wiped his brow, and considered his answer before he spoke. "Yes and no," he said. "Yes, Toon had some support from the Soviets early on. We believe that they saw his activities as a way to set a Communist anchor in central Asia, a flanking ally underneath China. But even the Soviets came to realize that Toon was utterly mad as well as ruthless. They cut off support six years ago. But it was too little too late. By that time, Toon didn't need them.

"Since then, they've been cooperating with us to some extent. That midnight refueling session you were involved in was one factor of their initiative. Once you are deployed, you will be refueled by Soviet aerial tankers."

Both Ryder and Woody whistled in disbelief.

"OK, so this guy Toon has a nuclear weapon," Woody said. "Why not just send in some B-52s, and carpet bomb the place?"

Moon shot a nervous look toward Jammer. "That's the hardest part of all this," Moon said, reaching for one of the Top Secret photos. The three men gathered around him.

"Here's a recent photo of part of the Iron Circle," Moon said. He pointed to a series of barracks-style buildings that were located next to what looked like a large igloo. "This is a prison camp. This strange-looking building is Toon's nuclear lab and weapons storage center. It was built almost exclusively with Iranian aid.

"Now there is a reason—a very *sinister* reason—why that nuclear storage center is next to that prison . . ."

"Which is . . . ?" Ryder asked.

He saw it was almost painful for Moon to answer. "Because, gentlemen, we believe that the two hundred prisoners in that camp are actually American POWs from the Vietnam War."

It was as if a bomb went off in the room. Both Ryder and Woody were stunned speechless.

"*But how?*" was all Ryder could get out finally.

"That we don't know . . ." Moon said. "Possibly he made a deal with Hanoi. Take these POWs off our hands and we'll give you all our old SAMs. Who knows? We've bombarded Hanoi with diplomatic protests—all in secret, of course. But to no avail, I'm afraid. They're hard nuts to crack, as you can imagine. So, especially in the past year while we have protest movements at home, begging the US government to do

334

something about the POWs, we've been sitting on this information that Toon has had them all along. And he was someone who we couldn't even get in touch with through channels, never mind sit down and talk rationally with."

"And Toon is using the POWs as hostages," Ryder surmised, "knowing we would be pretty hard pressed to carpet bomb the place and take the lives of those soldiers."

"That's it," Moon said. "But let me tell you, that's still an option. Though a grim one . . ."

"Why not just shoot the missile out of the air once he launches it?" Woody asked.

Moon frowned again. "We have found out that not only does Toon have a nuclear capability, his warheads are manufactured with a particularly 'dirty' strain of uranium. I'm not a nuclear physicist, but I've had it explained to me that these warheads are capable of spreading enormous amounts of radioactivity once they've exploded. So much hot stuff that by far more people would die of the radioactivity effects than would die in the blast.

"You see, Toon's weapons have little military value. He cannot conquer any territory by launching them. He, in fact, will have nothing at all to gain—other than pulling off the largest terrorist bombing ever. One that won't just kill a few dozen people at an airport somewhere. But one that could kill millions . . ."

They were all silent for a while. For Ryder it was like a bad dream turning into a full-blown nightmare, and then having it come true.

"How about a cruise missile strike?" Ryder asked. "That simulated bomb on our airplane is very much like a cruise . . ."

"True," Moon answered. "But with the in-depth defense that Toon has arranged—along with the thousands of SAMs at his disposal, the chances of a cruise missile getting through are less than one in a hundred. Plus, Toon has access to nearly five squadrons of fighters. MiGs. Fitters, you name it. Again, most supplied by the Vietnamese.

"So that's what you've been training for, gentlemen. We have determined that an air strike, carried out by two highly trained, innovative pilots who can fly their way into the target

335

and destroy it, has the better chance at succeeding."

"Better chance?" Woody asked. "What are the odds?"

Moon shook his head. "I'll be up front with you," he said. "The chances are only up to one in ten that you'll survive . . ."

Suddenly everything came together for Ryder. The fake obits. The extensive training at Top Gun. The bizarreness of War Heaven. They were going on a suicide mission, plain and simple.

"So what's the plan?" Ryder asked.

Moon referred to another of the Top Secret papers. "We get you and some support crews into a secure place in Burma, just over the Thailand border. You will have to operate just as you did here, because once you're down, you'll be on your own. You'll have to innovate. Create your opportunities.

"Meanwhile, we'll have a clandestine force move right to the south of the Iron Circle, create some diversion, tying up some of Toon's troops. That force, gentlemen, will be made up of your former adversaries, the Gray Army.

"When the time is right, we launch a rescue raid. We'll send in an airborne assault force—made up of Blue Army soldiers—to the prison camp. They'll be covered by air support from your colleagues, Reinhart, Chauvagne, Sammett, and Lancaster, plus, we hope, some further fighter cover.

"Once the POWs are safe, you will go in and bomb the target. That's the plan . . ."

Again, a silence filled the room.

Moon spread out another photo. It was an overall shot of the inner defense lines of the Iron Circle. The center of Toon's empire was at the end of a valley exactly like the holographic projection in Cartoon Valley.

"Here's a photo of your target," Moon explained. "You'll have to get to know this territory like the back of your hand. It has the highest concentration of SAMs in the whole Iron Circle.

"Someone, somewhere dubbed it Thunder Alley . . ."

PART THREE

Thunder Alley

63

Maureen woke up with a splitting headache.

She was in a totally dark room, lying on a bed. Her last memory was of her brief struggle with Jammer and the nurse who gave her the injection. Now she didn't know if it was day or night or how long she'd been out. Her first sensation was an ache in her stomach, a nauseating up and down motion that was making her stomach do flips. She was groggy, her teeth hurt, and she was feeling very uncomfortable.

It took a few moments for her to realize she was on a ship and that she was getting seasick . . .

She painfully got to her feet and walked unsteadily to the door. It took all her strength to open it, and when she did, she was met by two sailors, obviously posted outside her room as guards.

"What the hell is going on here?" she asked one of them. "Where am I?"

The sailor nodded to his partner. "Go get the doc," he said. "Tell him she's awake . . ."

Ten minutes later Maureen was back on the bed watching a Navy doctor checking her blood pressure.

"You got through the anesthesia very well, Miss O'Brien," the doctor said, smiling. "You'll be a little out of it for a while. But it will pass. I'll also send down some seasick pills for you."

"Where the hell am I?" she demanded. "Or are you going to play secret agent, too?"

The doctor smiled. "You are aboard the US Navy aircraft carrier, *Ben Franklin*," he said. "We are about an hour out of San Diego, cruising west."

"Where are we going?" she asked, cradling her uneasy stomach. "And why was I drugged and brought aboard?"

"We are heading for the Indian Ocean," he replied. "And, as I understand it, you were sedated in order to make it easy for you and us to get you aboard."

"This is an outrage!" Maureen said with all the seriousness she could muster. "I am a citizen . . ."

"*You* are a security risk, Miss O'Brien," the doctor said, quietly but firmly. "Now I don't know all that much about why we are heading toward our destination. But I do know that the most intense security measures I have ever witnessed in thirty-plus years in the Navy have been in force for this voyage. If they brought you along, Miss O'Brien, it must be for some very important reason . . ."

"I am a prisoner, aren't I?" she asked dejectedly.

"Not quite," he answered. "I believe the captain will allow you to leave your cabin with an escort. However you will not be permitted to discuss what you know—and what you've seen back in Nevada—with anyone."

Maureen felt her feverish head. "I feel terrible," she confessed.

"Don't worry," the doctor said. "I'll send down something for you to take. Then, when you are feeling better, I suggest you ask one of the guards outside to get you some food. You'll feel much better after eating."

With that the doctor got up and left, leaving her once again in the darkened room.

Oddly, with everything that was overflowing in her mind, she found herself wondering where Ryder was at that moment . . .

64

The Huey helicopter skimmed low over the Thai jungle and set down in a clearing just inside Burmese territory.

Ryder, Woody, Moon, and Moon's assistant Sergeant Bronco sat huddled in the Huey's passenger compartment. They were dressed in nondescript camouflage uniforms, jungle boots, and netted Marine Corps helmets. Each man was carrying an M-16 and a week's worth of field rations. Five ten-gallon cans of water were strapped into the Huey's cargo hold in back of their seats. Four boxes of real M-16 ammunition sat stacked in the middle of the four men.

"Time to saddle up," Woody said, gathering in his ration pack and field sack. "Hope the neighbors don't mind us dropping in . . ."

Ryder was the first to step out. He was hit full in the face with a blast of hot tropical air. Unlike the hot desert air, this breath could be cut with a knife, its humidity was so thick. He felt himself perspiring even before he was completely off the aircraft.

There was a rustling in the bushes near the landing site causing all four men to raise their M-16s.

"Friend!" a voice called out from the bush. "Friend, USA!"

A small, dark-complexioned Oriental man emerged holding his hands high. "Sim-mer Baroong!" the man said. *"Sim-mer Baroong!"*

"It's OK, guys," Moon said, lowering his M-16. "This is Baroong, our guide . . ."

Although Burmese, Baroong was a member of the Thai Army's Special Forces. He knew the jungle like the back of his hand. He would lead them to their base and stay with them as an adviser.

The chopper pilot gave them the thumbs-up and took off, quickly disappearing off to the south. The men helped each other put on their field packs and load up the ammunition and the water. Then, with Baroong in the lead, the small band set out into the jungle.

They would have to walk twenty miles to their destination.

The lush jungle looked like paradise. But the beauty of the fauna belied the danger that lurked about. The closest settlement was a place called Mong Hsat and the Thai Army Intelligence service had reported that elements of Toon's army had been seen in the area just three nights before. Therefore, their hike through the bush would have to be done as quickly and as silently as possible. This gave Ryder the opportunity to reflect on the group's recent activities.

They had left the Nevada desert two weeks to the day, leaving their F-14 and Spookbase behind. An AWACs plane brought them to Hawaii, where they were briefed by an assistant secretary of defense and a controlling group of three generals and an admiral.

A C-130 took them to Clark Air Force Base in Manila. Then they were transported to Subic Bay where they were put aboard the aircraft carrier, USS *Ben Franklin*. The Franklin set sail at midnight; four days later, they were in the Bay of Bengal, a hundred miles off the Thai coast.

All during the trip they were kept in isolation, not just from the crew but from each other. Ryder used some of the time in his cabin to read old magazines, watch the ship's closed-circuit TV, and stuff himself with his three generous meals per day. But most of the time—usually for hours on end—he spent going over the maneuvers he would have to perform over the *real* Thunder Alley.

Whatever minutes he had left, he used by dreaming of Maureen. She was still with him—in spirit anyway. A closeness that allowed him to recall exactly what she looked like, how she talked, how she moved. It was so unlike him to be romantic, he told himself. But she had touched something deep inside him, and he knew, whatever happened he would carry it—and her memory—into battle with him.

He had asked Moon what would happen to Smiling Jack's and Moon had told him the town no longer existed. Ryder didn't press the young officer at the time as to what exactly he had meant. Some things were better off not being known.

*   *   *

Earlier that morning, the USS *Ben Franklin* had moved in closer to the Thai coast and Ryder was told to get up on deck.

Moon and Bronco then appeared and they started packing up the Thai helicopter that had landed on the aircraft carrier several hours earlier. Although the four foreign pilots were nowhere to be seen—Moon explained they had already shipped out—Woody soon appeared. It was the first time Ryder had seen his partner since leaving Manila. Under orders, none of them had shaved during the trip, so both Ryder and Woody were wearing two-week growths when they met on the deck of the Franklin.

"Very distinguished, Major Woods," Ryder had told him.

"Wish I could say the same for you, Major Ryder," Woody had said. It was true. While Ryder's growth made him look more like a motorcycle gang member, whiskers made the Wiz look downright professorial.

They walked about seven miles in three hours, following the twists and turns of a jungle stream before reaching a small clearing. Ryder saw they were approaching a small mountain, one side of which was flattened out like a plateau. This was their destination.

Two more hours of climbing and they reached the leveled cliff.

Even before they reached the site, Ryder could appreciate the selection of the place. Unlike the beauty of the jungle, the mountain site was eerie. It was surrounded by a mist and the plateau part was almost totally hidden from three sides by the parent mountain. It looked like something Ryder had once seen in a movie, but he couldn't place which one. Woody did it for him.

"Jeesuz, this place looks right out of *King Kong!*" the Wiz said. "Remember the scene where he carried the girl to the cliff and had to kick ass on the big bird?"

That was it, Ryder knew. Their mountain base looked like something better found on Kong Island. It was so authentic, Ryder wouldn't have been surprised if the Big Monkey himself came climbing up the side.

Yet, the place was large enough to sustain several small

barracks, a hangar, and some take-off and landing space. A satellite dish lay hidden in the underbrush, as did a radar system. A waterfall fell conveniently nearby.

There were seven other soldiers at the base—all of them members of Moon's Spookbase crew. They had a reunion of sorts with the members of the 1245th, who were in the process of constructing another field catapult. Ryder and the others quickly lugged their gear to the small living quarters that were hidden under a vinelike overhang which fell from the nearby mountaintop. That done, Ryder, Woody, and Moon walked to the far end of the base to the small hangar.

Yanking the door open, they experienced a bit of déjà vu. Sitting inside was their beautiful F-14.

"How the hell they got this baby here, I'll never know," Woody exclaimed.

"Houdini might know," Ryder said, rubbing the nose of the VF-333.

"It came packed in crates," Moon explained. "We had a crew break it down the day after we left Nevada. They put it in a C-5, flew it nonstop to Manila where they picked up an Air Force maintenance crew who had been training for the past few months on how to put together F-14s. You think you guys were wondering about what the hell was going on! They all loaded up into the C-5, flew to Bangkok. Then the Thais moved it up here, crate by crate, and dropped the Air Force guys in. They put it together in three days, with help from my guys. It's all tested and checked out. Just like back in War Heaven."

But there was one big difference. Slung under the wings of the F-14, and stacked in the back of the small hangar were weapons—*real* weapons.

"This is amazing," Ryder said, shaking his head. "Putting an F-14 together in the middle of the jungle. It's an engineering marvel. Too bad it had to be done for such a critical situation."

"Most feats are done in situations like these, Major," Moon said, almost wistfully. "People rise to the occasion, despite the danger."

Moon knew his philosophical side was showing and he quickly changed the subject.

"The catapult will be finished this time tomorrow night," he told them as they walked toward the outer edge of the plateau.

"How about the arresting gear?" Woody asked.

Moon hesitated before answering. "The arresting situation will be a little different up here," he said.

"Different how?" Ryder asked.

"Well, no sense in coloring it over," Moon answered. "We'll only be able to install one cable. At the far end."

They turned back and looked at the area. "That's simple enough," Ryder said. "Miss the cable and smash into the hangar."

"I'm afraid so," Moon said. "This location was selected because of its height, the head winds, the concealability factor, and its relative closeness to friendly territory. The drawback was the limited space with which to work in the arresting cable."

They reached the outer edge and felt the high winds that blew around the side of the mountain. The strong breeze was hot and steamy, but they knew it would be very beneficial when launching the F-14.

"Where are the others?" Ryder asked Moon. "Lancaster, Reinhart, Chauvagne, and Sammett?"

"Out there, somewhere . . ." Moon said, spreading his arms out before him. "They're at similar bases. Lancaster and Sammett are working with the Blues. Reinhart and Chauvagne are with the Gray advance column. The poor bastards. I'd rather be here."

Just then they heard a shout. It was one of Moon's men, the radar technician. "Enemy aircraft approaching!" the man was yelling.

"*Damn!*" Moon cursed, running back toward the base's quarters. "Everyone to the hangar! Lower the netting! Turn off that radar!"

As they ran back toward the hangar, Ryder saw that a camouflage netting was automatically being draped over all the "unnatural" objects on the plateau.

They reached the hangar just as the netting was covering it. Then they waited . . .

Within a minute they heard an approaching roar.

"Sounds like a bunch of them . . ." Woody said.

"They passed over last night," one of Moon's men said. "Only two of them. It was too dark for an ID . . ."

"There they are . . ." Woody said. "Up near eleven o'clock . . ."

"MiG-21s . . ." Ryder said. "Six of them . . ."

They were flying in three pairs, way up. Their fuselages were silver with a strange green-and-black ball as an insignia.

"Those are Libyans . . ." Moon said. "Strutting their scrotums around. The Thais have reported them in this area before. They say Toon himself sometimes flies with them."

"What a newspaper story that would make," Woody said as the six jets passed over. "I can see the headline now: 'Libyan Air Force jets spotted in Burma.'"

"What about 'US forces spotted in Burma,'" Ryder added. "That would make a hell of a story, too . . ."

"This is Burma in name only," Moon said. "From what I hear, the army—what there is of it—has enough problems in their cities, never mind wandering around out here in the boondocks."

"So much for the sovereignty of nations," Woody said.

"Well, with crazy bastards like Toon running around," Ryder said, "the sovereignty of their nation is the least of Burma's problems . . ."

65

The palace stunk of incense and candle wax. The Iranian officer, a member of the Reovlutionary Guards, was shown into an anteroom and told to wait. His nose immediately began to run—the smell of the place, combined with the humidity of the land, made the air thick as mud.

Another man—the Iranian believed he was one of Toon's Pakistani scientists—was also waiting in the anteroom. They didn't speak to each other—the Iranian had no use for the

346

Paki. But he did notice that his nose was also running.

The Iranian was an adviser to Toon on military affairs, a well-paid, powerful position. And for once he was not worried about his impending meeting with the bizarre colonel. He had good news to deliver. The American aircraft carrier USS *Benjamin Franklin*, having arrived in the Bay of Bengal several days before just a hundred miles off the coast of Thailand, had left, steamed away with its entourage of support ships. This according to Toon's spies in Bangkok.

The door to the colonel's chamber opened and an aide beckoned the Iranian forward. He was walked into the chamber, which was ablaze with red and white candles. The man himself, looking all the world like a Mandarin emperor, sat on an ornate throne, four buckets of incense creating a cloud around him.

"Greetings, Colonel," the Iranian said. "Are you well today?"

The colonel nodded slowly. He was thin and wiry, but looked much younger than his supposed fifty-five years. His face was tight, leathery, his hair jet black and long. His eyes spoke of an Indochinese intensity—every day was a battle, every day a victory must be won.

"You have news?" Toon asked in English, the common language between the men.

"Yes, sir," the Iranian answered. "The US aircraft carrier has left the Bay of Bengal. Its support ships are gone also."

Toon smiled. Another victory. Then he asked, "What do you think it means?"

The Iranian carefully worded his answer. "It may mean nothing, sir," he said. "As you know, US warships frequently visit Thailand, as they are allies. They stay a few days and leave. However, this ship was in the northern part of the bay and we had not seen them up this far before . . ."

"How many aircraft was the ship carrying?" Toon asked.

"Maybe as many as three squadrons . . ." the Iranian said.

"F-14s? F-18s? A-6s?" Toon asked.

"All of those, sir," the Iranian answered.

"Do you think they intended on attacking us?" Toon asked calmly.

Again, the Iranian was careful with his answer. He felt as if

Toon was playing a game with him. "It was possible, but not likely," he said. "The Americans undoubtedly know that a massive air strike would be disastrous both for their attacking aircraft and for . . . for the people in this part of the world."

Toon gave a sinister chuckle. "You choose your words well," he said. "But if the Americans *did* attack, how would our defenses have reacted?"

The Iranian produced a list and read from it. "We had fifty fighters at the ready, sir," he said boastfully. "Your own fine squadrons, plus the Libyans, the North Koreans, and our Revolutionary pilots. Had they chosen to strike at us, we would have outnumbered them by a wide margin."

Toon smiled again. "That's good," he said. "You have answered well. Personally, I was convinced all along that the Americans were too nervous to strike us. They have not carried out a logical, coherent, successful air strike since we fought them over Hanoi. They trip over themselves. They worry about what their newspapers will say. Their own caution is their worst enemy . . ."

"How true, sir," the Iranian said, not wanting to mention that the Libyans might dispute Toon's claim that the US couldn't carry out a successful air strike.

"And how did our SAM teams react to the alert?" Toon asked.

"The crews were drilling around the clock," the Iranian answered. "Now that the danger has passed, their morale remains high . . ."

"Then we were ready for them!" Toon declared with a clap of his hands. "You may tell our soldiers that the mighty US Navy turned tail and ran because they feared what would happen to them if they struck us. Our determination won this battle. Our determination will win all our battles!"

Toon dismissed the Iranian and told his aide to bring the Pakistani in.

"Greetings, Colonel," the small, dark man said with a reverent bow. "You are well today?"

Toon waved the salutation away, his high spirits quickly

evaporating. "What is our schedule, Doctor?"

The Pakistani quickly straightened up. "Five more days, sir . . ." he said nervously.

"*Five days!*" Toon shouted. "Why is it that every time I ask you this question, we never get any closer to Zero Hour?"

"Sir, the equipment the Iranians gave us is not the best in the world . . ." the Pakistani said meekly. "We are continually resetting it. The calibrations alone take hours and they must be done several times a day . . ."

"These are unacceptable excuses!" Toon bellowed. "We have the ability to be one of the world's superpowers! Do you know what that means? It is something your government has been trying to do for years! And now you tell me that we are five days behind?"

"It is out of our control, sir," the Pakistani doctor offered. "The equipment . . ."

"To the devil with the equipment!" the colonel shouted. "Do you know that we must send a message to the world? We must launch! We must show them what we can do! And you and your miserable clique of scientists are standing in the way of that progress!"

The Pakistani was silent, terrified at what Toon might say next.

"You are lucky, Doctor," Toon said finally. "Lucky that the Americans chose to run from us again. Because they have dared not to set one foot into our territory, you have been reprieved. But realize this: their cowardice has bought you and your gang only a little more time."

The Pakistani bowed again. "We will work harder, sir," he said.

"You would be wise to do just that, Doctor," Toon said. "If not, I might just designate your miserable country as our first target!

"*Dismissed!*"

Sergeant C.T. Johnson, most recently of the Gray Army, adjusted his electronic binoculars and started counting trucks.

"OK, there's four two-by-twos, six jeeps, a portable AAA

gun and a fuel truck," he whispered to his corporal. "Looks like some kind of a long-range recon patrol. They've stopped for some reason."

They were hidden on top of a ridge overlooking the Burmese village of Kemg Sing watching a small convoy of Toon's soldiers. The soldiers had called out all of the villagers and now appeared to be searching them.

The PRA soldiers singled out one man and crowded around him, questioning him. The man, possibly the chief of the village, looked frightened. For good reason. One of the PRA soldiers, apparently dissatisfied with the man's answers, whacked his gun butt across the man's jaw. The man fell to the ground, holding his face. As the horrified villagers looked on, another soldier fired a single shot into the man's leg, causing him to yelp in pain.

With that, the villagers started emptying their pockets into a basket the soldiers had produced.

"Just as I thought," Johnson said. "It's a tax patrol."

It all took about ten minutes, then the soldiers climbed back into their trucks and roared away, leaving the wounded man on the ground writhing in pain.

"OK," Johnson said to his corporal. "Let's move out . . ."

The two American soldiers scrambled off the ridge and down to the battered truck they were using for transport. They quickly moved down the road, being careful not to trail the last truck in the PRA convoy too closely. According to their map, the next village, Song Keng, was four miles to the south. Johnson assumed the PRA soldiers would be heading there.

They reached a crossroads and stopped. Johnson took out a device that looked like a small flashlight and pointed it into the nearby woods. He moved it in a slow, left-to-right motion until he heard a low buzzing sound.

"There they are . . ." he said to the corporal. Johnson hit a button on the device eight times, stopped and heard a return signal buzz eight times. Seconds later, two American soldiers emerged from the woods.

"Did you see them?" Johnson asked one of the soldiers.

The man nodded. "Twelve trucks . . ."

"Yeah, that's them," Johnson said. "All right, let's get going."

Silently, quickly, more than three dozen soldiers emerged from the woods, each one carrying a heavy field sack. They double timed it up the road for two miles, letting Johnson's truck lead the way. The soldiers, all formerly of the Gray Army, appreciated their tough desert training now. If they could run with full pack in the heat of Nevada, they could run with full packs anywhere.

The troop reached a predetermined spot. Johnson hid the truck under some brush as the forty Americans divided into two groups and melted back into the bush. There they waited.

An hour went by. Then Johnson heard the sound of the convoy moving back down the road. Using hand signals, he passed the word to the other Americans to get ready. Johnson then had three soldiers help him push the battered truck back out onto the road. They lifted the hood then jumped back into the jungle again.

The convoy rumbled down the dusty road, its soldiers happy and unsuspecting, its trucks filled with money-ladened baskets. The patrol commander spotted the truck and raised his hand to halt the convoy. Two PRA soldiers climbed out of the commander's jeep and walked forward to inspect the truck.

One of them happened to look closely into the woods nearby. At first he thought he was seeing things. He thought he saw twenty blackened faces staring out at him.

He turned to yell back to the convoy when a bullet caught him in the throat. He grabbed his Adam's apple, felt the warm ooze of blood flowing out, then fell facedown on the road, dead before he hit the ground.

Suddenly gunfire erupted from both sides of the roadway, ripping into the convoy. A rocket-propelled grenade hit the fuel truck, blowing it ten feet up in the air in a sharp, violent explosion. Machine gun fire ripped into the PRA troop trucks, several hand grenades took care of the jeeps. Only the mobile AAA truck was spared, its drivers killed instantly by sniper shots to the head.

It was all over in less than a minute.

The Americans emerged from the woods and checked to make sure all of the PRA soldiers were dead. Twelve soldiers piled on the AAA truck and quickly drove away. Other soldiers retrieved the baskets of tax money from the backs of the trucks and loaded them on to Johnson's vehicle. Meanwhile the American sergeant scattered a dozen Ace of Spades playing cards over the dead bodies of the PRA soldiers. Then, the rest of the Americans climbed aboard three workable vehicles and quickly left the scene of the ambush.

66

Ryder stood over the satellite dish operator's shoulder and watched as an image slowly materialized on a small TV screen.

The operator pushed a button and hard copy of the image began feeding out of the side of his console. Ryder ripped the page from the processor and studied it. "It is very clear," he said, noting the detail of the electronic photo. "That satellite must be right over us."

The photo was the latest to be shot over Toon's territory. It showed in vivid detail the launching tower at the end of Toon's valley, plus the weapons storage building and the POW barracks.

Ryder immediately brought the photo to the living quarters, which now doubled as the small base's Ops Building.

"Looks like the launch pad is nearly complete," Moon said, studying the photo. "Just that and the final arming of their first missile's warhead is the only thing holding them back . . ."

Ryder looked at the photo and shook his head in disgust. "Does anybody have any idea what their first target might be?" he asked.

Moon shrugged. "I've seen CIA evaluation papers on the

subject," he said. "Never anything definite. There's a theory that Toon's missiles could reach the West Coast of the US, although their payload would have to be minimal."

"But that wouldn't make any difference," Ryder said. "A dirty bomb is a dirty bomb. Even a lightweight one would be disastrous."

"That's right," Moon said. "His warheads could easily hit Japan with a good-size load. Melbourne, Beijing, even Moscow, though that's unlikely. Toon knows the Russians will carpet bomb him in a second, the risk to the rest of the world's population be damned.

"Toon is basically a terrorist. His idea of detonating a nuclear warhead is to make a statement—however perverse it may be. Kill people, make the headlines. Imagine what would happen if he decided to unload on Jerusalem? He can hold the world hostage and he knows it. He thinks he's got all the bases covered, and some people reluctantly agree with him."

Just then the radio operator appeared. "Just came in from Central Command, sir," he said, handing a slip of paper to Moon. The young officer read it and handed it to Ryder.

"Well, it's started," Moon said, handing the paper to Ryder. "The Gray boys just wiped out one of his tax convoys about seventy-five miles from here."

"Part of the plan?" Ryder asked.

"Yes," Moon said. "We were certain that Toon's spies knew the *Ben Franklin* was up close in the Bay of Bengal. So close, the whole Iron Circle went on top alert. Their SAM sites started radiating and it allowed us to pinpoint them more accurately. That was one reason the *Franklin* came up so far north. We saw that it takes them very little time to go to full alert.

"The second idea was to bluff Toon. Just as his people knew the *Franklin* was just a stone's throw away, they now know that it sailed yesterday. According to Toon's profile, he's probably convinced their defenses caused the Navy to rethink an air strike."

Ryder nodded. "But it really was a cover for our deployment the whole time."

"That's right," Moon said. "Now, when Toon hears that one

of his tax convoys was bounced, he's going to wonder who the hell did it. He won't know who he's up against. It will keep him off balance. Or at least we hope it will."

"He'll certainly know he's up against someone better than those bananas in the Burmese National Guard," Ryder said.

"The plan is for the Grays to heat things up in the south, on a very selective basis," Moon explained. "We hope to draw some of Toon's troops to that area. We hope they'll be led to believe that a good-size unit is operating against them. They've been so invulnerable before, just the thought that someone would dare attack one of his tax convoys should send him off raving. If we guess right, he'll dispatch a disproportionate number of troops to the area. Little does he know there's seventy-five hundred Grays hiding right over the border in Thailand."

Ryder whistled. "That's risky, infiltrating in nearly half a division."

"Sure it is," Moon said. "But that's what all the training in War Heaven was about. Like it or not, the Grays performed superbly back in Nevada. They never let up. They were always going for those points, you know that. They were merciless against us and the Blues and the Greens. Think what they'll do to the PRA . . ."

"So when the time is right, the Grays will attack in full force?" Ryder asked.

"That's the idea," Moon confirmed. "Get some of Toon's boys into a good old-fashioned shooting war. Against real troops. Then, when his attention is diverted, we hit him."

"It should drive him nuts," Ryder said. "That is, if he isn't completely nuts already . . ."

"That's the down side of it all," Moon said solemnly. "We will be forcing his hand. He'll feel pressure and he'll hurry up his guys to put the finishing touches on the launch pad. And finish the warhead. That's why it's important that when the time is right, we knock him out *quick*."

It was three A.M. the next day when Ryder and Woody first launched the F-14.

The field catapult worked flawlessly thanks to Moon and his men. Experts in field launchers at this point, the 1245th team had put the thing together in record time, and worked out such intricacies as the difference of mineral content between the oily water they had used in Nevada and the water drained from the waterfall nearby.

They waited until past midnight to test the catapult itself. The three no-loads test went off without a hitch, the only drawback being the two loud bangs coming from the launcher, which echoed throughout the jungle.

The reason for the late-night launch was a message the base received earlier that evening. A Soviet aerial tanker would be waiting for the F-14 at 40,000 feet directly over the base at 0330 hours. At present, the Tomcat had only about quarter tanks of fuel, and a lot of fuel was the only thing that was impossible to lug overland to the mountain base. And everyone knew they would have to get as much gas as possible to complete their mission.

After launching, Ryder put the Tomcat on its tail and streaked up to thirty-five thousand feet. The last thing he wanted was to be detected by some rinky-dink radar on an MiG-21 cruising the area. Once up at thirty-five thousand, he leveled out and climbed gradually to the prescribed height of forty thousand.

The tanker—a Myasishchev M-4 Bison B—turned out to be fifteen minutes late. Woody had picked it up a hundred miles out heading up from the southeast, ironically probably originating from the old US air base at Da Nang, Vietnam. They successfully made the rendezvous with the aircraft and began the refueling process much like the practice run over the Pacific two weeks before.

But halfway through the operation, things started to go wrong . . .

Woody came on the line, tension evident in his voice. "Ghost, I'm picking up some bogies . . ." he reported.

"*Damn!*" Ryder called back. "How many and where?"

"Got three coming out of the due north, flying at thirty-two thousand feet, about eighty-five miles from us," Woody answered.

Ryder bit his lip. "Any type ID?" he asked.

"Getting an I-Band reading," Woody answered. "Might not be MiGs. Could be SU-Fitters . . ."

"Fitters?" Ryder said. "Libyans got Fitters . . ."

"We don't need any witnesses here, Ghost," Woody said, adding, "Targets now at seventy-five miles and closing . . ."

"I wonder if our friends here see them?" Ryder said, referring to the Soviet tanker crew.

"I'd guess no," Woody said. "Their radars are shit and if they did, they would have broke off by now."

"True," Ryder agreed. He checked his fuel reserve indicator needle. The operation still had about seven minutes to go. The trouble was he couldn't communicate with the tanker crew to break off the refueling.

"Targets at 65 and closing," Woody reported.

"Any way of determining whether they've seen us or not?" Ryder asked.

"Hard to say," Woody answered. "They're flying with their radars wide open and hot. So they might not know we're up here. Or they might just be dumb and not realize the best intercept procedure is to run your radar off and on."

Another tense minute passed.

"Targets at 45 and still closing," Woody said. "Climbing slightly to 36-5 . . ."

While the Soviet fuel gushed into the Tomcat's tanks, Ryder went over their options. The bogies were now four minutes away. The refueling operaiton had five minutes to go, not counting the time for disconnect. Should the Fitters catch them still connected, they were dead ducks.

"Targets at 35 and closing," Woody said. "Speed up to 440. Altitude at 38,500 . . ."

Ryder checked his weapons load. They were carrying four Sidewinders and two Phoenix missiles, the most sophisticated long-range air-to-airs in the world. The problem was Ryder couldn't arm any of the missiles, as any danger of a spark during the mid-air refueling operation would blow both the F-14 and the Soviet tanker to Kingdom Come.

"Targets at 25 and closing," Woody said. "Altitude up to 40,000, speed still at 440."

Ryder tried mind-reading. The bogies were heading right for them, but only at cruising speed. They were still two miles lower than the Tomcat, yet they'd been climbing steadily. They were running with the radars on, yet he had to assume their radars had at least a twenty-five-mile range.

"Ghost, they're now at 15 and still closing," Woody reported. "We'll be able to see their lights very soon at three o'clock. Speed picked up to 500. Altitude at 42,000."

Ryder knew it was getting serious. He knew he would have to break off the refueling operation prematurely. But how?

That's when Ryder got an idea . . .

During the practice run with the Soviets two weeks before, the Russians had communicated by flashing a light to Morse Code. Ryder now had to attempt the same thing.

Using his powerful nose lantern he quickly began flashing: "U-N-H-O-O-K."

It took several times but finally someone on the tanker got the message. The refueling hose went slack, allowing Ryder to disengage from the boom. The tanker crew immediately began reeling in the hose, so quickly that some of the excess fuel splashed across the Tomcat's windshield.

"Just what we need," Ryder cursed as he watched the fuel freeze up and crystallize. But he had no time to concern himself with a dirty windshield.

"Ghost, they've switched off their radars!" Woody called ahead. "I got them on scan reading. They're up to 550 and increasing. Altitude now 46,500 and climbing. They've just armed their missiles. They're at eight miles and coming up."

Ryder looked out his right side and saw the three trails of navigation lights. The Soviet tanker crew had finally finished reeling in the fuel hose and had started to bank away.

"OK, Wiz, hang on . . ." Ryder called back. "Keep an eye on those guys. I'm going to try and get us out of here . . ."

He banked the F-14 hard to port, away from the closing fighters. The Soviet tanker pilot took his cue and did the same thing. Both airplanes dove, hoping to get away while the approaching fighters had their radars turned off.

But the maneuver was too little too late . . .

"Ghost, I'm getting a low warning *pre*-warning," Woody

357

reported. Ryder knew this was the indication that an enemy missile was about to go hot.

"OK, arm our weapons," Ryder said, still diving, the Soviet tanker doing the same.

"Low warning!" Woody reported. "They're about to fire. They've switched their radars back on and got our mark . . ."

"Well, that rips it," Ryder said.

Suddenly the high warning buzzer went off in the F-14's cockpit.

"They've launched, Ghost!" Woody yelled out. "Two missiles. Infrareds. Go to evasive . . ."

"Roger," Ryder replied, putting the F-14 into a hard counterturn toward the bogies, cutting down the angle of the missiles' effectiveness.

He saw the missiles streak high and fast above him. The first one was shot wide and quickly disappeared from sight. But the second found its mark . . .

The Soviet-built AA-2 Atoll missile slammed into the rear quarter of the Soviet-built Bison tanker. It immediately ignited the fuel remaining in the Bison's tanks and in a great flash the airplane was completely obliterated.

"Jeesuz! The fuckers got them!" Woody yelled as Ryder put the F-14 into a controlled spin away from the blinding fire.

Now Ryder had to decide whether to melt away or fight. His instinct told him to fight. The Atoll missile could have hit the F-14 just as soon as it hit the Soviet tanker and Ryder didn't like the idea of someone trying to kill him.

On the other hand, the PRA pilots may not have realized that the F-14 was even in the area. If he cut and run, it might preserve their "undercover" status.

But it was the high warning buzzer that finally made up his mind for him.

"Ghost! They've launched again!" Woody called ahead. "Two missiles coming right at us . . ."

"OK, partner, we're going evasive," Ryder said, turning the F-14 hard left, spinning three times quickly to further confuse the missile's homing system.

"Light our Sidewinders," Ryder told Woody. "Give me a reading on the lead jet . . ."

Ryder saw the taillights of the Fitters about eight miles to his starboard. He turned hard toward them and booted in the airplane's afterburner. Within seconds, the F-14 crossed in front of the three attacking jets.

On seeing the F-14, the Fitters immediately scattered. "This is the last airplane they thought they were shooting at," Ryder called back to Woody. "How are the weapons?"

"Missile Fox one hot," the Wiz called. "Ready to launch . . ."

Ryder lined up the lead Fitter in his HUD screen, using an infrared filter as a kind of night vision device. The enemy pilot banked hard right and was diving, trying his best to get away from the awesome Tomcat. Ryder lined up the electronic crosshairs and squeezed the missile launch trigger.

"Fox One away!" Woody reported as they both heard the somewhat familiar noise of the Sidewinder launch.

The missile tracked perfectly, slamming into the Fitter's tail section inside of ten seconds. Once again the night sky was illuminated with a brilliant flash. When the light and smoke cleared, there was nothing left of the Soviet-built jet . . .

"Jeesuz, *that* was no Zootmissile!" Woody yelled out.

"No, it wasn't . . ." Ryder said, somewhat solemnly. He took two seconds to contemplate that he had just killed another human being.

The game-playing is really over now, he thought.

Sticks' call ahead broke his train of thought. "Fox Two ready for launch!" the Wiz reported. "Target two, eleven miles out at altitude, moving away . . ."

Ryder turned the big 'Cat toward the fleeing fighter and lined up another shot on the HUD. He squeezed the missile launch trigger a second time.

"Fox Two away!" Woody reported, as the missile flashed out from the F-14's port side wing.

They both watched the Sidewinder's trail streak across the inky black sky. It caught the Fitter on its starboard wing, blowing it off and flipping the airplane over. The Fitter quickly went into an uncontrolled dive, disappearing into a low cloud bank trailing smoke and fire.

"Scratch two . . ." Woody said as the bogie disappeared from

359

the AWG screen.

"Where's the third guy?" Ryder asked. They knew they couldn't let him get away.

Woody quickly consulted the AWG. "He's twenty-two miles out, heading due north," he told Ryder. "Down at 35,000 and diving. . . . We'd better hurry."

Ryder knew it was a job for the long-range Phoenix. "Heat up the big one," he called back to the pit, turning the airplane north.

"It's hot!" Woody reported just three seconds later.

Ryder checked his long-range target numbers on the HUD and let the Phoenix fly. The F-14 jumped as the large missile streaked away.

"It's got a solid lock . . ." Woody reported, tracking the missile's progress. "Speed up to Mach 4! Shit, that thing can move . . ."

Ryder kept his eyes glued to the HUD, watching the numbers which digitally kept track of the missile's flight path.

"C'mon, catch the bastard . . ." he whispered.

The Fitter was now thirty-two miles away and still diving. But his numbers told him the Phoenix was diving, too.

Suddenly they saw a brilliant orange flash way off in the distance. At the same time Woody called out, "Bingo! We got him!"

Ryder booted the F-14 and they soon passed through the airspace where the third Fitter had been hit. There wasn't so much as a smoke puff left.

"Jeesuz, those goddamn things really work," Ryder said, turning the F-14 south and heading back for the mountain base.

67

The Muong Sing River moves through eastern Burma like a snake, eventually flowing into the Nam Tha River, which in turn empties into the infamous Mekong River.

Colonel Toon had long ago declared the Moung Sing as the eastern border of his territory. It was at the time a sound military decision. The Muong Sing was wide in many places and it was dotted with many large islands—perfect bases for the PRA to repel an unlikely attack from neighboring Laos.

But because they were assigned to the outlying areas, the PRA troops stationed on the Muong Sing islands were isolated from the pad-locked defense perimeters of the inner Iron Circle. Typical of border guards, the troops were tough, but bored. There wasn't an army within five hundred miles that would want to challenge their tight-fisted grip on the river. To relieve the tedium, they frequently launched forays into the villages on the river's edge, killing residents, raping women, collecting taxes that Colonal Toon would never see.

Lank Sat was a major island base, a terminal through which many years before, equipment from Vietnam was processed after a long trip up the Mekong and Nam Tha rivers. Much of Toon's outdated Vietnamese SAM equipment had also passed through Lank Sat. So did many American POWs being transferred to the Iron Circle. In the course of these shipments, the island's PRA commander had asked Toon to leave a small contingent of POWs on Lank Sat, so his troops would be relieved of doing menial labor on the island. Toon had agreed, adhering to a basic terrorist tenet of not keeping all of one's hostages in a single location. So, for several years, twelve American POWs had lived on the island, living an existence akin to slaves, long since giving up any hope of ever going home.

That was about to change . . .

The three Blackhawk X-7X helicopters streaked along the winding Muong Sing so low, the gunners felt the spray of the river in their faces. Out ahead two Cobra attack choppers led the way. It was midnight and a monsoon-type storm had just passed through. The jungle, still hot from day, was now steaming and smoking like a cooking pot.

Major Maxwell was at the controls of the lead Blackhawk, Lieutenant Bo Simons was serving as his crew chief and radio operator. Captain Esposito was behind the controls of the Blackhawk on his left. Straight ahead was the island of Lank Sat.

The Blackhawk X-7X choppers were on loan from a classified US Army unit, known only as Task Force 32. The chopper's secret was their ultraquiet engines. Unlike the racket usually associated with most helicopters, the X-7X engine gave off a low, purring sound. It was the ideal aircraft with which to carry out a sneak attack . . .

"Two minutes, Major," Simons called ahead.

"OK, boys," Maxwell said over the chopper's intercom to the Blackhawk's eight-man strike team. "This is what we were training for back in the desert. If you could perform as well as you did there, you can do it anywhere. So get ready, and go in shooting. And let's all contribute . . ."

The eight soldiers buckled their helmets and checked their weapons. Five men were armed with M-16s equipped with NightScopes, three men carried rocket-propelled grenade launchers. Simons was armed with a lightweight Uzi; Major Max was carrying his trusty sawed-off shotgun. The Blackhawk's waist gunners were cradling M-60 machine guns, weapons so powerful that the large caliber shell was more suited to tearing up armor than flesh. No one expected that convention to be followed on this particular night.

"One minute, Major," Simons called ahead after a quick conversation with the SuperCobra attack choppers up ahead. These copters were also fitted with super-quiet engines. "We should see the flare in about thirty seconds . . ."

Maxwell eased back on the chopper's throttle. He saw a single light flash from Espo's chopper, indicating his team was also ready.

Maxwell clipped down his NightScope goggles, and with the aid of the flares, started recognizing targets of opportunity.

Just in from the beach he saw a compound containing three barracks, several machine gun posts, and two guard towers. At the far edge of the compound he could see a line of small shacks, almost resembling doghouses. But it was what he *didn't* see that counted. There were no antiaircraft weapons in the compound.

Maxwell clicked his radio twice, a predetermined signal to the other choppers. Seconds later, each SuperCobra fired a single flare rocket. The rockets streaked directly over the island and burst, releasing a parachute flare so bright, it illuminated a full third of the island.

Maxwell pulled a cigar from his uniform pocket and lit it. "Hang on, boys," he yelled. "Here we go!"

The SuperCobras opened up first, each sending a stream of rockets into the compound's guard towers on their first pass. Maxwell flew his Blackhawk right over the PRA base, allowing his waist gunners to rip up the barracks with murderous M-60 machine gun fire. Espo's gunners concentrated on the compound's machine gun posts, several of which contained sleeping guards.

Maxwell swung his Blackhawk back over the compound and put it into a hover. He switched on an ultrapowerful searchlight in the chopper's nose and trained it on the front of the barracks. Those PRA soldiers who survived the initial M-60 barrage and tried to flee out the front door were instantly cut down by the waist gunners. Meanwhile, the two SuperCobras were destroying one of the two remaining guard towers.

Maxwell quickly put the chopper down right in the middle of the compound, instructing his right waist gunner to continue blazing away at the barracks. One of the chopper's troopers alighted and instantly put a RPG round into the building blowing out its entire rear section. A second soldier took out the last guard tower.

Espo's Blackhawk then swooped down into the compound, its heavy guns trained on a concentration of enemy fire coming from one corner of the camp. Once that was suppressed, the remaining soldiers in both choppers jumped out.

The attack had taken place so quickly, there were only

scattered PRA soldiers remaining. After telling his co-pilot to keep his chopper's engines turning, Maxwell jumped out, linked up with Simons and two troopers and headed for the small shacks at the far end of the compound.

Simons sprinted ahead and was the first to reach the decrepit structures. They looked like something out of Bridge Over the River Kwai, which, in effect, they were.

Simons kicked open the door of the first shack he came to and peered in.

There was a man inside, scrunched up in the corner farthest from the door. He was thin, weak-looking, a straggily gray beard making him look older than he was. Yet what struck Simons was the look in the man's eyes. There was light there. A thin, candlepower of hope . . .

"We're Americans . . ." Simons said to the man, reaching in to touch him. "We've come to take you home . . ."

68

Colonel Toon was furious.

"I want answers!" he screamed. "The first man who gives me an excuse will be shot!"

Standing before his emperor's throne was the Iranian military adviser, the commander of the Libyan air squadron, the commander of the PRA ground forces, and the officer in charge of the Iron Circle's border guards.

"One of our tax convoys wiped out!" Toon shouted. "By who?"

"It must have been the villagers, sir," the PRA ground commander answered.

"Villagers?" Toon said, his voice an angry whisper. "Do you think, Commander, that a bunch of stupid villagers could destroy a convoy of our heavily armed soldiers?"

"The tax money was gone when we discovered the convoy, sir . . ." the commander said. "Who else could it be?"

Toon turned his attention to the Libyan squadron commander. "Did villagers shoot down your three airplanes, Commander?" he asked the man.

"We are still investigating the matter, sir," the air commander said.

Toon was past the point of boiling over. "And what happened at Lank Sat?" he asked the border guard commander.

"A sneak attack, sir," the man answered. "We believe bandits from Laos were responsible."

Toon smiled an evil, tooth-gaped grin. He had found his scapegoat. "Laotian rebels in helicopters, Commander?" he asked. "Laotian rebels who utterly destroyed our base and took the Americans along with them?"

The man fell silent for a moment then said, "We, too, are investigating this incident . . ."

"Commander, do you realize what will happen if those Americans reach a friendly country?" Toon asked, delighted the man was so intent on digging his own grave.

The man fell silent.

"I didn't think so," Toon said quickly. He motioned for two guards to take the man away.

"Make yourself a hat, Commander," he told the man. "A dunce hat. You will print your crimes on your hat and we will make a parade for you. This way everyone will know what a fool looks like . . ."

Toon dismissed the whole lot of them. Once he was alone, he sat back and contemplated the situation.

Who was attacking him? In two days, a tax convoy utterly wiped out. Three jet fighters shot out of the sky in the middle of the night. The border island base destroyed, a dozen American POWs gone. . . . Certainly the Americans could not be behind all this. Hadn't they just sailed away, just as they did in Lebanon years before, their tail between their legs? And if it were them, how could they do it? Certainly his spies would have found out if the attacks were coming from Thailand. Yet it would take a force of some numbers to coordinate the destruction of the tax convoy and the island base, not to mention the downing of the three jets.

Toon shook off an uneasy feeling. His thoughts were turning crazy. Neither the Americans nor anyone else had the courage, the dedication, the *innovation,* to train and infiltrate such a large force into his territory.

And besides, in four days, when the first warhead was ready, it wouldn't make any difference at all . . .

Ryder had slept for four hours, the longest time he'd spent asleep since arriving at the mountain base.

He had pulled himself out of his cot dragging on his fatigues and stumbled to the far end of the living quarters where he knew a coffeepot was brewing.

Woody was already awake, sitting at the small mess table in the tent's miniature kitchen area, staring into his coffee cup.

"Hey, Wiz," Ryder said wearily. "What's cooking?"

Woody just shook his head and said nothing. Ryder immediately knew something was bothering his partner.

"OK," he said, not even stopping at the coffeepot, "what's the buzz . . ."

"Nothing really, Ghost," the pilot said, barely looking up.

"Bullshit," Ryder told him. "You usually can't shut you up this time of day. So what the hell is up?"

Woody rubbed his scraggily beard. "This whole thing," he said, almost whispering. "It might be getting to me . . ."

Ryder shook his head. "It got to me a long time ago," he said.

"No, I mean now," Woody said. "Here. In the middle of the jungle. I mean, at least in Nevada, we knew we were close to home. Shit, man, we're *really* out in the middle of nowhere."

Ryder got serious. "This is our job," he said. "There's not much calling for this type of work in Hawaii, or Boise, or New York City."

"I know all this," Woody said. "But the truth is—and you know it as well as I—we could be bounced tomorrow and they wouldn't even search for the wreckage. I guess what I'm saying is that we're all so damned expendable! And the chances of both of us getting out of this are . . ."

"Are very high, because we know what the hell we're doing," Ryder said, cutting him off. "What do you think this is, the movies or something?"

Woody looked up at him for the first time. "Yes," he said. "That's exactly what I mean. In the movies, one of the two partners always gets it. It's like Nature intends it that way . . ."

"Hey, partner," Ryder said in all earnestness. "Neither one of us is getting it. *This ain't the goddamn movies.* We're the best goddamn crew ever to step into a Tomcat. Don't you see that's just what they wanted? All the ballbusting at Top Gun, the weirdness in War Heaven? We fit the profile, man. We're the best. You just haven't been paying attention."

Woody thought it over and finally managed a grin.

"You're right . . ." he said. "We're tight. We're on top of things . . ."

"You bet your ass," Ryder said, finally rising to get a cup of java. "And when we get out, your first stop is the University of San Diego library. Your second stop is the bar at Fightertown with that gorgeous librarian."

Woody reached out his hand and grabbed Ryder's in a handshake. "Tight, man. Stay tight . . ." Ryder told him. "You're the best. And everyone from Top Gun to Toon will know it soon enough, if they don't already . . ."

Woody finally gulped down his coffee. His smile widened and the color came back to his face. "OK, I'm psyched . . ." he said. "But tell me, Ghost, what the hell are *you* going to do when it's over? Where's *your* first stop?"

Ryder turned and looked him straight in the eye. "Good question, partner . . ." he said.

The USS *Ben Franklin* was two days out from the American naval base at Diego Garcia when the captain finally agreed to see Maureen.

She had requested the meeting one day after coming out of her sedation. She hadn't eaten but a little food in that time. And although she was permitted to go to some areas of the ship with an escort, she spent all her time locked inside her cabin, secretly working on her story and wondering what ever happened to Captain Ryder Long.

Two female sailors came to her door at nine that morning and escorted her to the captain's quarters. While she waited, a cook brought in a pot of coffee and some Danish, two of which Maureen quickly ate. The captain appeared ten minutes later.

He was a tall, blond-haired, ruddy-complexioned man, everything the captain of the huge ship should look like. His name was O'Leary and Maureen immediately made the psychic link that all Irish strangers do upon meeting for the first time.

"Miss O'Brien, first of all, my apologies for the inconvenience you've endured," the captain said, sitting across from her at the small round table. "But I won't belabor you with all the reasons why it was necessary. I understand that you already know a great deal about the operation. More than the vast majority of the people on this ship, I'm sure . . ."

Maureen nodded. She, too, was tired of bitching about being kidnapped, bitching about her rights being violated, bitching about going home. Something big was happening. She was a reporter. She couldn't think of being in a better place to get the story than on the operation's command ship, although her chances of ever getting to print it were probably nil. Her father knew she was safe, he would understand and that's really all that mattered for now.

Except one thing . . .

"Captain, did you meet any of the pilots who are taking part in the operation?" she asked.

He poured them each a cup of coffee. "Yes, I met all of them, in fact," he said. "Amazing individuals. Trained under the most intense conditions ever devised."

Maureen sipped her coffee and felt it warm her insides.

"Do you recall a Captain Ryder Long?" she asked, her heart leaping a beat on mentioning the name.

O'Leary nodded slowly. "Yes, I talked with Long several times," he said. He didn't dare tell her that Long and the others had been aboard the ship during its voyage from Manila to the Bay of Bengal. In fact, unbeknownst to either her or Long, they were actually just a few cabins apart during the trip.

"Ryder Long was promoted to major, by the way," O'Leary told her. "But why do you ask about him? Is he a friend of yours?"

Maureen lowered her eyes. "I met him, once . . ." she said softly.

O'Leary smiled, a twinkle running across his eyes. "And?" he said.

"And nothing," she replied, sounding like a reticent teenager. The last thing she wanted was to blurt out her feelings to the officer.

But O'Leary read her look right away. "I understand your father works in the Pentagon," he said.

Maureen nodded. "He did," she said. "I'm afraid I might have gotten him into some trouble . . ."

"You didn't," O'Leary told her. "He's on leave. But not for disciplinary reasons. They just don't want any, shall we say, complications arising at this critical junction."

Maureen brightened a little. She was glad her old man was OK.

"So you've been thinking about this guy, Ryder Long?" O'Leary asked with a fatherly smile.

Maureen opened her mouth but nothing came out.

O'Leary laughed. "That was a good answer . . ." he said. He reached into his pocket and pulled out his wallet. He retrieved two photos from its inside flap and showed them to Maureen.

"These are my daughters," he said. "One of them, Mary Ellen, is about your age. I'd like to think she's as pretty as you are. She has a boyfriend. She thinks about him all the time, too."

"Are *any* of them going to make it, Captain?" Maureen suddenly blurted out.

O'Leary felt the smile drain from his face. Suddenly the seriousness of the operation came crashing back to him. Now it was he who was at a loss for words.

"There's no way of knowing, Miss O'Brien" was all he could say.

Reinhart fired up his Tomcat's engines and quickly brought them to trim. Chauvagne spent his time checking and rechecking the aircraft's radar/fire control system. Everything came back "green" on the weapons load of four Sidewinders and two Phoenix missiles slung underneath the F-14.

Their base was at the bottom of a rocky canyon thirty-five miles north of the Burmese village of Houei Sai. Their catapult, using the water from a nearby stream for steam, had been set up and working when they trekked in several days before. They found the canyon base surrounded by members of the Gray Army, the same troopers who just two weeks before had pounded them nonstop with Supertears, Crab Gas, and Puke Gas. Now they were their protectors.

The wind that whipped down the canyon reached twenty-five knots on occasion. That and the field catapult was enough to get the F-14 up and flying with an afterburner-assisted take-off. Unlike the mountain base 120 miles to the east, the canyon base had a store of JP-5 aviation fuel—enough to launch the 'Cat on three extended combat sorties, as well as two test launchings.

Reinhart rechecked the rest of his controls then taxied the F-14 up and over the catapult's pressure gauge. A sergeant from the 1245th—a veteran of Spookbase—went through the steam weight/pressure procedure to ensure a safe take-off. Three minutes later, he gave Reinhart the thumbs-up signal and the Tomcat roared away.

At the same time, two North Korean MiGs were taking off from the PRA's main airfield within the Iron Circle. The North Korean aircraft were antique MiG-19s, jets that were relics even before the outbreak of the Vietnam War. Far from being dogfighters, the MiG-19s had long ago been relegated to Ground Attack status.

No sooner had Reinhart leveled off the Tomcat at 25,000 feet, when Chauvagne reported he'd picked up two targets—the two MiGs—moving toward the canyon base.

"Are they acting hostile?" Reinhart asked the French officer.

"No, Captain, not as yet . . ." the weapons officer answered.

Reinhart had simply intended to take the 'Cat on a quick

370

orientation flight and then set it back down. But now the two MiGs had changed those plans.

"Their altitude, Lieutenant?" Reinhart asked.

"Climbing through 17,500 feet, sir," Chauvagne answered. "They are emitting only a weak radar signal. Not intercept modes at all. Possibly they are attack aircraft . . ."

"Possibly, Lieutenant," Reinhart answered, raising their own altitude to 27,000 feet. "Please arm our weapons . . ."

Chauvagne did so, then checked back on the targets. "Bogies now at 18,000 feet, sir," he reported. "Still no high emissions readings . . ."

Reinhart knew he had to make a quick decision. If he chose to land now, he would have to be sure that they could set the F-14 down at the canyon base on the first try—not a certainty by any means. If their attempt was unsuccessful and they had to fly a go-around—and the MiGs stayed on their present course—they would be seen and the canyon base would be detected.

Reinhart decided not to set down. He was only carrying half a tank of fuel. As such, he hoped to avoid any dogfighting if possible. Instead he climbed to 55,000 feet, way above the antique jets' service ceiling and waited.

The North Korean pilots continued their southerly course, the flight simply meant to be a training mission, although both were carrying two five hundred-pound bombs each.

Per orders, the flight leader contacted the commander of a PRA battalion which was moving south toward the Thai border. The area had been the site of a recent tax convoy ambush and the troops were being sent in to secure the area and look for the mysterious culprits.

The North Korean flight leader contacted the ground forces on the third try. The battalion was moving down a winding highway, its troops hitching rides on a variety of vehicles such as trailer trucks, school buses and even an ancient Coca-Cola truck. Through an interpreter, the North Korean pilot proposed they fly low over the convoy, affecting a ground support role. The ground commander agreed and passed the word down the line to his troop sergeants.

The MiGs then dove to a height of a thousand feet and began a visual search for the convoy. The air was misty with jungle humidity, making the visual search more difficult. And as the day heated up, the mist would soon turn into a soupy fog. Calls back and forth to the ground commander were of little help. The North Korean pilots were at a loss to find the column.

They decided to split up and continue to search individually. The flight leader headed twenty-five miles to the south, while his wingman flew back to the north to double back over the territory already covered.

With a thickening mist rising from the jungle, the flight leader sought out a terrain that lent itself to atmospheric clearing, such as a wide river, a mountain pass, or a river canyon . . .

The Gray Army soldier manning the Roland antiaircraft battery at the canyon base adjusted his search scope. He had picked up a blip—a slow-moving aircraft still thirty-five miles from the base but heading right for them.

He quickly sounded an alarm and the soldiers at the base snapped into action. Everything not hidden under cliffs or in the caves along the bottom of the valley, was quickly covered over with camouflage netting. The base's radio operator sent a burst transmission to Reinhart's F-14, still orbiting high overhead. "Target intercepted. Flight course toward base."

Several minutes later, the MiG appeared. Its pilot was zigzagging through the clear air of the canyon, looking on either side for the highway being used by the PRA battalion.

The MiG passed right over the hidden Gray base and continued on its way, its pilot not suspecting that more than 550 American soldiers lay hidden nearby. But then, the same high winds that allowed the F-14 to lift off from the bottom of the canyon came into play with the MiG, with more disastrous results.

The North Korean pilot suddenly felt the nose of his airplane lift up. He quickly realized that he'd been caught in a strong cross wind whipping up from the canyon. He nosed the airplane down to regain control, but in doing so overcompensated, immediately stalling the engine. He hit the airplane's throttle, only to find the engine had flamed out.

He instantly lost control of the old plane, which gyrated to the starboard, flipped over on its back, and smashed into the canyon wall, just a hundred feet from the edge of the Gray Army's turf.

The Pakistani scientists working inside Toon's nuclear weapons laboratory came to attention when the colonel himself walked in.

It was never a pleasant occasion when Toon decided to inspect the place and this time proved to be the worst visit of all. Toon immediately began berating the thirty-five scientists who were lined up like recruits in a boot camp.

"All I want to know is 'why?'" Toon shouted nearly in the face of the lead scientist. "Why has it taken so long to do something you assured me would be ready months ago? I don't think anyone here realizes that we have the opportunity—no, the destiny—to become a world power. A *superpower*. We have the opportunity to become the leaders of the unaligned countries, to smite the impure American criminals and the others.

"But this destiny is being wasted, because you people are just too slow. You are standing in the way of progress. You are standing in the way of the destiny of the People's Revolutionary Army!"

Toon's face was boiling red with anger. His lips and eyes were squinting in fury. But then a sly smile came across his face.

"I don't accept excuses, comrades," he said. "And if you file outside, you will see what happens to one who chooses to offer excuses as impediments to destiny . . ."

Three PRA guards, each toting an AK-47 assault rifle, herded the Pakistani scientists out of the igloolike building. Other units of the PRA were already lined up along a parade route which ran through the center of Toon's major base.

The units were called to attention and watched as a jeep

slowly made its way down the route. Standing in the back, stooped over and wearing a huge crudely fashioned dunce hat was the former commander of the PRA border guards.

The jeep rolled to a stop in front of the Pakistani scientists and the man in the dunce cap was hauled down by Toon's personal bodyguards. He was pushed and kicked to a small platform that had been hastily erected next to the igloo building.

Toon himself waited on the platform, a silver pistol in his hand. The former border guard commander was led up to the platform, terror in his eyes. Toon raised the pistol over the man's head and announced, "This man has disgraced me. He has disgraced our cause. The People have convicted him of this crime. The People will carry out the sentence."

Toon then calmly placed the pistol to the man's temple and pulled the trigger . . .

The shot—a grisly *crack!*—echoed throughout the base, sending a shudder through all the witnesses, especially the Pakistanis. The man stood completely upright for a few grotesque seconds, a stream of blood squirting from his forehead. Then he collapsed backward, landing hard on the platform steps.

Toon looked out at the assembled units and waved them away with a sharp: *"Dismissed!"*

Just then, one of Toon's officers ran up and whispered a message to him.

Toon listened intently, then motioned a jeep forward. "Take me to the airfield," he told the driver.

The crash of the North Korean MiG-19 had already sent ripples through Toon's military complex, as well as that of the Americans.

Shortly after the crash, the second MiG-19 arrived at the scene, surveyed the wreckage, and radioed the news back to his base. Meanwhile, the convoy of PRA soldiers the dead pilot had been searching for, arrived near the crash site. As the Gray soldiers watched from their hiding places, the PRA troops scrambled down the canyon intent on reaching the crash site.

And high above it all, Reinhart and Chauvagne waited, the fuel reserves getting lower by the minute . . .

The first squad of PRA soldiers to reach the site found little remained of the MiG-19 or its pilot. The airplane was torn in two—the major part of the fuselage was sitting in the canyon river, a large section of the wing was jammed up against the rocks of the canyon wall itself. Smaller debris was scattered everywhere. The sergeant in charge of the PRA squad ordered his men to retrieve whatever they could.

It was when two of the PRA soldiers, attempting to recover a piece of the airplane's landing gear, stumbled across a steam pipe leading to the catapult that the first shots of the final battle of the Iron Circle were fired . . .

69

"Reinhart's in trouble . . ." was the message Moon brought to Ryder and Woody as the pilots were recalibrating the flight computer in the F-14.

"We've just got a burst transmission from their canyon base," Moon continued. "A North Korean MiG pilot cracked up just a stone's throw from their catapult and the place was soon crawling with PRA troops. Reinhart was up on an orientation flight and now he's stuck at 35,000 and running out of fuel . . ."

"Christ, can he divert here?" Ryder asked.

"Negative . . ." Moon answered. "He's got about ten minutes of fuel left. But there's more: We've picked up a lot of activity at Toon's airbase. I think they're sending up a flight to cover the rescue efforts."

"Shit and Shiloh," Woody said. "This will crack it open."

Ryder thought for a moment. Reinhart was going to have to land at the canyon base during the inevitable firefight that would soon break out between the Grays and the PRA. If more of Toon's aircraft were on the way, that meant Reinhart and the Grays would need air support.

"Let's go . . ." Ryder said. "We've got to launch—right now!"

The entire base rallied to push the F-14 out of its camouflaged hangar and connect it to the catapult. It took only three minutes for the steam pressure to rise, and less than six minutes after receiving the report, Ryder and Woody were airborne.

Colonel Toon himself led the flight of six MiG-21s down to the crash site. By the time the half dozen planes reached the area, a sharp firefight between the Grays and the PRA battalion had already broken out.

While the PRA troops were scurrying down to the canyon floor, the Gray troops had crawled out of the hiding places and had set up on the road being used by the PRA convoy. The two PRA soldiers who discovered the steam pipe were immediately cut down, as were those soldiers retrieving pieces of the North Korean jet. The PRA soldiers still remaining on the highway immediately went into a defensive posture while waiting for their commander to issue orders. That's when the Gray troops opened up on the tail end of the column with machine fire and RPGs.

The firefight was going full tilt when the MiG-21s arrived. Without warning, two of the jets swooped down and strafed the end of the column, killing Gray troopers and hapless PRA soldiers alike. The wild strafing run caused the Gray soldiers to wisely melt back into the jungle.

High above, Reinhart knew he had to start descending to land. His fuel reserves were down to three minutes of flying time. With all need of secrecy now gone, he openly called the flight officer of the Grays and asked for a status report on the arresting system. The answer came back that for the moment the arresting system was secure, but that status could change at any moment.

Reinhart put the F-14 into a slow descent, passing through layers of thick clouds. Chauvagne had picked up the five MiG-21s that were at various points over the battle scene. When the F-14 passed through 20,000 feet, both pilots could see two of the MiG-21s twelve miles off their port side. Two more were down at 750, buzzing the column. Then Chauvagne reported the single remaining MiG was orbiting way out at thirty-two miles, almost as if the pilot was watching and waiting for something to develop.

"Arm all the weapons," Reinhart called back to Chauvagne. "I don't see how we can avoid a fight . . ."

"Targets 3 and 4, turning toward us," Chauvagne reported. Reinhart turned to see the visual bogies had spotted them. The normally humorless Reinhart was forced to chuckle. "Well, the lid is off," he said. "Imagine their surprise when they see an F-14 . . ."

The two MiGs in visual turned toward the Tomcat. Reinhart remembered back to the key phrase of their War Heaven training: *Innovate.*

He didn't hesitate another second. He squeezed the missile launch trigger and a Sidewinder flashed out from underneath his right wing. No sooner had he fired when he turned the F-14 into a thick cloud bank.

The missile flew straight and true and impacted on one of the MiG's starboard wing. The MiG exploded immediately, sending the ruptured fuselage cartwheeling across the sky. The stricken MiG's wingman immediately dove to avoid being hit by the wreckage. At that moment Reinhart's F-14 passed out of the cloud bank. The German immediately fired a second Sidewinder, then banked to another thick stack of cumulus nearby.

The second air-to-air missile struck the MiG-21 on its ass end, blowing off the jet's tail section. The pilot ejected just moments before the airplane's fuel caught fire and exploded. It was a sterling first encounter for Reinhart and Chauvagne. Two targets destroyed and not a single missile fired at them.

But both the German and the Frenchman knew the game of high speed hide-and-seek was over. They were now without any missiles and had less than two minutes' fuel left and the two MiGs that were originally flying low over the battle area were now climbing to meet them. Judging by the accuracy of their intercept, Reinhart knew they must have been flying under direction of the MiG orbiting on the fringe of the action.

Below in the canyon base, Gray soldiers were scrambling to make sure the arresting gear was still operating while other troopers sprayed the top of the road with covering fire.

The F-14 reached ten thousand feet when the main reserve tank pumped the last of its fuel. Reinhart switched over to his emergency reserve which had exactly one minute of fuel, and that was if he continued descending.

But the two MiGs were now just two miles away and getting into attack position.

"They're arming . . ." Chauvagne reported from the pit. As if to underscore the point, the F-14's low warning buzzer came on.

"They've got a track . . ." the Frenchman continued. "Lead ship has radar lock . . ."

The high warning buzzer went off. Reinhart banked the F-14 first left then right, but knew his maneuverability was limited to just that—banking back and forth. He reached down and switched on the Tomcat's ECM device hoping it would screw up the MiG's targeting and direction finder.

"Lead ship firing!" Chauvagne called out. "Two missiles, infra-red homing . . ."

Reinhart pulled the airplane up sharply and faced it right toward the oncoming missiles. It was a risky move, but he knew that infrared air-to-airs rarely caught a target head-on. Sure enough, both missiles streaked right over them and disappeared into a cloud.

But the life-saving maneuver had used up all their gas. Reinhart was again faced with a difficult choice. Try to catch the arresting hook and bring the Tomcat in for a dead-stick landing—probably while under fire—or eject.

The second MiG's firing of two missiles solved the dilemma for him.

"Prepare to eject," he called back to Chauvagne. Then Reinhart pulled the F-14's nose up one more time, leveling off the disabled warplane. He counted to three and then yelled, "*Eject!*"

The Tomcat's canopy blew off immediately and both pilots were literally blasted out of the cockpit. They were sucked into the high winds at seventy-five hundred feet and were blown nearly a quarter of a mile before their chutes opened. The F-14 dipped down into an all-out nosedive, spinning as it went. As he watched the ship plunge, Reinhart's only consolation was that the F-14 would hit with such speed nothing of any value would survive intact.

But now the two pilots had a new threat to worry about. The MiG pilot who had chosen to stay on the periphery of the action was now zooming in toward them. They watched in horror as he opened up on them with his 30mm nose cannon.

"*You bastard!*" Reinhart screamed as the MiG-21 flashed by them. Then, in one horrible second, both pilots were riddled with cannon fire. Their bloody, lifeless bodies drifted off to land in the middle of the dense Burmese jungle.

That's when Ryder and Woody appeared on the scene . . .

They had been watching the action via the AWG radar. Ryder knew that he had no time to arm and fire a missile at the MiG shooting at the parachuting pilots. Instead he booted the F-14 into afterburner and intercepted the MiG as it was coming out of its turn.

He laid a heavy barrage from his own nose cannon right across the MiG's tail, chopping off its rear elevator controls and approximately a quarter of its vertical tail. Ryder knew the MiG pilot had been taken by surprise. He watched as the stricken Soviet-built plane dived into the nearest cloud for cover.

"Two targets dead ahead," Woody radioed ahead.

Ryder stared out of his HUD display and saw the paired MiGs coming right for them.

"Arm Fox One and Two," he called back to Woody, putting the Tomcat into a wicked climb. He topped out at eight thousand feet, looped around and put the sun at his back. Then he kicked in the afterburner, and in a matter of seconds, found himself right on the tail of the trailing MiG.

"Just like in school," he said to himself as he lined the MiG up in the crosshairs of the HUD. Everything came together, his flight computer rang telling him it was the optimum time to fire. He instantly squeezed the trigger and watched the Sidewinder smash into the MiG's tail no more than fifteen hundred feet away from them.

Ryder immediately went after the second MiG of the pair. Its pilot had banked hard left when the wingman was bounced, but Ryder had stayed right on his tail.

"*Fly this mutha, Ghost!*" Woody yelled in anger. "Make them pay!"

Both Americans were numb—two of their comrades had just been horribly murdered.

Ryder was glued to the MiG's tail, anticipating his every move. Once he knew he was in close enough for a cannon shot, he squeezed the Vulcan gun's trigger. He watched as the stream of shells shattered the MiG's port wing. A second burst hit the airplane's wing tank, igniting it. The MiG began to spin out of control and the pilot wisely hit the silks. Ryder suppressed an urge to riddle the man with bullets.

"Anyone else left?" he called back to Woody.

"Nope . . ." the Wiz replied. "The guy who iced Reinhart and Chauvagne split. I got him at forty-five miles out and retreating. Fucking coward is heading back to his base, I'd say."

Ryder shook his head. Not only had that particular pilot shown a murderous, ruthless side, he showed considerable flying skills escaping as he did in a shot-up airplane. Something in Ryder's gut told him this was no ordinary gomer.

"I don't think we've seen the last of that guy," he radioed back to Woody.

"I hope not . . ." Woody said.

Back on the ground there was considerable confusion resulting from the strafing of the PRA troops. Between this and the air battle that had raged some ten miles away, a lull had settled over the fighting on the roadway. The time allowed those Gray troopers stationed in the canyon to escape downriver, leaving behind delayed fused bombs which destroyed the catapult, the arresting gear, and anything they couldn't carry. Those Gray troopers who had moved into the jungle were presently circling back around and heading for the predetermined rendezvous point with the rest of their group.

The PRA commander was in the process of ordering his men to clear the roadway of debris and bodies when he heard a terrifying screech overhead. He looked up and saw the ghost-gray F-14 bearing down on the roadway, its nose lit up like a flamethrower.

He didn't even have a chance to call out a warning to his troops. The Tomcat's cannon was already ripping up vehicles at the head of the column. The commander was frozen in his tracks. Strange questions flashed through his mind. Who were these mysterious soldiers? he thought. Who could infiltrate hundreds of troops into the Burmese jungle, troops equipped with catapults and high-performance jets so sophisticated he'd never seen anything like them before? In an instant the commander realized that Toon's claim of the invulnerability of the Iron Circle and its outlying territories was hollow. And as he stood in shock, unable to move as the airplane chopped up his finest troops, he knew he, too, was about to pay the price . . .

70

The airfield at Toon's base had no emergency equipment, no capability of foaming down the runway in case a crippled airplane had to make a landing.

Toon's airplane was smoking heavily as it circled the base. He had no control over the rear quarter steering surfaces and his engine had flamed out a dozen times during the return flight. Only a handful of pilots in the world could have brought the shot-up MiG back to base. Toon was one of those pilots . . .

After jettisoning the remaining fuel and ammunition, Toon brought the MiG in for a wheels-up landing. The MiG floated in, hit once *hard,* bounced up then came down on its left wing sending up a shower of sparks. The MiG spun around three times before finally coming to rest.

Toon was up and walking away from the crashed airplane before anyone reached the wreckage. He was shaken, but more with anger than fear. There was a secret army—a well-trained, well-equipped force—hiding in his southern territory. And unlike most of his soldiers, Toon knew an F-14 when he saw one.

"Those devil Americans!" he cursed, wiping a spot of blood from his forehead. *"Those bastards!"*

A jeep finally reached him and he ordered the driver to take him directly to the weapons research lab. The driver had sense enough not to argue with the leader. He immediately floored the jeep and was pulling up to the lab just minutes later.

The head Pakistani doctor met Toon at the entrance to the lab.

"Doctor!" Toon screamed. "I demand that you have that warhead ready by sundown or I will personally shoot you and your clique of hooligans!"

The doctor surprised Toon. He had berated the man to scare him. Yet the Pakistani was smiling.

"You have reason to laugh?" Toon raged.

"Yes, sir," the Pakistani said. "Because, you see, the warhead is ready now . . ."

"We have to move against them within the next twenty-four hours," Ryder told Moon.

They were sitting in the mountain base's Ops Building. The entire group of base personnel was on hand, having listened to the report of the action at the canyon base. An angry sadness enveloped the base. Everyone there had known both Reinhart and Chauvagne. Now they would all be present while the officers determined the next course of action.

"They know we are here," Ryder continued. "We've stung

them a few times, but remember, these were isolated actions, and we called the spots and the shots. Now, they're going to be out looking for us."

"The question is: Are we ready to take them on?" Moon said.

"No . . ." Ryder said quickly. "The question is can we afford to wait? If anything, these skirmishes will speed up their timetable. We know the launch pad is operational. The first missile is in place. All it takes now is for them to attach the warhead . . ."

Moon thought it over, then said, "We would have to send a message to the *Ben Franklin*. Then they would have to contact the Blues and Grays . . ."

"I don't think we have a choice," Ryder said. "We've got to finally push the button on Distant Thunder . . ."

Major Maxwell had finally gotten to sleep for the first time in what seemed like weeks when someone shook him awake.

It was Simons. "We've received a top priority burst from the *Franklin,* sir," the young lieutenant told him. "For your eyes only . . ."

Maxwell quickly got up and climbed into his fatigues and made his way to his base's operations shack.

The Blues had located their base in dense jungle at the far southeastern edge of the Iron Circle. It was an isolated part of Burma, the nearest village was nearly thirty-five miles to the north. The tall trees provided perfect coverage for the group's twenty-two Blackhawk helicopters and twelve Cobra attack ships. And the tall grass nearby served as perfect camouflage for the field catapult used to launch the F-14 . . .

Lancaster and Sammett were waiting in the ops shack when Major Max swaggered in, trailing a cloud of cigar smoke.

"When did it come in?" he asked, taking the sealed slip of yellow paper from the radio operator.

"Just five minutes ago, sir," the man answered.

Maxwell read the message once, then twice, then ripped it up into tiny pieces.

He turned to Lancaster and Sammett.

Maxwell quickly asked, "How soon can you guys get airborne?"

Lancaster thought a moment. They had been the last element put into place in Burma, and therefore were the last of the three F-14s to launch. They had just finished setting up the field catapult that morning and the F-14 checked out later in the day. Now, the sun was setting.

"We could give it a try at midnight," the RAF officer said. "Best scenario would be at dawn tomorrow."

"Can you split the difference and be ready to launch around 3 A.M. if we had to?" Maxwell asked.

Lancaster looked to Sammett for agreement then nodded. "Yes . . ." he answered.

Maxwell took the cigar from his mouth and ran his hand through his hair.

"The Grays had a major battle with the PRA today," Maxwell told them. "Ryder and Woody downed two MiGs; Reinhart and Chauvagne got another two, but . . ."

"But what?" Lancaster asked.

"I'm afraid your friends Reinhart and Chauvagne have been killed," he said. "Machinegunned by a MiG while they were parachuting."

The news hit Lancaster like a shot in the stomach.

There was a long silence in the ops shack. Somehow Lancaster had convinced himself that just because the Blues had leveled the PRA island border base and snatched the American POWs without a scratch, then everything might go forward without casualties. But now, with Reinhart and Chauvagne gone, things were starting to look a little different . . .

"So what's Central Command want us to do?" Lancaster asked.

"They want us to go in," Maxwell said slowly. "Ready or not, the mission will go off at dawn tomorrow . . ."

It was close to 2100 hours when the three-man Thai Army Special Forces team reached the mountain base.

They were brought directly to the Ops Building where Ryder, Woody, and Moon were going over the last few grim details of the mission. Each of the Thais was carrying a heavy backpack.

Using Barrong as a translator, the Thai soldiers explained a helicopter from the USS *Benjamin Franklin* had landed at their base at mid-afternoon. All the pilot said was the two cases had to be delivered to the pilots on the mountain base immediately.

Ryder immediately began ripping open the packs. One of them contained—of all things—a VCR. The other contained a small TV and seven video tapes.

Woody and Moon hastily set up the VCR and plugged in the first tape. It showed what had to be the most recent footage shot of Toon's inner defense perimeter.

"This must have been shot this morning," Moon said, studying the tape. "The missile is being fueled, you can tell by those streams of smoke. Plus his men are all wearing protective suits."

The first tape ended and they quickly fed in the second one. It showed movement in the courtyard where the American POWs were kept.

"Looks like they're making them stay outside," Woody said.

"They're showing them to us," Ryder said. "They want us to know they've got them and that they'll be killed if we launch an air strike . . ."

The third tape showed three passes over Toon's airfield. There were more than fifty airplanes—Soviet-built models of all types—out on the flight line, obviously getting fueled up.

"That's what you'll be up against," Moon said. "Not much quality, but a lot of quantity . . ."

"Just like at Top Gun," Woody said.

"Someone once said that Quantity in itself is a Quality," Ryder said.

The fourth tape was a look at the target's outer defenses.

"SAMs every thousand yards," Moon observed. "SA-2s, they'll hit anything flying above five hundred feet . . ."

Tape number five showed the second line of antiaircraft defenses.

"SAMs every five hundred yards," Moon said. "Plus radar-controlled AAA guns . . ."

Tape 6 showed the inner ring—the third line. Moon whistled. "A missile site every hundred yards, with two AAA guns for every SAM . . ."

The last tape started out with a video display readout of the entire defense lines. Even without looking at the final tape, Ryder knew the terrain by heart.

At the bottom of the tape box was a sealed envelope. Ryder was surprised to see it was addressed to him personally.

Ryder excused himself and went to the far end of the Ops Building. He ripped open the envelope and found it contained a letter. It was from Maureen.

> *Dear Ryder:*
>
> *I am aboard the* Ben Franklin *and Captain O'Leary has allowed me to write this brief note to you. Funny thing is, I don't know what to say, not a good trait for a newspaper reporter.*
>
> *So, here's my picture: I already have yours. Be careful and I pray we meet again.*
>
> *Maureen*

Ryder reached inside the envelope and pulled out a District of Columbia driver's license with Maureen's photo on it. Even the antiphotogenic DC Registry of Motor Vehicles camera couldn't dissuade her beauty. He found himself shaking as he stared at the photo, trying to memorize the face. He knew he *did* have a reason to come back from Distant Thunder.

One by one, the huge C-5 Galaxy cargo airplanes roared in and touched down at Thailand's Udom Air Base. Each airplane quickly doused its running lights as soon as it touched down and taxied to a dark corner of the airfield.

Inside eight of the airplanes sat a pair of F-5 Aggressor jet fighters. Inside the remaining eight C-5s were members of a special US Marine Corps unit—formerly called the Green Army—along with a number of APCs and M-1 tanks.

The mission of the sixteen large craft was twofold. They

were charged with bringing in the remaining units of Project Distant Thunder. And, if the project was successful, they would be used to ferry out the two hundred American POWs.

Commander John Slade was the first Aggressor pilot to bound off the C-5. He stood on the darkened runway and stretched. He had been cooped up inside the Galaxy for eighteen hours, and this after being cooped up at Hickam Air Force Base in Hawaii for the past two weeks. He breathed deeply. But his first gulp of the thick Asian air made him long for the dry atmosphere of Nevada's War Heaven.

Slade had been finally briefed on Distant Thunder the day after he and the rest of the Spookbase crew—with the exception of Ryder and Woody—had been choppered out of the desert airstrip. His first surprise came when they told him he would soon be shipping out to Burma. His second surprise came when they told him he'd be flying with the Aggressors. Now, as he sat on the step of the C-5 loading ramp, he went over the very ambitious plan once again.

Once the mission got underway and the Gray Army opened up its "wide front" attacks against the Iron Circle's southern border, the Blue Army's choppers would fly in, attack, and hold, at least temporarily, Toon's airfield. Hold it long enough for ten Galaxies to touch down and unload the "Green" Marines and their armor. The Greens would then battle their way into Toon's compound and free the American POWs, ferry them back to the airport where they would be picked up by the waiting C-5s and flown to freedom.

This part of the plan hinged on surprise and on the CIA's assessment that when attacked Toon would order his remaining ground troops to protect the ICBM launch facilities and, theoretically, leave the POWs under little or no guard. His job—and that of the other Aggressors—would be to escort the C-5s in and out, staying over the field—and out of the murderous SAM path known as Thunder Alley.

He knew that suicidal airspace was reserved for Ryder and Woody . . .

Slade took another deep gulp of the thick air and counted the number of things that could go wrong with the mission. Toon might not fall for the Gray Army feint and deploy a lot of his troops to the south. The Blues might not be able to neutralize the airfield long enough for the C-5s to land. The Greens might not be able to break out of the airport and reach the POWs. Toon might have standing orders to his troop to shoot the POWs should anything go wrong.

There were a million things that could go wrong. As a military man, Slade knew any operation had a high degree of risk. Now he knew why all the secrecy surrounding Distant Thunder was so necessary. The integrity of the mission aside, if the mission fucked up, not many people would want to be associated with it.

But he also knew that even if ninety-nine percent of the mission got screwed up, there was one aspect that couldn't go wrong. That was the destruction of the warhead—ideally after all the POWs had been carried out of harm's way. That was why the F-14s were infiltrated into Burma in the first place and why they were not a part of the POW rescue operation. Because even if everything else went wrong, that ICBM had to be iced. Slade knew that was where Ryder and Woody came in. He wouldn't want to change places with them for a million dollars.

71

Ryder, Woody, and Moon spent the hours following the delivery of the equipment by the Thai soldiers going over the all-important seventh videotape. They continually watched and rewound, watched and rewound—over and over studying the route they would have to take to try and dodge the SAMs of Thunder Alley and lay the "down burst" bomb onto the missile pad before someone hit the ICBM's launch button.

According to Moon, the ICBM, which was built with the help of East German scientists using stolen or off-the-shelf parts, appeared to be ongoing a "full load" fueling. This gave a clue as to what Toon's first target would be.

"If he fueled up at half load, then the missile might be targeted to a low sub-orbital flight and hit Tokyo, or somewhere in the Mideast," the young officer explained. "A third load might indicate Beijing or Melbourne was the target. A quarter load could mean New Delhi or Islamabad."

"But what about a 'full-load?'" Ryder asked, already guessing at the answer.

Moon looked worried and for good reason.

"San Diego. Los Angeles. Seattle," he said grimly. "Phoenix or Denver depending on the upper wind speeds at launch time . . ."

"San Diego . . ." Woody said slowly under his breath.

"The bad news is that it doesn't make much difference where the damn warhead comes down," Moon said. "It's an air burst. It's designed to go off at twenty-five thousand feet. It could go off over the frigging Pacific and the winds would blow that hot dirt all up and down the West Coast. Some would even make it into the cross streams and reach as far as Chicago, even the East Coast."

"I suppose there's no doubt that Toon will hit the launch button . . ." Ryder asked. "You know, last minute attack of conscience?"

Moon shook his head. "Not a chance . . ." he said. "He fits all of the terrorists' profiles. Determined. Fanatical. And worse, he's operating on his own turf. Some of these bozos lose their nerve the farther they get from home. But Toon is home. The combination makes it a sure bet that when the time comes, he'll push the big button.

"That's why you guys got to get in there before that *mutha* takes off . . ."

It was after midnight when Ryder and Woody watched the seventh videotape for the last time.

"We got this dicked," Woody said after viewing the tape for the seventy-fifth time. "Shut-eye and fly . . ."

Ryder agreed with him. They already knew that the Gray

389

attacks started earlier that day. One positive report from a Thai long-range recon patrol said that two battalions of PRA troops—half of Toon's ground forces—were heading to engage the "mystery army" in the south. The lead force was made up of Toon's mercenaries, the second battalion was reportedly made up of crack Vietnamese troops.

The plan called for the Blues to attack Toon's air base at 0600 hours while it was still dark. The C-5s would go in at 0615, carrying equipment and the Marine-armored column. If everything went well, the Greens would strike out for Toon's main compound and possibly reach the POWs by 0700.

Ryder and Woody were scheduled to launch at 0710 hours. The flight up to the target would take only twenty minutes on afterburner, the bomb run only seven minutes at low speed. After that, they would only have about fifteen minutes of fuel left—the action in the canyon earlier in the day had burnt up their reserves and they were sure the Soviets weren't going to be forthcoming with another mid-air fill-up.

It was strange, Ryder thought as he finally lay down on his bunk, continuously going over his memorized maneuver patterns. In all the planning, no one had mentioned to them where *they* should land after the mission was completed.

He knew he had to try and sleep, but his mind was running in too many directions at once. There would be no turning back now—the mission would be flown tomorrow. The mission that started the day he was plucked out of the C-130 toilet paper run in Utah and found himself at Top Gun. Then to War Heaven. Then to Burma. It all made his experience of finding Simons in the desert seem positively mild by comparison.

Then, his thoughts turned to Maureen. All he wanted was to see her again. Sometime. Somewhere. He never wanted anything more in his life . . .

Then, as his eyelids finally got heavy, his thoughts turned to his father. Lost in skies not far from here so many years ago. He wondered what he would have thought of all this . . .

It was just after midnight when Toon entered his Planning Room.

The dozen officers assembled there snapped to attention. Toon took center stage in front of a crudely drawn map of the Iron Circle, and using a sword as a pointer, indicated an area at his territory's southern fringe.

"A ragtag band of mercenaries has infiltrated our southern flank," Toon began, angry and tight-lipped. "They are little more then bandits. Criminals. Rebels from the eastern part of this puny country. They have brazenly attacked our tax convoys. They have tried to bluff us by attacking one of our western border posts.

"We must exterminate them at once . . ."

The twelve officers, still standing at attention, were shocked. Up until that time, they were under the impression that not a "band" of mercenaries but an army of American special units had not just "infiltrated" but *invaded* the southern territory. And that the Americans had heavy-duty air support—attack helicopters and jet fighters. But for some reason, Toon had chosen not to face the facts.

"I have already dispatched one of our finest battalions to the south," Toon continued. "I will send another before dawn this morning. They are under orders to kill every person they come in contact with . . ."

"Excuse me, sir," the commander of Toon's ground forces spoke up. "I believe you meant to say 'kill every person who *resists*' . . ."

"*No!*" Toon raved, smashing the sword against the map. "My orders are for them to kill everyone and anyone in that sector. Only then can we send a message to those who are foolish enough to enter our territory. We will *cleanse* that area!"

Silence descended on the room.

"All of our troops will be on top alert as of this moment," Toon continued. "I want four patrols of our aircraft in the air at all times. And I want another four patrols to be ready to take off at a moment's notice."

Major Ling, Toon's trusted adviser and overall commander of the air forces, added the figures in his head. Each patrol consisted of five airplanes. That meant twenty airplanes in the air at all times, with twenty more waiting on standby. More than half their force would be involved.

Toon went on. "To prevent sabotage, I want all our aircraft brought out of their hangars and lined up out on the tarmac where our guards can watch over them . . ."

Major Ling spoke up. "A thousand pardons, sir," he said. "But in this configuration, we are very vulnerable to an attack from the air . . ."

Only Ling could have gotten away with such a question of Toon's judgment.

"*Major*," Toon said, his angry voice barely a whisper. "There is no threat from the air! Neither to the air base or our launch facilities. These rebels have no airplanes. Do not believe what you have heard from our people in the South. They have become hysterical in the heat of battle."

The assembled officers shifted uneasily. They knew that in the past three days, more than a half dozen of their jet fighters had disappeared and that Toon's own personal airplane had been shot up.

Toon sensed their discomfort.

"Rest easy, my officers," the colonel said. "We have our radar stations on the outlying areas. We'll have four patrols in the air at all times to protect our fighters on the ground. We have more surface-to-air missiles per square foot than anywhere in the world to protect our launch pad. No pilot is foolish enough to attack us through those SAMs. And even a concentrated air attack on our airfield would not destroy all our planes. After all, bombs can only do so much . . ."

An odd smile came across Toon's face. "Besides, my officers, today is to be our proudest day!" he continued. "Today we take our place among the superpowers of the planet. Today, our history will be made . . .

"Today, we launch '*Long Struggle*,' our glorious Rocket of the People!"

72

The last of the five Libyan "dawn patrol" fighters had just taken off when air crews working the flight line looked up to see two powerful lights approaching the air base from the east.

Major Ling was on the flight line at the time. He strained his eyes to see what was behind the powerful beams. It took a few seconds, but then the dark, insect-shaped aircraft came into full view.

"Cobras . . ." he said, almost to himself, recognizing the much-feared American attack chopper. How did they get by our radar? he wondered. Then he screamed, "Sound the alarm!"

As the air mechanics scrambled for cover, the Cobras swooped in on the base's control tower and sent a quick but accurate barrage of rockets into the structure. The glass-enclosed room at the top of the tower immediately exploded in a burst of flames. Two traffic controllers were thrown completely out of the tower, their bodies ripped and bleeding from the blizzard of broken glass. The large radio antenna on top of the tower first bent over, then was toppled in the explosion.

The Cobras made a tight turn and came in for a second pass, firing their heavy caliber nose machine guns into the burning tower. Then they roared away.

Five more PRA aircraft had been warming up at the time of the attack and their pilots hastily took off. Major Ling immediately got on the base's loudspeaker system and ordered all available aircraft to launch. He knew that despite Toon's misguided assurances just hours before, the Cobra attack was just the beginning. He also knew that it was important to get as many PRA aircraft into the air as quickly as possible.

But total confusion resulted from the "all launch" order. Stunned flight crews and pilots found themselves trying to take off without direction from a control tower, all the while looking over their shoulders for the return of the deadly choppers.

But it was an aircraft of a different kind that came over the

Commander Slade did a radio check on his four-plane flight then advised everyone to get down to attack level. The F-5 Aggressors, unmarked and still retaining their Soviet-style camouflage markings, leveled out to an attack height of five hundred feet, below the enemy base's radar capacity.

Two miles out from the airfield, Slade called back to his flight to prepare for the final attack approach. As he approached the field, Slade could see three enemy fighters were taking off on various runways. He knew he had to let them go. His mission was not to engage the enemy fighter pilots in the air—it was to neutralize those still on the ground.

"Flight, engage attack profile," Slade called back to the three F-5s behind him.

Taking the lead, the Navy commander pulled out in front, the point jet in the single-file formation. Within seconds he was over the field. The confusion on the ground was apparent—he could see soldiers, pilots, and mechanics running in every direction. He fingered his bomb-release lever, counted to three, and pulled it. Two canisters dropped from the F-5's wings, exploding in the middle of a cluster of North Korean jets. Slade pulled up immediately and, looking over his shoulder, saw two clouds rising up from the airbase. He knew the mist was not Supertears, or Crab Gas or Puke Gas. It was C-11, a gas which when inhaled fused the membranes in the lungs, suffocating anyone breathing it in less than a minute.

In sequence, the three other F-5s swooped in and dropped their deadly canisters. Within thirty seconds, the base was enveloped in a fog of poison gas.

Not like playtime in War Heaven, Slade thought as he watched the pink cloud. He knew that for the plan to work the enemy base personnel had to be neutralized—quickly. Some jobs, bombs just won't do. Gassing someone might appear inhumane—but then again, so was launching a "Super-Dirty" nuclear warhead . . .

*   *   *

High above the base, a lone F-14 was circling.

RAF Group Captain Lancaster listened as Sammett listed off the twelve separate targets on his AWG radar.

"Four Fitters, flying at 22,000 feet, circling in a wide-out orbit," Sammett said. "Four MiG-21s, down low, twenty-two miles east of the base. Two MiG-19s are approaching the field, possibly low on fuel. Two more MiG-19s about ten miles behind them . . ."

"Thank you, Lieutenant," Lancaster called back to the Indian officer. The RAF officer knew he now had to assign threat priorities to the enemy airplanes. The MiG-19s he decided to forget about. They were probably low on gas and therefore wouldn't be a factor.

The MiG-21s flying around the edge of the base were probably the flight that took off just before the gas attack. The Libyan Fitters had been airborne for a while, most likely waiting for instructions from the control tower which now no longer existed.

He decided to go after the Libyans first. "Lock up the two lead Fitters with our Phoenixes," Lancaster told Sammett. "Give me the go when ready . . ."

Sammett pushed a series of tracking and arming buttons. The long-range Phoenix missiles were ready to launch in under a minute.

"Launch, Captain . . ." Sammett reported.

Lancaster squeezed the missile launch trigger twice. With a shudder and a flash of light, the two large air-to-airs streaked out from underneath the Tomcat's wing and quickly disappeared off into the clouds. The RAF captain knew it could be as long as several minutes before the missiles reached their targets, but he didn't have to worry about them anymore. The Phoenix missile was the epitomy of a "fire and forget" weapon. It had a mind of its own . . .

Lancaster put the F-14 into a sharp turn and headed for the four MiG-21s.

"Emission data, please, Lieutenant?" he called back to Sammett.

"Targets emitting only local track, sir," the Indian officer answered. "They don't see us . . ."

"Excellent, Lieutenant, thank you," Lancaster answered. "Please arm up two 'Winders and give me a go-ahead when ready . . ."

Once again Sammett pushed the correct buttons. Meanwhile, Lancaster had moved the Tomcat within eight miles of the MiG-21 flight, giving him a visual target to shoot at. Sammett came back to Lancaster with the range and coordinates of the MiG-21s and the British officer let loose with two Sidewinders.

They watched as the missiles streaked off in a burst of flame and smoke, running a parallel course toward the two trailing MiGs. On cue, the missiles hit both airplanes dead-on, resulting in two nearly identical explosions.

"Good shooting!" Lancaster cried out.

At almost the same moment, Sammett came on the line: "Confirm two Phoenix kills, Captain," he said.

Lancaster had to shake his head. Only an F-14, with its load of deadly Phoenix and Sidewinder missiles, could track, engage, and destroy so many targets in so little time. In fact, the Phoenixes were so "user friendly"—but expensive—they were hardly even mentioned during his brief tenure at Top Gun or the days in War Heaven.

As he thought, the surviving airplanes in both flights simply fled the scene. They had no choice: this was not a dogfight. They were outmanned and outgunned and they knew it.

Lancaster put the F-14 into a high orbit above the airbase and switched his radio to a FM frequency.

"Cat Two to Blue Scarf," he called. "Airspace above target area cleared for time being. Will continue air cap . . ."

"Roger, Captain" the answer came back. "Thanks for the house cleaning. Keep an eye out for us . . ."

Major Maxwell hung up his chopper's microphone and checked his force.

The thirty helicopters of the Blue Army were skimming low over the jungle, the pilots of the lead aircraft wearing night goggles to see their way through the predawn darkness.

"OK, guys, Lancaster has opened up a great big hole for us," Maxwell called to all the pilots. "And the Aggressors have laid down the suppression gas. Everyone hook up to your air systems and check it with your buddy. This is what we've trained for. So let's go win us some medals!"

The helicopter pilots throttled up and doubled their speed. They had to make it to the airbase before Toon could think of sending in reinforcements. Inside the Blackhawks, members of the 15th Special Forces unit hooked up their gas masks and tied their blue scarves around their neck for easy identification when the shooting started. As they roared over the countryside, isolated Burmese villagers saw the chopper force and cheered. Somehow they knew the men in the helicopters were going against the evil Toon.

Maxwell knew that if they were lucky, the main chopper force would arrive if not unopposed, at least unexpected. While the two lead Cobras had taken out the control tower just minutes before, four other teams of Cobras had attacked several of Toon's radar stations thirty miles out.

Maxwell himself hooked up his gas mask as he saw the airbase come into vew. The objective of the chopper force was twofold. The Cobras would shoot up as many of Toon's fighters on the ground as possible. And while no one expected to ice all of the enemy fighters, the more that were bounced on the ground, the better the chances of the C-5 landings would be.

The second objective was to land the troops in the Blackhawks and secure the airfield allowing the C-5s to come in.

"Crew chiefs, check everyone's air masks," Maxwell called to all the Blackhawks. "Three minutes from touchdown."

Up ahead, Major Max could see the airbase was still surrounded by the gas cloud, the rising sun shooting its rays through the sickly pink color. Although he could see several jet fighters moving toward take-off, the base for the most part was very still.

"Check weapons!" Maxwell called out. "Cobra Leader, break off!"

He watched as, one by one, the ten Cobras banked to the right and climbed slightly, each chopper increasing its speed.

"Two minutes . . ." Maxwell called out. "Count off in landing priority!"

Each Blackhawk pilot then began calling in in the order that they had been assigned to land. Maxwell's four-chopper squad would go in first, followed by Esposito's four copters, and so on.

As he listened to each pilot call in, Maxwell could see the Cobras begin their first strafing runs. "Come on, boys," he urged. "Give it to them good . . ."

Major Ling couldn't believe his eyes . . .

He was holed up in what remained of the control tower. The top of the structure had been completely blown off, so now what was once the second-to-highest story was now the very top of the building. It was a good hiding place. It gave him a commanding view of the airfield and, for some reason, a telephone linked directly to Toon's headquarters was still working. Yet, safe as he was, he was afraid to report what he was seeing—or what he thought he was seeing—in front of him.

As a young man, Ling had been a Viet Cong soldier and thus had seen many American helicopter assaults. But now, as he looked out over the cloud of poison gas that covered a major part of the airfield, he thought he was dreaming. Out of the mist, it looked as if the American helicopters were coming again.

"Am I losing my mind?" he wondered, struggling with the gas mask he'd been able to find just after the gas attack. "Did I whiff some of this gas and it's affecting me?"

Everything had happened so fast at the airbase, his head was swimming. The first Cobra attack had been a complete surprise as was the gas attack by the Soviet-painted jet fighters. But after each one, he had contacted Colonel Toon directly on the phone link and each time the answer came back that the attacks on the airbase were not serious—the real enemy lay far to the south.

"These are feints, Ling," Toon had assured him. "Not even the Americans would be stupid enough to attack us here, at the heart of our territory . . ."

But now, Ling knew Toon had been wrong. American troop-carrying helicopters were touching down all over the runways, while the smaller attack Cobras were riddling the rows of parked jet fighters with cannon and rocket fire.

In the fires of the explosions, Ling could see his men—pilots and aircraft workers alike—sprawled everywhere, dead or in their death throes as a result of the gas attack. I can't believe the Americans gassed us . . . he thought. I can't believe that they would land troops here . . .

The helicopters just kept coming. They would touch down just long enough to disgorge their gas-masked troops, then they would fly away, churning up great swirls of gas as they departed. The troops were running across the runways, moving carefully in close precision, heading for the airbase's buildings. Meanwhile, the Cobras were ripping up all of their precious jet fighters.

He felt a pounding sensation in his temples. Suddenly he felt very hot. He began sweating profusely. Everything seemed to go into slow motion. He could smell the odor of the rice paddies, the stink of the elephant grass. All of a sudden he wasn't in Burma anymore—he was back in Vietnam, watching another American helicopter assault.

He felt something go *snap!*, his brain, and then he heard himself screaming. Uncontrollably. He knew it was his job to lead the defense of the airfield, but he couldn't. The pain of the memories exploding in his head was too much. He had heard that some American Vietnam veterans had been afflicted with something called "post-Vietnam syndrome." But in that instant he knew it wasn't only the American soldiers who had been handed such an affliction . . .

He took his pistol from his holster, put it in his mouth, and slowly pulled the trigger . . .

Bo Simons was the first man off Maxwell's helicopter. He adjusted his gas mask and checked his M-16, then sprinted forward, ready to shoot anything that moved.

He ran around a clump of dead flight mechanics, their faces twisted in evidence of a painful gas death. He passed a MiG-21, its engines turning, its pilot dead inside the open cockpit. Simons quickly unhooked a hand grenade, pulled the pin and threw it in front of the jet's intake nozzle and ran like hell. The grenade was sucked in in an instant and ignited, blowing the MiG ten feet off the ground.

Simons kept going. He was vaguely aware that he was leading the American charge. Everywhere he looked he saw dead or dying men and burning jet airplanes. Explosions were going off all around him. The deadly mist was lifting, but he was smart enough to keep his breathing apparatus on. He knew the lingering effects of the gas were still dangerous.

Ahead of him was a string of buildings, the center one being the control tower with its roof blown off. Every few seconds one of the Cobras would streak over, firing at the parked jet fighters still ahead of the advancing Americans.

Simons ran around the back of a burning fighter and spotted two PRA soldiers struggling with a SA-7 shoulder-launched SAM. He cut them down with two quick bursts from his M-16. Two more soldiers took pot shots at him from their position under an intact MiG-19. One of the bullets skinned his boot before he hit the ground. He instantly fired his M-16, not at the enemy soldiers, but at the fuel tank on the MiG. Three bursts and the tank exploded, dousing the soldiers with flaming aviation fuel.

He ignored their screams and kept running. He set his sights on the bottom of the wrecked control tower. If he and his men reached the building they'd be able to set up a radio post from which to call in the C-5s.

A jeep full of PRA gunmen appeared at the end of a line of burning MiGs. They spotted Simons and opened fire on him. He returned the fire just long enough to take cover. Two Blue troopers were at his side, one carrying a rocket-propelled grenade launcher.

The enemy jeep approached, the five men on board firing continuously. With Simons and the other trooper giving covering fire, the RPG man stood up and placed a grenade right through the jeep's radiator grill. There was a two-second delay, but then the jeep exploded, throwing the ripped-apart enemy soldiers in all directions.

Simons didn't stop to look, he was up and sprinting toward the control tower again. He dodged a few more shots and someone threw a grenade at him that failed to go off.

Finally he reached what was left of the control tower. He was sweating and out of breath, but none the worse for wear. He checked his watch. It was almost 0700 hours.

Colonel Toon was vaguely aware of the sound of gunfire coming from the airbase seven miles away, but it didn't concern him too much.

He was too busy overseeing the last-minute checks of the warhead atop the ICBM. Standing at the top of the work tower next to the rocket, Toon watched every movement of the operation. The Pakistani doctors, nervous that the colonel was present, nevertheless went about their work in a timely manner.

Despite the working conditions, the lead Pakistani was proud of his work. He and his group had fashioned a self-contained, self-arming air burst nuclear warhead which, by necessity, would work on a timer independent of the ICBM. It was small, no bigger than a soldier's field pack. And the Pakistani knew the bomb would work just as easily if dropped from an airplane, or set on a timer and driven in a truck somewhere as part of a suicide bombing. The Paki knew that if Toon was successful, they'd be able to sell their "dirty" nukes to a variety of clients and allies—Iran, Libya, the glut of terrorists in Lebanon's Bekaa Valley.

The warhead in place, Toon dismissed the Pakistani doctors and called in the people responsible for building the ICBM, the three Harvard-educated Iranians. He was always amazed at how the Americans could be so stupid as to train their own enemies. The Iranians were bought off for just a million dollars each—all of which Toon knew they had sent back home to support their country's gyrating revolution. The parts for the rocket had been easily purchased or manufactured, the fuel mix was simply kerosene. The launch pad was built from photos and drawings found in American news and science magazines. It had been all so simple.

The Iranians checked over the final details of the rocket. Its tanks were full, its gyros set, and its ignition sequence set.

"All that remains is your approval to start the countdown," the head Iranian told Toon.

Toon smiled. It was just getting dark on the American West Coast. The terror and blaze of the nuclear bomb—over San Diego—would be more effective at night.

"Start the countdown now," Toon said. "We launch within the hour . . ."

Ryder gently urged the F-14 over the catapult, watching as Moon directed his way.

He had only slept a few hours—a deep, surprisingly soothing sleep, as if his psyche was preparing itself for the events to come. He woke when it was still dark and spent the time doing a final check out of the airplane and the special downburst bomb. Everything was in top working order.

They were getting sporadic reports on the progress of the operation so far. The fighting was heavy on the southern front. The Grays were going toe-to-toe with the PRA troops, all without the benefit of the covering fire from an F-14. The attack on Toon's airbase had started, and at last report, the Blues were down and battling for control of the runways. Apparently Lancaster and Sammett were doing a bang-up job watching over the operation. At least four enemy airplanes had already been shot down and others were simply flying around the periphery of the action, waiting for orders.

Everyone at Ryder's mountain base knew the operation was now irreversible. Each man had come up to wish both he and Woody the best of luck on their mission. Ryder saw in their eyes the look of men that thought they'd never see them again. But Ryder himself was beyond wondering about that possibility . . .

The steam in the catapult was building to the correct pressure when Moon appeared on the F-14's access ladder.

"The latest news," he said. "Just down from the satellite."

"We're all ears," Woody said.

"The C-5s and the Greens are down at the airbase," he said excitedly. "They're broken out and are heading for the POW camp . . ."

"So far, so good," Ryder said.

"Set your radio to 1278 on the low band," Moon said. "We'll pump the action reports to you from here."

"Just what we need," Woody said. "A play-by-play report . . ."

Moon checked his watch. It was now 0712.

"Two minutes, guys," he said.

Ryder reached out of the cockpit and shook the man's hand. Woody did likewise.

"Thanks, Lieutenant," Ryder told him. "You were the linchpin. You made it work . . ."

Moon nearly went speechless. "You guys are the heroes," the young officer said. "Good luck. You'll make the best chapters in my book . . ."

Ryder gave him a crisp salute and lowered the canopy. Now he and Woody were back in their own world again. He revved the F-14's engines. So it all comes down to this, he thought. He reached into his boot, took out the photo of Maureen, and carefully positioned it just below his HUD screen. It suddenly struck him as the act of a romantic, something he'd never been accused of before. Well, he thought, people change . . .

Moon himself gave the thumbs-up sign, indicating they were ready for launch. Ryder checked his watch, then gave Moon another salute. He felt the catapult lurch forward and the F-14 was flung out off the mountain.

They were on their way . . .

73

USAF Lt. Colonel Jerry Steed had his eye pressed up against a crack in the barracks wall. A crowd of thin, frail men was gathered at his feet, waiting.

"What the hell is going on out there, Jerry?" one of the men asked. "What's all the commotion?"

Steed was six four, tall for a pilot in his day. There was only one crack in the otherwise completely-boarded-up barracks building that gave a view to the front gate of the prison camp. Only Steed, standing on his toes, could reach the spot. Plus he was the senior officer of the barracks. Therefore it was left to him to be the designated lookout.

"It's definitely gunfire," Steed reported. "It's getting closer . . ."

The prisoners, two hundred of them in all, had been hearing what sounded like gunfire and explosions since before dawn. The guards had burst in shortly afterwards and ordered the prisoners to stay in their racks, then they proceeded to board up the barracks tight.

Except for the one crack where the sunlight streamed in . . .

For the past thirty minutes, Steed had been watching a cloud of black smoke rising above the eastern horizon, coming from the general direction of the airbase. Now there was great commotion at the front of the missile complex with PRA troops—some on foot, others in trucks—being rushed toward the airfield.

Steed also saw a lot of activity around the missile launch pad a mile and a half from the barracks.

"Jesus, could it be his own men turned against him?" one of the prisoners asked.

"Could it be a large army of Burmese rebels?" another said.

"Either way, we're sunk," a third said.

"Listen!" Steed cried out. "Whatever it is, it's getting closer . . ."

He watched as several PRA vehicles came speeding through the main gate, stopping quickly to allow the troops in back to get off. These soldiers immediately took up defensive positions near and around the gate and started firing at someone approaching down the road. The far-off popping and cracking sounds they'd been hearing all morning were now getting louder and more concentrated. Steed thought he could also hear a mechanized sound.

Suddenly there was a tremendous explosion which caused the entire base to shudder. The force of the shaking was so intense, Steed was knocked back from the wall.

When he regained his position he saw that half the main gate of the complex had been blown away and a huge fire was blazing nearby. Just then, the barracks was sprayed with gunfire, some of the shells piercing the heavy wooden walls.

"Everyone down!" Steed yelled out. "Under your racks. Hurry!"

However, he stayed at his position, watching . . .

There was another large explosion and he could see the PRA soldiers falling back. The mechanized sound got louder, more distinct. Whoever was coming down the road was packing a mighty wallop, he thought. And they were coming fast . . .

"Whoever they are, they're coming through the gate now!" Steed shouted.

Just then, the barracks was hit with another barrage of gunfire. One bullet hit near Steed's peephole, sending a spray of burning splinters into his face. Yet he was determined to stay at his post . . .

He cleared the burning bits of wood from his face and pressed his eyes against the peephole once again. That's when he saw the huge M-1 Abrams tank come flying through the main gate . . .

Just then, a third barrage of bullets hit the barracks wall. Steed could see that it was the PRA soldiers who were firing on the building, possibly in a desperate attempt to kill them before the camp was liberated.

But oddly enough, this barrage only served to open more holes in the barracks walls. *Now the sunlight streamed in in a hundred places.* And now a hundred of the prisoners could look out . . .

"Holy Christ!" someone yelled out. "If these guys are Burmese rebels, where the hell did they get a tank like that?!"

Another shouted, "What kind of tank *is* that?!"

"Maybe it's the Russians!" someone else called out.

"Stay down, guys!" Steed yelled out, knowing it was probably useless.

Another tank burst through the gate, its turret machine gunner firing wildly, its cannon firing point-blank at the PRA troops.

"Kill the bastards!" one of the prisoners screamed. "Kill them all!"

Two more tanks crashed in, followed by a pair of armored personal carriers and an armored jeep.

Steed tried to get a focus on the faces of the attacking soldiers, but his eyes had dulled over his more than twenty years of captivity. Plus, he thought he felt tears welling up in their corners . . .

One of the APCs charged right toward their barracks, the top gunner spraying a nearby group of PRA soldiers with a heavy caliber machine gun. The armored vehicle crashed through the barbed wire fence surrounding the barracks and screeched to a halt outside the front door.

"*Everyone down!*" Steed yelled, this time heeding his own advice. "*Everyone get their asses on the floor!*"

Two explosions went off outside, followed by yet another barrage of gunfire against the barracks wall. Steed could hear the gunner on the APC firing back, followed by a number of loud shouts.

Suddenly they all heard someone pounding on the barracks door. No one moved . . .

Then they heard someone kicking at the door.

Still, no one dared move . . .

"Please, Lord," Steed whispered. Suddenly more than two decades of captivity flashed before his eyes. "*Please . . .*"

The door was finally kicked in and Steed looked up. It was a very young man, wearing a jungle camouflage uniform and a helmet that looked all the world like a Nazi-style tinpot from World War II. The entire uniform looked so strange, Steed had absolutely no idea what army the man was from.

That's when the young soldier spoke the words they had all been waiting years to hear:

"We're Americans!" the soldier yelled. "*We're here to take you home!*"

74

Colonel Toon knew it was no time to panic.

He was atop the missile launch tower, watching through binoculars, as the fighting around the barracks raged.

"The vermin!" he screamed, cursing his hired ground troops. He knew they had failed to carry out his orders to blow up the barracks and kill the American prisoners should anything like this happen. After all, what good were hostages if the captor didn't follow through and kill them when things went wrong?

But Toon also knew it was no time to dwell on the POWs. His main priority now was the launch of the *Long Struggle,* an act that would put millions of Americans to death. So they were, in effect, his *new* hostages. Then he would make his escape, just as he did years before when the world through he was dead. His only helicopter—a Soviet-built Hind given to him by the North Koreans—was standing by with a loyal pilot at the controls. But Toon would leave only when he was sure the missile launch could not be stopped.

He was not surprised that many of his mercenaries fled when the attackers reached the outskirts of his compound. He expected little else from hired help. They simply had no cause—no revolutionary *fervor*—to keep them around. It made no difference to him—let the Iranians and the Libyans and the North Koreans and the Pakis and the rest walk back through the jungle to their pathetic little countries.

"The fools!" he laughed, watching the fighting taper off around the POW barracks more than a mile away. The attackers were Americans—he was sure of that now. But he was also sure they were aware of the limitations they faced in attacking his complex. They might be able to free the POWs, but not a one was moving toward the launch tower. Even the plundering Americans knew that a single stray bullet could ignite the missile fuel or even explode the nuclear warhead. Either way, it would kill everyone—soldier and precious POW alike—for miles around.

Besides, two of his loyal Vietnamese battalions were racing back from the south. They were just a few miles away and they would strike the Americans as they were withdrawing back toward the airport.

Much American blood would be shed yet!

Toon scanned his SAM sites and was heartened to see they were still manned. He congratulated himself for a decision he had made when he first set up the base. That was to station only trustworthy Vietnamese comrades at the missile sites, under the control of his old friend, Major Trang. From this he gathered comfort. The attacking ground troops would not dare approach the launch pad, and no airplane, flying high or low, would dare attack the facility from the air. His launch, now reaching the thirty-minute mark of the countdown, was safe . . .

Bo Simons was sitting in the co-pilot seat of the Blackhawk helicopter, listening to the radio.

The airwaves were a confused symphony of calls back and forth between members of the Green Army Marines. Simons had been trying as best he could to make some sense of it all.

From what he could decipher, the Greens had reached the POW barracks and had freed the roughly two hundred prisoners held there. They were now heading back to the airport, using the APCs, M-1s, and some two-and-a-half-ton trucks they'd commandeered along the way.

So far everything had been going fairly smoothly. The casualties to the American force had been light—the gassing at the airport and the Tomcat clearing the skies above it had a lot to do with that.

But now there was a new complication . . .

One of the Blue Army's Cobra scout ships had spotted a large force five clicks away and heading for the airport.

"Two battalions," the pilot reported. "They've got transport and they're moving quick . . ."

"Can you tell whether they are mercenaries or not?" Simons asked.

"They're all wearing the same uniform," the pilot answered. "If I had to guess, I'd say they were Vietnamese."

Simons immediately called Maxwell who was stationed at

the far edge of the base and told him the news.

"OK, we'll have to disperse into Plan Delta Five," Maxwell said quickly. "Get it going, Bo, and good luck . . ."

Simons knew immediately what Plan Delta Five was. It was a holding action, a fall-back defense plan that would slow down the advancing column long enough for the Greens and the POWs to get back on the C-5s and clear out. The irony of the situation was not lost on Simons. Plan Delta Five was the last exercise the Blues had participated in back at War Heaven.

Simons quickly passed the word to implement Plan Delta Five. Within a minute he saw two-thirds of the Blues, Blackhawks, and all of the Cobras lift off and head south to cut off the approaching enemy column. He gave the thumbs-up sign to his pilot and they lifted off, quickly joining the other choppers.

Ryder put the F-14 on its tail and streaked up to 45,000 feet.

"How's the package?" he called back to Woody.

"Still 'green,'" the Wiz replied.

"OK," Ryder said, checking his own instruments. "One minute to arming . . ."

Looking back over their shoulders, the pilots could see the faint wisps of smoke coming from the battle area a hundred miles to the north. The sky over Toon's base was a furball of vapor trails, evidence of the intense dogfight going on between Toon's fighters and the Aggressors.

"Lancaster and Sammett are in the middle of that, somewhere," Ryder said to Woody.

"Yeah," Woody said. "Some guys have all the fun . . ."

The F-14 passed the crucial 52,500-foot mark.

"Payload still green?" Ryder asked.

"That's affirmative," Woody said. "Initiating arming sequence, now . . ."

Ryder slowly leveled out the Tomcat and began a wide circle. He let Woody do his work. The bomb they were carrying needed to get to "critical heat"—actually a series of arming procedures, each one needing precise timing. Inside its warhead were hundreds of depleted uranium pellets. If they were able to deliver the bomb and it exploded on the proper "down burst" the pellets would penetrate Toon's own nuclear device and hopefully render it inoperable.

Finally, Woody called ahead. "I see all 'green,'" he told Ryder. "I just hope this baby behaves itself when we drop below fifty-two-five . . ."

"Only one way to find out," Ryder said. "Hang on . . ."

He pushed the 'Cat's controls forward, putting the airplane into a steep dive. A few nervous seconds passed, then the F-14 slipped below the critical height.

"Well, we're still here . . ." Ryder said.

"And, it's still ticking . . ." the Wiz reported.

Ryder checked the time. It was now 0730.

"Only a few minutes to go, partner . . ." he told Woody. "Then it's our turn . . ."

The pilot of Toon's Hind helicopter was getting nervous.

Just about everyone in the vicinity of the launch pad was gone—everyone except Toon and a few remaining missile technicians. This scattering of personnel told the chopper pilot that the ICBM was going to launch very soon. And he wished he could put as many miles as possible between himself and the rocket when it took off.

If it took off, that is. Few people at the base believed the missile would ever make it off the launch pad. Just one meeting with the Iranian missile "experts" was all one needed to question the airworthiness of the built-off-the-shelf ICBM. Just like the mercenaries who had long since fled the area, the chopper pilot didn't want to be around when the missile blew and the dirty warhead started spitting out its deadly contents.

Up in the tower, Toon was making his technicians take one last look at the weapon's arming mechanism.

"It *will* arm at 70,100 feet, sir," the extremely nervous Paki doctor told him. "And explode at the same height on descent . . ."

"It had better, *doctor,*" Toon said, finally dismissing the man.

* * *

Now Toon was alone in the tower. He surveyed his realm one last time. The fighting at the POW barracks was over. It was up to his two battalions to prevent the Americans from accomplishing their rescue mission.

He turned and surveyed the canyon itself. He knew the SAMs were still manned, Major Trang's loyal troops at the controls with orders to stay until the missile had launched and was out of sight.

High above, he could see the confused contrails of the air battles still going between his fighters and the Americans. He knew an F-14 was up there, somewhere, along with that strange group of American airplanes that carried Soviet markings.

Certain that he had pulled it off, Toon majestically descended the tower stairs and joined the Pakistani and the Iranians in the already-crowded helicopter.

Lieutenant Major Nguyen Li was riding in the lead vehicle of the Vietnamese relief column when he first saw the American helicopters high overhead.

Up until that moment, Li had been looking forward to leading his troops into battle. A member of Toon's original cadre back in the glory days of the war for Vietnam reunification, he was anxious to win a victory for his old comrade. Now that Burmese rebels had foolishly made a suicide attack on the airbase, Toon had given the chance. Instead of joining the fighting in the south of the Iron Circle, Toon had asked Li to about-face and return to repulse the airbase attackers.

But not once had Toon mentioned anything about the attackers having helicopters . . .

Li quickly counted eight helicopters above him then immediately ordered his troops to dismount off their trucks and take defense positions in the woods. Within seconds, the first chopper swooped in and strafed the thirty-five-vehicle convoy.

"An American Cobra?" Li whispered, taking cover himself in a road ditch. "What Burmese bandit would have access to such a machine?"

A second Cobra streaked over, firing rockets into several

troop trucks at the end of the convoy. A few of his men fired on the copter with their rifles, but the buglike machine was moving too fast for any of the return to do any good.

Li screamed for his antiaircraft cadre to come up. Just after a third chopper passed overhead, the SAM team, equipped with shoulder-launched SA-7 antiaircraft missile, took up a position close by him.

A fourth chopper went over and the team fired its five-foot-long missile. The rocket streaked wildly up into the sky and caught the American helicopter on its tail rotor, blowing it off completely. The stricken Cobra immediately flipped over and crashed into the woods next to the road, the resulting explosion shaking the ground under Li's feet.

He knew some of his men died as a result of the crash, but he couldn't worry about that now. He had to get to the airport.

He passed the word down the line for his troops to move up. He was only a quarter of a mile from the crossroads connecting to the airport road, and just over a mile from the airport itself. Li sent a dozen of his fastest men to scout the airport road ahead. He was hoping it would be clear of the enemy.

The Cobras made two more passes, ripping up three platoons in the middle of the convoy, then they flew off to the east. The lightning-quick air strike had killed about fifty of his troop and yet it had lasted only two minutes.

A few more minutes passed then one of his runners returned. The crossroads appeared clear for the moment although helicopters were seen overhead. Li sent the word down for the troops to move out. Quickly. But they would have to hoof it—the Cobras had destroyed so many of his trucks, the roadway was now virtually impassable.

"Here they come . . ." Simons said, watching as the lead element of the Vietnamese column appeared at the crossroad. "Wait until my order . . ."

The woods opposite the airport road was filled with Blue Army troops. In a field beyond were a dozen Blackhawk 7-X7 choppers, their muffled engines turning.

Simons watched as first twenty, then thirty, then fifty Vietnamese soldiers appeared at the crossroads and cautiously

412

turned toward the airport.

"OK, get ready," Simons said. "*Now!*"

His RPG men opened up first, spinning a dozen rocket-propelled grenades toward the enemy soldiers. Even as the grenades were blowing up, Simons' riflemen opened up, spraying the Communist troops. It was all over in less than a half minute. The Vietnamese advance force—fifty men—lay dead or dying at the crossroads.

Simons ordered his men back to the helicopters . . .

"Tomcat . . . Tomcat, this is Mountain Base Alpha . . ."

"Go ahead, Alpha," Ryder answered, instantly recognizing Moon's voice.

"Major, we have a delay in the operation . . ." Moon told him. "Trouble at the airport road . . ."

"What kind of trouble?" Ryder asked, checking his fuel supply. They had not a gallon to spare.

"There are two of Toon's battalions moving toward the airport," Moon said. "The Greens are already there. And they got the POWs. But if these troops of Toon's break through, they could jeopardize the C-5 take-offs . . ."

"Is anyone engaging these guys?" Ryder asked.

"The Blues are fighting a holding action against them now," Moon said, his voice filled with static. "But it'll be tough. The Vietnamese have portable SAMs."

Ryder was getting impatient. Besides the fact that he was flying around, wasting gas and carrying a volatile "antinuke" under his wing, he knew that with all the action, Toon had most certainly started his launch sequence already.

"How long a delay, Lieutenant?" Ryder asked, putting the F-14 into yet another high-altitude turn.

"Ten to fifteen minutes," Moon answered. "Maybe more."

"Damn!" Woody cursed as Moon signed off. "This could blow the whole wad. What now?"

"We wait . . ." Ryder said, checking his watch. "For twelve minutes from right now. Then, no matter what, we go in . . ."

The Cobras hit the Vietnamese twice more, and Simons set

up one more "running ambush." Although a third of the enemy troops were now out of the action, more than a thousand of Major Li's soldiers were now closing in on the airport.

Simons had landed his Blackhawks at and around the entrance to the airport, determined to make a final stand. He knew the Communist troops would soon be within mortar range of the runways. If that happened, then there'd be real trouble . . .

Out on the tarmac, Major Maxwell had made a tough decision. As overall commander of the operation, he knew he had to get everyone—strike force soldiers and POWs—out as quickly as possible. The POWs were just now being loaded onto one of the C-5s, along with the Green Army Marine wounded. But there was still room to spare on the big airship. Maxwell knew that if they left *all* the equipment behind, they could all fit on two of the C-5s.

It was a multi-*billion*-dollar decree, but at that point, Maxwell couldn't have cared less. He passed his decision on to the Green Army Marine commander: They would leave behind four of the C-5s, plus all of the Green armor and Blue Army choppers.

Within a minute of making his decision, several squads of Green Army Marines were sent out to blow up four of the huge C-5s.

Just then, the first mortar rounds fired by the Vietnamese troops started landing on the runways . . .

"Mountain Base Alpha, this is Tomcat," Ryder called.

"This is Alpha . . ." came Moon's reply.

"What's the latest, Lieutenant?" Ryder asked.

There was a loud burst of static. "Not sure, Major," they heard Moon say through the interference. "We overheard one report from an Aggressor pilot that said one of the C-5s was airborne. But he also said he saw four C-5s burning on the runway . . ."

"*Jeesuz* . . ." Woody whistled.

Moon continued. "He also reported that he saw a number of

414

wrecked choppers and armor. Plus the Vietnamese column was mortaring the runways . . ."

"What about the missile complex?" Ryder asked.

"The SAMs are still active," Moon reported. "This Aggressor pilot had a couple shot at him, and he was up around twenty thousand feet . . ."

"OK, Lieutenant," Ryder said finally. "We can't wait any longer. . . . We'll have to assume the C-5 that got off was carrying the POWs.

"*We're going in* . . ."

75

Major Trang never left his post. He stayed despite the sounds of battle coming from both the airport and the POW camp. He stayed despite the air battle that raged between the invading jets and Colonel Toon's air force high above for more than an hour. And now he stayed even though he knew that the colonel was long gone, spirited away in a helicopter, most likely after setting the *Long Struggle* on automatic.

"Our revolutionary duty is to remain here . . ." he told the officers who had assembled in the SAM net's main tracking house. "Go back and make sure your cadres stay alert."

But no sooner had his officers filed out when his officer in charge of radar called to him.

"Sir, we have a low target approaching from the south," the man said.

Trang was instantly standing over the radar operator's shoulder watching the large green radar screen. Sure enough, he saw a small blip out on the very periphery of the radar arm's sweep, but obviously heading their way.

Trang was shocked. What pilot would be foolish enough to fly the gauntlet of SAMs that dotted the canyon? Whoever it was, it made little difference. The intruder would be destroyed within seconds of entering the SAM "free fire" zone.

Instantly the tracking house was a scene of controlled confusion. Trang ordered that all SAM units, 1,453 sites in all, arm up and start their radars. A similar order was passed to the four hundred AAA gun sites.

Trang checked the radar sweep once again. The target was within ten miles of entering the valley and therefore the SAM zone. It was flying low and fast. Trang knew it was probably some kind of high-performance jet. It was undoubtedly heading to destroy the ICBM.

Trang grabbed the SAM net microphone. "All units," he shouted. "Arm missiles. First line commanders, target will be in your airspace in one minute!"

The moment he never thought would happen had arrived. Someone was actually going to challenge the air defenses of Thunder Alley . . .

"Thirty seconds, Ghost . . ." Woody called ahead to Ryder. "I got emission signals going up all over . . ."

"What's your reading from the missile?" Ryder asked, bringing the Tomcat down to just treetop level. By tracking a high band radio frequency, they had been able to pick up the radio-controlled automatic countdown sequence set by Toon's missile technicians.

"Getting hotter," Woody reported. "If I had to guess, I'd say we got less than five minutes to launch . . ."

"Damn!" Ryder cursed under his breath. The delay at the airport *had* robbed them of valuable time. It had been estimated earlier that running the SAMs of Thunder Alley would take nearly seven minutes. Even if they made it, they could be two full minutes late.

Just then, up ahead, the valley came into view. Although it was his first time seeing the actual item, Ryder felt like he'd seen the place before. The holographic recreation at Cartoon Valley had been *amazingly* accurate.

He pushed a button and the HUD appeared in front of him. Already it was lit up with the various red, orange, and yellow "threat" cones. Once again, the readings were identical to those over the Nevada holographic display—frighteningly so.

"OK, start up the ECM," Ryder told Woody. Instantly Woody cranked on the electronic interference gear.

"Flare release status?" Ryder asked. Woody checked the flare storage attachment. There were more than 350 small missile-deflecting flares at the ready.

"Flares set," Woody reported. "ECM on and emitting."

Ryder reached down and turned off his low- and high-warning threat indicators. He knew they'd be facing so many SAMs the noise would only be a distraction. All he wanted on was the special ICBM launch indicator and the cockpit intercom.

"Major Woods?" Ryder said. "Are *you* ready to save civilization as we know it?"

"Are *you* kidding?" came back the reply. "I already got a bet down on next year's Super Bowl . . ."

Ryder hunkered down in his seat and got a firm grip on the Tomcat's control stick.

"OK," he said. *"Then hang on, partner . . ."*

The commander of the first defense line couldn't believe his eyes . . .

The approaching jet fighter was still two miles away yet it had already started acting strange. It was gyrating wildly, spinning, twisting, turning, yet obviously under control. He had never seen an aircraft act that way ever. It reminded him of a dancer doing some wild, almost out-of-control step, yet keeping up with a rhythm only known to the individual.

"Fire!" he called out loudly.

In seconds a barrage of SAMs lifted off, themselves twisting toward the low-flying fluttering jet fighter. Immediately he saw the pilot start to release a steady pump of deflecting flares.

The officer was astonished. Somehow the jet was working its way through the barrage of SAMs. It was as if the pilot had memorized every inch of safe airspace and was using it to his maximum advantage.

"This is impossible!" the officer cried out. Before he knew

417

it, the wildly maneuvering aircraft was over his head and streaking off to the north. It had passed through the first line of defense unscathed. None of the missiles had even come near it. "How can this be?" the officer asked himself.

"OK, we made it through the first round," Ryder said, leveling the airplane out for a few moments. "Keep those flares coming . . ."

"Roger, Ghost," Woody answered. "I'm getting a reading on the missile. Still getting hotter. The computer says three and a half minutes to launch . . ."

Ryder increased the 'Cat's speed. He knew flying this low this fast was dangerous. But he had no other choice. They were terribly behind schedule.

"Second line coming up!" Woody called out.

Ryder put the F-14 into its gyratics once again, whispering the moves he'd memorized over the past ten weeks all the while watching his HUD screen.

"*Hard right twist. Hard left twist. Snap up . . .*"

He was barely aware of the SAMs flying all around them. He was too busy maneuvering the airplane through the safety cones.

"*Hard twist left. Full roll. Go inverted. Hold for three . . .*"

A missile exploded very close to them, buffeting the airplane with two violent shock waves.

"That was close . . ." he whispered, getting the airplane back into its maneuvering pattern.

"*Roll, hold for two. Snap left. Go inverted. Count to five. Snap back. Pitch. Snap. Pitch . . .*"

Another missile exploded right off their tail, putting the F-14 into an involuntary pitch.

Ryder quickly regained control, noting the rear elevator controls were sluggish in their response. Again, he had little time to worry about it.

"*Snap over. Two rolls. Inverted for eight count. Pitch down . . .*"

Just then a missile exploded right in front of them. The flash blinded Ryder for a few precious seconds. When he could see clearly again, the jet had passed through the smoke and debris and was in a shallow dive.

Ryder yanked back on the controls. They responded slowly. "Get up, baby," Ryder urged, going in a mandatory roll. The airplane finally came around.

That's when Woody came on the line.

"I'm getting a red-hot warning from the missile!" the Wiz reported in an excited voice. "Two minutes, Ghost!"

"Jesus Christ!" Ryder yelled. "We can't make it in two minutes . . ."

Just then they passed out of the second SAM zone. Ryder leveled out for ten seconds, quickly checking his important gauges.

"How are the flares holding out?" he yelled back to Woody.

"Flares are OK," the answer came back. "How are the controls?"

"They're getting touchy," Ryder answered honestly. "Hang on, here we go again . . ."

They quickly flashed into the third, most concentrated, line of SAMs. Now Ryder would have to not only perform each maneuver quicker, but there would be more of them.

"Full pitch. Hold for two. Hard right snap. Full roll, snap down . . ."

Another missile exploded off their port wing.

"Two full rolls. Snap up . . ."

Two SAMs then collided just ahead of them, causing Ryder to bank hard left to avoid the debris.

"Pitch back. Pitch back. Snap. Roll once. Twice. Go inverted . . ."

Now Ryder *was* fully aware that SAMs were exploding all around them. The air was filled with shockwaves. These and the damaged controls would cause the F-14 to veer out of control for a few moments at a time. It was all Ryder could do to keep his hands on the control stick.

"One minute warning from the missile!" Woody shouted over the pandemonium.

Ryder had to increase the F-14's speed, making the insane movements even crazier . . .

"Snap left. Snap right. Inverted for a seven count. Roll one. Roll

419

two. Pitch. Snap right again . . ."

His mind was recalling and acting on the memorized maneuvers at an incredible rate. The ground was flashing by them at such a tremendous speed, it looked like no more than a fiery blur. Yet despite all the craziness, they had the feeling that they were actually going to make it . . .

"Come on, Ghostman!" Woody was yelling. "Fly this motherfucker! Fly your pants off! Go, baby. Go!"

Suddenly, Ryder saw it. He was inverted at the time, but it was still unmistakable. Three miles, dead ahead was the ICBM launch pad.

All of sudden there were no more SAMs. They were in the clear. They'd made the impossible run through Thunder Alley . . .

But there was no time to celebrate. They might have run the deadliest electronic gauntlet ever, but they'd been too late . .

"Twenty seconds to launch!" Woody yelled out.

"Damn! We'll never make it!" Ryder yelled out.

"Fifteen seconds!"

He quickly began the "pop-up" maneuver, booting the F-14 into afterburner. But he could already see clouds of smoke shooting out from under the missile.

"Ten seconds!" Woody shouted. "Deflect, Ghost! Deflect, we're not going to make it!"

Suddenly the cockpit was filled with the ultra-screech of feedback indicating the missile's launch warning.

"It's taking off!" Woody yelled. *"Deflect!"*

Ryder knew it was hopeless. He banked to the left and watched in horror as the ICBM blasted off . . .

"Jeesuz, Ghost," Woody said grimly. "All this . . . *for nothing!"*

76

Although the battle at the airport was going full tilt, soldiers on both sides stopped shooting to wach the ICBM slowly climb into the sky.

"Oh, God," Maxwell said as he watched the missile ride the fiery plume up into the clouds. "Ryder and Woods didn't make it . . ."

He was standing on the ramp of the second C-5 as the huge airplane taxied toward the runway. The Vietnamese soldiers were inside the airport perimeter. Simons and a handful of Blue Army soldiers were hopscotching across the tarmac, using the two last available Blackhawks as cover.

Maxwell grabbed his portable radio and called Simons. "OK, Bo, get your asses on those choppers! Meet us at the end of the runway. We're getting the hell out of here!"

Simons did as ordered. He literally threw two of his men aboard his helicopter and screamed for the pilot to take off. They did just as a Vietnamese mortar shell came crashing down almost on the exact spot where the helicopter was sitting just seconds before. Side by side, the Blackhawks rose up just high enough to move forward, speeding toward a rendezvous point with the slowly taxiing C-5.

It was then that Maxwell looked up and saw a curious sight. A single MiG-21 was roaring down the runway, lifting into a full afterburner take-off.

"Who the hell is that?" he yelled out as the MiG flashed by the rolling C-5.

"Ghost! I got a gomer heading right for us!"

Ryder took his eyes off the ICBM to look at his instruments. "Range and speed!" he called back to Woody.

"Three miles out, hitting supersonic," the Wiz answered. "He's dead behind us . . . he's following us up!"

Ryder set his sights back onto the ICBM. He was determined to stop the missile either by a Phoenix, a Sidewinder, or his cannon. If all else failed, he was prepared to ram it . . .

"Gomer closing in . . ." Woody reported. "Two mile back . . ."

Ryder switched the low- and high-warning threat buzze back on, then squeezed off a Phoenix missile. He watched a the air-to-air climbed toward the ICBM, only to see it quickl veer off course.

"The magnetic field around that missile must screw up th Phoenix homing system," Woody called ahead. "Either that o the missile's launch vortex is ruining its guidance system."

Ryder pushed his Sidewinder select button and squeezed of two of his four missiles. Both flashed out from underneath th 'Cat's belly and raced toward the slowly rising ICBM now jus eight miles away.

But just like the Phoenix, the Sidewinders quickly starte behaving erratically and fell off course.

Suddenly the F-14's high-warning buzzer went off.

"The Gomer took a shot at us," Woody yelled.

Ryder instantly banked the F-14 away. The obsolete Aphi air-to-air missile streaked by them harmlessly.

"Ghost, I think we've got to deal with this guy," Wood said.

"But we can't let that missile get away!" Ryder responded "We can't let it get above seventy thousand feet and arm!"

Ryder put the F-14 into a straight vertical climb and kicke in the afterburner.

"Let's try to outrun him . . ." Ryder said.

But then to his surprise, he looked across from him to se the MiG-21 pull up beside them.

"Jeesuz! Look at that guy!" Woody yelled.

One glance and Ryder knew who it was. An older man longish hair, World War II-type goggles, an old-fashione flying cap on his head. And he was shaking his fist at them

"It's got to be Toon himself!" Woody said.

Ryder immediately booted the airplane into fourth gear. Th powerful Tomcat easily pulled away from the MiG. Bu suddenly, Toon opened up with his cannon.

"Jeesuz," Woody yelled. "I thought Russian guns couldn' fire on the vertical!"

"I guess he must have an American gun," Ryder said as h

rolled over the top and began a spiral downward. Toon did the same and soon both aircraft were in a "rolling scissors," each one trying like hell to get a good angle on the other.

"He's trying to drag us down to his speed!" Ryder yelled back to Woody as he felt their airspeed slow down drastically. "He can turn and handle better at three hundred knots!"

Ryder booted the F-14 again, managing to put a mile between him and Toon. Then he rolled over and went vertical again, intent on taking down the renegade pilot. But to his surprise, Toon once again mimicked his maneuver.

"Christ! He must have an American engine in that rig, too!" Woody shouted ahead.

Once again, Ryder booted it, pulling away from Toon in the vertical. Once again, the Communist pilot fired off a barrage from his cannon. Ryder flipped the 'Cat over on its back and he and Toon got into the rolling scissors again.

"He's trying to delay us!" Woody yelled. "The longer we screw around with him, the farther away that missile gets!"

But then Ryder got a flash of intuition. He jinked left when Toon jinked right, then they both banked inwards. They were coming at each other, almost head-on, each blazing away with their cannons. Once again, they both went into a vertical climb.

But that's when Toon made a fatal mistake . . .

Instead of repeating the steep climb maneuver for the third time, Ryder yanked back on his throttles, pulling the engine to near-idle. The sudden jolt nearly threw Woody through his console, but it also caused Toon to streak by them at full throttle.

Now Ryder finally had the angles on the MiG-21. Toon went right over the top and into a dead vertical dive. Ryder knew that the pilot was thinking a Sidewinder shot at this angle could get screwed up. The Sidewinder's heat-seeking system didn't cotton to being fired straight down, simply because there was a lot of heat in the earth's surface and this tended to confuse the missile's guidance system.

But that didn't mean his cannon couldn't work . . .

He put the Tomcat into afterburner and caught up to the MiG-21. Without a moment's hesitation, he opened up with the Vulcan.

"C'mon," Ryder urged the cannon fire, trying to put some English on it. "Eat him up!"

Finally the stream of cannon shells found Toon's tail section. They quickly ripped away some of the metal covering, chopping away the airplane's exhaust fuselage. Ryder didn't let up on the cannon for a second. Now bullets were finding Toon's starboard wing.

Just then, a giant streak of flame erupted from under the MiG's wing. Still Ryder kept firing. The airplane began to turn over slowly. Still, Ryder poured shells into it. Parts of the wing then came flying off, a large piece hitting the Tomcat's canopy. But Ryder never once let up on the trigger.

Suddenly the MiG-21 exploded with a great flash of fire. Ryder was so close to the MiG he turned only at the last second to avoid being caught in blast.

"Yeah! Ghost!" Woody screamed as Ryder yanked back on the F-14's controls. "You just greased the greasiest bastard on earth!"

But Ryder knew they had no time to celebrate . . .

"Yeah, but now we got to find his toy," Ryder said, pointing the F-14 up and toward the east. "And we're running on empty."

They streaked upwards in silence, as if their chatter would use up precious fuel.

Then Woody called out with the word Ryder had been waiting to hear.

"I got it, Ghost!" the Wiz cried out. "It's about sixty-six miles downrange."

"What's the altitude?" Ryder called back, urging the Tomcat on.

"I got him at 56,250 and climbing . . ." Woody reported. "It's turned over to a forty-degree angle . . ."

"Jeesuz, that will give us the time," Ryder said. "But we just don't have the gas . . ."

Still they climbed, approaching Mach 2.1.

"Got it at twenty-three miles, Ghost," Woody reported.

Ryder looked at his fuel indicators. Every one of them was on empty. Yet they were still flying at twice the speed of sound.

"Closing to fifteen miles . . ." Woody yelled. "Go, Ghost-man. *Go!*"

It was getting almost dreamlike. The Tomcat was out of gas, yet they were still climbing. Still accelerating.

"*Ten miles,* Ghost!" Woody yelled excitedly. "Can you see the bastard?"

Ryder looked up. Sure enough, through the thin cloud layer, he could see the twin flames of the *Long Struggle*.

He checked his altimeter. They were at 62,000, the missile was 67,500. They were already past the safe operating ceiling of the F-14. Ryder knew at this height, anything could happen to the airplane. And still, they had no fuel.

"*Five miles, Ghost!*" Woody called out, his voice sounding strange at the high altitude. "*Four miles!*"

The missile was at 68,200, they were just passing through 66,000 feet. And they were still accelerating.

"This is giving me the creeps!" Woody yelled out. "We're going close to Mach 3. No Tomcat has ever gone this fast!"

Ryder didn't want to think about it. He knew that sometimes strange things happen. This was one of them.

"*Two fucking miles, Ghost!*" Woody yelled, his voice cracking.

The 'Cat's throttles were wide open. Yet, Ryder gave them a hard slap and felt the F-14 lurch ahead even faster.

"*Jesus Christ!*" Woody yelled, pressed hard against his seat from the force of the Tomcat's speed. "One mile . . ."

They were now at 68,200, the missile passing through 69,000. Just a thousand feet and the missile would be irreversibly armed.

They closed to within a half mile. The exhaust from the ICBM was kicking up a hurricane of turbulance. The F-14 was shaking all over. Still Ryder kept the airplane steady.

"Cross your fingers!" he yelled to Woody. Then he squeezed the cannon's trigger. The fiery stream flashed out from the Cat's nose, streaking across the thin air nearly fourteen miles above the earth.

Ryder saw the shells bounce off the ICBM's rear quarter. Then he saw a vapor trail come out of one of the holes. Then another and another. Suddenly the ICBM started slowly

425

spinning sideways. More vapor trails appeared. The air was so turbulent, Ryder's hand was bleeding just trying to keep the F-14 steady.

More shells hit the mark. Ryder glanced down at his speed indicator and couldn't believe his eyes. They were approaching Mach 3!

"Jeesuz, Ghost!" Woody screamed as they watched the shells hit the spinning ICBM. *"It's going to blow!"*

No sooner had the word left his lips when the ICBM exploded in a great ball of yellow fire . . .

The force of the blast knocked the F-14 head over tails.

Then the airplane went into an uncontrolled dive, pieces of flaming debris battering them as they fell.

Still they dove, the airplane spinning wildly. Both Ryder and Woody were passing in and out of consciousness. Ryder's head was so light, he felt drunk. All fear of death was gone. The image of the ICBM detonating was burned onto his retinas. And still, the image of Maureen was burned on his soul.

"It's over . . ." he whispered as he passed once again into unconsciousness. *"It's finally over . . ."*

The assistant secretary could barely hold the telex paper in his hand. He picked up the telephone and banged in an access code. A phone just outside the Oval Office rang once.

"Let me speak to the secretary," he said firmly. "He is with the President . . ."

The person on the other end recognized his voice and patched him through. "Mr. Secretary," the assistant secretary said slowly. "The missile has been destroyed . . ."

There was a long silence at the other end of the line. The assistant secretary knew the news was being passed on to the President.

Then the secretary asked, "Are you absolutely certain?"

"Yes, sir," the assistant secretary said. "NORAD has confirmed it . . ."

"What about the pilots?" the secretary asked. "Any word from them?"

The telex message did fall out of the assistant secretary's

hand at this point. "No, sir," he said slowly. "Not yet . . ."

Captain O'Leary poured a cup of coffee for Maureen, then for himself.

"The mission is over . . ." he said simply.

Maureen felt a wave of relief and fear come over her. She was afraid to just come right out and ask about Ryder. Instead, she let her newspaper person instincts take over.

"What can you tell me about it, Captain?" she asked. "Was it successful?"

"Yes, it was . . ." O'Leary said. Then, after thinking for a moment, continued. "I can tell you that the action took place in Burma. We had a substantial number of troops in that country—a lot of the same troops you saw in Nevada. Those troops completed their mission. They took some casualties. They are now being withdrawn. Apparently a lot of equipment was left behind, but this is a relatively minor point."

"Just what *was* it all about, Captain?" Maureen asked, still avoiding the big question. "Was it all necessary? The secrecy, the cover stories, the training?"

"Yes," the captain answered emphatically. "There was a madman—a renegade Vietnamese colonel—who was able to buy himself an ICBM with a highly radioactive warhead. He fired that missile at San Diego early this morning. Your friend Ryder Long and his partner shot down that missile."

"Oh, my God . . ." Maureen said in a half whisper. "Did they make it?"

O'Leary shrugged. "Officially, it's too early to tell," he said.

"And what about '*un*-officially?'" she asked quickly.

O'Leary smiled. "Your pilot, Major Long—and his partner—are OK," he said. "But I can't give you any details. Not right now.

"I do know they have already been awarded the Navy Cross. I'm sure they are the first Air Force officers to receive it."

Maureen felt like a great weight had been lifted from her shoulders.

"I'm so glad . . ." she said, hoping she wouldn't tear up. "But what happens to me now? Do I have to make a pledge that

427

I will never utter a word of this to anyone? Isn't there some oath a citizen takes, promising never to reveal a top secret they've stumbled upon?"

"There is such an oath," O'Leary said. "But I doubt if you will be asked to take it, Miss O'Brien. Quite the contrary . . ."

The comment caught Maureen off guard. "What do you mean, Captain?" she asked.

"I mean that you have one hell of an exclusive," O'Leary said, his face betraying a smile. "I've just been in contact with the office of the secretary of defense. They will be making a statement on the mission this afternoon, Washington time, just as soon as we are sure all of our troops have been withdrawn.

"Now, I'm sure you'll agree that you have the inside track on this story . . ."

Maureen was stunned. "You mean, the Pentagon is actually going to make all this public?"

"Of course," O'Leary said. "The Pentagon has just successfully pulled off one of the most elaborate military operations ever conceived. They have thwarted a real nuclear terrorist. And they recovered more than two hundred of our missing POWs! You don't think they would want to keep all that secret, do you? Good God, the newspapers will be filled with this tomorrow and for weeks to come. You won't be able to turn on a TV without hearing about every little detail. I see news documentaries, books, a miniseries . . ."

Maureen could only agree with him. "That's the American way, I guess," she said, glad she had covertly been keeping detailed notes.

"And, I might add, Miss O'Brien," O'Leary said. "You are pretty enough to play yourself when they make the movie . . ."

Shortly before his meeting with Maureen, O'Leary had been privy to a secret report coming out of Thailand.

About an hour before, the control tower at Udorn Air Base in northern Thailand had picked up an unidentified aircraft on their radar screen, descending from 65,000 feet. They tried raising the airplane on the radio but got no reply. Two Thai Air Force jets that happened to be flying nearby were vectored toward the unidentified airplane, and intercepted it at 53,000 feet.

It was they who first identified the aircraft as an F-14 . . .

The Tomcat had no power. It was gliding, like the space shuttle returning from space. There had been just enough time to foam the runway. Emergency vehicles were standing by. After several anxious moments, the F-14 simply appeared out of the clouds and came in for a successful, if nerve-rattling, dead-stick landing.

Both pilots were semiconscious, wounded and bleeding, when base personnel reached them. They were immediately rushed to the base hospital, suffering from a number of ailments. Both were in bad shape but were expected to recover.

American officials at the base said they were certain the battered F-14 had taken part in the Distant Thunder Operation. But they were at a loss to explain how the airplane—without fuel and with many of its controls damaged—had made it over hundreds of miles back to the only friendly base in the area.

Ironically, shortly before the F-14 landed, two C-5s that had taken place in the Distant Thunder operation had departed for Clark Air Force Base in Manila, escorted by the six U.S. Aggressor F-5s and a single F-14.

Those airplanes arrived in the Philippines several hours later. In one of the C-5s were the survivors from the Blue and Green forces, Bo Simons and Major Maxwell among them.

The second C-5 was carrying the 207 POWs liberated from Toon's camp.

An Army major who had worked in War Heaven as a referee and who was now acting as a repatriation officer for the POWs, walked among the men on the airplane, gathering information on each of them, such as how long they'd been in captivity, when they had been shot down, and so on.

As he listed each ex-POW's name and serial number, he

came upon a tall, thin man, distinguished by his thick shock of gray hair. He was frail, but healthier than most of the rescued men.

The Army major took down the information from the man: He was an Air Force officer, shot down over Hanoi in his F-4 Phantom in April of 1967. This information wasn't too unusual—most of the POWs had been missing for more than twenty-five years.

It was the man's name that caught the major's attention.

"Ryder Long, Sr.," the major read it over again.

For some reason, the name sounded familiar . . .